Christopher Evans was born in
and educated at Cardiff Univers
been a freelance writer since 1978
Golden Eyes (1980) and *The Insic*

By the same author

Capella's Golden Eyes
The Insider

CHRISTOPHER EVANS

In Limbo

PANTHER
Granada Publishing

Panther Books
Granada Publishing Ltd
8 Grafton Street, London W1X 3LA

Published by Panther Books 1985

ISBN 0-586-06338-2

Printed and bound in Great Britain by
Collins, Glasgow

Set in Plantin

The author would like to acknowledge the assistance of the Arts Council of Great Britain in the writing of this book.

To Randal Flynn, Joe Unsworth and Tom Disch

'Things close in'
James Thurber

1
Marking Time

Most mornings the alarm outside Carpenter's door startled him from sleep, but this particular morning he woke early to the whiteness of his cell with the feeling that he had had an important dream during the night. Usually his dreams were pleasant, aimless affairs in which he would wander through summery meadows or lie on a beach at sunset or sit snug beside a fire watching the rain fall through a window. He was always alone. The dreams were pleasant because they were dominated by a comfortable lack of urgency, by a feeling that *this might go on for ever*. They were an idyllic reflection of his waking life.

The alarm went off, startling Carpenter even though he had been steeling himself for it, sensing that it was almost eight o'clock despite the absence of clocks and sunlight. He remembered the dream: he had been exploring a labyrinthine library, filled with leather-bound books; a vast library containing all the knowledge in the world, like something out of a story by Borges. He was searching for – he didn't know what. At first he had been strolling leisurely through room after book-lined room; but then a sense of urgency had slowly overtaken him until finally he was running through wood-panelled passageways, feeling something approaching panic.

The dream had ended at that point. He pondered its significance and drew a blank. The alarm cut off, and presently he heard footsteps in the corridor outside before the bolt was drawn back on his door. He closed his eyes, pretending sleep.

Snider entered, carrying a pair of white gym shorts, a towel and a battery razor. He wore slate-blue coveralls and cropped blond hair; there was a name-tag on his breast. A lean but muscular man, Snider affected a smart appearance and an uncompromising attitude towards matters of discipline. Carpenter often thought of him as a throwback to the Gestapo, even his surname sounding suitably Germanic. His coveralls were always clean and uncrumpled; each morning he seemed to have been recreated anew, brought forth fresh from a mould.

Snider put the towel and razor on the ledge above the washbasin and tossed the shorts on the bed.

'Five minutes, Carpenter,' he said, then went out.

The bolt thunked shut behind him. Through the wall Carpenter could hear Sinnott in the cell next door getting out of bed as his door was opened.

Carpenter still felt tired. He would have dearly loved to roll over and go straight back to sleep, but he knew that Snider would only haul him out of bed and frogmarch him off to the gym where Blythe would be waiting, ready to take them through another twenty minutes of physical torment. *Bend* at the hip. *Stretch* those arms. *Lift* those legs. Something ought to be done about people like Blythe.

He threw back the bedclothes and put his feet down on the concrete floor. He wore striped pyjamas, and there were canvas slippers beside the bed. His cell was a twelve by nine foot chamber, painted entirely white. It was unornamented and the blankness of the walls was relieved only by the washbasin to the left of the door and a circular light at the centre of the ceiling. The washbasin had three taps, delivering hot water, liquid soap and cold water respectively. A toothbrush, comb and a tube of SR stood in a clear plastic beaker, and a small rectangular mirror was set into the wall above. Under his bed was a plastic chamber-pot which he had never used. The central light was a hemisphere of opaque glass with a metal nipple at its centre which made it look like an artificial breast; it was dimmed at night but never extinguished. There were similar lights throughout Limbo and each contained a hidden spy camera so that the inmates were under surveillance practically everywhere they went. White walls and bare concrete floors predominated in the corridors and rooms, with functional modern furniture and a minimum of decoration. Most of the rooms were less spartan than the cells; but none had windows.

Carpenter crossed to the washbasin and examined his face in the mirror for signs of decay. He would be thirty this coming October and his health worried him greatly; he had never had a serious illness in his life and felt that it was only a matter of time before he came down with something complicated and incurable. In the meantime Blythe was doing his best to kill him off through sheer over-exertion. During his first month in Limbo he had developed aches in muscles he hadn't known existed, and he still refused to believe that Blythe had his well-being at heart. Most fitness freaks had masochistic tendencies, and to become a PT instructor you had to be a sadist as well.

Carpenter washed his face before switching on the razor. Monday, he thought vaguely. It was a Monday.

*

'Now try it with one hand,' Blythe directed Sinnott, ignoring the fact that Sinnott could barely manage the requisite twenty-five press-ups with two tremulous hands splayed on the parquet floor. Sinnott's thin, post-adolescent body was frail enough, but his arms were even spindlier. Ever eager to please, he lifted his left hand and promptly collapsed, his head banging against the floor.

He's knocked himself out, Carpenter thought as he hastily completed his own quota. Then Sinnott groaned and rolled over, pushing back his long hair from his face. He looked more downcast than hurt.

Carpenter took the weight off his arms and rested his cheek against the herringbone wood. His innards felt as if they had been stretched on a rack. He decided that if ever he became Dictator of the World he'd have all PT instructors shot and outlaw press-ups by decree. They were a very British form of torture, just like cold showers and boarding-schools.

Blythe had turned his attention to Riley. Riley's portly, middle-aged body was ill-suited to any kind of contortion, but he always entered into the spirit of the gym sessions with gusto. As usual he was panting and groaning with effort, his head bobbing up and down in opposition to his behind while his arms remained motionless. It was the classic schoolboy simulation of a press-up.

'Bend those arms,' Blythe told him, putting a foot to his ample backside and forcing his body down. Riley's pot-belly flattened against the floor, his elbows jutting upwards. He made no attempt to rise.

'Come on,' Blythe urged him. 'You've got at least fifteen more to do.'

Riley let his arms go limp and lay there, panting. He looked like a stranded turtle. The soles of his feet were grey with dust from the floor.

'You're not finished,' Blythe insisted.

'My heart's given out. Leave me in peace to die.'

Off to the right, Treadwell was continuing with his routine, blind to everything around him. Carpenter watched with a mixture of envy and irritation as he jerked his body up and down with supreme ease. He had the physique of a lightweight boxer, muscular but trim, and the only sound he made was the hiss of air through his nostrils as his chest brushed the floor before his arms straightened without a quiver to raise his rigid torso once more.

In theory Carpenter would have loved to emulate Treadwell's effortless athleticism, but Treadwell added insult to injury by always doing double the number of required exercises. His relish for such strenuous and sweaty activities was a mystery to Carpenter, but he tried not to let it bother him too much, oppressed as he was by much thornier problems.

'Everybody hup!' Blythe shouted.

He took a stopwatch from the hip pocket of his grey flannel tracksuit. The session was almost at an end, and they now only had to complete five minutes of running on the spot before they would be released.

The gym was the only room in Limbo with a wooden floor. Apart from that, it was like all the others: bare and white-painted. There was a storeroom next to the entrance from which Blythe would occasionally produce medicine balls for them to hurl at one another or weights to strain their muscles with. On one occasion he had even dragged out a trampoline and a vaulting box and had been flattened when Riley had come sailing over the latter like a human cannonball and hit him in the small of the back. That was the last they had seen of the trampoline. Carpenter had never dared peer into the storeroom, his secret fear being that it also contained a set of collapsible wall-bars which Blythe would erect one morning before commanding them to mount the bars and hang there until he counted to one million. 'Back-hanging from the top wall-bar' was an order which echoed down the years from Carpenter's schooldays, and he never recalled it without wincing.

In the doorway Snider was watching over the lanky figure of Wright, who was still in his pyjamas. Wright was the only one of the inmates who refused to participate in the gym sessions; he forfeited breakfast as a result. Snider stood at his shoulder, his arms folded across his chest, his austere face as impassive as ever. Although Snider never revealed any emotion or bias towards his charges, Carpenter suspected that he actively disliked Wright and would not hesitate to bend his body into unusual postures should he step out of line.

'I want you to lift those legs high,' Blythe said. 'And run as fast as you can, clear?'

He studied his stopwatch and began to give the countdown for the exercise. He was a beefy, florid man in his late forties who always looked at once superbly fit and on the verge of a fatal coronary. Carpenter stared hard at him, thinking dark thoughts. On Saturday he had read an article in the *Reader's Digest* which had suggested that positive and negative emotional waves could be transmitted from the brain across free space and exert a palpable effect on other people. Carpenter was entertaining a vision of Blythe turning purple and crumpling to the ground in the hope of inducing a real seizure which would free them from the ritual torment of the gym sessions.

But Blythe completed the countdown as hale as ever. 'Go!' he shouted, and the four of them began running on the spot, Riley lifting his legs so high that he resembled a demented grape-treader. Carpenter squeezed his eyes shut and concentrated even harder on thinking Blythe to death.

*

Released from the gym, they assembled outside the bathroom for a shower. Hemmings, the slovenly guard who assisted Snider on the eight till four shift, was standing outside with the bathtowels.

'Morning,' he said brightly to no one in particular.

They were admitted one by one to the bathroom and allowed a maximum of five minutes per shower: Hemmings kept track on his wrist-watch. Riley was at the head of the queue, scratching his curly hair and yawning. Next to him was Treadwell, who stood erect and looked remarkably unruffled after the gym; he always awaited his turn with infinite patience. Sinnott, by contrast always looked edgy, as if he wished he was somewhere else; he seemed to be giving the blank stretch of wall before his eyes particular scrutiny.

Carpenter went to the end of the queue, standing behind Wright, who was now completely naked. He always insisted on stripping off as soon as the gym session was over, and he wore his nakedness proudly, as a sign of his defiance. No one paid much attention to him in this state, though Carpenter always noticed how much better endowed he was than himself.

The rest of them were allowed to retain their shorts until they entered the shower. Afterwards, wrapped in bathtowels, they departed to their individual cells, where a white cotton shirt and a pair of navy-blue serge trousers would be draped across the bed. This was their uniform in Limbo, with grey worsted socks, plain black shoes and a pair of white Y-fronts. The shirts and underwear were changed every other day, and every fortnight there was a clean pair of trousers. They had just completed their third month in Limbo, and there was no indication of when, if ever, they would be released.

*

The traditional English breakfast was one of the best things about Limbo, and the only thing that made Carpenter endure the gym sessions. Fruit juice and cereal would be followed by permutations of eggs, bacon, sausages, mushrooms, black pudding, baked beans and fried bread, with plenty of toast, marmalade and tea or coffee. It sometimes seemed to Carpenter that Limbo's catering department – whoever they were – worked in direct opposition to Blythe, being intent on clotting the inmates' veins and arteries with cholesterol as soon as Blythe had finished removing the previous day's deposits in the gym. But Carpenter always tried not to think of his health when eating; food was one of the few pleasures remaining to him.

They gathered in the small room which was set aside for meals and locked at other times. Hemmings doled out their breakfast from portable metal bins of the kind used in hospitals. He also gave Carpenter a fresh packet of Silk Cut and the blue disposable lighter which Carpenter had been using ever since he'd been in Limbo. He was allowed one packet of cigarettes per day, and these were taken from him before bedtime and a fresh packet provided every morning. Since he seldom smoked a full packet in a day he often wondered if Peacock, the evening shift guard who always collected his cigarettes and apparently didn't smoke himself, sold off those that were left to other guards or people in the outside world. Every prison traditionally had a racket.

Wright sat at the head of the table, disdaining the solitary glass of water which had been provided for him. He rested his elbows on the blue formica table-top and leaned forward, his eyes taking in everyone.

'I don't understand why you continue to submit yourselves to the indignity of the gym every day,' he said. 'I look upon it as a form of corporal punishment.'

Carpenter felt his spirits sag, and he kept his eyes fixed on his food; Wright was about to embark on his morning lecture.

Treadwell dabbed at his moustache with a paper napkin.

'Exercise is good for you,' he said. 'It has to hurt a little to be of any benefit.'

'That's where you're wrong, my friend. The notion that things must hurt in order to do you any good is a fallacy which arises from the Protestant Work Ethic.'

Treadwell stared at Wright with patent incomprehension.

'The Protestant Work Ethic,' Wright explained, 'underlies most of Western civilization. It's rooted in the Christian doctrine that pleasure is, in itself, an unhealthy thing, that to enjoy something you must first suffer hardship and toil.'

'What hardship?' Treadwell looked puzzled. 'It's fun.'

'It may be fun for someone like you who's fit and naturally enjoys exercise. But what about someone like, say, Riley there, who's obviously in no condition to enjoy it? How do you think he feels?'

Riley stifled a burp.

'I feel indigestion coming on,' he said.

'Exercise doesn't have to hurt to do you good,' Wright told Treadwell. 'Essentially, all you have to do is raise your heart-rate under exercise by gradual stages until you reach the level of fitness you desire. You don't have to sweat blood.'

'Who's sweating blood?' Treadwell said.

'I was speaking metaphorically.'

Riley, munching toast, let out a longer, louder burp. Wright kept his attention on Treadwell. 'Anyway you sidetracked me. I wasn't really making a point about the merits of exercise – I believe in it myself – but about the fact that there's no element of choice involved in whether we exercise or not.'

'I'd do it anyway,' Treadwell said. 'I enjoy it.'

Wright sighed. 'I know you would. But that's not the issue. What I'm arguing is that the gym sessions should not be compulsory. We should be free to participate if, and only if, we want to.'

'But *you* don't participate,' Treadwell said.

'I don't get any breakfast because I refuse, do I? How many of the others do you think would be with you in the gym each morning of their own free choice if it wasn't for the fact that they'd forfeit breakfast if they didn't?'

Carpenter could see that Treadwell was lost in the convolutions of this last sentence. He considered sticking a sausage in Wright's mouth to shut him up but rejected the idea since it was likely to have the opposite effect.

'They're treating us like criminals, don't you see?' A film of spittle had formed at both corners of his mouth. 'They're attempting to dictate our behaviour with a system of rewards and punishments, to compel us to do things we may not want to do. That's the point. We're not criminals. What gives them the right to treat us this way? What have we done to deserve it?'

'Why are we here?' Sinnott murmured.

That, thought Carpenter, is the sixty-four-thousand-dollar question.

*

After breakfast they retired to what was popularly known as the lounge, a spacious room holding black vinyl armchairs, melamine coffee tables and a colour television set. On the walls hung cheerless abstract prints. Athena prints. There was something about Athena prints which always made Carpenter think of colour supplements and long, boring Sundays. He'd disliked Sundays ever since he'd been a young child and had had to go to Sunday School while most of his friends were out playing football or teaching themselves to smoke. Even when religious disillusionment had finally overcome him and he'd stopped going, he'd still found that Sundays remained boring or were prone to disruption by bad news. Maybe it was God's way of getting His own back.

The morning papers were sitting on the central coffee table and Carpenter selected a *Daily Star*, feeling a twinge of guilt as he did so. Wright would have no truck with any of the popular newspapers and was always chastising Carpenter for not reading a 'quality' paper such as *The Times* or the *Guardian*. Carpenter agreed that these were indeed good newspapers and worthy of his attention, but he continued to avoid reading them for the very reason that they contained a lot of important news and considered analysis of current affairs. The issues were invariably so complex that he could never form any coherent opinions on them and always ended up wishing that he hadn't bothered to apprise himself of the facts in the first place. Since he'd been in Limbo he'd stuck resolutely to the tabloids with their more comforting diet of sex, sport and showbusiness. If this meant that his mind was going to seed, so much the better.

Despite his strong opinions on the press, Wright did not in fact read any newspapers in Limbo or watch any television. He had explained that since Limbo was an enclosed environment, since they knew nothing about what was happening in the outside world except what they read in the newspapers or saw on television, it was possible that all their incoming information was doctored – censored or even fabricated – to suit the mysterious purposes of those who were keeping them in captivity.

Wright had evolved the provisional theory that their enforced incarceration in Limbo was some form of unprecedented sociological experiment whose purpose was simply to study the reactions of five randomly chosen men to such an unexplained and unjust imprisonment. In comparison to Riley's notion that they had been press-ganged and were aboard a spaceship en route to another planet, this seemed to Carpenter quite a reasonable idea: after all, sociologists and psychologists were renowned for doing arcane studies in which the layman could see no practical relevance whatsoever. But he didn't believe that they were receiving faked or censored news. He could think of no earthly reason for such a subterfuge, and there were practical difficulties, too. Imagine having to invent a special set of newspapers each day, in addition to persuading all the television newsreaders to do extra broadcasts of made-up news just for their benefit – it simply wasn't on. Wright, however, remained unmoved by these arguments, contending that anything was possible under the bizarre circumstances in which they found themselves and that it was prudent to trust nothing.

Carpenter stared at the front-page story in the *Telegraph* Treadwell was reading – a report of an earthquake in Ecuador. Even assuming that their news input *was* faked, the point seemed pretty academic to him. The world outside was doubtless in as much confusion as it had been before they'd been spirited away to Limbo, and did it really matter if it was an earthquake in Ecuador or a plague in Pakistan that was presently causing misery for thousands or millions of people? Well, yes, strictly speaking it did; to the Ecuadorians and the Pakistanis at least, it probably mattered a hell of a lot. But what about the typical Britisher, shielded from such gross catastrophes by the luck of geography and history? What did it really matter to him who was dying and where? Tragedies tended to blur into one another when viewed through the cosy medium of print or screen; and anyway, you could only absorb so much bad news before your brain clicked into neutral. Take Northern Ireland, for example: there was a perfect case of so much horror building up that eventually you became inured to it.

Carpenter immediately stopped himself from thinking about Northern Ireland. Northern Ireland was one of those thorny problems which seemed so impervious to rational contemplation that he tried to relegate it to a dark corner of his mind with all the other questions to which he could find no answers. He turned to the back page, looking for some news of Manchester United. Sometimes it seemed strange that he should be so concerned about the fortunes of a football team when there were many larger issues which ought to be occupying his mind. Wright, for example, disapproved of all team sports, claiming that they promoted regimentation and the mob ethos. He had been expostulating on that very subject the Saturday afternoon of the Wales–England rugby international when Riley had poured a cup of coffee in his lap.

As if on cue, Wright emerged from his cell, where, Carpenter knew, he had been exercising. Wright was almost as keen on physical fitness as Treadwell, and would surely have enjoyed the gym sessions had he not been ordered to participate. The question of whether Wright's behaviour was symptomatic of an absolute integrity or an ineluctable stupidity was one which continued to haunt Carpenter. Wright, a rangy six-footer with a pointed nose and a shock of mousy hair which hung over his widow's peak like a wave about to break on the shore of his forehead, did at least possess the firmness of mind which Carpenter knew he lacked himself. Wright believed in things; he had strong opinions on a wide range of subjects; he was committed. This naturally made him hell to live with.

Carpenter lit his first Silk Cut of the day. This is the one, he thought as he drew on it, which will trigger one of my cells into a riot of replication. Within a year or two I'll be dead, consumed by a cancerous hunger. Why am I doing this to myself?

Of all the grisly ends which Carpenter conceived for himself, the thought of cancer was the most terrible. In this he knew he was representative of his time. Wright believed that the general fear of cancer arose from the fact that most people instinctively understood and were appalled at the thought that they were dying through self-cannibalization, being eaten by themselves, as it were. Like most of his ideas it suffered, Carpenter felt, from over-intellectualization. He doubted that most people had sufficient knowledge of the exact nature of the disease to conceptualize their fears in such a fashion. As far as he was concerned there was a much simpler and more plausible reason for the general horror of cancer: most people who got it eventually died of it.

As soon as Wright saw Carpenter light up, he walked straight through the lounge and into the games room where Sinnott was practising his snooker. Perhaps the only good reason Carpenter could give himself for continuing to smoke was that it would ensure

Wright's abrupt departure from whatever room they happened to be in. Wright detested cigarettes, and espoused the theory that they were substitute nipples; smoking, according to him, was as much an oral comfort harking back to breast-feeding as it was a nicotine addiction. Carpenter was quite happy to subscribe to this theory: how much nicer it was to think of a cigarette as the end of a tit than as a tube of potentially lethal tar.

He was thinking too much, he knew, and about all sorts of unpleasant and unfruitful subjects. That was the trouble with Limbo: you had so much time on your hands you invariably spent a lot of it in thought.

'Listen to this,' Riley said, and read out an amusing story from the *Daily Mirror* about a man who had climbed a tree to rescue a cat only to have the animal leap upon his head and hang there, tearing out half of his hair before he brought it to ground.

Riley showed him a photograph of the man, who looked like an alopecia victim. Treadwell peered over the top of his paper and smiled in a way which suggested he had no idea why Riley was displaying the photograph.

'If I was him,' Riley said, 'I'd claim damages from the cat. Demand a graft of its hair to cover the missing bits.'

Carpenter returned to his own paper, unhappily stirred by the story to thoughts of his own receding hairline. Baldness, he had reluctantly decided, was aesthetically unappealing. One of his girlfriends had once told him that bald or partially bald men were often very attractive to women, but to him this simply implied by a kind of negative emphasis that most, in fact, were not. And anyway, to be losing your hair at twenty-nine was . . . well, it made you worry like hell and caused your hair to fall out even faster. It was a vicious circle, a destructive self-perpetuating cycle, as most of his habits seemed to be.

Riley was peering at him.

'You all right?' he asked.

Carpenter pointed a forefinger to the side of his head and twirled it around. His brain was in overdrive today.

'Darts?' Riley suggested.

Carpenter decided that a game would be most welcome. Darts were always good for staving off thought.

They went into the games room. Sinnott was knocking balls around the snooker table, waiting for Treadwell to finish his newspaper; Treadwell was the only one who could really compete with him on green felt. Wright was sitting in an armchair beside the dartboard, reading a copy of *The Listener*.

Riley put a rag to the scoreboard. A cloud of chalkdust began to descend on Wright.

'Do you mind?' he said.

'Do I mind what?' Riley asked.

'Do you mind not showering me with chalkdust.'

'No,' said Riley, 'I don't mind.'

Wright glared at him, then returned to his reading, smoothing out the page emphatically. 'Don't think I'm going to move just because you've come in here to annoy me.'

Riley took the darts from the board and walked back to the eight foot mark.

'Up for bull,' he said, handing Carpenter a dart.

Carpenter aimed and threw. Riley followed. He was closer.

'I'm warning you, Riley,' said Wright as he plucked out the darts, 'if you hit me I'll bloody throttle you.'

'What if I hit you in the head?'

'If you so much as graze me, I'll throttle you.'

'Not if I hit you in the head. You'll be dead.'

'Are you threatening me?'

'Just pointing out the dangers. The brain is in the head, you know.'

'I don't need you to give me an anatomy lesson. I knew where the brain was when I was five years old.'

Riley looked impressed. He walked back to the mark.

'When I was five years old,' he said to Carpenter, 'all I could do was dribble. I was a late developer.'

'Late?' said Wright. 'You never got started.' He gave a porcine snort.

'I was eight before I learned to talk,' Riley told him.

'And you've talked a lot of drivel ever since.'

'It's all to do with upbringing. My parents neglected me. They left me with my uncle a lot. He was a bit eccentric. He used to tell me funny stories.'

Wright studiously returned to his reading. Riley looked as if he was recalling fond memories.

'I'll never forget what he told me about Santa Claus. Did you believe in Santa Claus when you were little?'

'Just go away,' said Wright.

'I did at first. But later I wasn't sure. I wanted to know how he made a living out of season. You know what my uncle told me?'

'I haven't the faintest idea and I couldn't care less.'

'He told me he delivered babies the rest of the year round. That's where babies came from – the North Pole. According to my uncle Santa went around in disguise as a rag-and-bone man, with an old tweed suit and a trilby in place of his usual outfit. And he shaved his beard off so that people wouldn't recognize him. He had this horse and cart, with all sorts of old junk on it. But under the junk was babies, ready for delivery. He'd sneak them into houses for women when the neighbours weren't looking.'

Wright had put a hand over his eyes as if to shut out the sound of Riley's voice. Riley made to throw, then paused. 'Whenever I heard a rag-and-bone man in the street I'd always rush outside and try to see what was in his cart, thinking that if I found any babies I'd steal one and take it home for my mother.'

Wright was staring at him. 'I can't believe I'm listening to such puerile nonsense from a fully grown man.'

'I was at an impressionable age,' Riley told him. 'And you can't blame my uncle – he was a bit peculiar. He had an accident when he was younger, in a pub. Someone hit him in the head with a dart.'

Wright surged to his feet, flinging down the magazine. 'You're not funny, Riley, you're just inane.' He stalked out.

Riley aimed at the dartboard and proceeded to throw. His first dart narrowly missed the double five. The second scored a double eighteen. The third hit the metal ribbing of the treble twenty and rebounded, embedding itself in the back of the chair in which Wright had been sitting.

Riley walked over to the chair. He cocked his head, looked rueful, then plucked out the dart.

Carpenter understood his disappointment. The dart would have got Wright between the eyes.

*

Within half an hour Carpenter was bored with darts. He and Riley challenged Treadwell to doubles at snooker. They were resoundingly beaten three games in a row. It was a mystery to Carpenter how Sinnott, a nervous lad at the best of times, always managed to steady himself when taking a crucial shot: the ball would inevitably thud into the pocket. Carpenter kept wishing that Snider would appear, for his presence was usually enough to put Sinnott off his game. But Snider had evidently gone off for his coffee break or whatever it was the guards did when they weren't around. Perhaps he was watching them at this very moment through the spy camera in the light fitting. Sinnott continued to play with perfect assurance, and Treadwell provided good support. By the third game Riley was telling Carpenter jokes across the table in the hope that this would distract them. It didn't.

Carpenter felt restless, as if he had something important to do but had forgotten what. Usually he was quite content to while away the morning hours with darts or snooker or cards or board-games – the place was well-stocked with amusements – but today something was bothering him. He shook his head to the suggestion of a fourth game and returned to the lounge.

Wright was evidently still in the library, for he was nowhere to be seen. Carpenter stretched out on a sofa, relieved to have a few moments to himself. Then Hemmings shambled into the room.

'Carpenter,' he said, as though greeting a long-lost friend. 'Just the man I've been looking for.'

He sat down beside Carpenter and offered him a piece of the large Cadbury's Fruit & Nut bar he was holding. Carpenter shook his head. He watched as Hemmings crammed chocolate into his mouth. Debris from the bar littered the chest of his coveralls and there were brown smears on his thighs.

'You're a scientist, right?' he said presently.

No, it was not right. He was a physics graduate who hadn't opened a modern physics book in years. To call him a scientist was about as accurate as calling a man who whistled a musician.

'Gravity,' said Hemmings. 'Gravity comes from the centre of the earth, right? It keeps us stuck to the ground. Anything that's thrown up in the air is always pulled back down again. Unless it's travelling fast enough to escape, like a rocket.' Hemmings paused to swallow. 'Then how come the moon doesn't fall on the earth?'

Carpenter wanted to get up and flee to the bathroom. But Hemmings was leaning across him.

'How come,' he went on, 'the earth doesn't fall into the sun? The sun has more gravity than the earth, right?'

He crammed more chocolate into his mouth. Carpenter backed off to the edge of the sofa, but Hemmings moved with him, maintaining his oppressive propinquity. As he chewed his mouth opened to reveal teeth coated with brown slime.

'Another thing,' he said. 'The universe is expanding, right? But what's it expanding *into*?'

Carpenter fished out a cigarette and lit up, blowing smoke into his face. This had no deterrent effect whatsoever.

'I don't get it. There must be something outside the universe. And how far does it go?'

Carpenter was now hopelessly cornered. He puffed on his cigarette, shrouding his head in a cloud of smoke. At this point Wright emerged from the library with a book.

'Morning,' Hemmings said jauntily as he sat down in an armchair. 'How are you this morning?'

'How do you think I am?' Wright said. 'How would you like to have your fundamental liberties removed without any justification whatsoever? How would you like to be treated like a caged animal?'

Hemmings put more chocolate into his mouth. He seemed to be considering Wright's questions. Then he turned back to Carpenter.

'I saw this programme the other night about experiments on animals. They were putting electrodes into dogs' brains and cutting the tails off rats and hamsters.'

'Hamsters do not have tails,' Wright informed him.

Carpenter tried to move, but Hemmings was leaning against him.

'They reckon that dolphins and whales communicate by mental telepathy,' he said.

'That,' said Wright, 'is a tautology. Telepathy cannot be anything but mental.'

Hemmings blinked and swallowed. Carpenter blew smoke in

Wright's direction before stubbing out his cigarette. But Wright didn't notice; he was too busy enjoying himself with Hemmings.

In most respects Hemmings was the antithesis of Snider. Snider was stern, punctilious and aloof, whereas Hemmings, an ungainly, slack-faced man in his late thirties, had cultivated a more informal approach towards Carpenter and the others. From the day of their arrival in Limbo he had been chatty and had made a special effort to get to know them. But there was something about him which was repellent. His conversational gambits seemed phoney and he had no concept of bodily space, tending to sit or stand too close to the person he was addressing. It made you want to push him away or leap backwards. And he was one of those people who conducted a conversation without really listening to what the other person was saying. No one felt comfortable with him, and Wright only tolerated his company because it gave him ample opportunities for disdainful demonstrations of his superior intelligence.

Hemmings had a faint accent which Carpenter couldn't identify. But then he had never been very good at identifying accents. Wright, by contrast, claimed to have a finely tuned ear; according to him Hemmings hailed from the Black Country, and he also claimed that he could pinpoint the native areas of Limbo's entire staff from the way each spoke. This had led him to devise a method for establishing Limbo's likely location. It ultimately involved drawing on a map a series of lines whose point of convergence would reveal precisely where Limbo was sited. Wright had huddled in the library for over a week with a pencil stub and a plastic ruler which one of the weekend guards had allowed him, making intricate networks of lines on the pocket atlas whenever he thought the guards weren't looking. At the end of it he had announced that Limbo was situated about forty miles south of Eastbourne.

Despite the scepticism of the others, Wright had insisted his method was valid. It was not at all unreasonable, he argued, to suppose that Limbo was sited in the middle of the Channel, probably on the sea bed. This conclusion might have been within the bounds of credibility were it not for the fact that the television programmes they received pointed to a London location. To Wright this was simply confirmation that they were receiving fake transmissions.

'So you disapprove of battery farming,' Wright was saying. 'What about concentration camps?'

Carpenter had no idea how the conversation had got around to battery farming, but he knew it was time to leave.

'Are human beings any less important than chickens?' Wright was asking the hapless Hemmings. 'Did you know that the British invented concentration camps? It's one of our more recent contributions to civilization.'

Carpenter edged off the sofa and fled.

*

'Check,' said Wright, moving his queen abreast Carpenter's king.

Carpenter gazed with dismay at the board, wondering why he had been so stupid as to play Wright in the first place. After fleeing into the games room from Hemmings he had taken the chessboard and box out of the store cupboard behind the dartboard for no other reason than to divert himself by pretending that he was a young British discovery engaged in a chequerboard tussle with some nefarious Russian grandmaster. Naturally he would win through in the end and become the first British chess champion of the world. Then Wright had spoiled it by sitting down opposite him and moving a pawn. Wright often played chess with himself, and Carpenter knew he had been seeking an opponent ever since they'd been in Limbo. Some automatic instinct had made him move an equivalent pawn, and then it was too late.

Carpenter decided that he hated chess. They had only been playing for ten minutes or so, and Wright already had him hemmed in with a queen, a rook and a battery of pawns. Carpenter's beleaguered king was hopelessly cornered, and Wright was casually picking off his other pieces, as if deliberately delaying the *coup de grâce* through sheer sadism. His main struggle now was resisting the urge to contrive an accident in which the pieces would be scattered over the floor.

Carpenter sighed. He had only ever won a handful of games since he had learned to play chess at school, and he wondered why he persisted in deluding himself that he was a competent player. Once, he'd sat down and tried to analyse why he usually lost, and he had come to the conclusion it was due to a surfeit of caution and anxiety. He spent so much time trying to determine his opponent's strategy that his own game dissolved under the welter of devilish possibilities which his brain conjured up. It was remarkable what brilliantly fiendish gambits he could imagine were being employed against him: far more brilliant and fiendish than actually turned out to be the case. He knew that if only he could play his own game as if he was his own opponent, he'd be unbeatable. As it was, he simply worked himself into such a state of agitation that within minutes he was actively longing to be put out of his misery.

On this occasion, however, deliverance of another sort was at hand. Snider entered and announced that Naughton wanted to see them all in his office immediately.

Carpenter's first thought was that he would steal back into the room as soon as Naughton released them and pile all the pieces back into their box.

'I think you'll find it's mate,' said Wright.

*

Carpenter's eyes were always drawn first to the red telephone.

Naughton stood behind his desk, his face fixed in the disapproving expression he had been cultivating throughout their stay in Limbo. He was a thin man with dark, wavy hair cropped unfashionably short around his ears. To Carpenter he always appeared nervous and tubercular, his cheeks hollow and his eyes too bright and bulbous. He was probably in his late thirties, but he looked younger, almost adolescent. He wore shabby, ill-fitting suits – a black barathea affair on this occasion – while his kipper ties were a wonder to behold. Today's was salmon-pink with crescent moons in royal blue and five-pointed stars in scarlet. So hideous that it transcended bad taste.

Summonses to Naughton's office tended to be rare – Carpenter guessed that he preferred to see as little of them as possible – but they always meant that he was upset about some aspect of their general conduct; particular infractions merited an individual interview. The office held a filing cabinet and a metal desk with the red telephone on it. The walls were painted a mustard colour, a neon tube glowed overhead, and a print of *The Fighting Temeraire* hung on the wall behind the desk. Despite all this, it seemed just as bare as the other rooms in Limbo. The desk was always devoid of paperwork and Carpenter had never seen Naughton use the red telephone or even heard it ringing.

On the floor next to the filing cabinet was a yellow plastic bowl containing a few smears of cat food. The cat was still hiding under Naughton's desk, but Carpenter was confident it would soon emerge.

Naughton launched into his preamble, which consisted of vague and generalized comments on reports he had received of minor breaches in discipline since he had last interviewed them. Carpenter had heard it all before in essence; he stifled a yawn and wondered if Naughton was married. On balance he thought not; it was hard to imagine any wife tolerating his taste in ties.

When Naughton was finished he studied them all gravely before telling Sinnott to stand still. This was a futile order, since Sinnott's nervous disposition did not permit immobility unless he was unconscious, but it was less a demand than a token display of power: Naughton knew that Sinnott was the only inmate who was intimidated by his authority and consequently he always found an excuse to pick on him.

As far as Carpenter could tell, Naughton worked a peculiarly staggered day in Limbo. It was never possible to be sure precisely when he was in attendance since the door to his office was normally closed; but he seemed to take a two-hour lunch break at noon and then a further two-hour break between five and seven o'clock before finally departing at ten o'clock. Saturdays and Sundays were his days off.

Naughton opened the middle drawer of his desk and produced two items of cutlery which he held up.

'Fork,' said Riley. 'Spoon.'

Naughton put both pieces down on the desk in front of him.

'These two pieces of cutlery went missing after dinner on Friday. The theft was reported to me this morning and your cells were promptly searched. They were found to have been secreted in a mattress.' Naughton was looking at Wright. 'Would you care to explain what they were doing there?'

'You know perfectly well what they were doing there,' said Wright. 'I am being kept a prisoner here, illegally. I intend to do everything in my power to escape.'

'This isn't Colditz, Wright. I won't tolerate these foolish displays of dramatics.'

'I'm in deadly earnest.'

Naughton gave a small sigh. 'Would you care to tell us what you were intending to do with them?'

'I'm not prepared to tell you anything which you might be able to use to your own advantage.'

Carpenter decided that this was a pretty good answer under the circumstances. No doubt Wright planned to use the fork and spoon as digging implements, but Carpenter still couldn't see what use they would be. A tunnel needed to have two ends, and it was necessary to dig towards a point outside the institution from which you wanted to escape. And this was the nub of the problem. Since Limbo had no windows, none of them knew which direction led out; they didn't even know where the exit was within the building: the corridors all led into one another, as did the doors between each room.

There had to be a way out, of course, for the staff came and went according to their rotas and evidently returned to the outside world when they were not on duty. But after three months none of them had succeeded in pinpointing a door or corridor which indubitably led outside. To Carpenter's right was a door which he had previously assumed led into Dr Dempster's office until it had dawned on him that there was no door in the corresponding wall there; so there had to be a small room or a corridor in between. Possibly the exit lay there, but it was more likely to be the monitor room where the guards kept watch over them from afar. But the door was always closed whenever they were summoned to Naughton's office, and Carpenter had never been able to get a glimpse of what lay beyond it.

Naughton was telling Wright how disappointed he was with his behaviour; he had hoped by now that they would have established an atmosphere of mutual respect and trust. But clearly not. Of course they were all responsible for one another's actions, therefore in future their cells would be searched before bedtime and after breakfast.

Was that it? Was that all? Evidently it was, and Naughton seemed satisfied that it was stern punishment indeed.

At this point the cat finally crawled out from under his desk. It was a large black cat named Mordred with long claws and malevolent yellow-green eyes. A leather lead tied to one of the desk legs kept it confined to the office, which was just as well. It had been installed by Naughton a month previously as an indirect result of Riley's inability to tie proper knots in his shoelaces.

The cat advanced on Sinnott, who tried smiling at it to fend off its approach, but without success. It pounced on his nearest foot and proceeded to flex its claws in the ragged leather. Sinnott began to squirm and gulp.

'What's the matter with you?' Naughton demanded of him. 'I haven't condemned you to death.' He was unaware of the cat's onslaught.

'Nothing,' said Sinnott, swallowing back the pain.

Sinnott lived in dread of incurring Naughton's displeasure and would not complain about the cat as a result. Mere youth could not explain his fear of authority, which was almost pathological and caused him to be exploited by practically everyone. Blythe pressed him to the limit in the gym, Snider could frighten him with a single glance, and Harris, one of the evening shift guards with a penchant for bullying, was always playing practical jokes on him such as putting cornflakes in his bed or a condom in his coffee.

Carpenter felt sorry for Sinnott since he seemed condemned to go through life moulding his own destiny to the whims of others. He was the classic orphan who had been raised in an institution with a strictly disciplinarian atmosphere which had inculcated into him a pervasive fear of falling foul of authority. Or, conversely, he had grown up without ever having any elders to supervise his upbringing and thus saw all figures of authority as parental substitutes whom he looked to for the guidance and approval he had never received in childhood. Carpenter found psychology a fascinating subject since it was always possible to arrive at two diametrically opposing theories from one set of observations.

He stretched out a foot and prodded the cat in the backside. It immediately relinquished its grip on Sinnott's toe and hissed at him before going down into a crouch. As it prepared to leap at him, Carpenter cupped his hands over his genitals like a footballer in a defensive wall.

'What are you doing, Carpenter?' Naughton demanded.

Carpenter pointed, and Naughton peered over the top of his desk.

'Mordred!' he shouted. 'Come here!' He fumbled under the desk for the lead.

The cat darted off to the other side of the room and squeezed itself behind the filing cabinet to glare evilly at Carpenter from the shadows, as if promising vengeance at a later date. Hemmings edged away from the wall where he had been lounging.

Today Riley's shoes were securely tied. Treadwell had lately been checking them every morning after breakfast since Riley seemed incapable of tying proper knots himself and often walked around with his shoelaces flapping. This had become a source of curiosity and perhaps even irritation to Treadwell, who was an orderly man in his habits; but Treadwell had shown his usual politeness when he had first asked Riley why his laces were always undone.

Riley had studied his shoes before saying, 'What's the point? I only have to undo them again at night when I go to bed.'

They were all sitting around in the lounge at the time; it was only their second week in Limbo, and they were still getting to know one another.

'Are you saying you don't do them up at all?'

Riley shrugged. 'It's a waste of time. Why do them up if you have to undo them all over again?'

Treadwell looked as if he had been forced to wrestle with some utterly new philosophical concept. Several moments passed before he said, 'That's not a good idea. It's dangerous. You could trip over them and fracture your skull.'

'He's having you on,' Wright interjected. 'He's just using an absurd argument to justify his laziness.'

'What's absurd about it?' said Riley, showing no indication that he had been joking.

'Oh, come on. You don't not do up your shoelaces just because you have to undo them at night. What do you take me for? If you took that sort of reasoning to its logical conclusion you'd walk around with your eyes closed because there'd be no point in opening them since you have to go to sleep each night. Wouldn't you?'

'That would be daft,' said Riley. 'If I walked around all day with my eyes closed I'd probably trip over my shoelaces and fracture my skull.'

Riley had a habit of standing on one foot and swinging his other leg. This caused his loose laces to make skittering noises on the bare floor of Naughton's office which sounded like the scampering of tiny feet. Hemmings had let slip that Naughton was convinced he had mice in his office, and Carpenter had subsequently noticed mousetraps and piles of poison in the corners of the room. Mordred was simply the latest in a line of rodent-repellents.

'I've noticed a progressive deterioration in standards of personal hygiene,' Naughton was saying; he had abandoned his attempt to bring Mordred to heel. 'I exempt Wright and Treadwell from this criticism, but you, Riley, are slovenly in appearance. And you, Sinnott, need your hair cut. I'll have the barber brought in tomorrow.'

'Let me have a pair of scissors,' Sinnott said. 'I'll trim it myself.'

'You'll have it cut for you like everyone else.'

'Please. You can have someone watch me.'

'Tomorrow morning, Sinnott. I don't want to hear any more about it.'

Sinnott looked devastated, and Carpenter knew that it was not simply a matter of pride, even though he always kept his shoulder-length hair carefully groomed. No, Sinnott had good reason to fear a haircut. Shortly after their arrival in Limbo a barber had been brought in by Naughton to cut their hair, and it was not an experience Carpenter was ever likely to forget. The barber was a squat, almost bald man wearing horn-rimmed glasses with lenses like the bottoms of milk bottles. He appeared to have learned his trade before the invention of electricity, for apart from the standard scissors he also wielded a pair of mechanical clippers. Carpenter had not seen such an implement in years, and in his hands they proved an exquisite instrument of torture, making Carpenter yelp with pain as they tore lumps of hair from his neck. He also suffered several minor cuts on the ears from misapplied scissors, the barber humming unconcernedly to himself throughout. He was to hair-dressing what Genghis Khan had been to diplomacy.

Afterwards Carpenter had felt humiliated and had vowed that he would do everything in his power to prevent the barber from ever getting near him again. His cropped head merely emphasized those expanding areas of his scalp where hair would never grow again, and there was little consolation in the fact that Riley, Treadwell and Wright had all suffered similarly. He had that awful, impotent feeling of looking ridiculous, a feeling he vividly remembered from his teens when overzealous barbers had been the cause of weeks of misery and mockery from friends. Only now, over two months later, was his hair beginning to look vaguely normal again.

Sinnott had escaped the slaughter on that day by the useful expedient of fainting; after seeing first Carpenter and then Riley emerge from the gym shorn and trembling he had keeled over as Wright took his turn. Snider had carried him off to his cell and he had not emerged until the following morning, looking far worse than any of them. Carpenter did not envy him his belated assignation with the demon barber.

Naughton now opened another drawer in his desk and produced a white pillowcase which he unfolded and held up. It was stained with several blurred red spots. Carpenter studied *The Fighting Temeraire* on the wall above Naughton's head, knowing what was coming.

'Last week's pillowcase, Carpenter,' said Naughton. 'Would you care to explain how it got into such a state?'

Carpenter did not care to. He shrugged.

'If you are suffering from nocturnal nosebleeds or some similar complaint, then I suggest you inform Dr Dempster and seek suitable treatment from her. Bloodstains are notoriously difficult to remove from linen and we can't constantly be supplying you with fresh pillowcases. This is not the first occasion I've had to warn you about this . . .'

The words became a drone. Carpenter concentrated on the painting, imagining that Naughton was aboard the ship and that he was a U-boat commander under the water with it square in his periscope sights. *Fire One! Fire Two! Fire Three!*

*

Carpenter sat in the toilet, thinking of the morning when he had awoken to find himself in Limbo. One night he had gone to bed as usual at his flat, but the next morning he had opened his eyes to find himself in a white windowless cell, lying under artificial light. He felt terrible, his head fuzzy with sleep, his whole body aching; but finally he had summoned the energy to get out of bed and try the door. It was locked. Soon afterwards someone had come along and marched him off without explanation to Naughton's office. This was Snider.

Naughton had been sitting at his desk, wearing a dishevelled grey suit and a violet and yellow paisley tie. Carpenter had simply stood there, dazed and disorientated, while Snider and another guard whom he later came to know as Hemmings had fetched four other men into the office whom Carpenter had never seen before. They all wore striped pyjamas like himself and all looked equally bewildered. None of them had said anything as Naughton had informed them of his name and of the fact that he was henceforward responsible for their welfare. He expected them to behave fittingly to their new status, and in return their needs would be catered to. He talked of rules and regulations, but Carpenter absorbed little of it at the time since he was feeling light-headed and his dearest wish was to lie down again. When Naughton was finally finished they were marched off to the bathroom for a shower and thence to breakfast.

A few days had passed before it dawned on them that they were effectively prisoners in some enclosed and windowless institution, their activities monitored and regulated by Naughton's guards. The guards refused to answer questions, and they were given no inkling of why they had been imprisoned. The regime was not especially repressive. Newspapers were delivered every day (and magazines each weekend), there was a television to watch and a variety of games with which to amuse themselves. They were provided with meals at set times, made to exercise each morning and were locked in their cells each night. Apart from this nothing seemed to be required of them apart from docile and accepting behaviour.

By the end of their first week Wright had forced them to accompany him to Naughton's office, where he had demanded an explanation for their imprisonment and their immediate release. Naughton had replied that he, Wright, was in no position to demand anything and was expected to behave himself. Wright had begun to protest more loudly and indignantly until finally Naughton had ordered Snider and Hemmings to drag him off to his cell and lock him inside for the rest of the day. That was the end of formal protests, though Wright's umbrage had not lessened in the slightest since then.

They were in Limbo, and in the absence of any official designation this became its name. Days turned into weeks, and with the exception of Wright they had accepted their new status stoically, lulled by its routine and lack of blatant outrages. Only Wright continued to rail against the injustice of their plight, but faced with the intransigence of the guards and the continuing bewilderment of his fellow inmates, there was little he could do except lecture them on their apathy and lack of moral fibre. In many ways he was the biggest nuisance in Limbo.

*

Lunch was omelettes with baked ham and pineapples. Riley always developed a healthy appetite before each meal, and he ate with such speed and gusto that he was finished before the rest of them were done with their soup. He went off to his cell to take a siesta. Conversation at the table was muted, with Wright being in a subdued mood for once. Carpenter was profoundly grateful; it was at meal-times that Wright usually launched into his tirades against whatever happened to be bothering him at the time. Sinnott seldom spoke unless he was first addressed; he had the appetite of a sparrow and spent most of his time at the table prodding and rearranging his food on his plate but actually eating little.

Carpenter fell to watching Treadwell, who was observing a strictly rectilinear approach to the cutting of his food. First he pared away the edges of his omelette to leave a perfect rectangle; then he began cutting off strips until the omelette was reduced to a square; this was finally sliced vertically and horizontally to give four smaller, mouth-sized squares. The omelette eaten, he repeated the procedure on his ham, then carved his pineapple into quarter segments and ate them.

Carpenter was fascinated by this ritual, which he had observed on many occasions. He also suspected that Treadwell reserved the same number of chews for a given piece of food, the number varying with different items and being directly dependent on the consistency and toughness of the food.

When he had finished eating, Treadwell laid his knife and fork along the centre of the plate, parallel to one another and with their points facing away from him. He then took a little water before wiping his lips with a paper napkin, crumpling it afterwards and placing it on his plate.

Carpenter knew that this was perfect table etiquette, for he had recently read an article on the subject in one of the Sunday supplements. Since he'd been in Limbo he had widened his general knowledge considerably from the magazines which were always lying around in the lounge, learning how to make tiny storage compartments out of used matchboxes, how to be more confident when giving public speeches, how to mount a beermat collection, how to shear sheep, how to reduce pre-menstrual tension, how to get more out of his sex life, how to identify common species of trees at a single glance, how to design a more efficient kitchen, and so on. His mind was turning into a litter bin for all sorts of useless bits of information. And he was, he realized, becoming obsessed by trivia such as Treadwell's eating habits.

Treadwell had the chiselled handsomeness of a Hollywood star, but there was no real spark of personality in his face so that he looked undistinguished. He was the most orderly person Carpenter had ever met, the fastidiousness with which he applied himself to his food being evident in every other aspect of his behaviour. He was always well turned out, and his manner with even the most obnoxious of the guards was perfectly correct. Carpenter had long felt that people whose lives were rigidly bound to formality and routine lacked imagination, and this certainly seemed to apply to Treadwell. While he was a polite and affable man, he also tended to obtuseness and gullibility.

There was an apple for dessert. Presently Treadwell picked his up and began slicing it into four segments before cutting out the cores with a delicacy which would have done credit to a surgeon. Not a lock of his bronze hair was ever out of place, his moustache was always immaculately trimmed and his sideboards had a perfect edge. Carpenter had never been able to shave properly with a dry razor and he continually marvelled at how Treadwell managed such geometrical perfection. Indeed, it periodically irritated him so much he would take to fantasizing that one day he'd sneak up on Treadwell with a pair of scissors and carve his moustache and sideboards into a mockery of their present neatness.

No doubt Treadwell shaved according to his favourite maxim: Time and Patience. He was fond of quoting maxims and adages by which he claimed to live his life, and Carpenter recalled the day Sinnott had become agitated about something and Treadwell had counselled him: 'Take your time and have patience. It's always the best policy.'

'Why?' Riley had wanted to know.

'You'll do things better if you take your time over them,' Treadwell had informed him.

'What if you're about to be trampled by a herd of rampaging elephants? Or being attacked by a lunatic with an axe who wants to hack you to pieces?'

It was clear that these were contingencies which Treadwell had not contemplated in this context. But Riley was merely warming to his theme. By a series of bizarre examples invoking terminally ill relatives, demented lodgers, mass riots and much else, he proceeded to demonstrate that honesty was not always the best policy, that you shouldn't always do as you would be done by, that many hands did not necessarily make light work, and so on. When he was finished, Treadwell looked utterly bemused, stunned by the irresistible power of Riley's illogic.

Carpenter became aware that Treadwell was studying him.

'Would you mind if I had a word with you?' he whispered. 'In the bathroom.'

It had to be important. The bathroom was the only place in Limbo where there were no spy cameras or guards; and since it was possible that the rooms were also wired for sound, the most secret conversations took place through the partition between the two toilet cubicles. Even there it was necessary to talk in whispers, the peculiar acoustics of the place tending to amplify normal sounds so that they often carried into the corridor outside.

Treadwell departed past Snider, who was on duty at the doorway. Carpenter counted slowly to thirty before rising and going after him.

The right-hand cubicle was closed, so Carpenter entered the other one. He automatically laid toilet paper around the seat even though he did not drop his trousers before sitting down; when he was young one of his aunts had told him a terrifying story about someone who had caught leprosy off a public toilet seat, and the habit was now entrenched. He pressed his ear to the partition.

'. . . the trouble with Wright,' Treadwell was already murmuring. 'He's always creating a fuss and that only makes the guards watch him more closely. I'm keeping a low profile so I don't arouse their suspicions.'

Carpenter was immediately intrigued. Did Treadwell have an escape plan?

'I'd be grateful if you kept this to yourself. Wright especially – I don't want him to know. Not for the time being, at least. He'd only do something silly so that Naughton would find out.'

Find out what? Carpenter wondered. He pressed his ear harder against the partition.

Treadwell continued talking, and gradually it became clear that there was a loose parquet tile in the gym. Treadwell had discovered it about a month after their arrival in Limbo, and since then he had been gripping the edges of the tile while doing press-ups, jerking himself up and down as hard as he could to loosen it further. Just yesterday he had finally freed it.

'I started work on the one next to it this morning,' he told Carpenter.

Each tile was about twelve inches by three, which meant that Treadwell would need to uproot about half a dozen before he would have a man-sized hole. And at the rate of two months per tile, this meant a year before they had a potential escape route. The only scrap of comfort Carpenter could draw from this was that it gave a reason for Treadwell's extreme devotion to press-ups.

'You don't happen to have anything I could use as a chisel?'

Carpenter decided that the question was rhetorical; they were allowed no personal accessories apart from a comb and a toothbrush. Occasionally they would be provided with scissors for trimming nails, but always under the supervision of a guard. Carpenter was tempted to ask Treadwell if the sledge-hammer he'd come by would serve instead, but he knew his sarcasm would be wasted. Then Treadwell explained that the parquet tiles were set in cement.

*

Afternoons were a dead time of the day for Carpenter. By then he had read all the tabloids and was bored with snooker, darts and all the other games which had been provided for them. Riley, whose company he found most stimulating, usually slept until the guards changed, Treadwell he could only take in small doses, Sinnott was always so edgy that he made Carpenter feel nervous himself, and Wright – well, Wright was beyond anyone's pale. On Friday evenings a fresh batch of magazines and periodicals were delivered, but Carpenter had usually read them all from cover to cover by Sunday evening, excepting the more serious ones such as *New Society* and *The New Statesman*, which he avoided. For a while he had taken to doing the crosswords in all the tabloids; but he had soon found himself becoming obsessive about having to complete every one he started, so he had given them up entirely.

He sat down in the lounge and lit a cigarette. Sinnott and Treadwell were playing snooker in the games room. There was no sign of Wright, or of Snider and Hemmings. Carpenter hummed tunelessly to himself. He stared up at the central light, wondering if a guard in the monitor room was watching him. Far from resenting this constant surveillance, he actually found it rather comforting and flattering; it made him feel special, important. He supposed that this was what most religious converts felt like, secure in the knowledge that their God was taking a paternal interest in their affairs. In this respect he regretted his own loss of faith.

Carpenter reminded himself that he was in danger of allowing his thoughts to stray on to a thorny problem. In his category of thorny problems the question of whether or not there was a God had once been paramount. It had slipped down the rankings in recent years, being displaced by such associated questions as: Is there a meaning to life? Is there life after death? Is there such a thing as human freedom? Is killing ever justifiable? Could any political system triumph over human greed? Were the sins of the fathers descended on the sons? And so on.

He knew that most of these questions were products of a religious upbringing. Carpenter had hoped that they would bother him less as he grew older, but most of them had instead loomed larger in his mind as he gained more experience of the world and became more confused by its complexities. No wonder most people looked back on their childhood with affection, no matter how awful they had actually been; it wasn't really because they had been young and innocent then but rather that they had taken everything in the world for granted and hadn't yet cultivated the morbid habit of thinking about it.

At this point Hemmings lumbered into the room. Carpenter immediately closed his eyes and let his body go limp in the hope that Hemmings would think he was dozing; but already he felt trapped.

Hemmings sat down beside him.

'Carpenter?' he said, leaning so close that Carpenter could feel his breath on his cheek. He continued to pretend that he was asleep, but the index and middle fingers of his right hand had started to grow warm.

Hemmings nudged him. 'Carpenter? Are you awake?'

Carpenter emitted a snorting sound designed to indicate that he was not awake, but he knew the pretence was an absurd one. His fingers were growing hot, and suddenly he remembered that he had left his cigarette burning between them. With a yelp he sprang to his feet, dropping the butt.

It was only a minor burn, but it stung. He flapped his fingers, then blew on them.

'That's what I was trying to tell you,' Hemmings said. 'I was trying to wake you to stop you from burning yourself.'

The butt had fallen down the back of the chair. While Hemmings rooted for it, Carpenter fled to the bathroom.

He pushed his hand under the cold-water tap. The soothing effect of the water was immediate. As a child he had been taught that the best cure for burns was to hold them as close to the fire as possible so that the burn would be 'sucked' out; but medical opinion had seemingly undergone a reversal since then. In a way this was worrying. Carpenter had once been willing to trust absolutely the expertise of doctors, but as he grew older and it became clear that treatments were constantly subject to refinement, modification and even debunking his confidence in them had waned. It was unnerving to think of all the illnesses that might afflict you which doctors would only make worse.

Illnesses were something he definitely did not want to think about. He turned off the tap and gingerly dried his hand with a paper towel. The two fingers were pulsing, but the pain was bearable. Still desirous of avoiding Hemmings, he slipped out of the bathroom and crept away to the library.

Wright was sitting at the head of the long table at the centre of the room, engrossed in a fat paperback. He did not look up when Carpenter entered.

The library was small, and it contained mostly paperbacks, stacked on white melamine shelves from floor to ceiling around three walls. Carpenter had done a lot of browsing there since his arrival in Limbo, but he had not actually read a single book. Once upon a time he had been a great reader.

The wall opposite the door was devoted to Penguins. The black spines of Classics were ranked with the grey spines of Modern Classics, followed by a preponderance of books with orange spines by writers who presumably hoped to attain classic status one day, probably by dying. Below these were shelves of blue Pelicans on every subject from cookery to cosmology. The two remaining walls had a more gaudy array of paperbacks from other publishers, and there were special sections for horror, romance, westerns, and so on. If he was feeling in a frivolous mood Carpenter would sometimes swap the books around, putting J. T. Edson into the romance section, slipping Agatha Christie among the westerns and Harold Robbins under horror. This was mostly a futile game since only Wright habitually used the library, but he had once succeeded in irritating Wright by filing Kafka's *America* under Travel; Wright had read a lot of Kafka since they'd been in Limbo.

On a whim he took a book at random from the shelves and

dragged a chair over to a corner beside the door where Hemmings would be unable to see him unless he walked in. He saw that Wright was reading Volume Two of *War and Peace*, a book Carpenter had often told himself he should read. Wright had once announced that he did not read novels by living writers since posterity was the only judge of a work of art. No doubt this was true, but death seemed a high price for any writer to pay for a readership.

Carpenter's book proved to be a science fiction novel, its cover showing a naked woman of buxom proportions cavorting with some kind of reptilian creature which looked like a cross between a lizard and an octopus. In the background a spaceship resembling a phallus was taking off into a moon-studded purple sky. Carpenter had once spent a very drunken night on a chilly mountaintop in the Pennines hoping to see a UFO. Needless to say, no extraterrestrial civilization had seen fit to manifest itself to him on that occasion and eventually he had fallen asleep. When he had awoken dawn was breaking, he was chilled to the bone and his chest was covered with beery vomit. He had often felt that there was some significance to what had happened to him that night, but the only conclusion he had ever been able to draw was the obvious one that you seldom found things when you went looking for them.

Carpenter started to read the book but gave up after a few pages, unable to make sense of what was going on. As far as he could judge the story was about a human colony on another world which had evolved an elaborate caste system and a complicated code of ethics and propriety. What ultimately confounded him was the jargon which the author had invented for the various castes and customs: words like *qwadut*, *cherkaui*, *liafianth*, *pfui*, *pterk* and even *pfui-pterk*. Had each of these terms been introduced gradually over a period of chapters, he might have had some success in comprehension; but when, only four pages into the book, he encountered the sentence: 'L'llala, cherkaui of liafianth, fourth-level qwadut, drew the vapours into her nostrils and entered the pfui-pterk mode' his mind went blank and he flung the book at the nearest wall.

Wright looked up with irritation. Carpenter smiled at him. He had always found the requisite silences in libraries utterly inimical to concentration; after a few minutes he would be possessed with the urge to whistle or imitate Tarzan.

'Have you seen Carpenter?' came a voice from the corridor.

It was Hemmings. Carpenter made semaphore signals at Wright to convey that he did not want to be found.

'There,' said Wright, pointing.

Hemmings entered, armed with a medical kit. Carpenter practised his death-ray stare on Wright while Hemmings proceeded to dress his fingers with Germolene and lint.

'How does that feel?' he said presently.

It actually felt much worse. Hemmings had taped the lint so tightly to his fingers that the burns were pulsing inside their cocoon. The tips of both fingers poked out from the ends. They now bore a strong resemblance to the spaceship on the cover of the book Carpenter had just been trying to read.

Wright looked smug. Carpenter made a V-sign of his bandaged fingers and flourished them at him. Snider walked in.

'What's going on here?' he wanted to know.

'Carpenter burnt himself with his cigarette,' Hemmings told him. 'I was just bandaging his fingers for him.'

Carpenter gave Snider a V-sign in proof of this.

'I think you ought to return to your duties,' Snider said.

'What's the matter?' said Wright, 'are you afraid he'll become contaminated if he spends too much time with us?' He gave a snort of disdain as Hemmings departed. 'A lackey of a lackey. It's pathetic.'

Snider did not move or say anything, but his eyes were fixed on Wright. Wright closed his book and rose.

'You're just as bad, Carpenter,' he said. 'You encourage them.' Then he stalked out.

Carpenter waited. Snider seemed about to say something to him. Then, as if abruptly changing his mind, he too departed.

Carpenter went over to where Wright had been sitting. He felt irritated and vindictive as he stood there, clawing the lint from his fingers and scattering the pieces over the floor. His fingers immediately began to feel better.

He picked up *War and Peace*. Dare he do it? Wouldn't it be petty and malicious, not to mention showing a disrespect for literature? To hell with it – he owed Wright one. Turning his back to the spy camera he coughed to cover the sound he made as he tore out the last few pages of the book.

*

Carpenter lingered in the library for a short while, gazing at the books on the shelves. He made no attempt to remove any. Even a small library such as this held titles by writers as remote from one another as Sophocles and Jacqueline Suzanne. We're filling the world up with words, he thought. So much effort, so many personal statements made by human beings who were mostly long-vanished from the earth, the residues of their lives encapsulated in dry, flat pages. Somehow it all seemed sad and inadequate.

There had been a time when he had enjoyed inspecting book shelves, their arrays of titles silently challenging him with the prospect of acquiring new or deeper knowledge. Now he felt daunted and deflated by the sight of them. Any given display always contained a preponderance of titles he would never manage to read, even if he spent the rest of his life doing nothing else. Once he had sought in books the learning and insights which he hoped would provide a focus and certainty in his own life. But all his reading had only succeeded in delineating more clearly how contingent and impossibly complex life was. Books betrayed you; they promised you wisdom but only emphasized the scope of your ignorance and the conditional nature of your beliefs.

*

Riley lay on his bed with his hands on his belly, soft snores issuing from his open mouth. His plump face was a picture of blissful sleep, and Carpenter envied his ability to doze off whenever he felt like it; sometimes it seemed to him that sleeping was the most desirable human activity of all.

Riley's dark, curly hair showed a hint of greyness throughout, but his chubby face was relatively unlined for his age. He was over forty, but he looked like an aged cherub sleeping off some hearty bacchanalia. Carpenter went over to the washbasin and doused the pages from *War and Peace* in water. Returning to Riley's bedside, he held the dripping wad over his head so that drops of water began plopping on his face. At first there was no reaction, but then Riley gave a great yawn and left his mouth open, seemingly content to let each drop fall into his throat. Carpenter squeezed the wad, and Riley began to blubber before finally giving out a wet belch and rolling over so that his face was pressed into the pillow.

Carpenter leant over him and began making snorting sounds in his ear. When this produced no reaction he redoubled his efforts until he was giving a passable imitation of a frenzied pig. Still Riley did not stir. It occurred to Carpenter that the guard on monitor duty might by now be taking an interest in his behaviour. What if he decided to investigate and discovered that Carpenter had been vandalizing library property? He stuffed the wad into his trouser pocket and departed.

The restless feeling which had possessed him earlier had returned. He entered the lounge, suddenly wishing he was in the outside world, if only for a few minutes. It was the beginning of April, and spring should be on the advance, with crocuses studding fields orange and lilac and white, and gusty showers washing the resurgent landscape. Spring had always been his favourite time of the year.

He sighed and picked up a newspaper, flicking through it until he came to the astrology section. As a physics graduate he had no faith in the scientific basis of astrology, but he seldom failed to take a discreet peek at his stars for the day. And while optimistic forecasts were always preferable, doom- or-danger-laden ones were usually more exciting, adding a certain piquancy to the day if you managed to remember them and giving you the comforting feeling that if something did go badly wrong you could always blame it on fate. Under Libra, his star-sign, he read:

The working week may begin on a somewhat confused or worrying note, but don't let anyone convince you that major plans and projects are impractical. Try to stay close to home today, for relatives and close associates may be looking to you for help or advice.

*

Shortly before four o'clock Snider and Hemmings would make a final tour of Limbo before they went off duty and were replaced by the evening shift guards, Harris and Peacock. The inmates were required to assemble in the lounge and wait there until the change-over had taken place. They always did so without protest, and Peacock would appear shortly afterwards with coffee and biscuits, a snack designed to sustain them until dinner at seven.

Today, however, Carpenter watched Snider depart and followed him down the corridor. He saw Snider enter Naughton's office and close the door behind him. Creeping up to the door, he put his ear to it.

He could make out a mumble of voices, but no words. Then everything went quiet.

Abruptly the door opened, almost sending Carpenter reeling into the room. Too late he realized that he *should* have gone reeling into the room in the hope of glimpsing what lay beyond the side door.

'What do you want, Carpenter?' asked Naughton.

He had changed into a fawn twill suit and a bottle-green tie decorated with sky-blue and lemon squiggles.

'I won't have you skulking around my office,' he said. He stood in the space between the door and jamb so that Carpenter could not see inside. 'Get away from here.'

Carpenter did not move.

'Get away!' Naughton shouted, and slammed the door in his face.

Carpenter returned to the lounge, where everyone apart from Wright was assembled. Wright never took coffee and biscuits because he disapproved of eating between meals. 'Then think of it as a meal,' Riley had counselled him; but Wright remained resistant to this logic.

Riley, fresh from his nap, was perusing a copy of *Woman's Own* which had somehow been included in the last batch of magazines. Treadwell and Sinnott were discussing American foreign policy. Treadwell was of the opinion that it was the duty of the United States to protect and support free governments throughout the world, while Sinnott cautiously asserted his view that if every soldier in every army in the world laid down his arms and refused to fight, world peace would be achieved overnight.

Thank God Wright isn't around, Carpenter thought. He took a seat and began anticipating a chocolate-covered digestive.

Having come to an amicable non-agreement on the solution to the world's problems, Treadwell and Sinnott fell silent. Sinnott was sitting on the edge of his chair with his legs crossed, and one leg was vibrating with such rapidity that Carpenter found it remarkable he was not conscious of it. He was picking at hangnails on his fingers, thus generating more, a process which would presumably keep him occupied for the rest of his life. How did he survive at such a constant pitch of anxiety? It was just as well he didn't smoke, for he'd probably be a hundred-a-day man.

Carpenter had taken a cigarette from his pocket, but he put it back, knowing that Peacock would soon be arriving with the coffee-trolley. He studied his burnt fingers. They still felt a little sensitive, but the pain was mostly gone. In front of him Treadwell was opening a pack of cards from the games room. Treadwell often amused himself by building houses of cards or pyramids of dominoes or doing origami on old newspapers and magazines. All of these activities were practically intolerable to the onlooker, so assiduously did he work. Carpenter sat back in his chair, trying to distance himself from Treadwell; but he was morbidly fascinated despite himself. After a while Treadwell began to hum to himself as he worked. The tune was 'Raindrops Keep Falling on My Head'.

Treadwell had completed the first two tiers of his card-house when Riley dropped the copy of *Woman's Own* on the coffee table. The impact caused the structure to collapse. But Treadwell showed not a trace of irritation, simply gathering up the cards and starting again.

'According to a woman in there,' said Riley with reference to the magazine, 'you can learn to control your dreams.'

A useful technique, thought Carpenter, especially if you could also learn to sleep all day. It reminded him of a film he'd once seen in the Saturday morning pictures as a child. In it the population were put into a kind of giant cinema and fed pleasant dreams which kept them docile and happy all day. Eventually the fatheaded hero of the story had brought about a revolution which had led to the destruction of the happiness cinemas; Carpenter's sympathies had been entirely with the authorities.

Sinnott would be an obvious beneficiary of dream control, he thought. He had once overheard him discussing his dreams with Treadwell, and they seemed to consist of frenzied nightmares about being pursued by giant wolves or having his heart cut out under local anaesthetic. Carpenter's own secret fear was the thought of being buried alive. Imagine waking up to find yourself entombed in a coffin, its lid only inches from your face, with six feet of earth on top of you . . .

No, he did not want to imagine it. When he made his will he hoped it would be possible to include a clause which insisted on him being given a lethal injection after he had been pronounced dead, just in case. Or perhaps cremation was a simpler option.

The rattle of the coffee-trolley brought a welcome distraction from this morbid line of thought. Treadwell's reconstructed card-house collapsed again as the trolley came through the door. Harris was at its helm. This was unusual, for he hardly ever performed this particular duty and was seldom seen abroad in Limbo.

Harris picked up a plate holding a cream bun and smiled benignly at them. Everyone immediately knew that something nasty was going to happen.

'Today is a special day,' he informed them. 'It's Sinnott's birthday.'

Judging by the expression on Sinnott's face, this was either untrue or he was heartily wishing it wasn't. He seemed to be trying to say something, though nothing was emerging.

'He's eighteen today,' Harris went on, his smile becoming broader and even more humourless.

He offered Sinnott the cream bun. Sinnott stared at it as if it was a hand grenade.

'Take it,' Harris said. 'It's a little treat for a special day.'

Sinnott took the bun and held it in front of his mouth.

'Eat up,' said Harris. He was a short, stocky man with ginger hair and a freckled face. He never looked more unpleasant than when he cajoled and smiled.

Sinnott bit into the bun. It was immediately clear that there was something wrong with it. But Sinnott suppressed his disgust and started chewing. Then he tried to swallow the mouthful, and gagged. Dropping the bun, he bolted for the bathroom.

Harris was beside himself with laughter. Carpenter retrieved the bun. The cream was shaving foam.

Harris was facing him as he straightened, a broad grin on his face, a grin that challenged Carpenter to do something about it.

Carpenter felt Riley take his arm and drag him away.

In the bathroom Sinnott was retching into the washbasin. When he was finished they helped him back to his cell and made him lie down. He was trembling all over.

Treadwell entered the cell.

'How is he?' he asked.

'He'll survive,' said Riley.

'I didn't think it was very funny. I think we ought to complain to Naughton.'

'No!' said Sinnott with some vehemence. He rolled over and lay with his face to the wall. 'Just leave me alone.'

★

'How long are we going to stand for this?' Wright demanded of them. Treadwell had just explained what had happened. 'They've not only taken our liberty, they're violating us physically and mentally. Are we just going to continue to let them treat us like cattle?'

No one said anything. Wright began to elaborate on his theme, talking of fundamental human rights and the dignity of the individual, and arguing that their docility encouraged the guards to take advantage of them. Carpenter showed more than his usual attentiveness, not disagreeing with the substance of what Wright was saying but feeling a growing irritation. Riley was ignoring him completely, but Carpenter noticed that Treadwell was also looking irritated. In fact he had begun to look positively angry.

'You get my bloody goat sometimes,' he suddenly thundered. 'Why don't you bloody go and see how he is, instead of standing here giving us a bloody lecture.'

Treadwell departed to the games room. Wright looked puzzled, as if he was genuinely unable to understand what had provoked the outburst.

Carpenter went after Treadwell and found him throwing the white ball around the table. He looked a little shamefaced.

Carpenter gave him a wink and a grin, then took two cues from the cupboard.

*

Carpenter crouched over the table, looking along the length of his cue. He needed the pink and black to win, and the pink ball was sitting right over one of the centre pockets, with the black nicely positioned near a corner pocket at the baulk end. Treadwell had thrashed him in all their games so far, but he had managed to make a few decent breaks in this one and was poised, if only he could keep his nerve, to break his duck.

Please, Carpenter whispered mentally to whatever unseen gods might be watching over him, let me get this one. It's all I ask.

Satisfied that he had the two balls correctly aligned, he drew back his cue. Just as he was making the shot a voice said, 'Carpenter!' in an imperative tone, and an instant later he heard not the sweet clack of a firmly struck ball but the scraping sound of a miscue.

The white ball trundled slowly down the table and nudged the pink. It wavered on the lip of the pocket, Carpenter staring hard at it, willing it to drop; then, to his amazement and inordinate delight, it did.

The white ball was separated from the black by almost half the table. It was not the kind of shot he would have wished for, but it wasn't impossible; at least he hadn't blown the game completely.

'Dr Dempster is waiting, Carpenter,' said Peacock.

He stood in the doorway, a sharp-featured man of fastidious manners and a superior air. If Harris was actively contemptuous of them, Peacock was merely resentful, as if he considered the job beneath his dignity. The guards' coveralls looked incongruous on him, and Carpenter always imagined that he was wearing a dinner suit underneath. He maintained a bored supervision of them in the evenings when there was nothing better to do than sit watching television. Presumably Harris spent his time with his feet up in the monitor room, perusing men's magazines or thinking up vindictive pranks to amuse himself.

Carpenter moved around the table and lined up the black. Wild horses wouldn't stop him from making this shot now. Out of the corner of his eye he saw Peacock moving towards him. He hit the cue ball hard, saw it rocket up the table and strike the black ball, which promptly vanished down the pocket with a rapidity which startled and thrilled him. He'd hurried the shot, but the ball had gone down. He'd done it! It was his first victory.

The cue ball was still rebounding off the cushions. A sudden sinking feeling replaced Carpenter's elation as he watched it roll up the table and disappear down the same pocket into which he had dispatched the black.

*

'Come in, Michael,' Dr Dempster said with her usual welcoming smile. 'Take a seat.'

Carpenter settled back in the tall leather armchair beside the desk. It was real leather, but he was careful never to shift his position too abruptly in case it made the same farting noises as the vinyl armchairs in the lounge. Dr Dempster's desk was of solid dark wood with brass handles, and there was a white telephone on it; but apart from the desk and telephone he might have been sitting in someone's cosy front room. The place was simply but elegantly furnished with embossed fleur-de-lys wallpaper and a thick buff carpet of real wool. On the walls were old prints of St Paul's and Westminster Abbey, while to the right of the desk was a glass-fronted cabinet holding medical textbooks. On top of the cabinet stood a vase of freshly cut daffodils.

The flowers were the first real vegetable life he'd seen in Limbo, and their presence was uplifting, manifest evidence that spring was advancing in the world outside.

Dr Dempster's handbag rested against the cabinet, reminding Carpenter that she was only visiting Limbo briefly. She usually came on Mondays, Wednesdays and Fridays at six o'clock, though this routine was flexible. Because she was not involved in the day-to-day running of the institution it was hard to think of her as one of the staff and hence an enemy. Besides, she was always very nice to him.

The white telephone gleamed under the café-light chandelier, looking as pristine as ever. Like Naughton's phone, it had never rung during Carpenter's time in Limbo and Dr Dempster had never so much as touched it.

She was in her late thirties or early forties, and she wore her white doctor's coat over a pale green blouse and a tweed skirt. Her sandy hair was swept back into a loose bun at the nape of her neck, revealing earrings like mistletoe berries. She always wore a minimum of make-up, just sufficient to highlight her elegant features. Hers was an effortless yet serious beauty which Carpenter found slightly forbidding.

'Tea?' she enquired, lifting the china pot which sat on a silver tray in front of her. There were two gold-rimmed cups and saucers, with a matching sugar bowl and milk jug. It had not really been a question; he always took tea with her.

He watched her as she poured, one delicate hand resting on the top of the pot. Her pale pink nails were immaculately manicured. An errant strand of hair curled down her neck behind her right ear.

Carpenter added milk to his cup and just one spoonful of sugar instead of his normal three. Sugar was another bad habit of his, and he always tried to show restraint in her company. She herself took a mere tip of a teaspoon, but it was nice to know that at least she possessed this small weakness.

The smell of expensive perfume emanated from her: a fragrant yet spicy aroma. Carpenter surreptitiously inhaled it as he raised his cup to his mouth. The tea was Earl Grey.

She was the only person in Limbo who called him 'Michael' and to him this seemed more formal than 'Carpenter'. He had always been Mike to his friends; no one apart from his parents had called him Michael in years.

'Any problems?' she asked him. 'Sleeping all right?'

He was sleeping perfectly well. He'd never had any difficulty sleeping in Limbo; his major struggle was getting up each morning. Every night at bedtime Peacock gave him a red sleeping tablet before locking him in his cell. But they always left him feeling groggy in the morning, and in recent weeks he had taken to slipping them under his tongue instead of swallowing them. As soon as he got into bed he would spit them out and hide them inside his pillowcase before flushing them down the washbasin in the morning. This was the origin of the red stains which had vexed Naughton.

As Limbo's medical officer, Dr Dempster doubtless prescribed the tablets, and Carpenter didn't dare tell her that he no longer used them. She seemed to take a special interest in his welfare, he being the only inmate who was ever summoned to her office. He didn't want her to think that she wasn't doing anything useful for him in case she ended their regular interviews over tea. He enjoyed the opportunity to relax for a short while in a room that hardly seemed part of Limbo.

But it was never long enough, and he knew he was to blame. Dr Dempster would always tell him that he shouldn't hesitate to talk to her about anything that might be troubling him, but Carpenter had no such inclination. She was, after all, one of Limbo's staff, and if he started complaining about minor irritations or the simple fact of their imprisonment he felt sure she would prove just as unhelpful as the guards. He preferred not to risk this possibility and keep their relationship on a polite and pleasant level of uncommunicativeness.

*

The others had already assembled for dinner by the time he emerged from Dr Dempster's office. Peacock was doling out the food: pork chops with carrots and roast potatoes. In general the dinners in Limbo tended to be wholesome if uninspired, but Carpenter had always been squeamish about eating pork, remembering a childhood story of a huge tapeworm which had emerged from a woman's mouth as a result of her eating undercooked meat. Though he now knew that the tale was apocryphal the light of this knowledge had never entirely banished the shadow of his unease. In a similar manner, while he was diligent about walking under ladders, letting black cats cross his path, eating cheese at bedtime, not having a bowel movement every day, and so on, he could never do so with complete assurance.

He consoled himself with the fact that it was treacle tart for dessert, one of his favourites. He waited until Peacock gave him a second helping of custard before he took his tray over to the table.

Sinnott was sitting next to Riley. He looked recovered from the cream bun incident but was clearly preoccupied with the prospect of a haircut. Treadwell had taken the chair at the head of the table, which meant that Carpenter had no alternative but to sit down next to Wright. And Wright was already in mid-exposition about something. About God, Carpenter realized with dismay. He was telling Riley that the notion of a Supreme Being was an outmoded concept and that until the human race came to terms with this fact and behaved morally from humanistic imperatives rather than the hypocritical expectation of some reward in an after-life, there would be no basis for a truly just and civilized society.

Riley was spooning treacle tart into his mouth throughout this, his lips yellow with custard. He was watching Wright as he ate like an overgrown baby listening contentedly to the cooings and murmurings of an adult without understanding, or needing to understand, a word of what was being said.

I can't stand it, Carpenter thought. He stuck out a foot, intending to drag back his chair from the table. But somehow he contrived to get it twisted between the legs of the chair and he immediately felt himself overbalancing. With the tray in his hands, there was nothing he could do to stop himself from falling. He went down to a clattering of utensils and the emphatic sound of crockery smashing.

*

'That wasn't very clever, was it?'

Carpenter turned his back to Harris and dropped the mop into the bucket of dirty water in which floated the residues of his dinner. He swirled it around a bit, imagining that it was Harris's head. Meanwhile Harris was inspecting the food bins.

'There's a few spuds and a carrot left,' he announced, picking them out. 'Do you want me to get you a plate?'

Harris was grinning at him, and Carpenter wondered why he didn't just heft the mop and ram it in his face. Maybe Wright had been talking sense for once. Maybe they ought to do something.

Harris threw the food back into the bins.

'Looks like you're out of luck,' he said. 'Looks like you slipped up.' He chuckled unpleasantly.

Carpenter smiled despite himself, for he had suddenly realized that he must have unconsciously precipitated the accident to avoid being a captive audience to a theology lecture from Wright. It had been a Freudian trip.

*

As he approached the lounge Carpenter could hear Wright talking; he sounded irate. Normally Wright spent his evenings reading in the library, thus allowing the rest of them to watch television in peace.

The television was, in fact, on, but no one was watching the horseriding it was showing. Sinnott and Treadwell were pretending to play dominoes, while Wright stood over Riley, shouting at him. Riley was slouched in an armchair but he looked as if he was assessing the likelihood of Wright leaping upon him and was considering suitable evasive action. There was no sign of Peacock.

Then Carpenter noticed the copy of *War and Peace* on the coffee table. He made to turn, intending to hide himself in the toilet until the storm had blown over. But Wright had spotted him.

'Some idiot's torn the pages out of the book I've been reading,' he said. Then he pointed at Riley: 'Him.'

Riley did not say anything.

'I know it was you,' said Wright. 'It's no good trying to play the innocent with me. No one else would do such an infantile thing.'

Carpenter hadn't expected Wright to discover that the pages were missing for some days since he was only halfway through the book. Had he taken a forward peek to find out what happened at the end? This thought cheered Carpenter, for if it was true it meant that Wright did sometimes behave like a normal human being.

'I can never understand,' Wright was saying, 'what prompts people into such petty and demeaning acts of vandalism. It shows such an utter lack of consideration for anyone else.'

Carpenter was profoundly aware of the wodge of damp pages in his pocket. Should he own up to the theft?

'Why don't you just turn the book around and start reading from the other end?' said Riley. 'That way you'd only miss the first few pages and you'd be able to fill in what happened as you went along.'

Wright's white-flecked lips began to tremble. A small vein started pulsing at the side of his head. Carpenter wondered if Wright was about to demonstrate that a human being could literally explode with anger. Or would he succumb to the heat of the moment, forget his conviction that violence was the last resort of the feeble-minded and leap upon Riley with flailing arms?

He did neither. Instead he snatched up the book and began tearing it into pieces. It was the first time that Carpenter had seen him display real anger, and a look of something resembling relish suffused his face as the dismemberment went on.

Peacock appeared in the middle of this. He started across the room.

'Get away from me!' Wright screamed at him.

Peacock immediately halted. No one moved. Wright continued tearing the book apart. On the television screen a woman rider went hurtling through a wall into a pool of water. But everyone was watching Wright.

When the deed was finally done and the pages of the book lay scattered all over the floor, Wright turned and stalked out with all the dignity of a monarch.

For a moment no one did anything. Then Peacock gathered himself and went off in pursuit of Wright. Seconds later Harris appeared in the doorway. He surveyed the littered room and went over to Riley.

'What's been going on here?'

Riley simply shrugged.

Harris took hold of his ear and began twisting it. 'I've had enough of you lot this evening. I asked you what was going on.'

'It wasn't him,' said Treadwell. 'Wright got a bit upset.'

'Did he now?' Harris continued to twist Riley's ear. 'And just where is our friend Wright?'

'He went out,' Treadwell said. 'Peacock's gone after him.'

'Is that a fact?'

'If you don't let go of my ear,' said Riley, 'I'm going to do something to you.'

This only made Harris smile and twist harder. He was about to say something, but the words never reached his lips. Riley elbowed him briskly in the groin.

Harris staggered back, clutching the injured part with both hands. Slowly he straightened, rage replacing the pain on his face. Then he leapt on Riley.

Riley twisted aside with surprising agility so that the brunt of Harris's weight fell on the coffee table, which promptly overturned. Both men began a wrestling match on the floor while the others looked on, dumbfounded. Peacock appeared and immediately went to Harris's aid. This was too much for Treadwell, who redressed the balance by leaping upon him.

Carpenter studied the scene with a curious feeling of detachment. Sinnott was huddled in the corner, frozen with fright. Skirting the mêlée, Carpenter went out into the corridor. He could hear rapid footsteps approaching: it had to be Naughton. He went off in the opposite direction.

Naughton had left the door to his office ajar. Carpenter immediately went to his desk and began searching through its drawers. He found a pencil, a few paper-clips, a Crunchie wrapper and some yellowing sheets of plain paper, but nothing else. It was the same story for the filing cabinet: all the drawers opened but none contained anything except office litter.

He went to the side door and turned the handle. It opened. The room was small and desolate-looking, its off-white walls scuffed and grimy. A battered chipboard table stood in one corner with two moulded grey plastic chairs. On the table were several used coffee mugs, an ashtray overflowing with cigarette butts, a pack of playing cards and a pile of newspapers and well-thumbed magazines. A small shelf above the table held more magazines and a few paperbacks: *Shogun*, *The Carpetbaggers*, *Thunderball* and *The Valley of the Dolls*. In the opposite corner a television set stood on a tall stand, and in front of it was a battered black armchair with straw-coloured foam poking out through gashes in the vinyl. A wastepaper bin beside the TV held balls of crumpled paper, breadcrusts, old newspapers and a detritus of ash and butts. Overhead burned a single electric bulb. That was all.

To his left was another door with a small square window in its upper half. He peered through the wire glass. A stretch of bare concrete corridor dimly lit by bulkhead lights in the ceiling receded into the gloom. He tried the door and found that it opened. A stale, lifeless smell emanated from the corridor.

Carpenter closed the door and returned to Naughton's office. The red telephone sat waiting on the desk. He was about to pick it up when suddenly Mordred leapt on the table-top and hissed at him.

He backed away and retreated to the adjoining room where he retrieved a newspaper from the table. Rolling it into a cylinder, he advanced on the cat, switching it in front of him. The cat suddenly raked the end of the newspaper with a speed that made Carpenter jump back. Again he advanced, and again the cat raked the newspaper. But Carpenter was able to reach out with his free hand and snatch up the receiver.

He heard the hurried march of footsteps in the corridor outside. Quickly he put the receiver to his ear. The line was dead.

*

'I've never witnessed such a disgraceful exhibition in my entire life,' Naughton was saying. He looked ruffled and his cheeks were red. 'I simply will not have this kind of behaviour. You have been repeatedly warned that breaches of discipline will not be tolerated, but evidently these warnings have gone unheeded.'

Carpenter stopped listening. He flexed his right arm, which felt a little sore after Harris had burst in on him in the office and twisted it up his back. His chin was also aching from the impact of Harris slamming him against the wall.

Although Naughton and the guards had subdued them, Treadwell and Riley looked unscathed. Treadwell was sporting a resolute, captured-British-Army-officer expression, while Riley looked completely unconcerned. It was Sinnott and Wright, neither of whom had actually participated in the scuffle, who were the most agitated. Sinnott was his usual frightened self, while Wright bristled with indignation.

Neither Harris nor Peacock looked injured, but Carpenter hoped that Harris was still in pain from Riley's elbow. He hoped it would ruin his sex life for weeks. People like Harris were warts on the body of creation.

The postmortem went on, with Naughton demanding a detailed account of the events leading up to the violence. Slowly the story emerged, with Naughton naturally favouring Harris's assertion of unprovoked assault by Riley over Treadwell's insistence that Harris was to blame. Riley himself said nothing until pressed by Naughton, whereupon he shrugged and said, 'He had it coming to him.'

Meanwhile Carpenter had been studying the red telephone, and he saw that there was a button just above the dial. If he had pressed this, would he have got a line to the outside world?

Naughton had finally pieced together a version of the events which suited him. He rose from his chair.

'Firstly,' he began, 'I will not countenance the destruction of property in this establishment, for whatever reason. There are no mitigating circumstances whatsoever. The library will therefore be off-limits for one week to you all.'

There was no immediate protest from Wright. Even Naughton looked surprised.

'Secondly,' he went on, 'I want the person who tore the missing pages from the book to own up.'

Carpenter felt trapped; the pages were still in his trouser pocket. Why hadn't he got rid of them before now, flushed them down the toilet? What if Naughton ordered them searched?

He knew that he should own up, if only to take the burden of guilt off Riley. But he remained silent, telling himself that he had done nothing which he felt ashamed or regretful about. Why should he pander to Naughton when Naughton had no rightful authority over him in the first place?

Naughton gave his 'I'm-disappointed-in-you' sigh, then said, 'I can see that I've been misguided in expecting your cooperation. I had hoped that we could deal with this matter as adult human beings, but it seems not. This is a most serious breach of discipline and I must move to protect the integrity of this establishment.'

'Integrity?' Wright pointed at Harris. 'He's nothing but a hooligan.'

'Be quiet, Wright. Do you seriously think I'm going to allow my staff to be assaulted? For the next week you will be confined to your rooms an hour earlier each evening and your coffee break will be suspended.'

He sat down heavily. 'I could be much harsher than this, but I'm still hoping it is possible to cultivate an atmosphere of cooperation and respect. But if there are any further outbreaks of this sort of behaviour, your privileges will be further reduced.'

'Privileges?' Wright was astounded. 'Privileges? This whole place is an outrage. Why should we cooperate with you? You have no right to expect anything but contempt from us.'

'Shut up, Wright.'

'Why are we being kept here? Tell me that. Have we committed any crime? Are we a danger to anyone? What gives you the authority to order us around? I demand to know.'

'If you don't shut up I'll have you locked up immediately. I'm appalled enough by your behaviour as it is.'

Naughton continued with his dismal lecture, and Carpenter switched off again. The door to the adjoining room had been closed by Harris immediately on subduing him, but Carpenter could not believe his luck in finding all the doors unlocked. Harris was a smoker, and the butts in the ashtray he had seen were doubtless his.

As Naughton talked on, it occurred to Carpenter that all his disciplinary measures were really so trivial as to suggest that his authority over them was quite limited. Really he was little more than a trumped-up headmaster. And Limbo itself was more akin to a school than a penal institution. He had never thought of this before.

*

On the television screen an American detective was having a gun battle with a hoodlum in a bowling alley. Then both men ran out of bullets. The hoodlum fled down one of the bowling alleys, but the detective rolled a bowling ball at him, knocking him over.

Carpenter yawned; he had seen it coming. He opened his cigarette packet and saw that there were only two cigarettes left; he always smoked more when he was bored.

Minutes later the detective was involved in a high-speed car chase along a dangerous mountain road as the story reached its climax. Carpenter had little idea of the plot, even though he had ostensibly been watching the programme for the best part of an hour. But it didn't seem to matter – not to him or to Riley, Treadwell and Sinnott, who were all gazing at the screen with a blank absorption.

Carpenter pursed his lips and tried to blow a smoke ring. All his friends had mastered the trick soon after they had started smoking, but he had never been able to manage it. Then suddenly, amongst the curlicues of smoke issuing from his mouth, there appeared a perfect ring which slowly expanded above his head.

He was about to draw Riley's attention to it when the door opened and the resulting draught obliterated the ring in an instant. It was Wright.

At a hairpin bend the villain's car smashed through a flimsy fence and went plummeting down the mountainside to explode into flames. On the clifftop an attractive young woman began to weep into the shoulder of the detective. He was a grizzled handsome man with strong features which indicated that he would act decisively when called upon to do so but was also a man of wisdom and honour.

'I'm so glad it's all over,' the girl sobbed. Carpenter couldn't have agreed with her more.

Wright crouched in front of the screen as the credits began to appear.

'I think it's time we all had a talk,' he said, making it sound as much like a suggestion as he was able.

When no one indicated any violent objection to this, Wright adjusted the volume of the TV, turning it up rather than down. A woman with an elaborate perm began to enthuse about cat food while cradling a fat and complacent-looking white Persian in her arms. In a loud voice Wright explained that he had turned the set up so that they wouldn't be overheard by the guards.

'What?' said Riley.

Wright turned the volume down a little.

'What happened this evening was very significant,' he said.

Everyone waited for him to explain why.

'I think it's safe to assume that we all want to get out of this place as soon as possible.'

What he said immediately after this was lost as a fanfare of trumpets blared out from the television to herald a huge sale of carpets at knockdown prices.

'The trouble is,' he was saying when Carpenter was able to hear him again, 'we haven't pulled together. We've all been going our separate ways and not presenting a united front against Naughton and his lackeys. When this evening we actually started fighting back as a team, we gave them something to think about.'

Carpenter found it remarkable that Wright could view the fracas as a coordinated offensive and even more remarkable that he had included himself in it. Somehow it was hard to picture Wright trading punches with anyone.

'Imagine what might have happened if all five of us had joined in.' The glance which he gave Carpenter and Sinnott was gently chastising but also magnanimous, as if he was so pleased by the evening's turn of events that he was prepared to forgive their non-involvement.

'Don't you agree it's time we settled our differences and started working together, as a team? We could make life really difficult for them if we adopt a policy of non-cooperation. But it has to be everyone if it's going to work. Just think of what we might achieve. We could refuse to exercise, refuse to wash or shave, ignore the guards completely. We could even go on hunger strike.'

This last suggestion was greeted with a notable lack of enthusiasm. Wright immediately strove to moderate his line: 'Naturally we would have to reach a democratic decision on what sort of disruptive action we should take, and naturally everyone would get an equal vote.'

But would they get an equal share in the arguments leading up to the vote? Wright would probably produce a whole portfolio of suggestions and strategies which he would force the rest of them to accept by brute argumentative force.

'We have to do *something*,' he insisted. 'We can't just sit here day after day and let them treat us like sheep. Unless we combine forces we might never get out of here. We've all been too apathetic about our situation.'

Carpenter knew that Wright was doing his best to be diplomatic;

what he really meant was that everyone but himself had been too apathetic.

'I think you're right,' Treadwell said. 'We've got to try to get out of here. And it's better if we work together.'

'Good,' said Wright. He studied the rest of them. Carpenter huddled behind Sinnott.

'Riley?'

Riley was intent on the news.

'What do you say? Can we count you in?'

'On what?'

'On presenting a united front against Naughton.'

'I'm not presenting a united anything against anybody.'

'It's for our own benefit. We're all in this together.'

Riley kept his eyes on the screen. The news reader was informing them that the situation was said to be deteriorating.

'Well?' said Wright.

'Well what?'

'Are you with us?'

'I'm not with anybody.'

'We're asking for your cooperation.'

'You do as you like. I'm not going to stop you.'

'We're not going to get out of here by sitting around on our backsides.'

'Who says I want to get out of here?'

'This is serious, Riley.'

Riley shrugged.

'Are you trying to tell us that you're not interested in escaping?'

'You're the one who's complaining, not me.'

'It's for all our benefit.'

'How come you're always so sure what's good for everyone else?'

Wright gave a small sigh. There was a pause, and then he turned to Sinnott.

'I take it we can count on your support?'

Sinnott didn't look at him either.

'Well?' said Wright.

'I don't want any trouble,' said Sinnott.

'I'm talking about insisting on our rights, on taking positive action to gain our liberty. We should be free men. They have no right to keep us here, and we have to do something about it.'

Sinnott fidgeted in his seat and picked at hangnails.

'If you're expecting Naughton to come along one day and tell you that you can leave, you're mistaken. The only way we're going to get out of here is through our own efforts.'

Sinnott continued to fidget, and he wouldn't look Wright in the eye. Wright was showing signs of exasperation.

'For once in your life show a little backbone, man. It's time you stood up for yourself.'

Sinnott did stand up, practically surging towards the door.

'Just leave me alone!' he cried as he hurried off in the direction of his cell.

His departure left Carpenter exposed. He also wanted to get up and leave, but he had left it too late.

'I think we should abide by the majority decision,' said Wright. 'It's up to you, Carpenter. What do you say?'

*

Carpenter sat between Riley and Sinnott, watching a repeat of a new religious programme which they had managed to avoid on Sunday evening. Now all three of them were mesmerized by it. The programme featured a folk group who sang pop-gospel songs with lines like:

Believe, believe, believe in Jesus
He's the only one who can relieve us

Even worse was the man who was presenting the programme, a large and incredibly hairy individual dressed in peach-coloured trousers and a black open-necked shirt with a gold cross hanging at the centre of his matted chest. His hair formed a dense black cloud around his head, and his mouth was almost invisible behind a profuse beard. Unfortunately this did not prevent him from talking. He used phrases such as 'a raising of Christian consciousness', and he had a high-powered and hysterical manner of delivery, like an especially obnoxious disc jockey.

Carpenter found the whole affair very undignified, and nothing like the kind of Christianity he remembered. His mother had sent him to the local Methodist church in Crumpsall every Sunday afternoon from an early age. He would sit in a corner on a hard wooden pew with a handful of other children, listening to his Sunday School teacher telling him of all the horrible things that would happen to people who weren't saved. He learned that God was watching over you all the time and would be aware of even the smallest sins you committed. His teacher had a squint, and Carpenter was never sure when he was looking directly at him. Somehow he came to think of God in a similar way: God spent most of His time keeping an eye on the affairs of important people, but everyone had to be on his guard in case He was peering at you out of the corner of His eye while you were doing something sinful.

The bearded man was now talking about 'moral rearmament against the forces of evil'. Though he had long abandoned church-going, Carpenter had never completely renounced his belief in God. Even now he considered himself an agnostic rather than an atheist. You simply never knew. The hard-line atheists he'd met had seemed just as religious in their denial of God's existence as any true believer, and who could be sure either way? His years of church-going had left him with the nagging worry that a Judgement Day might yet await him beyond death. Agnosticism was a way of hedging your bets so that if it did turn out that God existed He might be inclined to treat you leniently for giving Him the benefit of the doubt.

The folk group had returned and were singing a song which compared Jesus to the Pied Piper of Hamelin; the rats represented people's sins. The song was mercifully brief, and after a snatch of sales talk from the hairy man, the camera switched to an older man seated in an armchair. He had the venerable and quietly holy appearance of a real minister and he started to read from Matthew in a warm resonant voice:

'The gate is wide and the way is broad that leads to destruction, and many go that way: because the gate is strait and the way is narrow that leads to life, and there are few that find it.'

Carpenter wondered what Riley and Sinnott were thinking; both were intent on the screen.

The minister read on for a while, then closed the Bible.

'What will it profit a man,' he concluded, 'if he gains the whole world but loses his soul?'

This was one of the many questions which Carpenter preferred not to have asked of him.

*

Net curtains billowed at the open window as rain poured from a stormy night sky. The girl was huddled in the corner of the gloomy bedroom, wearing only a flimsy nightdress. A single candle highlighted her frightened face.

There was a flash of lightning, followed by a crescendo of thunder and a gust of wind which extinguished the candle, plunging the bedroom into darkness. Then there came a scratching sound.

'Who's there?' the girl whimpered.

Peacock stepped in front of the television and turned it off.

'Bedtime,' he told everyone.

No one complained, even though the horror film had just started to get interesting. Riley and Treadwell rose, both looking ready for bed; Sinnott and Wright had departed to their cells earlier. Peacock gathered up Carpenter's lighter and cigarette packet. The packet was empty.

While Peacock locked the others in, Carpenter undressed quickly, transferring the wodge of pages from *War and Peace* into his pyjama jacket pocket. Peacock appeared and cursorily searched his cell before handing Carpenter his sleeping tablet. Then he picked up his clothes and departed.

The bolt thunked shut behind him. Carpenter put the tablet into his pocket with the wodge of paper. Tomorrow he would flush both down the toilet.

He got into bed. Presently his light dimmed. By Limbo's standards it had been a highly eventful day, not least in Wright's attempt to create a sense of solidarity between them. It had finally forced Carpenter to admit that the restless feeling that had been bothering him all day was not primarily a result of boredom or vexation at his imprisonment. On the contrary: when Wright had asked him for his support he had suddenly realized that despite the routine and restrictions and petty irritations of Limbo, despite its whole unfairness as a principle and a fact, it was in a strange way the most exciting thing that had ever happened to him. He had felt anxious at the thought of abandoning it, and so he had finally spoken up, looking Wright full in the face and saying: 'No.'

2

Making Waves

For almost as long as he could remember, Carpenter had always felt that some special destiny lay in store for him.

As a young boy he liked to hide himself in the cupboard under the stairs, sitting snug in the darkness and relishing the feeling that no one knew where he was. He remained aware that beyond the cupboard his father still sat in the living room reading his newspaper while his mother pottered in the kitchen; but alone, his mind was free to roam.

In truth, he seldom did more than revel in the sheer fact of his seclusion. Sometimes – usually after Sunday School – he would find himself thinking about God and would try to imagine what it would be like to live for ever in Heaven. The idea vaguely terrified him. Or he would imagine himself as an adult, returning home to visit his parents after a lengthy absence. He invariably entered the house to find his father sitting with his newspaper on his lap and his aproned mother with her hands still wet from the sink.

In adolescence, the cupboard renounced for the more spacious sanctuary of his bedroom, his dreams took on a more traditional and romantic flavour: his abiding passion was by now football, and he became a United hero who could do no wrong. Later he flirted with the idea of being a famous pop star, and then a scientific genius; he would be respected and admired by everyone – but especially by girls. Later still, in the heady years of university, he felt himself like a sponge, absorbing multifarious influences and experiences for future use in some unspecified endeavour which would Make His Name. And even in the sobering post-university years, when disillusionment gradually seeped through his being like rising damp, he held to the implicit faith that Big Things lay in store for him; he was marked for glory, was special, unique, and need only bide his time.

This was the thread which held his days, weeks, months, years together through good times and bad. It kept him patient, steadfast, accepting. But in retrospect it also made all those days, weeks, months and years something of a rehearsal for What Was To Come. Real life was somehow always just around the corner; it was never quite here-and-now.

Carpenter lay marooned in his bed, deserted by sleep. He knew that much of his outlook on life had been conditioned by a Christian education. As a young boy his impressionable mind had been filled with ideas of eternal damnation or the prospect of Life Everlasting – concepts which tended to instil both high expectations and high anxieties into an individual, marking him for life.

At the time it had never struck him as odd that his parents were not regular church goers. His mother was a short and active woman who seemed to spend most of her time in the kitchen, cooking, cleaning, mending and washing up; she was always far too busy for him. His father, by contrast, was grave and sedate, old beyond his years and grey-haired even when Carpenter was small. He worked nights six days a week as a security guard at a local factory and slept till late in the afternoons. He seldom had much to say and always seemed to be engrossed in his newspaper. It was as if life had worn every spark of vitality out of him. The young Carpenter moved around him as if he was a piece of furniture, his mother constantly warning him that his father was tired and shouldn't be bothered. He was a fixture in Carpenter's childhood in the most strict and limited sense.

Carpenter's first real disillusionment had been with the church, though it had come upon him gradually. In his early teens he had gone through a phase in which he had eagerly anticipated conversion, having been inspired by the precedent of a girl in his Sunday School class who had one day declared herself saved by the certain knowledge of Christ's salvation. In the weeks that followed, several other members of Carpenter's class had undergone similar conversions until Carpenter felt left out. He grew ever more keen to receive his own call to salvation. It was clear to him that those who had been converted had discovered a conviction and commitment which he himself woefully lacked. He envisaged his own moment of conversion as an abrupt and immediately transforming flood of divine illumination; like Saul on the road to Tarsus, he would experience a blinding moment of revelation in which God would come to him in all His glory and he would be accepted into the fold.

But nothing happened, and as he progressed through his teens he found himself increasingly distracted by the simpler pleasures of the real world. There was football, pop music and the ambiguous attractions of the opposite sex. He had finally been lured away from church by the Sunday afternoon fishing trips to the local reservoir with his best friend, Graham Stoneley.

To think of Graham made him feel uncomfortable and vaguely agitated. They had become friends at the age of ten when the Stoneley family had moved into a house in the next street. Graham was blond and blue-eyed, handsome and full of enthusiasms even in those days. His father was a tall, jovial man, and there was an older sister, Beryl, who was always feeding them biscuits and glasses of raspberryade. The Stoneley house was far more lively than his own and he spent a lot of time there, with Graham's father making them pram-wheeled trolleys, repairing their bicycles and showing them how to carve wood for arrows. Carpenter always assumed that Graham's mother was dead, and it was only years later that he learned she had run off with another man before the family moved to his neighbourhood.

It was Graham's father who first took Carpenter to Old Trafford and fired him with a passion for Manchester United. An ardent supporter himself, he taught Carpenter the litany of those who had died in the Munich air crash and made an article of faith of the fact that Duncan Edwards was the greatest footballer who had ever lived. Their fortnightly trips to Old Trafford became a highlight of Carpenter's youth, giving him a new focus for his religious fervour. Graham, however, never became similarly inspired, and as soon as they were old enough to attend matches by themselves, he stopped going and began to spend his Saturday afternoons practising on an acoustic guitar which he had picked up for £5 at a market stall. Soon Carpenter was caught up in his obsession with becoming a famous musician.

This time it was Carpenter who failed his calling and not his calling which failed him. When Graham formed a group at school, Carpenter provided its name – Gray Stone and the Rockrollers – but his contribution went little further than this, even though he bought himself a harmonica and a pair of maracas as a sign of good faith. He was far too self-conscious actually to sing at the group gatherings which Graham began to organize in the Stoneley front room; he preferred to play records and pose in front of the bedroom mirror pretending that he was already famous rather than spend his time learning to sing or play an instrument. Graham quickly mastered the basic chords and riffs, but Carpenter's maracas gathered dust on his dressing table and he finally sold his harmonica to the boy who was drafted in to replace him in the group and who actually had a passable singing voice.

It was typical, really; Graham was always a person of great enthusiasms, and Carpenter inevitably got carried along in his wake. He continued to attend the group's rehearsals, where he was expected to give frank appraisals of their performances. Frankly, he thought they were pretty awful, only Graham seeming blessed with any natural ability, however crude. But he always made encouraging noises, knowing that it meant a lot to Graham. He was beginning to understand that things never turned out as perfectly as one hoped or imagined. And he was to receive his severest lesson in this fact not long afterwards, when he fell in love.

Carpenter fell in love shortly before his fourteenth birthday, when a new girl came to his class in school. Her name was Gail Renshaw, and she was quite simply the most beautiful creature he had ever seen. She was blonde and graceful and had a smile which captivated him and made him long to be the object of it. From that moment on she became the centre of his romantic fantasies, though he was never able to speak to her except on the most passing and mundane of terms. For two years he told no one of his infatuation until finally he confessed all to Graham one evening outside the fish-and-chip shop a few days before the school's Christmas party. He was determined to declare his passion for her at the party, but he didn't know how to go about it. Graham, already popular and confident with girls, assured him that it would be no problem; he would fix them up at the dance.

Carpenter still cringed whenever he thought of it. On the night of the party he had arrived wearing white hipster trousers and a white shirt over a scarlet bri-nylon polo-neck. He was quietly confident that he looked the part, but when he entered the dance hall and the cluster of girls beside the door glanced at him, his immediate impulse was to flee. Gail was amongst them, looking gorgeous and utterly unattainable in cream knee-length boots, a lemon miniskirt and a white cheesecloth blouse.

He kept to the shadows from then on, rejecting Graham's suggestion that they go talk to Gail and huddling with a group of fifth-formers who all disdained dancing and professed no interest in girls; they lounged against the wall, ostentatiously keeping time with the music and making caustic remarks about any boy who had the temerity to dance. Carpenter contributed his share of cutting comments, but he couldn't keep his eyes off Gail. Graham had now gone across to talk to her, and Carpenter's heart started to palpitate as he anticipated the moment when Graham would lead her over to him. What would he say? What would *she* say? What was he supposed to do? Again he felt the urge to bolt and hide himself in the toilet.

But Graham took Gail on to the dance floor as the disc jockey – a prefect trusted by the staff – put on 'Substitute' by The Who. This was followed by The Spencer Davis Group with 'Keep on Running', and now Graham and Gail were dancing closer and even holding one another's arms. They were talking earnestly together, though neither glanced in Carpenter's direction. The record ended and was replaced by The Monkees and 'I'm A Believer'. Graham professed not to like The Monkees, but still he was dancing with Gail and they were laughing together.

Carpenter huddled even deeper into the shadows when Graham and Gail left about an hour later, arm in arm. They looked the perfect couple. He did not move for a long while, and remembered only that he wanted to vanish, to disappear down some dark hole and never emerge. Then he noticed that one of Gail's friends was staring at him with interest. She was renowned for her sharp tongue, but she had always been friendly towards him. The dance was now winding down, and she was standing by the doorway, alone. Did he detect a faint smile on her lips?

This is it, he thought with a resurgence of hope. Plucking up his courage, he strode across to her. Before he could say anything she told him he looked like a polar bear that had had its throat cut.

The next day Graham claimed that Gail had actually asked him,

Graham, out before he could broach the matter of Carpenter's attraction to her. He assured Carpenter that he was simply playing for time; he would continue to take her out until the moment was ripe to tell her that he was actually acting on behalf of his best friend. Carpenter did not know what to say to this; even if it was true, it sounded like a recipe for disaster. He adopted his usual strategy of letting events unfold without influence by him. Two years later, when he departed to university, Graham and Gail were still going strong.

*

The light still burned in his cell, and the night seemed endless. The memories were crowding in, clamouring for his attention. He had denied them all for months, and wanted to forget them all now. But to think of Gail was to think of the other women who had dominated and defined much of his life ever since that time. Veronica. Karen. Eleanor. Penny. He was a victim of romance, or some warped idea of romance. Veronica. Karen. Eleanor. Penny. A roll-call of guilt and confusion and even anger.

He turned over, face to the wall, dragging the blankets right up to his chin, forcing his eyes shut. He wasn't going to think about them now.

You've got to face up to the facts, Veronica said.

Carpenter knew that the voice was his own, but its tone was unmistakably that of Veronicas. It did not surprise him that she should be insistent on being heard, for she of all his girlfriends had been the most forceful and self-assured.

He took the sleeping pill from his pyjama pocket, stared at it, then put it away again. Limbo was utterly silent around him, and there was no escape.

Escape from what? He had done nothing wrong – at least nothing worse than any ordinary man. But he knew that the facts were really irrelevant. It wasn't what you did that mattered, but how you felt about what you did.

He rolled over again, feeling tired despite his agitation. He would sleep. Sleep would rescue him. He thought this without conviction, but it seemed only moments later that he was waking startled by the sound of the morning bell.

*

That afternoon – the barber was late – Sinnott had his hair reduced to stubble in a matter of fifteen minutes. He was not seen for the rest of the day, and the guards informed the rest of them that he had asked to be confined to his cell.

It was a quiet, uneventful day, and Carpenter retired early that night. To his relief, he slept immediately and heavily, waking only seconds before the alarm. He could not remember having dreamt; the night was just a blank.

When Sinnott emerged from his cell he looked devastated and at least ten years younger than before. He refused to meet anyone's eyes and stood apart from the rest of them during the gym session.

Over breakfast Carpenter and the others tried to cheer him up, but to no avail. He wouldn't talk to any of them, responding only with movements of the head. Snider was on hand to caution them that they should not press him if he wanted to be left alone.

Immediately after breakfast, Sinnott retired to his cell and did not emerge until lunch. He ate little and was as uncommunicative as ever, departing back to his cell as soon as he could. By now Carpenter and the others were worried, but Sinnott refused to greet visitors. He lay on his bed with his face to the wall and would not move or speak.

Carpenter knew that he had to do something about it. As soon as Dr Dempster arrived that evening, he went straight to her office, knocking on her door and opening it.

'Michael,' she said. 'You're very prompt.'

'I'd like to have a word with you.'

She stared at him for a moment, then nodded vigorously. 'Sit down. Sit down.'

'I'm worried about Sinnott,' Carpenter told her, then explained about his haircut and the effect it had had on him.

Dr Dempster listened without comment and was silent for a while after he had finished speaking. The tea-tray was already sitting on her desk, but she made no move to fill their cups.

Carpenter tried to read her expression. If anything, she looked confused.

'I'm afraid you've caught me a little bit at a loss,' she confessed. 'What exactly has been happening?'

Was it possible that Naughton did not keep her informed about the day-to-day events in Limbo? Carpenter decided that it was – especially if he felt that she might be sympathetic to their plight. He did his best to give her all the relevant details of their last summons to his office.

This time she did not say anything for a long while. Her face was carefully neutral, and it was as if she was engaged in some complex and intricate mental calculation.

At length she said, 'Have you tried talking to him?'

'We've all tried.'

'All?'

'All four of us. He just nods or shakes his head. Mostly not even that.'

There was a pause before she said, 'Do you think he's likely to do something drastic?'

'Anything's possible. Being cooped up here tends to get you down at times, and Sinnott was very proud of his hair.'

'Yes. Of course.'

She had taken out her silver ballpoint pen and was doodling on a pad.

'Would it help if I talked to him?'

'I doubt it.'

'Why not?'

Carpenter wasn't sure why he had said this. He shrugged. 'He's probably frightened of you. He's frightened of everyone.'

'Everyone?'

'Naughton. The guards. Even his own shadow, I think.'

'I see. So what would you suggest?'

'He's always being picked on. It isn't fair – he never causes any trouble. They ought to leave him alone.'

He was hoping she would put pressure to bear on Naughton, but he didn't like to ask her direct.

She drew spirals on the notepaper. 'What about the others? The other three?'

'What about them?'

'Any problems with them?'

Carpenter shrugged. 'They're much the same as ever.'

This was not exactly true. Wright and Treadwell had decided to go ahead with their campaign of resistance to Naughton and had formed a two-man escape committee. Carpenter had no idea what they were plotting, but he supposed that Treadwell had told Wright about the loose floor tile in the gym. No doubt they were hoping to gain possession of a heavy-duty soup spoon or some similar implement and would begin gouging their way to freedom at the earliest opportunity.

Dr Dempster appeared to be waiting for him to say something further. Carpenter had an abrupt feeling that he had already said too much. The silence lengthened, but still she waited.

'I won't be needing any more sleeping tablets,' he said.

'Have you been sleeping without them?'

He nodded. 'For the last week or so.' He didn't like to admit that he had stopped taking them several weeks ago. 'I've been rinsing them down the washbasin.'

She smiled faintly and began to push the pen to and fro between her fingers. Carpenter found this very stimulating.

'You don't mind?' he said.

'Not if you feel you don't need them. You've had no problems sleeping?'

'No,' he lied.

'Not waking in the middle of the night?'

'No.' This, at least, was true.

'Bad dreams? Nightmares? Anything of that sort?'

'No.'

'Good. Good.'

She looked genuinely pleased. Then it occurred to him that in presenting her with a clean bill of health he might be putting his regular appointments with her in jeopardy.

'I've been getting these headaches,' he said.

*

Dr Dempster advised Carpenter to keep an eye on Sinnott and let her know of his progress; she prescribed aspirin for his headaches. Over the next two days Sinnott showed no sign of improvement. His shorn hair made him look like a pitiable young convict; he seldom emerged from his cell and spoke only rarely. Carpenter tried to get him talking about football, a subject in which he had previously shown some interest; but it was no use. All the guards except Snider left him alone. Snider would watch over him at breakfast and lunch and would not allow him to leave the table until he had eaten something. Naughton remained in his office, and no summons were received from him.

In the gym Treadwell was more vigorous than ever in his press-ups, no doubt in the hope of speeding up the tile-loosening process, though this was not evident from his technique. Blythe had instituted a new regime of knee-bends to replace the running on the spot which Riley had sabotaged by making a pantomime of it. This brought a new worry for Carpenter, who could hear the dodgy cartilage in his left knee making crackling noises as he went through the motions. It seemed only a matter of time before he did sudden and excruciating damage to his knee.

'Do you get any pain?' Dr Dempster asked, her cool fingers delicately probing his knee.

'Only when I bath,' Carpenter said.

She looked puzzled at this, and he regretted the feeble attempt at humour. But it was too late to back down now.

'Sometimes it seems to swell up under hot water,' he said vaguely. In fact pain was the last thing on his mind at that moment. His trouser-leg was rolled up to his thigh, and Dr Dempster had her other hand cupped under his knee.

'It's a kind of crunching sensation,' he said. 'I'm afraid it might go at any moment. My father had to have a cartilage removed when he was younger. Perhaps it's hereditary.'

She stared at him for a moment. 'Did your father play a lot of sport or have a physically active job?'

'No, not particularly.'

'What did he do?'

'He was a nightwatchman.'

She did a bit more probing, then gave his knee a concluding pat.

'I shouldn't worry too much about it if I were you. As long as you're not *too* vigorous with it you should be all right.'

Carpenter was disappointed. He had been hoping that she might have him excused from the gym sessions on medical grounds.

She returned to her desk, her perfume lingering. Carpenter suddenly thought of something.

'How did you know my father was dead?' he asked.

She stared back at him. 'It's on your medical records.'

He fell silent, disappointed on one hand that she had been reading up on him without his knowledge, yet aware that this was only to be expected under the circumstances.

She poured the teas, and put his cup down in front of him.

'Headaches?' she asked.

'They've stopped.'

'And how is your friend Sinnott?'

'Much the same.'

'Does he trust you?'

'I suppose so.'

'Then try a little gentle bullying.'

*

Carpenter decided to follow Dr Dempster's advice. That evening he kept Sinnott occupied with games of snooker and darts, insisting that he continue playing when he complained that he wanted to return to his cell. By the end of the evening he was exhausted by his efforts and Sinnott looked positively relieved that it was time for bed. Carpenter reflected that people were never more of a nuisance than when they were hell-bent on helping others. But he was determined to jolly Sinnott out of his gloom, and he was helped by the fact that the next day was a Saturday.

Saturdays and Sundays were always more relaxed than weekdays. Naughton was absent and his deputy, Brookes, was an amiable man who disliked confrontations and did his best to keep the inmates happy. The weekend guards, Grant and Fairbrother, were on duty throughout the day, and they were also easygoing. After breakfast on Saturday morning Carpenter approached Grant and suggested a soccer match in the gym that afternoon between the inmates and the guards.

Grant was a cheerful, stocky man in his early thirties, and Carpenter knew he was an Arsenal supporter because he always waited for their result on *Grandstand* at a quarter to five. He immediately looked interested in Carpenter's proposal, but said the main problem might be getting hold of a ball. He would see what he could do.

Carpenter informed Riley and Treadwell of the prospective match, but said nothing to Sinnott for the time being. Wright was ensconced in his cell with a pile of books which Brookes had allowed him to take out of the library; given his stated views on team sports, Carpenter did not suppose he would be remotely interested in playing. If Riley agreed to referee, that would leave himself, Sinnott and Treadwell to make up the team.

As they were finishing lunch, Grant entered with a leather football. Brookes had given them the go-ahead for the game and had even offered to act as referee. Fairbrother had agreed to play, and they had enlisted another man for their team. Kick-off was at three o'clock.

Carpenter immediately set about organizing his own team. This did not prove as straightforward as he had expected, for both Riley and Wright insisted that they wanted to play. Sinnott was, in fact, the only inmate who showed no enthusiasm for the game; he wanted to spend the afternoon alone in his cell. This prompted Carpenter to insist that he was going to play even if they had to use him as the ball.

But there was now an even greater imbalance in the teams. Carpenter spent the next five minutes juggling with the idea of second-half substitutes until the problem was solved by Treadwell volunteering to play on the guards' side. Wright was vehemently opposed to such a defection, but everyone else agreed that it was the simplest solution and he was overruled.

They assembled in the gym at a quarter to three. Grant had managed to obtain training shoes, shorts and two sets of shirts, in red and green.

'We'll take red,' Carpenter said instantly, having spotted the number 9 shirt which he was determined to wear.

Grant shook his head; red was also Arsenal's colour.

They tossed a coin. To Carpenter's delight, he won.

Brookes appeared, dressed in a natty black tracksuit with white piping which looked as if it had been bought especially for the occasion. An affable and avuncular man in his late forties, Brookes was not exactly a forceful personality, and Carpenter wondered how he would fare in controlling the game. He suspected it would be a spirited affair.

Both guards and inmates donned their kit. The extra member of the guards' team was called Loftus; he was an appropriately tall man whom none of the inmates had ever seen before. He proved to be the strong, silent type, only speaking if spoken to. Carpenter decided that he probably manned the surveillance monitors on weekends and had only reluctantly been persuaded to take part in the game.

Carpenter surveyed the opposition. Loftus looked as if he lacked coordination, while Fairbrother, squat and stout, would probably be short on stamina. But Grant appeared sturdy and fit, while Treadwell would be a major threat by virtue of sheer athleticism unless he did the decent thing and deliberately played badly. Against them he had Riley, who was unlikely to last more than five minutes, Wright, who had probably not played football since primary school, and Sinnott, who looked painfully fragile, his shirt hanging on him. Overall the odds were against them.

Then Sinnott announced that he wanted to play in goal, and Carpenter's spirits sank even further. He had earmarked the place for Riley since it seemed the only position in which he would see out the game. But Riley was keen to play outfield, and it was too late to argue now.

The goal posts were four medicine balls taken from Blythe's storeroom. Carpenter and Grant had previously agreed on a loose set of rules which permitted practically everything short of grievous bodily harm. As self-appointed captain he assigned Riley to defence, with himself in midfield and Wright as striker. Loftus had gone into goal for the guards, with Fairbrother defending, Treadwell in midfield and Grant up front. Brookes insisted that the two captains shake hands before they kicked off.

'Let's have a nice clean game,' he told them, then blew his whistle.

Wild confusion immediately ensued, with everyone charging pell-mell after the ball wherever it went. There were numerous collisions and knocks from flailing elbows and knees in the first five minutes until exhaustion began to force some semblance of order on the game. This was just as well, for Brookes's attempts at arbitration were having only a marginal effect.

After about ten minutes, the guards scored: a lofted ball from Fairbrother dropped at Riley's feet, causing Riley to fall over as he tried to kick it and leaving Grant free to shoot past the helpless Sinnott. As a result of this Sinnott began to shout instructions to Riley each time the guards mounted an attack. But Riley was utterly incapable of responding to any of it since he lacked speed, balance and coordination. In fact he was a positive asset to the opposition.

Each half was to last twenty minutes, and shortly before half-time the guards scored again through a penalty awarded by Brookes after Wright had hacked down Treadwell when he came charging upfield. Wright had been playing with a manic aggression since the start of the game and would have long been sent off by any referee less lenient than Brookes. Carpenter had been correct in assuming that Wright had no talent for football, but his vicious charges at his opponents had had something of a deterrent effect up to that point. He was especially vehement when confronted by Treadwell, and Carpenter sympathized with him on this score since Treadwell was playing with complete commitment to his side. He lacked basic ability but his very fitness enabled him to keep running into free space, thus providing an extra man in attack. Carpenter had been doing his best to support Wright, but Wright preferred to run back and scythe down attacking players rather than stay forward in his appointed position. It was a shambles.

When the whistle blew for half-time, Carpenter was surprised that they had only conceded two goals; a rout seemed inevitable. Riley lay flat on his back, panting and moaning that he was dying. Carpenter was about to suggest a change of formation when Sinnott announced that Riley would go into goal, while he would take Carpenter's place in midfield, with Carpenter himself going into attack and Wright defending. He told Wright that he should try to force any attacking players out on to the flanks so that his fouls could be committed outside the penalty area. This was very professional advice, and when he directed Carpenter to push as far forward as possible, Carpenter was eager to oblige, aware of the number 9 on his shirt.

The game resumed again. Carpenter noted that he did not feel at all weary or stiff; evidently the gym sessions had had some beneficial effect. He moved into the guards' half, Fairbrother shadowing him everywhere. Grant and Treadwell mounted an attack, but Sinnott plucked the ball from Grant's feet, sold a dummy to Treadwell and came surging forward. Fairbrother rushed to meet him, but Sinnott pushed the ball through his legs and ran around him before striking the ball hard and low past Loftus. 2–1.

From that moment on Sinnott's mastery of the game was undeniable. Grant was a more than competent footballer, but Sinnott easily surpassed him and Carpenter began to wonder why no First Division team had signed him up. Or was it just that the rest of them were so inept that they made Sinnott look good? Carpenter had been entertaining the fantasy that he was Denis Law at the head of the Manchester United attack, but his actual achievements on the field of play continued to conspire against this dream. Sinnott was now giving him good possession with perfectly weighted passes, but Carpenter was seldom able to put his foot to the end of them. In his mind he was engaged in a European Cup Final with Bobby Charlton, George Best and the rest of the United greats; in reality he was playing like a clown.

As the second half progressed, Sinnott's composure in defence meant that Riley had not been required to make a single save in goal, and Carpenter saw that he was now sitting on one of the medicine balls, picking his nose. Then suddenly Grant managed to get past Sinnott with the ball. He passed it to Treadwell, who leapt over the lunging Wright, then raced after the ball as it trickled towards Riley.

Riley did a kind of frog-leap from a sitting position and smothered the ball just as Treadwell reached it. Treadwell went down like a felled tree, and Carpenter closed his eyes at the thought of another penalty. But Brookes deemed the challenge a fair one and theatrically waved play on as if he was performing in front of the *Match of the Day* cameras.

Riley punted the ball up the gym. It soared over everyone and dropped at Carpenter's feet. Loftus advanced out of goal as Carpenter readied himself for a shot. This was the moment Carpenter had been waiting for. No United fan of any standing would ever forget that Nat Lofthouse of Bolton Wanderers had brought about United's defeat in the 1958 Cup Final by barging Harry Gregg, United's 'keeper, over the goal line: a doubly cruel blow since United were fielding a makeshift side after the Busby Babes had been decimated in the Munich air crash. Even before the game had started Carpenter had begun to think of Loftus as Lofthouse, and now he was going to repay the insult by humiliating him with his ball control.

Carpenter prodded the ball forward, then tried to drive it through Loftus's legs; but he miskicked and the ball hit Loftus in the knee before rebounding into Carpenter's face. There was an instant fiery red pain, and he fell, clutching his nose.

When he opened his eyes everyone was clustered around him. After a moment he sat up.

'I'm all right,' he said manfully, though his nostrils felt as if they had been scoured with a wire brush. He struggled to his feet, blood seeming to slosh around in his head.

'You're bleeding,' Treadwell said.

He was aware of the drops plopping on to his chest.

'I'm all right,' he insisted. 'It's a red shirt.'

No one seemed to think that this had any relevance; they all wanted him to abandon the game. But he was adamant that he would play on. Brookes delved into his pocket and produced a wad of cotton wool.

Just to touch cotton wool had always made Carpenter cringe. But anything was better than running around dripping blood everywhere. He tore off two pieces and hastily stuffed one up each nostril. They made his nose feel enormous.

'If anybody says anything,' he began, then shut up. He sounded ridiculous.

The game resumed, and Carpenter made strenuous efforts to

prove that he could shrug off his injury by doing more running and chasing than ever. Within minutes he was feeling sick. Then Sinnott levelled the scores with a dipping shot which deceived Loftus, and for a while an honourable draw seemed the most likely outcome. But in the last minute Riley fumbled a back pass from Wright and Grant prodded the ball home. 3–2 to the guards.

Everyone – even Wright – seemed agreed that the game had been a success; everyone, that is, except Carpenter. He felt awful, and had to go and lie down for the rest of the day.

*

On Monday morning Wright vouchsafed Carpenter the nature of the escape plan he had evolved with Treadwell. This began in the form of an entreaty to be careful when he visited the right-hand cubicle of the toilet. Carpenter was suitably intrigued, and Wright went on to explain that he and Treadwell had loosened several tiles from the wall immediately below the toilet cistern and were in the process of gouging through the mortar underneath with the cistern handle, which could be unscrewed from its mounting.

'Neat,' said Carpenter.

'One of us keeps an eye on the guards while the other's at work,' Wright told him. 'That's the advantage of working as a team.'

Wright was very enthusiastic about the plan. It had, he informed Carpenter, three major advantages. First and foremost, there was no surveillance camera in the bathroom (he had deemed Treadwell's plan to escape by tunnelling through the gymnasium floor impractical for this very reason); second, the mortar was quite soft, which meant that they could make good progress; and third, the gouged-out mortar could be flushed down the toilet and the tiles replaced so that the guards would not suspect what was going on. Carpenter was warned that he should do nothing to arouse their suspicions and that he was not to tamper with the tiles.

'Cross my heart,' he said. 'It's nice of you to make me privy to the plan.'

As soon as Wright left him alone, he went to the bathroom and entered the right-hand cubicle. The tiles came away easily to reveal their handiwork. They had removed six in all, to give a potential tunnel about two feet in diameter. Carpenter stuck his thumb into the hole they had so far gouged. It was about a quarter of an inch deep, and this in roughly one week's work. How thick would the wall be? A foot? Two feet? More?

He resisted the temptation to perform a calculation; Wright and Treadwell would devote the rest of their lives to the task if necessary. But he couldn't understand why they hadn't simply removed just one tile at first until they had some idea of the thickness of the wall. Even then there was no guarantee that it would lead outside. And how did Wright square this operation with his belief that Limbo was in the middle of the Channel?

It took him about ten minutes to reposition the tiles correctly. He swabbed the powdered mortar from the floor with damp toilet paper and flushed this away. Snider was waiting for him when he emerged.

Carpenter went through an elaborate routine of lathering and rinsing his hands at the washbasin while peering at Snider in the mirror. Snider had pushed the cubicle door open with his foot and was staring inside. Carpenter held his breath. Finally Snider turned to face him, the door swinging shut. Carpenter went to the roller-towel and began to wipe his hands. Snider had said nothing, but the expression on his face was eloquent. It said, *I'm watching you, Carpenter.*

*

That evening Carpenter told Dr Dempster about the football match and its success in revitalizing Sinnott. Since then Sinnott had reverted to his normal self, and while this was hardly a healthy state in absolute terms, at least he was no longer in danger of going completely to pieces.

Dr Dempster praised him for his initiative. This made Carpenter feel like a schoolboy who had just turned in his best essay for his favourite teacher. When she smiled, small lines formed at either side of her mouth. They were very appealing lines. She was wearing a pink satin blouse beneath her white coat, and he found himself wondering what it would be like to run his hands over the silky material, preferably with her still inside it and lying beneath him.

This immediately struck him as a highly improper thought. Until now the general subject of sex had been far from his mind all the time he'd been in Limbo.

'. . . wouldn't you say?'

'Pardon?' He could feel himself blushing.

'Help from others is important to all of us sometimes.'

'Oh, yes.'

'It's like friendship. We all need friendship.'

'I suppose we do.' He thought of hermits and lighthouse keepers.

'One can't get by without companionship and moral support from other people.'

'No man is an island. Or woman, for that matter.'

'Precisely. I always think we should value everyone close to us and cherish their company.'

'Absolutely.'

A silence fell which became more uncomfortable as it lengthened.

'How is your knee?' she asked.

*

To distract himself from thoughts of sex, Carpenter sat in the lounge and watched a science programme about the new discipline of sociobiology, which he was told aimed to trace the biological basis of human and animal behaviour. By the end of it he had learned that sociobiologists considered all human behaviour to have its roots in the blind biological urge to propagate genes. Humans and animals existed for the prime purpose of producing further humans and animals, and their activities were thus dominated by reproductive imperatives programmed into their DNA.

There was something profoundly dispiriting about this, despite all the talk of the modifying effects of culture and intellect. But then he had long ceased to expect illumination of an elevating nature from any system of rational inquiry. He had opted for sciences in the sixth form at school because physics and mathematics had seemed to him to represent the most fundamental and rigorous method of investigating and interpreting the world. Disillusioned with the promises of religion and increasingly perplexed by personal relationships, he saw in science a precision-built analytical instrument which gave concrete results about natural phenomena and made testable predictions. It was an area of human activity where everything was quantifiable and certainties could be arrived at. The scientific process was simply a matter of providing more and more precise measurements and formulating more and more exact and comprehensive theories to explain the behaviour of the physical universe. If it was no help at all in personal and spiritual problems, at least it was better than nothing.

But in the sixth form his teachers began to give him a more sophisticated grounding in the subject, and the sands began to shift beneath his feet. Physics up to the fifth form had been firmly rooted in Newtonian mechanics whose laws and their effects on bodies were perfectly amenable to him because he was always able to form mental pictures to represent their actions and consequences. Now he was introduced to such ideas as probability theory, the wave-particle duality of matter and the concept of entropy. These indicated that it was not always possible to obtain precise measurements, that matter could behave like radiation and vice versa, and that the whole universe was tending towards a state of increasing randomness in which complete disorder would eventually prevail.

These ideas were not exactly in line with his original vision of a universe which resembled a sophisticated machine whose working parts could be isolated and their functions explained. But it was at university that his faith in absolutes was finally undermined. In his first term he was confronted with quantum mechanics, which destroyed for ever his notion of the atom as a miniature solar system having discrete electrons orbiting a solid nucleus and replaced it with three-dimensional stationary wave systems in which the position and velocity of the electrons could never be specified with perfect accuracy. Allied to this was Heisenberg's Uncertainty Principle, which told him that the more precisely one tried to determine a specific property of a particle, the less precisely could another property be determined; the very act of measurement influenced the result obtained so that it was, in effect, impossible to be a completely detached observer.

His mind started to boggle, for he could conjure up no handy mental pictures for three-dimensional stationary waves and associated quantum mechanical notions, while the Uncertainty Principle made it clear that accurate measurements were not possible beyond a certain limit. Far from being an intricate machine accessible to progressively finer scrutiny, the universe was beginning to resemble a picture on a television screen which became fuzzy and chaotic if you peered at it too closely. Then came relativity.

Relativity was the last straw for Carpenter, because it told him that no frame of reference was absolute and that the universe had, as it were, no focal point. Everything depended on the status of the observer, and if you were elsewhere (or elsewhen) you might see things quite differently. There were many other bizarre implications too, and he strived to master the idea of a universe that was finite but boundless, to think of time as another dimension, to accept that the mass and physical dimensions of an object altered as its velocity changed, to imagine gravity warping the very fabric of space. It was all incredible and thoroughly perplexing, as though the universe had been designed for the express purpose of being unimaginable to the human mind.

*

Captive to the television, Carpenter found himself watching a documentary about the extinction of a tribe of Amazonian Indians. Normally this was the sort of programme he avoided like the plague, but something compelled him to stay where he was.

The reporter was walking through a stretch of tribal homeland which had been sprayed with defoliants. The stench, he told his audience, was unbelievable. The camera lingered on rotting vegetation and the decaying carcasses of small animals. Then the scene switched to a huge new concrete reservoir which the Brazilian government had flooded mile upon mile of virgin rainforest to create. There were more horror stories of pollution, wanton destruction of irreplaceable habitats and the ruthless activities of new settlers and farmers. Carpenter began to feel miserable and helpless.

You see, said Veronica. This is what happens when people don't face up to their responsibilities.

From that point on, Veronica's insistent voice formed a kind of counterpoint to the actual documentary, with the difference that her condemnatory tone was addressed at him and him alone. Carpenter fidgeted in his seat, appalled at what he was seeing and hearing, but unable to move. At length the documentary came to an end with the image of a native Indian standing knee-deep in a jungle stream, morosely jabbing a wooden spear at passing fish while puffing on a cigarette. And Veronica was saying: How can you possibly complain about your own situation when millions of people all over the world are dying of starvation, disease and neglect?

Carpenter fled to his cell, knowing he couldn't escape. Veronica had haunted him for years before Limbo, and she had returned to haunt him again. No matter that he knew it was his own conscience finding its voice through her: if anything, that only made it worse.

Lying on his bed, he focused on the blank expanse of the ceiling. To his relief, the images of death and destruction began to pass away and were gradually replaced by thoughts of sex. At first he was shocked by the association, but it was no less welcome for that. In some ways Veronica still exemplified the idea of sex for him, not because she was either sensuous or promiscuous but because it was she who finally delivered him of his virginity.

He had met her at Cardiff in his second year at university. He had gone to Cardiff because it was far away from Manchester and he hoped to escape the effects of his unrequited passion for Gail. Both Graham and Gail were staying put in Manchester, Gail to attend teaching college, Graham to play with his new group, somewhat mystically called The Beyond, who were doing the Manchester club circuit and hoping for a big break. Carpenter was now on friendly terms with Gail, but her commitment to Graham was total and at times unbearable to him. He hoped that absence would make the heart grow less fond.

Carpenter spent his first year in university being a typical first-year student – that is to say he discovered excess in the form of alcohol, marijuana and all-night parties. Freed from the stultifying influence of his home, he grew his hair long and took to wearing tie-dyed vests and garish paisley shirts with bell-bottomed jeans and a parka. Everyone around him was colourful, unconventional and, it seemed to him, clever. Carpenter was determined to match them in every way.

There was only one small problem: he was a virgin and had never had a genuine relationship with a girl. He had dated a few girls in the sixth form at school, but all of them had known of his passion for Gail and none had lasted. At university there were plenty of girls around who knew nothing about Gail; several were even quite friendly to him, but somehow it never went beyond that. In the final analysis he was always too afraid to ask them out for fear that they might say no and humiliate him. Before he knew it his first year was over, and he returned to Manchester convinced that he was the only male university student in the country who had never experienced the delights of sexual congress.

In his second year at Cardiff he determined to be bolder with the female student body. But his old habits of self-consciousness and emotional cowardice continued to conspire against his most passionate intentions. Weeks turned into months, and he seemed further away than ever from finding himself a girlfriend. It was then that Veronica unexpectedly entered his life.

They met by accident shortly before Christmas when Carpenter wandered into a Students Action Group meeting by mistake, thinking that it was the party to which he had been invited. The Students Action Group were a small but vociferous band of activists who espoused radical causes. They called themselves STAG for short, though outside the group they were known as SAG and considered far too earnest for the spirit of the times. Before Carpenter knew it he had been ushered to a seat at the front of the room where a tall, pale girl wearing gold-rimmed grannie glasses and a grey knitted dress was delivering a denunciation of an economics lecturer whom she claimed had offered her flatmate a lift home in his car 'with blatantly sexual intentions'. Afterwards, when her motion of censure had been defeated on the grounds of insufficient evidence, she introduced herself to him and said that she had been impressed by his thoughtful air during the debate. He had, in fact, spent the whole time trying to think of some way to escape the meeting short of faking a nosebleed, which he lacked the nerve to do.

She seemed interested in him and asked his opinions on a number of issues arising out of the debate. He had practically no idea of what they had been talking about, but somehow he cobbled together a few generalized comments which evidently satisfied her. She had a thin, intense face, and her straw-coloured hair was severely parted down the centre of her scalp and hung straight down to her shoulders on either side. He asked her if she wanted to go to a party with him, and to his surprise she said yes.

Three-quarters of an hour later they had still not managed to find it, so Veronica suggested that they share a bottle of wine at her place. It proved to be a spacious ground floor flat in a large Victorian house near Sophia Gardens which she shared with another girl named Alison, who was not at home. The wine was retsina, which Carpenter had never tasted before. It made him want to gag, but he swallowed it manfully and listened as she told him all about the aims of STAG, which she finally summarized as being to ensure that the democratic rights of students were not threatened by bureaucracy, snobbery, elitism, pedagogy, establishment politics and male sexual harassment. At this point Carpenter abandoned his fantasy of being invited to stay the night and asked her if she was thinking of becoming an MP when she left university.

This had been a perfectly serious question, but she told him not to be ridiculous and informed him that she was a sociology student and that her future plans included doing Voluntary Service Overseas in Black Africa, touring the Middle East, visiting Athens, Istanbul and Rome, and working with underprivileged groups in Britain. Carpenter was impressed; Veronica seemed to see her future in remarkably concrete terms, whereas he had no idea what he was going to do. But then she was firm on most things, giving him her views on capital punishment, the war in Vietnam, the British class system, nuclear power, capitalism and much else. She was negative about all of them. Carpenter managed to bring up the subject of sexual promiscuity, and he learned that she was against sex for the sole purpose of physical gratification but believed it to be an integral part of any adult relationship based on mutual trust. Did he not agree? Carpenter nodded, doing his damnedest to look adult and utterly trustworthy. Then she announced that he would have to excuse her because the retsina had given her a headache and she really had to go to bed.

He left with an invitation to dinner the following day. Veronica was a vegetarian, and the meal comprised boiled rice and a variety of curried vegetables; to his surprise he found it tasty. That evening he also met Alison, an attractive, cheerful girl with dark auburn hair and an amply proportioned body whom he gathered was always bringing boys back to her room for bouts of loudly expressive lovemaking. She was a first-year student whom Veronica, in her second year like Carpenter, had taken under her wing. He soon learned that she was referred to as Slack Alison around the university, a nickname which drove Veronica into a fury of denunciation. Why is it, she complained to Carpenter, that when a man sleeps around a lot he's regarded as a stud, whereas if a woman does the same she's branded a slut? It's sheer hypocrisy and sexual stereotyping. Carpenter agreed, but he could not fail to notice that in practice Veronica thoroughly disapproved of Alison's behaviour and frequently chastised her for allowing herself to be taken advantage of.

Because he began spending much of his free time at Veronica's, Carpenter often became embroiled in the aftermath of Alison's liaisons, and he was the sympathetic ear in contrast to Veronica's stern tongue. If a boyfriend had let her down especially badly, Alison would sit tearfully on the bed and pour her heart out to Carpenter while Veronica brooded in the kitchen, having lost patience with her. Carpenter was seldom able to offer any constructive advice, but Alison seemed content just to have someone who would listen to her current tale of woe. She would usually be completely recovered by the next day and ready for a fresh skirmish on the sexual battleground.

She's her own worst enemy, Veronica would say of her, and it was undeniably true that Alison was the complaisant type who simply didn't like to say no. But it also seemed to him that she thoroughly enjoyed the company of the opposite sex and sex itself for its own sake. Her crises and disappointments tended to be short-lived, and Carpenter came to suspect that she was basically quite a tough and independent person. She was at least determined to follow her own urges without the support or approval of anyone else. Veronica, on the other hand, seemed to function best when she was striving to persuade and mobilize others.

Opposites attract, Carpenter thought to himself, for it seemed that Veronica had chosen both a flatmate and a boyfriend who were quite unlike herself. She had soon discovered that he possessed no firm opinions on any important subjects apart from football, and she became determined to 'educate and politicize' him. He was obliged to accompany her to meetings on pressing issues, of which there was at least one a week.

It was a time of brash radicalism and experimentation, but Carpenter swam against the tide by discovering in himself a growing sense of caution. He would dutifully sit listening to all the arguments and then emerge less committed than when he had entered. The more ardent the rhetoric, the greater his doubts about the point of view or the course of action he was being asked to accept. Veronica would become exasperated with him when their postmortems invariably revealed a strengthening of his irresolution, and she would redouble her efforts to convert him to a particular cause, be it the boycotting of South African goods or a sit-in at a hall of residence to protest against the petty regulations which refused to recognize students as adults. But the more pressure she put on him, the more fluid he became.

It was, in fact, a constant mystery to him that Veronica continued to tolerate his company and even seemed quite content with it on those rare occasions when they were not arguing over important issues. She had a few qualms about his drinking habits, it was true, and despised his smoking, frequently reminding him in unnecessary detail of the appalling damage he was doing to his body; but somehow she saw something in him which he could not see himself. He supposed it was a fascination akin to that of a priest who is inspired by the challenge of converting an especially hardened unbeliever.

In the early weeks of their relationship they did little more than exchange a few chaste kisses while sitting on the sofa at Veronica's in the evenings. Gradually their bouts of kissing grew more intense, though Carpenter was always careful to let Veronica dictate the pace. It was five weeks before he finally summoned the courage to put a hand on her breast, and when she made no protest he felt relief and a vague sense of anticlimax. Alone in the privacy of his bedsitter he would masturbate frantically to visions of women who were not Veronica or even Gail but stereotypes of wantonness who would do anything he wished. Then one Tuesday night six weeks after they had first met, Veronica announced that she wanted him to spend the night with her.

He was taken completely by surprise, since he had only got as far as fondling both her breasts through her clothing and had assumed that the etiquette of such matters demanded that he progress to more nether regions before a full consummation took place. But he managed to swallow his surprise and indicate that it was all right by him.

He spent ten minutes preparing himself in the bathroom, his stomach beginning to churn with anxiety and anticipation. The idea of finally losing his virginity, of actually making love to a real, live woman, was one which had obsessed him since his arrival at Cardiff, but it hardly seemed possible that it was finally about to happen. What if he bungled the job through his total lack of experience? He had all the theoretical knowledge of someone painfully lacking in practical expertise, and this now seemed a positive hindrance since he was only too aware of the possible problems from impotence to premature ejaculation which might make the whole experience a humiliating disaster.

But there was no going back now, nor did he want to. He brushed his teeth, sprayed under his armpits with deodorant from one of Alison's array of cans, then decided that he had overdone it and swabbed them with a wet flannel. He gave his face and neck and genitals a thorough washing before taking off his shoes and socks and doing likewise to his feet. Then he dressed again. He was ready. This was it.

Veronica had already undressed and got into bed when he entered her room. The first thing he noticed was how strange and vulnerable she looked without her glasses. The bedclothes were drawn up to her neck. She had turned off the light, and he undressed quickly in the sodium glow of the streetlamp outside before slipping into bed and sliding his arms around the naked body he had never seen or touched before.

Veronica jumped at the contact, and told him that his hands were cold. He warmed them between his knees for a few minutes, lying there beside her without touching her while wondering what was going to happen next and whether he was up to it. Physically he definitely wasn't at the moment. To stave off further thought he put his arms around her again. Her skin felt smooth and dry. He started to kiss her and stroke her arms and back and eventually her breasts.

After about ten minutes of this he was feeling extremely randy but was still in no position to act, being utterly limp. He wondered what Veronica was thinking or feeling; she was not saying or doing anything to indicate any sense of excitement but simply lay there, unmoving. Experimentally he slid his hand below her waist. She did not protest. He continued onwards, encountering surprisingly coarse pubic hair. And onwards, down and around towards the territory of his most fervent desires. Veronica shifted, opened her legs. The front door banged open.

They both heard Alison's giggles, interspersed with a man's voice. She sounded drunk. Then there was a tapping on the door, and Alison was asking if anyone was at home. We're in bed, Veronica called back, and Carpenter felt immensely proud since he knew that Alison would know exactly what she meant. He heard her enter her own bedroom next door, exchanging patter with her companion. The door closed and a silence descended.

It lasted only a few minutes.

I want to sleep, Veronica told him a few minutes later. Carpenter didn't blame her: the sounds of passionate lovemaking which were filtering through the wall made their own performance seem like practising the mouth organ while the London Symphony Orchestra was in full flow next door. Nevertheless he was crestfallen and consumed with frustration. For a long time he lay there in the darkness, listening to every gasp and groan of delight from Alison and thinking *damn, damn, damn*. Beside him Veronica lay so still and silent he was pretty sure that she was awake, too.

It's just first-night nerves, he told himself about his own performance; but the worrying conviction took root that he was a victim of some kind of mental block, that he would never be able to rise to the occasion when actually faced with a warm, living body rather than the nubile nymphomaniacs of his fantasies. He had been completely aroused in all but the vital hydraulic sense, and that seemed far worse than not being aroused at all. Was he destined to remain a virgin for the rest of his life through some mental quirk? Or what if it was organic? But how could it be organic if he could get it up when he was on his own? He was still awake some hours later when Alison and her bedfellow started up again. This time it was less urgent and demonstrative than earlier, but it went on far longer.

He awoke in the early hours of the morning with an erection and the instant awareness that Veronica was also awake and somehow waiting for him. They looped their arms around one another and lazily started kissing. Carpenter immediately knew that at last he was going to do it, and something in the back of his mind started telling him that this was one of the most important moments of his life and that he had to hang on to every impression he could. The thought became increasingly persistent, threatening to divert him from the actual task at hand. He could not allow that to happen. Better to minimize the requisite foreplay and get on with it lest he risk a disastrous loss of capability; more important than the experience being earth-shaking was the fact that it actually occurred.

It was not as straightforward as he had anticipated; their bodies did not meld together as simply and exquisitely as they always did in his fantasies: he had to probe and prod before finally, almost unexpectedly, resistance gave way to slick access. Even then it proved impossible to perform as two bodies in perfect working harmony; so urgent was he in his movements that he slipped out again. And then, after a frantically fumbling re-entry, Veronica shifted her position, arching her back and raising her thighs to an angle that presumably gave her more comfort or pleasure but actually gave him less. Yet the sheer fact that he was doing it at last was incredible, thrust, wonderful, thrust, amazing, thrust.

He came. It went on for quite a while, spasm after spasm. And then it was over, and again he was aware of Veronica lying beneath him, around him. Gently he lowered himself across her and began kissing her cheeks and chin. She was silent, though he could feel her heart pounding against his chest. He kissed her eyebrows, the tip of her nose, then finally, delicately, extracted himself and rolled over. She immediately reached for the box of tissues on the bedside table and began swabbing her thighs.

When this was done she allowed him to hold her again and he

told her how good it had been for him and apologized for not having been able to go on for as long as he would have liked because he had been so aroused with her. Had it been all right for her, too? Yes, she said simply, but he should have asked her if she was on the pill before they had started; it was typical of men to take it for granted and it was just as well she had taken precautions in advance. He was genuinely chastened, for the thought had never entered his head, so overwhelmed had he been by the blinding prospect of penetration. There was, in fact, a packet of Durex in his parka pocket which he had been carrying around for the past month in anticipation of the event; he had even been practising putting them on.

Despite this criticism, Veronica seemed satisfied overall, or perhaps it was simply relief that they had finally gone the whole hog and could now relax a little. She had been rather stiff and undemonstrative, but that was only to be expected the first time. She had previously told him that she was not a virgin but had only made love once, to an Austrian boy while on holiday in the Tyrol when she was seventeen. He had informed her that he'd slept with two girlfriends while living in Manchester. Two seemed just about the right number, making him seem neither a philanderer nor an outright novice.

Later that morning he wandered into the kitchen in a spare dressing gown to find Alison there, cooking breakfast. He felt as if he was wearing his long-delayed badge of full manhood on his breast for all to see, and it seemed odd that she greeted him with a simple 'Hello' and went on cooking her bacon and eggs as if nothing had happened.

He imagined that he and Veronica would now progress to a state of blissful mutual gratification when they made love, but it was not to be. They did indeed sleep together at least once a week from that time on, and gradually grew more expert in the sheer physical act of lovemaking. But somehow it remained an intrinsically serious and demanding activity, not least because Veronica revealed a continuing inability to attain orgasm, or even approach it. Once the initial period of excitement and discovery was over, this fact began to loom over them every time they went to bed like a bad examination result; all of his efforts were of no avail in solving the problem.

After a while she began to insist that it was not important, that the act itself was pleasurable enough and that the constant striving for her climax was in itself inhibiting and counter-productive. This was undoubtedly true, though he could not help feeling that he was somehow to blame. Yet by now he was also wondering if a little variety and experimentation might do the trick. They always made love in the dark and in the missionary position; he wanted to suggest new routines from the sex manuals he'd taken to perusing, a little soft lighting and even a mirror or two. But custom had crystallized into orthodoxy, and he was sure that Veronica would see any suggestion of a change in procedure as an implied criticism of her or even an indication that he had discovered something new from a different partner.

Still, he was learning much from his first genuine relationship with a woman. Most of all he was learning how incredibly complicated the female body was. Veronica always suffered badly just before, during and after her period, getting cramps, headaches and being generally irritable. At these times Carpenter would be afraid to touch her for fear of upsetting the intricate balance of her system, and when she complained that men had it easy in all aspects of their sexuality, he had to agree. Apart from its complexity, female sexuality seemed altogether more noble than its male equivalent since it tended to be more intimately connected with non-sexual emotions. There were times when just the sight of a passing woman would be enough to send him off into a lurid sexual fantasy. And while these bouts of mental infidelity did not affect his basic commitment to Veronica, they seemed somehow demeaning to her.

That summer Veronica went home to her parents in Hampshire while Carpenter returned to Manchester to work in the Co-op biscuit factory. When he arrived back in Cardiff in October he found that Veronica had stopped taking the pill. She was worried about the side-effects, she told him, and had opted for the coil instead. But the coil proved unsatisfactory, giving her discomfort, as did the cap she tried next. She complained that it was always left to the woman to arrange contraception, so he started using condoms. The problem now became one of sensitivity; for a while their lovemaking sessions grew to the marathon proportions of their earliest days not through a resurgence of excitement but because insufficient stimulus made ejaculation a considerable task. Frequently Carpenter would give up through sheer exhaustion.

Meanwhile outside the bedroom Veronica remained unrelenting in her efforts to make him a man of firm convictions. He would sit at meetings and listen to her present cogent arguments for her position on everything from the situation in Rhodesia to the seating arrangements in the Students' Union. Cardiff was hardly a hotbed of student activism even in those heady days, but Veronica was a woman for all causes. She even spoke in support of the Welsh nationalists who were spraying out English roadsigns in the region and replacing them with their Welsh equivalents: Language is an expression of cultural consciousness, she argued; it's the prime symbol of national identity and must be preserved at all costs. In this last respect she showed a true radical's disinterested support for the worthy cause since she did not speak Welsh and had once confessed to him in an unguarded moment that as a language she thought it sounded unpleasant.

Despite Veronica's efforts, Carpenter remained obdurate in his uncertainty. For one thing he could never quite be convinced either that he was being presented with all the facts or that the facts themselves weren't incorrect or biased or both. His experiences with religion and science had taught him that the more facts you amassed, the less certain you became about anything, and he could only suppose that people with strong opinions – and especially *young* people with strong opinions – were either inadequately informed or wilfully blinding themselves to those facts which might conflict with their convictions. And why did there have to be only one correct viewpoint on a given issue? Wasn't it possible that a variety of viewpoints could be tolerated and perhaps even reconciled to produce a more comprehensive picture?

On hearing this sort of argument Veronica would stare at him with patent impatience before talking of appeasement and what that had led to in Europe in the 1930s. He was simply suffering from moral paralysis and was trying to rationalize his inability to commit himself. Radical problems demanded radical solutions, and there was no place for fence-sitters in today's world. His was a bland liberalism which was always trying to see both sides of the question. If only it were that simple, Carpenter would think; my trouble is that I tend to see six or seven or eight sides of the question.

Continually pressed by Veronica for some positive statement of his beliefs, he finally gave way and presented her with a framework which he felt embraced them. If he was disillusioned with the actual subject matter of his degree course, his knowledge of modern physics nevertheless provided him with basis for formulating what he came to think of as Carpenter's Theory of Relativity. Einstein had shown that all motion was relative, and Carpenter had come to the conclusion that this was also true for truth. Just as it was impossible to determine absolute motion because its measurement was dependent on the motion of the observer, so there was no absolute truth about any given subject; the various opinions on it derived from the persons' philosophical and ideological prejudices, which were in turn products of their particular upbringings over which they had little influence.

Einstein's theory had led to the concept of a four-dimensional space-time continuum, and in a similar manner Carpenter's theory led to a multidimensional opinion continuum in which all beliefs were valid. This was not to say that some weren't more defensible or desirable than others, only that Carpenter was quite capable of accepting the existence of even the more perverse or objectionable beliefs: they were perverse and objectionable to him, he supposed, because they arose out of formative experiences which were quite alien to his own.

Carpenter was pleased with his theory, even though it appeared to have no practical use whatsoever; if it did not clear away his confusion, at least it enabled him not to get too upset or perplexed when faced with people who were espousing views which he personally found disagreeable or just plain stupid. The multiplicity of world-views which existed merely reflected the diversity of the human species. Everyone needed to put his faith in something, and faith was essentially a religious impulse. All philosophies and political dogmas could therefore be viewed as secular offshoots of religion which attracted adherents through some intricate process of psychological osmosis rather than through any intrinsic truths which they might contain. You chose your ideological uniform to match your mental complexion.

That's all very well, said Veronica, but it's neither very new nor very useful. They were lying in bed at her place after an evening at the Union; Carpenter was a little drunk, otherwise he would not have explained himself at such length. Veronica told him that most of his ideas had been prefigured by the Sceptic school of philosophers in Ancient Greece. She herself rejected relativism utterly because it encouraged intellectual and moral cowardice.

There's nothing new under the sun, Carpenter thought, but his chief feeling was a sense that he had betrayed himself by giving Veronica such a coherent statement of his attitudes. He had made a tactical blunder, for Veronica was never happier than when she was arguing on points of principle. She finally had his number.

He and Veronica had been together for two years, but the following evening, which he spent alone in his bedsitter, he came to the realization that he no longer wanted to continue with their relationship. The truth was that he had never actually experienced a completely unselfish longing for her, and he saw that she had always been less important to him as a person in her own right than as someone who provided him with sexual fulfilment and female companionship. But sex was no longer much fun, and he was not sure that he had ever really found her physically desirable in herself.

Life with Veronica had never been less than stimulating, and it had certainly taught him a lot. Most of all it had taught him how easy it was to settle into a relationship and ignore its nagging dissatisfactions for the sake of cosiness. But if they were to continue together in the long term there had to be some kind of reconciliation in beliefs and interests. It was on this rock that he saw himself foundering. He could never be the person Veronica wanted him to be – and it was he who would have to do the changing if the tensions between them weren't to become unbearable. It was time to end their affair.

Carpenter had no idea how he would go about detaching himself from her, but events conspired in his favour as it turned out. He had previously agreed to accompany her to London that coming Saturday for the demonstration outside the US Embassy against the Nixon administration's policy in South-East Asia. But as everyone was assembling outside the embassy, he slipped away. And while Veronica stood in the drizzle chanting anti-American slogans, he was at White Hart Lane watching United play Spurs. He had crossed the Rubicon in the only way he knew how.

*

'Oooh-aah-gaa-doo-goo,' said Riley after breakfast.

Carpenter looked up from his newspaper. Riley repeated the sound and then passed him a magazine entitled *Quizzwhiz*, pointing to the relevant entry in the answers section. It read, *Ouagadougou*.

'It's the capital of the Upper Volta,' Riley informed him. 'An interesting word.' He paused. 'I didn't even know there was an Upper Volta. It sounds like an Olympics event.'

'It's a country in West Africa,' Wright informed him over the top of *The Times*, which he had taken to reading in recent days. 'It has one of the lowest per capita incomes in the world.'

'Is that a fact?' said Riley. 'Are they poor as well?'

Wright glared at him.

'They speak Swahili in Africa,' Riley told Sinnott.

'The official language is French,' said Wright. 'It was once the centre of the Mossi empire which resisted Arab invasions of the area. We're always too ready to assume that Africa was just a place of jungles and mud huts, but it had its own advanced cultures while much of Europe was still little more than barbaric.'

Wright's smile was faintly patronizing, and he was clearly warming up for a lecture on African political history. He had been in a more convivial mood since the commencement of the escape tunnel in the toilet. It made him equally unbearable in a different sort of way.

Riley was peering into Wright's face.

'Is something wrong?' Wright asked.

'Have you noticed,' said Riley, 'how the fronts of people's heads are much more interesting than the backs?'

A blank silence greeted this observation.

'It's true,' Riley insisted. 'All the useful bits are at the front.'

'What about the ears?' said Treadwell. 'They're on the side of the head.'

'But they point forwards. And besides, they're for balance. If you chopped someone's ears off, he'd keep falling over all the time.'

'Balderdash,' said Wright. 'The organs of balance are located in the *inner* ear. Chopping off one's ears would have no effect whatsoever on balance.'

'How do you know?'

'The outer ear is merely a fleshy receptacle for gathering sound. Many people have lost their ears and it in no way affects their stability.'

'Both ears? Do you know anyone who's lost both ears?'

'I don't see what that has to do with it.'

'How do you know that losing both ears doesn't affect your balance?'

For a moment Wright looked as if he was mustering a sophisticated line of argument which would demolish Riley's reasoning. Then he seemed to think better of it and simply said, 'You don't believe that yourself. You're simply trying to be provocative in your bumbling, idiotic way.'

A silence descended. Riley stared at his toes and sucked on his teeth.

'Balderdash,' he said presently to Sinnott, 'is a Swahili word.'

'No it isn't,' Wright said instantly.

'You're thinking of "bungalow",' Treadwell told him.

'No he's not,' Wright snapped. 'Bungalow is a Hindi word.'

'Indian? What sort of Indian?'

'Hindi!'

'Then what's balderdash?' Treadwell wanted to know.

'It means nonsense, piffle – the kind of thing you two have just been talking.'

'When I was a boy I always wanted to visit Swahililand,' said Riley.

Wright restrained himself from making any comment on this. A further silence ensued. Carpenter waited.

'"Piffle",' said Riley at length. 'Another interesting word.'

*

'If I could have anything I wanted,' Treadwell said to Carpenter, 'I'd have a tiger.'

They were playing darts in the games room, and Carpenter was winning.

'A tiger? Why?'

'I just think they're beautiful animals.'

This seemed as good a reason as any to Carpenter, though he wondered about the practical details.

'Where would you keep it?'

'I'd have a big garden with a high wall around it so that the tiger could roam around as it wanted. And I'd feed it hunks of meat from a helicopter.'

Treadwell had obviously done some detailed thinking on the subject, and Carpenter could only admire its fanciful nature.

'Tigers might soon be extinct,' Treadwell told him.

'Your throw,' Carpenter said, not wanting to dwell on this. What sort of world would it be without tigers? Much the same, and that was the trouble.

Treadwell threw, scoring thirty-six. Carpenter was ahead by over a hundred and practically in sight of a double. At least the desire to own a tiger proved that Treadwell had an imagination. It was possible that he secretly had a vivid and quixotic inner life; you never knew with people.

Carpenter scored eighty with his first two darts, leaving him on thirty-nine. He aimed and scored a seven with his final throw. Double sixteen was all he needed.

'I used to have this pet mouse when I was a boy,' he told Treadwell. 'I wasn't allowed to have a dog or anything like that because it would be too much trouble around the house. So I had this mouse. It was white with red eyes. A horrible thing, really, but I liked it.'

'What was it called?'

'It didn't have a name. It was just a mouse.'

'Did you bury it in the bottom of the garden when it died?'

This seemed rather a morbid question.

'It escaped from its box and got eaten by next door's cat. At least I think the cat ate it. Short of cutting it open I could never be sure.'

Life was like that: you could never be sure about most things. At the time he had wanted to strangle the cat, a scruffy tabby called, if memory served him correctly, Tiger. Life was also full of little coincidences.

Treadwell threw again, and this time he scored a hundred and thirty-eight. Suddenly he was close to double figures.

Carpenter took his turn. He missed the double with his first two darts, then scored a single sixteen.

'I wish you'd help with the you-know-what,' said Treadwell.

'What?'

Treadwell mouthed the word: 'Tunnel.'

'Wright getting on your nerves?'

'It isn't that. It would just help.'

He fired off three darts in rapid succession. The final dart left him needing double twenty.

'Good darts,' said Carpenter, hating him.

He handed Carpenter the darts. 'That sounded like *Goo dar*.'

'Eh?'

'I've been getting this ringing in my ears.'

'Since when?'

'Since the football match. I banged my head on the floor when Wright tackled me. It comes and goes. Sometimes it sounds like electricity and sometimes the sea. If it happens when someone's talking to me, their words go all funny.'

Carpenter studied him. 'It's probably nothing to worry about.'

'Probably not.'

Carpenter concentrated on the next throw, trying not to imagine what sorts of horrendous ailments he would suspect if it was happening to him. Come on, he told himself as he prepared to throw; this is your last chance.

He threw. A single eight. He threw again, and knew that the dart was hopelessly misaimed the instant it left his hand. It stuck sideways in the three, dangling down. Carpenter willed it to fall out, but it did not. He was left on five. He aimed again and threw his final dart. It hit the double rather than single one, leaving him on three. He wanted to scream.

'Maybe you just need to have your ears syringed,' he said to Treadwell, hoping it would distract him. But Treadwell obviously scented victory.

Carpenter watched him throw, knowing he had lost. A single twenty. No score. A six. He needed double seven, and Carpenter had another chance.

He quickly took the darts and threw each one with a minimum of fuss. A single one. No score. Double one. He was already plucking out the darts before it dawned on him that he had won.

Treadwell was regarding him with a faint smile which seemed devoid of resentment. Why was it that victory was always less thrilling than its anticipation? And why had he allowed himself to become so worked up about a trivial game of darts? He felt like suggesting that Treadwell be awarded the game by moral default and better sportsmanship. But instead he concentrated on feeling magnanimous in victory. But not magnanimous enough to advise that Treadwell visit Dr Dempster about the ringing in his ears. He had been resisting the suggestion since he had thought of it, and he realized that he was jealous of his monopoly of her time.

Snider materialized in the doorway at this point.

'You're wanted, Carpenter.'

Carpenter accompanied him to Naughton's office. Naughton raised himself from his chair, putting his fists down on the desk top. Today his tie was a mottled affair in lemon, lime and black which clashed wonderfully with the oxblood pinstripe suit he was wearing. The suit was double-breasted with baggy trousers, and several sizes too big. It made him look like a pubescent gangster.

'Dr Dempster informs me that you're unhappy with the behaviour of the staff here.'

Carpenter decided that this must refer to his request for Sinnott to be shown more leniency. He explained this to Naughton.

'Do you wish to make a formal complaint?'

Naughton sounded annoyed but also a little concerned, as if he was hoping he would not. On the desk in front of him was a large writing pad and a ballpoint pen, presumably for putting his complaint in writing.

'Who would I complain to?'

'Myself.'

'And what would happen then?'

'If I considered it serious enough I would be obliged to refer it to a higher authority.'

'What higher authority?'

'That needn't concern you.'

'I'm not concerned. I'm just interested. I'd like to know.'

'I'm not prepared to discuss the details of our administrative structure with you. Are you going to make a formal, written complaint?'

'What would this higher authority do if you passed it on?'

'They would give it due consideration.'

'And then?'

'And then they would come to a decision on what action should be taken.'

'And what sort of action would they be likely to advise?'

'It is not within my jurisdiction to stipulate that.'

Naughton sounded as if he was reading from a manual, and Carpenter felt like strangling him. There was a movement under his desk, and Carpenter saw Mordred there. The cat was gnawing intently on its lead.

'And if you didn't consider it serious enough to pass on?' Carpenter asked.

'I would deal with it myself.'

He saw that he was stymied. Naughton already knew what he was complaining about, and he knew that he would do nothing.

'Just keep Harris on a tight rein,' he said. 'Any more funny business from him and you might have a riot on your hands.'

'Are you threatening me?'

'It's a warning,' Carpenter said, and then he walked out without waiting to be dismissed.

*

Hemmings was on the prowl again. Carpenter wanted to be left in peace, so he grabbed a magazine from the lounge and fled to the bathroom, locking himself in the left-hand toilet.

'Who's that?' came a whispered voice from next door. It was Treadwell.

Carpenter said nothing. Treadwell frantically began clearing up. Finally the toilet flushed and the door opened.

'It's all right,' he heard Wright say tartly. 'I told you I'd keep watch for the guards.'

A brief recapitulation of logistics ensued, with Wright telling Treadwell that he had to trust him if they were to make efficient progress with their tunnel.

'Carpenter?' said Treadwell. 'Is that you in there?'

Still Carpenter remained silent.

'Of course it's him,' said Wright. 'I saw him come in here. He's just being bloody-minded as usual.'

Carpenter heard the cubicle door opening again, and then Wright was complaining to Treadwell that he hadn't cleared up the powdered plaster properly.

'I was in a hurry,' Treadwell told him. 'I thought it might be Snider.'

'If it was Snider I would have warned you. Use your head, for God's sake. We've got to be careful not to leave any tell-tale signs of our work. The important thing is not to panic.'

'Having a little chat, are we?' said the voice of Hemmings.

'It's none of your business,' said Wright, panicking. The cubicle door banged shut. 'Can't we have any privacy around here?'

Carpenter heard him stalk out.

'What's up with him?' Hemmings asked. He was chewing something and making loud slurping sounds.

'I think he was looking for Carpenter,' Treadwell said wanly.

'Where is he?'

'He's – I haven't seen him.'

'Who's in there?'

'I don't know.'

'Carpenter? Is that you?'

Carpenter continued to remain silent.

'Carpenter? Are you all right?' Hemmings tapped on the door.

There was a pause. The slurping sounds grew more rapid.

'Perhaps he's had a heart attack in there,' said Hemmings.

Carpenter was, in fact, staring at the magazine which lay open on his knees to an advertisement which showed a naked woman lying beneath a sun lamp. It was a small black-and-white photograph of no great eroticism, but it had already provided him with his first erection since he'd been in Limbo. He began to wish that Treadwell and Hemmings would leave him alone so that he could at least indulge himself in a few private minutes of physical gratification. Then Hemmings began to pound on the door.

★

'Where's the coffee?' Riley asked Peacock when he made a belated appearance in the lounge. They hadn't seen a guard since Snider and Hemmings had gone off duty at least an hour ago.

'There isn't any,' said Peacock.

'Why not?'

'Because I say so,' said Harris, coming in behind him.

'On whose authority?' Wright wanted to know.

'On *my* authority,' he replied.

Carpenter wondered if it was just his imagination that Harris seemed to be talking primarily for his benefit. Had Naughton told him about the complaint he'd made? And were they now being baited so that Harris could demonstrate just how futile such complaints were? By trying to help Sinnott, had he only made things worse for all of them?

Without pausing to deliberate further, Carpenter left the room and strode down the corridor to Naughton's office. He twisted the door handle while maintaining his forward momentum, intending to burst in on Naughton and hurl denunciations at him. But the door was locked and his face rebounded off it, his nose taking the brunt of the impact. He reeled back in pain, his right hand coming up to cover his face. His nostrils had only just stopped feeling sensitive after the football game, and now the pain was worse than ever.

'You should have tried knocking first,' said a voice behind him.

Harris had followed him and was standing close by, hands on hips. He was grinning.

Carpenter was almost overwhelmed with the urge to kick him in the crotch. Then he felt the palm of his hand growing warm and saw blood trickling out from between his fingers.

★

'Cabbage,' said Sinnott, giving it the same connotation as 'poison'. He pushed his plate away from him.

It did indeed look distinctly unappetizing, being mashed to such a pulp that it resembled a pale green frogspawn. It was accompanied by greyish potatoes and a strip of beef cut so thin that it fell apart as soon as you put a fork into it. The gravy was the colour of mahogany and the consistency of water.

'This is disgraceful,' Wright said, also pushing his plate aside. He looked across at Peacock, who was standing beside the door. 'We can't eat this. It's not fit to be served to animals.'

Peacock merely shrugged, as if to say that he was only responsible for serving it.

'Look at it,' said Wright. 'Would you put that on your own dinner table?'

Reluctantly Peacock approached the table, but he did not even glance at the food.

'Do you want me to take it away?'

'Take it,' said Wright. 'How many times has it been reheated? It's probably crawling with salmonella.'

'Anyone else?' asked Peacock.

Sinnott also surrendered his plate. But Riley had already cleared most of his, and Treadwell continued to eat in his usual fastidious manner. Carpenter decided to stick with his, too, though he could have done without the reference to salmonella. Eating was a rather uncomfortable process for him at the moment because he had to breathe through his nose and his nostrils felt like scorched tubes. The bleeding had been stanched with more wads of cotton wool which he had only recently removed and flushed down the toilet. It occurred to him that he might get out of Limbo by faking an appendicitis attack or something similar. But he immediately rejected the idea; he didn't want to tempt fate.

Peacock departed with the discarded plates.

'You're setting a dangerous precedent, don't you see?' said Wright. 'If we accept substandard food once, that gives them the excuse to continue serving pap to us.'

Peacock returned and doled out the baked apple desserts.

'I'm not eating that,' said Wright.

'I'll take it,' said Riley.

'Do you want mine?' Sinnott asked Treadwell.

It's like a children's birthday party, thought Carpenter.

*

'How is your nose?' Treadwell asked Carpenter after dinner.

'Delicate,' Carpenter told him. 'How are your ears?'

'They're not too bad. But I'm feeling a bit bilious.'

Treadwell had already visited the bathroom twice since dinner, but Carpenter had assumed that he was merely being diligent in getting on with the escape tunnel. Then he started getting ominous pains in his own stomach.

They were all sitting in the lounge watching television. Peacock had taken up his usual position at the back of the room, but no one was paying him any attention. Riley had just emitted a fart so rank it was clear evidence of digestive disorder, and no one was now sitting within a yard of him.

Carpenter said nothing about his own discomfort, for he knew that Wright would only gloat and remind him that he had advised against eating dinner. But Carpenter was convinced the food had been deliberately adulterated. His baked apple had had a slightly bitter taste which he had ignored at the time; now he felt sure that Harris had doctored it with laxative as another of his little 'jokes'. Something would have to be done about Harris.

His stomach lurched at that moment, and he thought his time had come. But the spasms ebbed away to leave an uneasy digestive calm. Treadwell departed to the bathroom once more. Both he and Riley had eaten two desserts each. Riley had not moved from his armchair since dinner, but he seemed capable of digesting anything short of nitroglycerine without discomfort.

Carpenter tried to concentrate on the television programme. A young woman was standing at a window, gazing out at a dismal back yard hemmed in by brick walls. She had been contemplating suicide for the last ten minutes, and Carpenter wondered why she didn't just get on with it. She lived in a dreary flat and had no money or friends; her parents were dead, she had been fired from her job, she was pregnant by the boyfriend who had deserted her on hearing the news, and to cap it all she had just discovered that he was suffering from VD.

If she puts on a Leonard Cohen record I'll scream, thought Carpenter. He felt sympathetic to her plight only insofar as she was a victim of dramatic overkill. Why didn't someone switch channels and find a cheerful documentary about battery farming or open-heart surgery?

Treadwell returned and sat down with some delicacy. Presently Riley let out an enormous burp which confirmed Carpenter's diagnosis of abnormal flatulence. The fact that Wright and Sinnott seemed unaffected was proof that something in the dinner was causing the trouble.

The girl finally climbed into a warm bath and was holding a razor blade to one of her wrists. To divert himself Carpenter tried to imagine her ten years younger, in pigtails and a summer frock, on a picnic with her parents and without a care in the world. The really messy things didn't usually start affecting most people until they reached adolescence – or at least they only started becoming aware of their misery then. Carpenter's ideal Utopia was a place run by benevolent machines which dispensed all the necessities of life including drugs which never allowed a person's physical and mental development to progress beyond the age of ten.

Before the girl could slash her wrists, a burglar broke into the flat. On hearing the sound of breaking glass, she wrapped a towel around herself and went to investigate. The burglar, caught in the act, grabbed her and slammed her head against the mantelpiece. She slumped to the floor. The burglar stood over her, panic slowly ebbing from his unwholesome features to be replaced by unmistakable lust. Slowly the camera began to track back to the accompaniment of a heartbeat which abruptly stopped as the scene froze with the burglar crouched over her, leaving the audience in no doubt of what was going to happen next.

'Melodrama at its crassest and most offensive,' said Wright.

For once Carpenter was in complete accord with him; the salted peanut commercial which followed seemed the epitome of good taste in comparison.

Carpenter wondered about his Utopia. Wouldn't it be better if instead of making its inhabitants permanent children he made them permanent adults who never had to suffer the mind-deforming experiences of childhood? Yes, this was a much better idea, for it meant that they would be able to enjoy the pleasures of sex, and guilt-free sex at that.

Did this change of emphasis mark a new maturity in his own mental development? Had he finally reached psychological puberty?

*

'That lighter could be useful to us,' said Wright.

It was late evening, and Carpenter's stomach finally felt sufficiently settled for him to risk smoking a cigarette. But he was having difficulty in getting the flame to catch.

'How?' he asked Wright.

'Surely you don't need me to tell you that.'

'He wants to set fire to the place as a diversion,' said Riley.

Wright ignored him. 'A lighter is a potential weapon. I'm surprised they let you have it.'

'A packet of cigarettes would be pretty useless without it.'

'Nevertheless, they're taking a risk.'

'Maybe they trust me.'

'Maybe he's a spy,' said Riley. 'Maybe we're all spies, watching *you*.'

Wright glanced at him in such a way as to suggest that he did not consider this idea beyond the bounds of possibility.

'It could be more constructively employed than in ruining your health by smoking.'

Carpenter flicked the lighter a few more times, still without getting a flame.

'Every cigarette you smoke shortens your life by five minutes,' said Treadwell.

'Don't you start!'

'It's quite telling that you've never thought of using it as an offensive weapon,' said Wright.

'What do you want me to do? Set fire to my mattress?'

'I think we could be more subtle than that.'

'How?'

'The lighter contains butane gas.'

'And?'

Wright sighed, as if he was loath to explain the obvious. Carpenter was by now convinced that he had no specific idea what to do with it.

'I know,' said Riley, 'we fill a paper bag with the gas, stick it over Harris's head, then run for it.'

'If you can't say anything constructive,' said Wright, 'then I wish you'd shut up.' He turned again to Carpenter. 'Butane is inflammable.'

Carpenter waited, resisting the urge to bellow that inflammability tended to be an important property of lighter fuels.

Sinnott said, 'Inflammable means it catches fire, doesn't it?'

'Yes,' said Wright impatiently.

'So what does flammable mean?'

'The same.'

'Then what's the difference?'

Carpenter saw his opportunity. He slid off the chair and headed for the bathroom, leaving the lighter on the coffee table. It was empty.

*

Carpenter woke in the middle of the night to the sound of footsteps in the corridor outside his cell: a slow, leisurely tread. He waited, wondering if one of the night-shift guards was about to look in on him. But the footsteps went past his door and a silence descended once more.

He began thinking about the girl in the television play: she had reminded him of Karen, with whom he had become involved after he had finally left Cardiff and gone to work for his uncle in Bristol. Karen was quite a different type from Veronica, and she had created a whole host of different problems for him. It was odd to recall that Veronica had been indirectly responsible for him meeting her, even though they had never met. Veronica had continued to exert her influence over his life long after their university days together.

It had taken him a while to leave Cardiff. He had graduated with a third class honours degree which he had always suspected had been awarded more for good attendance than academic performance. Afterwards he had decided to stay on at his bedsitter and had spent a further fourteen months in the city, supporting himself by working as a bus conductor for Cardiff Corporation. In the evenings he would visit the Union bar to drink with student friends of his who remained. It was an arrangement which had all the advantages and none of the disadvantages of actually being a student, chiefly in that he had much more money and did not have to worry about exams.

Veronica had obtained an upper second honours degree, and she departed to Glasgow, where she took a job at a hostel for alcoholics and down-and-outs. They had not split up immediately on their return from London after his defection from the demonstration, but their relationship was effectively over from that point. With their finals looming they saw one another only briefly in the evenings, and Carpenter was never again invited to stay the night. Their relationship remained amicable and conversational, but what little passion there had been was now entirely spent. Finally it became clear to everyone around them that they had become ex-lovers. At this point Carpenter felt relieved, for he had imagined that the end of their affair would be marked by a blazing argument and a tirade of character assassination from Veronica. In fact she seemed as reluctant as he did to go through the verbal motions of breaking up; the drift occurred naturally and without a postmortem.

It proved, however, only a temporary reticence on her part. When she left Cardiff she told him that she wanted to keep in touch with him and would write. He dutifully promised to write back, never imagining that anything would come of it. But Veronica, always true to her word, began to send him long letters every few months in which she gave him detailed accounts of her work and life coupled with retrospective appraisals of their time together. The latter chiefly involved an analysis of the flaws in his character, and while the details sometimes varied, the thrust of her criticism was that he was still immature and afraid to accept any sort of responsibility, as evidenced by his inability to leave Cardiff and take on a job which really taxed him. Carpenter always wrote a polite note in reply, thanking her for her comments and saying that he hoped she was well.

When he went home that Christmas he sensed that his parents

were a little worried that he was drifting along, though they said nothing directly. Carpenter had no great desire to take a job which utilized his scientific training, and there was nothing else that immediately appealed to him. He knew only that he wanted to live a little before he committed himself to the demands of a career and the ties of respectability.

Graham, meanwhile, had formed a new group with a name inspired by Carpenter's physics studies: Quantum Mechanics. Carpenter privately thought that this was even worse than Gray Stone and the Rockrollers, but he said nothing. Graham now had a reputation as one of the best young guitarists in Manchester, and he was undisputed leader of the five-piece group of experienced musicians who played sophisticated rock after the fashion of Yes and Roxy Music. They were attracting considerable interest and had played at several major London venues in recent months; rumours of a recording contract were afoot. Graham had grown a scraggly goatee which Carpenter noted with pride did not compare with the full facial growth which he had cultivated in the past year. But otherwise he felt pale in comparison with him; Graham was full of grandiose plans to do a concept album and tour America, and Carpenter saw his own years in university as little more than an extension of school when measured against the romance and excitement of Graham's life. Meanwhile Gail was as desirable and as unattainable as ever. She had obtained a teaching post at an infants' school in Salford and seemed to have accommodated herself to Graham's itinerant life; when they were together they were inseparable.

Most of Carpenter's remaining friends in Cardiff left the following summer, and he felt abruptly abandoned. As autumn gathered his mother wrote to him that his uncle, who ran a small engineering company in Bristol, was looking for a junior manager to help with the administrative side of the business at a reasonable salary. The job was his for the asking.

His uncle was a large and hearty man whose back-slapping manner did not disguise his basic lack of interest in anyone but himself. His business was in the drab and run-down St Philip's area of Bristol, close to Temple Meads station, and the 'offices' proved to be a converted storeroom above the engineering shop. Carpenter was consigned to an enclosure little bigger than a privy, with an ancient wooden desk crammed up against a grime-crusted window and an even more ancient typewriter planted at its centre. It was a large, black machine which looked as if it might have antique value. One of Carpenter's first tasks was to teach himself to type.

The company manufactured a particular kind of valve used in sewage treatment systems; his uncle told him proudly that they were the only suppliers in the country. Despite this, he and his uncle constituted the entire management, with six men being employed in the workshop below. The junior manager's title sounded reasonably impressive, but in practice it entailed taking incoming calls, dealing with routine correspondence, and trying to bring some order to the filing system, which consisted of a four-foot pile of cardboard document wallets which his uncle had deposited in the only free corner of his office on the morning he started work. About once a fortnight he would be required to write a memo on behalf of his uncle, telling the men in the workshop to refrain from playing their radios above a reasonable volume, to use the ashtrays provided and not drop their cigarette butts on the floor, to desist from putting obscene pin-ups on the back of the lavatory door, and other such matters of vital concern to the future of the business.

His uncle had very little contact with the workforce, and Carpenter supposed that his memos were a way of reminding them that he existed. The men themselves were clannish and taciturn; they never gave him any indication of what they thought of his uncle, though he suspected the word 'Prick' would have been an adequate summary of their feelings. Most mornings his uncle would be absent on mysterious errands with the generic title of 'meeting clients'; he would often return late in the afternoon, smelling of liquor and unbearably garrulous. When he was in attendance he divided his time between long visits to the toilet and even longer telephone calls to arrange dinner dates with various women; he was a widower and evidently something of a ladies' man. Carpenter was never invited to his home, and their relationship was always to remain strictly formal and confined to business hours.

It soon dawned on him that he was little more than a glorified clerk. He had a lot of free time on his hands, and since he was under orders to keep the office manned from nine o'clock till five-thirty, he spent it reading newspapers and magazines from end to end. With some difficulty he managed to clear the grime from the outside of the window, but the view now afforded him was a dismal prospect of sheds and loading yards facing the stagnant waters of the Floating Harbour. On rainy days when the landscape was deserted it gave him the feeling that he was the only person left alive on Earth.

Gradually, though, he grew to like being left alone. He started buying second-hand paperbacks from a bookshop nearby, and soon found that on a typical day he could complete a 200 page book before it was time to go home. With the exception of several evenings spent in joyless contemplation of texts by Marx and Sartre at Veronica's urging, he had done no serious reading apart from course texts in his life. Now his instincts led him to select books completely by whim, and before long he was reading everything from history books to detective novels. This activity gradually extended into his evenings. His uncle had found him a two-roomed flat in Ashley Down, not far from the cricket ground; he sent monthly rent-cheques to the landlady, who lived in Clifton, and she never bothered him. The flat was luxurious after four years in his attic bedsitter and he was content to spend most of his evenings at home, not finding the average Bristolian particularly welcoming towards strangers. Occasionally he would visit Ashton Gate or Eastville on a Saturday afternoon, but football matches did not have the same lure when United were not involved.

Every month or so he would make a pilgrimage across the Severn to Cardiff, where only three of his close friends remained. These were Ian Duffy, a fellow physics graduate who hailed from Liverpool and was now embarked on a PhD, Tim Bullivant, whose wealthy family were subsidizing his fifth year as an economics undergraduate, and Alison, who had missed her final year through illness while Carpenter had been working on the buses. Duffy was an earthy, pragmatic soul, while Bullivant was cheerful and irresponsible and claimed that his ambition was to remain an undergraduate for the rest of his life. They invariably got him drunk within hours of his arrival at the Union. Meanwhile Alison was going out with a huge South African called Naas Van Dyk who played rugby for UWIST and had hands which looked powerful enough to squeeze a human head to pulp. He was swarthy and stolid and Carpenter found him dull, though he took great care never to annoy him. Alison remained her cheerful, easy-going self, getting drunk with the rest of them while Van Dyk sipped a glass of Mackeson all evening and gazed at them with the impassive rectitude of a minister from the Dutch Reformed Church.

Carpenter enjoyed these hectic, alcoholic weekends, yet he always felt vaguely deflated when he returned to Bristol on Sunday; he knew that he was grimly hanging on to a world which was inexorably slipping away. He comforted himself with the fact that at least he was earning a regular and respectable wage which allowed him to continue adding to his record collection and to buy a new stereo. If people asked what he did, he would tell them that he was in 'purification systems', though with Duffy and Bullivant this became 'crap disposal'. In a dull sort of way he was content; the job offered no challenges but consequently few pressures.

Shortly before his departure to Manchester for Christmas he wrote to Veronica, describing his quiet, even studious existence. He assumed she would approve, but she wrote back by return of post to say he was simply creating a womb for himself. Over Christmas he had a frustrating encounter with a cousin of Gail's whom he fancied but who remained utterly immune to his blandishments. He returned to Bristol painfully aware that he was lacking female companionship in his life.

A few days later a letter arrived addressed to his predecessor, a young woman named Karen Newcombe. Carpenter had never met her, but from regular callers to the office he had gained the impression that she was an attractive and personable girl. Without saying anything to his uncle, he checked through his old desk diaries and eventually found her address. The letter looked personal, and he decided that he was going to deliver it by hand that evening.

It was a ten-minute walk from his workplace. The address proved to be a squat and dilapidated block of flats in crumbling red brick with rusting iron windows. The number he wanted was on the second floor. The bell didn't work, so he hammered on the knocker.

Presently the door was opened by a stocky, bearded young man dressed in a grimy T-shirt and bleached jeans. He had dark eyes and a glowering, impatient expression. The smell of stale cooking emanated from the flat, though the door was not opened more than a body's width.

Carpenter explained about the letter, saying that he had decided to deliver it personally because it looked important. It did not, in fact, look anything of the sort, and was quite possibly a belated Christmas card. The other man regarded him with a bored fixity. Then he shrugged, told him that she didn't live there any longer, and made to close the door.

Carpenter trapped it with his foot. Did he happen to know where she might be living now? Gone home for all I know, was the reply. And did he happen to know where home was? Did he possibly have the address? The man gave a heavy, exasperated sigh and told him to wait.

Carpenter studied the stretch of wall that was available to his vision through the crack in the door. A large poster of a naked woman astride a chaise longue was taped to the striped wallpaper. Three darts were embedded in the woman's navel and a pink balloon was pinned above her head, the word THINKS written on it in black marker pen.

The man returned and recited the address. Carpenter hastily wrote it down on the back of a cigarette packet as the door was closed in his face. As he made to depart, vibrant rock music erupted from the flat. It was Led Zeppelin singing 'Communication Breakdown'.

The new address was in Redlands, closer to where he was living. He took a bus. It turned out to be an ordinary Victorian terraced house hidden behind an overgrown privet hedge. As he walked up the path, he could hear the theme music from *Coronation Street* issuing from the house.

He rang the doorbell several times while a deodorant advertisement blared out in all its glory. Finally the door opened to reveal a short, blonde girl in her late teens, dressed in a white shirt and black cords. She was pretty. Are you Karen Olive Newcombe? Carpenter asked her, giving the full name on the envelope and raising his voice above the sound of the television. She frowned, nodded, then gave a nervous smile as Carpenter handed her the letter and explained how he had come by it.

She tore the envelope open. It was, as he had anticipated, a belated Christmas card. It's from my mother, she told him. I hate the name Olive, but she always writes my full name. There was something winsomely vulnerable about her, her ready smile seeming designed to defuse hostility. Carpenter imagined himself hugging her, and the idea was very pleasant.

He quickly established that her father was dead and that her mother had remarried and was now living in St Ives; their only contact in the last few years had been an exchange of Christmas cards. They didn't get on well since she had remarried, Karen explained; this was her grandparents' house.

They must be suffering from advanced deafness, Carpenter thought, for it was not easy to converse above housewives waxing lyrical about soap powders or jingles for building societies. He explained about his earlier visit to the block of flats, and she informed him that the man he had met there was Derek, her ex-boyfriend, who had thrown her out of the flat they had shared about a month after she had lost her job at his uncle's firm.

You *lost* your job? said Carpenter. She nodded and said that his uncle had given her the sack after telling her that he was getting someone more qualified.

Carpenter was mortified. He was aware that his parents must have put pressure on his uncle to get him the job, but it had never occurred to him that someone else would have been fired to make way for him.

He told her this, but she assured him that it was all right, she had a new job now at the Wills factory and was better off than before, with more money and shorter hours. But Carpenter insisted that he was going to resign in protest at the way she had been treated.

She told him that there was no need, it really had been all for the best in the long run. She didn't mind that she and Derek had split up; he had a terrible temper and was always going out with his friends and getting drunk. Carpenter said that it was a point of principle: he had obtained the job under false pretences. She replied that it was too late to do anything about it now; giving up his job wouldn't help her get it back, even if she wanted it. Which she didn't.

She was smiling at him. He smiled back. She told him that it was very kind of him to have brought the letter and did he want to come in for a cup of tea? Carpenter told her that that would be very nice.

Inside it was a typical old people's house from its dark brown paintwork and anaglypta-covered walls to the oppressive, elderly smell which pervaded the hallway. Karen led him into the living room where her grandparents sat on a faded green sofa. Neither of them seemed to register his passage into the kitchen, being intent on a quiz show. They both looked remarkably similar, like wizened fraternal twins. The television stood scarcely a foot from their knees, and it would have been impossible to talk in the room above its volume. He saw no evidence of hearing-aids or even an ear trumpet. Karen closed the kitchen door behind them, which muffled the noise a little. Do they always have it on that loud? he asked, to which she nodded and shrugged and said that you got used to it.

He sat down at an oilcloth-topped table while she set about making tea. This took the form of putting four teabags into an aluminium teapot which she then topped up with cold water and put on a lighted gas ring.

To distract himself Carpenter asked her some questions about her grandparents' general state of health and what it was like living with them. He learned that they were quite healthy and mobile for their age, suffering only from advanced deafness and a reluctance to communicate with anyone else. They insisted on doing all their own washing and cooking, even though she had offered to help. They were very independent and didn't interfere with her much. She paid them £5 a week for her own room upstairs and the use of the kitchen. She spent most evenings listening to records. No, she didn't really have any close friends, having grown up in Weston-super-Mare. Her parents had only moved back to Bristol three years ago, and her father had died shortly afterwards. When her mother remarried a year later and moved to Cornwall, she had left school and gone to work for his uncle. But she had plenty of company at the factory now, and she liked to have time to herself in the evenings.

It sounded a dismal sort of existence, made more pathetic by her attempts to put a brave face on it. Carpenter studied her as she put two mugs and a bottle of milk down on the table. A warm, protective feeling welled up in him: she was young and pretty and deserved better than this. He recalled Veronica's last letter, in which she had argued that the kind of life he was now leading was designed to shield him from new experiences and demonstrated the fundamental caution which dominated his behaviour; he had always been afraid of taking risks and of grasping the nettle of life.

This criticism had stung, and now he saw the opportunity to prove that he was not always thus hidebound. Before he had time to dwell on his decision to be bold, he was telling Karen that there was a settee in the front room at his place and she was welcome to sleep there any time she wanted. He knew how it was to live with old people, they sometimes got you down, so if she found she needed to get away for just a night or even simply wanted someone to talk to for a few hours one evening, she could always come to him, as a friend, and he would always be prepared to put her up or take her out for a few drinks, with no strings attached.

All this was accompanied by a vision of himself and Karen grappling nude on the very settee he was offering her. Not that his offer wasn't genuine as it stood: only that he hoped it would quickly lead to greater and more passionate things. His own reference to old people had been in regard to his parents, and he felt ashamed of himself for the implicit suggestion that they resembled Karen's grandparents; considerations of honesty and nobility were never more lacking than when he was trying to ingratiate himself with a member of the opposite sex.

Karen was smiling at him in her hesitant fashion and saying that she didn't deserve his kindness. Her modesty only made her more appealing to him, and he found the idea of a romance between them coming easily to him and offering greater attractions than the intellectual rigours of life with Veronica. Meanwhile the teapot had begun to emit steam from its spout. Karen removed it from the gas ring and set it down on the table. The smell of melting oilcloth reached Carpenter's nostrils.

When he left about an hour later he had written down his address on one of his uncle's business cards and told her that his offer was still open if ever she cared to take him up on it. But she had not risen to the bait, or even to his suggestion that they go out for a drink together one evening. It was not that she wasn't interested in him, he felt, rather that she seemed to consider herself unworthy of his attentions. But she had been friendly enough, and he decided that he might call on her again in a few days' time and ask her out. He felt pretty sure he would enjoy her company as long as he didn't have to drink her tea again.

The next day was a Friday, and Carpenter departed to Cardiff for the weekend. It proved the usual mixture of camaraderie and drunkenness, highlighted by a party at Van Dyk's plush flat in Rhiwbina on the Saturday evening to celebrate Alison's birthday. Bullivant fell asleep in the bathroom, Duffy was copiously sick over the record player, while Alison became amorous in her drunkenness towards practically every male in sight, but in particular himself. At first Carpenter enjoyed her advances, but they were conducted under the increasingly baleful gaze of Van Dyk, and eventually Carpenter locked himself in the outside toilet for a spell lest the South African be provoked into wrenching his head from his shoulders and punting it through the window. The party went on well into the night, and he returned to Bristol the following evening feeling dissipated, forlorn and unbearably randy.

He was lying on the settee imagining that he was having exquisite sex with one of his fantasy females when the doorbell rang. He leapt guiltily to his feet and made himself respectable before going to the door.

It was Karen. She stood there in a blue duffle coat and jeans, holding a plastic carrier bag crammed with clothing. Did he mind if she came in? Did he mind if she spent the night there? She'd had a row with her grandparents and she just had to get away from them for a few hours.

Of course he didn't mind, not at all. His pent-up sexual lust made him want to throw her on the settee and ravish her there and then, but he did his best to appear calm and matter-of-fact. She put her carrier bag on a chair and told him what a nice place he had. I'm glad you like it, said Carpenter, wishing that he hadn't left his dirty underwear in front of the fire. She took off her coat and draped it over the carrier bag. She was wearing a check blouse in blue-and-white. It was a cold night outside, and she was bright-eyed and rosy-cheeked.

What did you have a row about? Carpenter asked her. She simply shrugged as if to say that it wasn't important or she didn't want to talk about it. She was standing close to him, and suddenly she came forward, put her arms around his neck and pressed a cheek against his chest. He could smell the medicated shampoo she had used on her hair.

Slowly he looped his arms around her waist. After a while she raised her head. Seizing the moment, Carpenter kissed her.

She immediately thrust her tongue into his mouth. Carpenter was taken by surprise. This can't be happening, he thought. But it was, and Karen's tongue was now writhing to great effect around his own. Her mouth tasted at once minty and medicinal, which immediately started him thinking that his own mouth must by contrast taste foul after all the smoking and drinking he had done the previous night. But Karen didn't seem to mind; her breath came hot and hard, her mouth was wet and warm, and Carpenter's loins were going into overdrive.

The settee stood about six feet away. After a respectable interval of tongue sucking Carpenter decided to edge them both towards it. This did not prove as easy as he had anticipated, even though Karen was neither large nor heavy; she had gone limp in his arms with the urgency of their kissing, so that it was like trying to drag a corpse across the room with infinite slowness. Carpenter felt that it was vital he kept kissing her as he did so, and he discovered that the most effective means of locomotion was to rock back and forth several times before putting one foot forward; then he would drag his trailing foot up and allow a pause before repeating the procedure.

Ten minutes later they were at the foot of the settee. Now Carpenter had to get the two of them flat on it without breaking lip contact. For a while this problem seemed insuperable until he had the inspiration to tilt them both sideways so that they collapsed on to it. Contact was, in fact, broken momentarily, but he quickly repositioned his mouth on hers.

She responded again, bringing a knee up to nuzzle his groin. This further inflamed him, though he was aware that physically he had not yet risen to the occasion.

There followed a lengthy period of wriggling and writhing and fumbling with buttons and clasps and zips and elasticated bands.

At the end of it, Karen's knickers were still wrapped around her thighs and Carpenter felt exhausted. She had not exactly helped him to undress her, burying her head in his shoulder and clinging leech-like to him the moment he started to unbutton her blouse. Her body was more compact than Veronica's, with small breasts which he managed to fondle only briefly before she had crushed them against his chest.

Now he was left with just her knickers. Her thighs were pressed together, and it would be impossible to remove them unless he lifted her bodily from the settee. It occurred to him that he might ask her to open her legs, but somehow he could not bring himself to do this; neither of them had spoken for at least half an hour, and he did not want to risk breaking the spell. Besides, he was still only half-erect, despite being fully aroused in a glandular sense. He needed to relax for a few minutes, get his breath back.

Gently he began to stroke the trim lines of her body, thinking that this was good strategy in any case: a spell of passionate writhing followed by a tender period of caressing before he took the final plunge. Assuming that he was able to take it. He ran his hands along her back, willing himself to stiffen. But nothing was happening. Was he physically exhausted after the weekend? Or was it a recurrence of the problem he'd initially had with Veronica? Would he never be able to get it up the first time with any woman?

After several minutes of stroking Carpenter realized that Karen had gone completely inert in his arms. He studied her face and saw that her eyes were closed. Her breathing was shallow and regular, and it dawned on him that she had fallen asleep.

She did not stir when he rose, or even when he returned with some spare blankets from his bedroom which he draped over her. Carpenter did not linger; he went straight to bed.

Within minutes of getting into bed he was achingly erect and profoundly aware of Karen lying in the next room. He wanted to sneak back and make mad, passionate love to her, awake or not. But such impulsiveness was foreign to his nature.

He was woken early the following morning by the sound of his front door opening. He got out of bed, quickly donned his dressing gown and went out into the hallway. Karen was fully dressed and on the point of leaving with her carrier bag.

She gave him an apologetic smile and said she hadn't wanted to disturb him. It was kind of him to have let her stay the night and she didn't know how to thank him. Carpenter told her to think nothing of it, repeated that she was welcome to stay whenever she wished, and then said why didn't she come to dinner one evening. When would suit her? Tuesday? Wednesday? Thursday? Thursday would be nice, she said. What was the best time for her? Six-thirty? Seven? Could she make it seven-thirty? Seven-thirty was fine by him, so seven-thirty it was, on Thursday evening. She seemed eager to get away, as if she felt she had overstayed her welcome. He gave her a brief kiss on the cheek before she departed.

Carpenter spent the next four days dwelling on the prospect. He was not the world's greatest cook, but Veronica had taught him to concoct a vegetable risotto which he felt would pass muster. But the meal itself preoccupied him far less than what would follow it. Karen had permitted him considerable liberties with her body on their first evening together, and he saw no reason why he should not make further progress on Thursday. One evening he visited the men's toilet at a local garage and got a fresh packet of Durex from the slot machine, just in case.

He went home early from work on the appointed day and immediately set about preparing all the ingredients for the meal. When everything was ready he took a shower and cleaned his teeth before donning his favourite denim shirt and a freshly laundered pair of jeans. The risotto could be cooked in under half an hour, a task he would set about immediately after greeting Karen with a glass of red wine.

It was now seven o'clock. He opened the wine bottle and poured himself a glass before sitting down to await her arrival. He promised himself that he would drink no more than three glasses of wine that evening so that his virility would not be impaired in any way. He felt fit, alert and eager for Karen's company.

By the time the wine bottle was empty, Carpenter felt drunk, muddled and profoundly miserable. It was approaching nine-thirty, and there was no sign of her. He swallowed the last mouthful of wine and realized that he was extremely hungry. Hungry enough to eat a vegetable risotto for two. He rose and went into the kitchen. The wine seemed to have gone straight to his head, which made it even more imperative that he eat. He was just about to add the onions to the frying pan when the doorbell rang.

Carpenter was at the door in an instant. As soon as he opened it Karen flung her arms around his neck and told him she was sorry, she'd had another row with her grandparents and hadn't been able to get away until now. Carpenter could smell the minty tang of her breath against his cheek, and he knew that he could not pretend to be irritated or dismissive. Already she was offering her mouth to him, and he accepted it wholeheartedly.

They continued kissing until she broke free and said she could smell something funny. Carpenter remembered the frying pan. He dashed off to the kitchen, found it filled with acrid fumes, and heaved the window open before thrusting the frying pan under the cold water tap. Hot steam billowed into his face, and he slopped water down his shirt-front.

Karen was sitting on the corner of the settee when he returned. She had removed her duffle coat to reveal a brown fisherman's sweater worn under dungarees. Carpenter was somewhat daunted by the sight of the latter, but she was smiling at him cheerfully enough. Was she ready to eat? She gave an apologetic smile. She wasn't really hungry; did he mind if she didn't have anything? Carpenter assured her that it was no problem, he wasn't particularly hungry himself.

He returned to the kitchen and switched everything off before scanning his larder for something to eat. He was randy but also ravenous. He popped three pickled onions into his mouth, crunched them and swallowed them. Too late he realized what this would do to his breath. He hurried into the bathroom and plastered his toothbrush with Macleans.

He emerged to find that Karen had been riffling through his record collection and was putting on an LP. Suddenly the abrasive guitar riff of 'Little Wing' by Derek and the Dominos erupted from the speakers with remarkable loudness. When, after half a minute of this, Karen showed no sign of turning it down, Carpenter began to wonder if deafness or at least an addiction to extreme volume ran in the family.

He was standing beside the settee. Karen now came across to him and put her arms around him again. Spurred by the wine,

Carpenter immediately pulled her down on the settee and they went into a clinch remarkably similar to that of Sunday evening. Karen responded as eagerly as before; indeed, in some respects she was more urgent, clutching the back of his shirt and sucking at his lips as they writhed together on the settee while Derek and the Dominos completed 'Little Wing', continued with 'It's Too Late' and then launched into 'Layla'. Every so often Carpenter would be compelled to surface for air and let out a discreet belch which was a disgusting combination of red wine and pickled onions.

Derek and the Dominos were now singing about the thorn tree in the garden. It was the last track on that particular side of the record, and Carpenter was suddenly possessed by a sense of urgency. After considerable effort he had managed to unbuckle Karen's dungarees and pull them down to her thighs. But her knickers were proving as recalcitrant as on Sunday evening, and Carpenter couldn't bear it. Despite the wine he had drunk, he was both thoroughly randy and fully equipped to do what he had been unable to do on Sunday. Throwing caution to the wind, he grabbed her dungarees and knickers simultaneously and tugged them down to her ankles in one forceful movement.

Karen immediately responded by grabbing him, unzipping him and thrusting her hand inside his Y-fronts. She began to manipulate him with some dexterity, and he thought: This is it! He kissed her, fondled her bottom and tried to get his hand between her legs. But she was lying in a position which prevented this, and as he tried to prise her legs apart she redoubled her efforts at his crotch. Abruptly he felt the accumulated lust of five days about to burst forth. He made a strangled sound which was meant to indicate that he wanted her to pause, but she only increased his rhythm yet more. Instinctively he twisted away, and then he was spurting all over the settee.

Neither of them moved for several minutes after this. Carpenter felt embarrassed in a sense which he could not quite determine. He wondered what she was thinking, and it came to him that he had been ready, indeed avid, to spill himself inside her without thinking to establish whether she had taken precautions. Hadn't Veronica chastised him on that very point? And hadn't he bought himself a fresh packet of Durex for that very eventuality?

Finally he rolled over and peered at her. She was lying with her head on one arm, and her eyes were closed. She looked attractively winsome and waif-like. He kissed the tip of her nose, and her eyes opened. That was nice, he told her. She smiled and said did he mind if she had a cup of tea?

He heard her enter the bathroom while he was waiting for the kettle to boil. Immediately he grabbed a box of tissues from his bedroom and hurriedly swabbed the settee before she returned. He stuffed the crumpled tissues into his jeans pocket, put a cushion over the damp spot and went back to the kitchen. It was like covering up the evidence of a crime.

She had put on David Bowie's *Hunky Dory* when he emerged with the tea; her smile once again had an edge of nervousness to it. They sipped their tea while Bowie sang about Andy Warhol, Bob Dylan and the Queen Bitch. There seemed to be nothing to say, although there was no sense of strain. Talking would have been difficult in any case over the music. 'There's a taste in my mouth,' sang Bowie, 'and it's no taste at all.' Carpenter let out another acidic belch.

At length Karen began to yawn. Carpenter put his arms around her and said why didn't they go to bed? She shrugged, looked sheepish. It's a double, he explained, with plenty of room for two. She gave a wan smile. Did he mind if she slept on the settee? She was always restless in bed and he wouldn't like it if her elbows and knees were everywhere; it used to drive Derek mad. The settee was very comfortable, and she really did feel worn out.

Carpenter fetched her blankets and a spare pillow. She was asleep when he returned and she did not stir as he tucked her in. When he awoke the following morning she had already left.

He did not see her again for over a week. At first he made no attempt to contact her because he kept expecting her to turn up each evening; but as the days went by with no sign of her he decided that she would not be returning. He had probably scared her off by being too forward in suggesting that they sleep together. He did not know whether to telephone her at work or bow gracefully out of her life. After a week had passed he concluded that their brief flirtation had died a natural death.

The following Friday evening he was sitting in front of the

television in an old pullover and baggy jeans when the doorbell rang. He immediately knew that it was Karen and immediately wished that he was better dressed for the occasion and not redolent of the fish and chips which he had just finished eating from a bag. But Karen was quick to apologize for not having contacted him in the past week; her grandparents had been making things difficult for her again and she simply hadn't had a moment's peace.

Carpenter did not care whether or not this was true: he was pleased that she was back. Soon she was kissing him in her usual hectic fashion, and while this was nice, he did not immediately feel up to the rigmarole of the settee and suggested that they go out to the pub for a drink.

In the pub Carpenter drank pints of Courage Bitter to Karen's halves of lager and lime. There was not a great deal of conversation between them, but he was content with the feel of her thigh against his. He drank steadily, and by ten o'clock felt perfectly relaxed and mellow. At this point Karen offered to buy a round, her first of the evening.

When she returned she was also carrying four packets of crisps, or rather had stuffed them under her jumper because her hands were full with the drinks. Four seemed rather an excessive number to Carpenter, but as he tore open a packet Karen casually told him that a box had been within arm's reach over the counter and she had simply grabbed a handful while the barman's back was turned.

You mean you didn't pay for them? said Carpenter, swallowing rapidly and lowering the crisp packet below the level of the table-top. She smiled in reply. For the rest of the evening he huddled in the alcove where they were sitting, convinced that at any moment the barman's beefy hand would descend on his shoulder and he would be forced to account for the stolen packets.

Within ten minutes of returning to his place they were once again grappling on the settee. Again Carpenter laboriously undressed her, wondering why they didn't simply strip down to their essentials before leaping on to the settee and doing what came naturally – things had been simpler with Veronica in this respect at least. But something told him that Karen wouldn't have wanted it that way; something told him that she didn't want it at all. As before she did not actively resist the removal of her clothing, but there was a stiffness, a tenseness in her body that was not merely nervousness.

Having reached the knickers-only stage, Carpenter paused and asked her if she was on the pill. She shook her head like someone vehemently denying an accusation. It's all right, he told her, I'll see to it. But as he reached for his jeans (in which he had earlier placed a packet of Durex in a rare moment of foresight) she took his wrist and made him look at her. It wasn't that she didn't like him, she said, and didn't enjoy what they were doing, but she didn't want to go any further at the moment, she hoped he understood. The thing was, she had gone to bed with Derek and she felt that he had lost his respect for her afterwards. She didn't want to risk that happening again until they got to know one another a little better.

That's all right, Carpenter assured her, experiencing only a mild desire to start banging his head against the wall. In truth he had half expected it, though it was hard to square her excuse with her earlier claim that she and Derek had lived together for six months. Presumably they had been sleeping together during that time, and if Derek had lost his respect for her because she had made herself sexually available to him, he had taken a long time to act on it. Or was he merely showing his ignorance of Derek's character? Or indeed Karen's? That night he was rampant in bed, and he wondered why he always felt at a disadvantage in his relationships with women.

The following morning he was awoken by the strains of Fleetwood Mac's 'The Green Manalishi'. The track was one of his favourites, but it was not yet nine o'clock on a Saturday morning. So far none of his neighbours had started hammering on the walls, but it seemed only a matter of time.

After breakfast she accompanied him on his weekly shopping expedition. Carpenter was filling up his basket at the local supermarket when he saw her take a tin off the shelf and slip it into the pocket of her duffle coat. He immediately froze and made a minute inspection of the ranks of HP sauce bottles in front of him. Karen moved on, and presently she slipped another item into her pocket. Carpenter was aghast. He hung back, hoping to lose her amongst the throng of Saturday shoppers; but when he cautiously approached the check-out counter with his basket, she materialized at his side.

Her pockets were bulging with stolen goods, and Carpenter's heart was pounding as they passed through the check-out; it seemed impossible that they would escape without having to fight off a horde of store detectives.

As soon as they were a safe distance from the supermarket, Carpenter turned on her and asked her what she thought she was doing. Didn't she know that shoplifting was a criminal offence? She gave him one of her disarming smiles and said that she had simply been getting him a few extras for his larder. This made him feel churlish and ungrateful, so he put his arm around her, told her it was all right and asked to see what she had got for him. One by one the items emerged from her pockets: a tin of prunes and another of tapioca pudding, a bottle of pickled gherkins, a jar of horseradish sauce, a packet of frozen puff pastry, a sachet of custard, a small turnip and a tin of Kennomeat. Carpenter had no pets.

They had baked beans on toast for lunch. Then Karen announced that she had to be getting back, her grandparents would be expecting her and she had to help them with their shopping. Earlier Carpenter had bought a pound and a half of fillet steak for their dinner, assuming that she would be staying for the rest of the day in the absence of any indication to the contrary. He suppressed the urge to bellow with frustration and simply asked when he would see her again. She told him that she couldn't be sure, it depended on her grandparents, but she would ring him at work as soon as she could and thanks for a lovely weekend.

The pattern of their relationship had been established. At the time Carpenter sensed that he had started something which was already out of his control; he had the helpless feeling that Karen's appearances at his flat could neither be predicted nor dictated by him. And so it proved. From then on she turned up at his flat at least once a week, but he never knew when she was coming until she arrived. There invariably followed a bout of wrestling and undressing on the settee before Carpenter was ultimately frustrated by her continued refusal to permit him penetration. At times he wondered why he carried on, though he knew it was simply lust. Every time she allowed him to undress her, he would become convinced that this time she would finally let him go the whole hog while simultaneously knowing that he was deluding himself. The tantalizing prospect of sexual gratification was enough to make a nonsense of logic and ordinary good judgement.

Her erratic timetable was usually explained by difficulties with her grandparents. Carpenter seldom bothered to press her on the details. She usually arrived around nine o'clock, in which case they would immediately get down to the business of necking and petting on the settee. If she came earlier he would let her play records at the usual ear-shattering volume, his neighbours being apparently immune to the noise. At the end of the evening she invariably fell asleep on the settee and he would depart to his own bed, consumed with frustration.

Carpenter never felt compelled to contact her in between visits, although the unpredictability of her appearances made it impossible to feel perfectly relaxed and comfortably alone except on those evenings immediately following an overnight stay. At these times he actively welcomed his solitude, and all the negative aspects of their relationship would loom large in his mind. Finally he wrote a letter to Veronica, describing what had been happening and explaining his dissatisfactions as well as he could. This was partly in response to a remarkably candid letter from her in which she had gone into great detail about the affair she was now having with a forty-five-year-old man who was married, a Roman Catholic and a Conservative supporter. She had explained at length the various moral dilemmas into which this had put her but had also emphasized that she had gained much in experience from their affair, not least in sexual terms. Donald (for that was her lover's name) was a caring and inventive partner who had enabled her to derive a greater satisfaction from the sexual experience so that for the first time she felt able to think of her body as an instrument of pleasure rather than merely a vessel for lust. There were numerous examples to indicate just how she had achieved this which read like letters from *Forum* and left Carpenter feeling that he was an utter novice in the sexual stakes.

Sensing that she had not actively been soliciting his advice on the problems inherent in her lover's status as a Tory Catholic in wedlock, he made only a passing reference to it and concentrated on giving her a detailed description of Karen and the circumstances which had brought them together before announcing that he was unhappy with their relationship, such as it was. Although he strove to be honest in the letter, he could not resist giving Karen a wholly misleading mysteriousness by referring to her as K throughout. Even as he was forcing himself to describe their wrestling matches on the settee and his subsequent frustration, he was anticipating a response which would condemn him for expecting sexual favours in return for a night's lodging. He imagined that Veronica would berate him for his selfishness, his lack of respect for the seflhood of the other person, his typically boorish male desire for sexual conquest. But she wrote back to say that in her opinion he had chosen someone who was less intelligent than himself and could not therefore provide him with the mental stimulus and the emotional intimacy which was necessary for a mature and lasting relationship.

This irritated Carpenter because it was so transparently true. There were occasions when he despaired of the gulf that existed between them, and he would long for the company of someone with whom he could discuss the meaning of life or even the awful prospect of United being relegated to the Second Division (they were having a bad season). But whenever he was feeling most frustrated with her, she would turn up at her most endearing, often bringing him provisions for his larder. It was impossible to be stern with her then, even though he knew the produce had been pilfered and that he had little use for packets of shredded coconut, cartons of glacé cherries or wrinkled lemons. It's the thought that counts, he would tell himself, while wondering exactly what the thought was. And there remained the continued teasing prospect of her body.

Carpenter had not managed to visit Cardiff since the turn of the year, but in March Duffy rang to say that he and his girlfriend, Liz, would be visiting him the weekend before Easter. Alison would also be accompanying them: Naas was going away on a rugby tour of North Wales. Duffy made it sound like a normal social visit, but Carpenter knew that Liverpool were playing at Bristol City on the Saturday.

Carpenter said nothing to Karen in the weeks that followed. When she turned up at the flat on the Thursday before Duffy and the others were due to arrive, Carpenter felt blessed with luck, for once she left in the morning he would surely not see her again until the following week; she had not stayed at his place on a weekend since she had shoplifted in the supermarket. Then she announced that her grandparents were going away on Saturday by courtesy of the social services so why didn't they do something special together this weekend?

Carpenter heard himself saying that it was a pity because he had to visit his dying grandmother in Lowestoft; at the same time he was thinking, *somehow she knows*, even though he knew this was impossible, given that the visit had been arranged over a single phonecall. Had he talked in his sleep and had she crept into his room and heard all the details? No, it was simply his usual bad luck.

By now Carpenter had concocted a tale fit to make a grown man weep: He was his grandmother's favourite, she having nursed him as a child when he was ill; she was now living alone, crippled and in the grip of a wasting desease; the doctors could do nothing for her, and she had been writing to him, pleading with him to visit her. She was unlikely to last more than a month.

Carpenter kept a solemn face throughout this recital, hoping that his real grandmothers weren't turning in their graves: both had died years before he was born.

Oh, said Karen presently, looking suitably sympathetic, that is a pity. But would he mind leaving the key with her then? She'd much prefer to spend the weekend at his place than at her grandparents' house. *Somehow she knows*, Carpenter thought again, searching frantically for a further excuse. He announced that he couldn't leave his key with her because his landlady had hinted that she might be making one of her spot checks this very weekend, which was another reason why he had decided to visit his grandmother, so that he would be out of the way. I can tell her I'm your sister, Karen announced. No, no, said Carpenter, she knows I'm an only child. Your cousin, then. No, that wouldn't be possible either, she's a friend of the family and might check up; he simply couldn't take the risk.

There was a silence. Carpenter felt despicable, and he was convinced that Karen knew he was lying. But there could be no going back now, nor did he want to except as a sop to his conscience. He recalled his original intention to resign his job on her behalf. What had happened to that grand gesture? He hadn't even told his uncle that he had met Karen, let alone of their peculiar relationship.

They were opposite one another in armchairs. Suddenly Karen got up and sat on his lap. She nestled her head in his shoulder so that Carpenter felt like a cruel Victorian landlord who had just given a poor orphan a notice to quit. Then she started nuzzling his neck, and before he knew it they were kissing. Her hand slipped down to his crotch and she unzipped him. He was already hard.

Then the utterly unexpected happened: she slid her head down to his lap.

What followed were some of the most blissful moments Carpenter had ever experienced. The sex-objects of his fantasies regularly performed fellatio on him, but this was the first time it had happened in the flesh, and it was sublime. Karen milked him like an expert, and when it was over he was left sprawled blissfully in the chair while she departed to the bathroom.

When she returned she had reverted to her usual timid self. She told him she wouldn't stay the night, it would be better if she went home. Please stay, Carpenter insisted, wanting her company more than ever after the service she had rendered him. She shook her head, was quietly adamant. He told her that he would be back by Sunday evening, aware that Duffy and the others would be gone by then. Why didn't she come for dinner?

She said that she might do that; but she collected up all her clothing when she departed, leaving not a scrap behind. Carpenter cursed himself for not having prepared a better lie. He wondered if she was gone from his life for good.

By the following morning, however, such considerations were outweighed by the prospect of the weekend. He stocked his fridge with beer and wine, and sat down in front of the television to wait for the arrival of Duffy and co. Five hours later he was still alone. It had all been in vain; they had decided not to come. Carpenter stumbled off to bed at one o'clock, intending to stay there until noon.

He was awoken at eight-thirty the next morning by the doorbell ringing. Duffy, Liz and Alison were standing outside. Duffy's car, a venerable Anglia, had expired on the M4 just outside Newport the previous evening, and they had been forced to get an early train to Bristol that morning instead.

Better late than never, said Carpenter. He cooked them breakfast, assisted by Alison. You're looking well, Mike, she told him, I hope you don't mind me coming. Mind? said Carpenter, I could hardly wait. As soon as this was out, it sounded precipitate, but Alison merely smiled and gave him a wink. She was wearing a low-necked T-shirt under a black cardigan and a black satin skirt with dark tights. She kept brushing against him as they worked together at the cooker, and it was all he could do to stop himself from falling on her there and then.

After breakfast they sat around listening to records for a few hours before he and Duffy departed for Ashton Gate. Alison and Liz were going shopping, and they arranged to rendezvous outside St Mary Redcliffe Church at six o'clock.

The game was not particularly exciting, but Liverpool won, which pleased Duffy, who also met up with a few old friends from his native city at the match. He and Carpenter were given a flagon of cider to share during the second half, and afterwards it seemed only polite to buy Duffy's friends a drink in return at a pub nearby.

When Carpenter next glanced at his watch he saw that it was almost eight o'clock. They were still in the pub, and he had two full pints of Courage Bitter lined up in front of him. Both he and Duffy agreed that it was now far too late to do anything about it. They would simply have to face the music when they got back later.

'Later' was after midnight. He and Duffy stumbled up the street with their arms around one another, Duffy chanting Kop slogans, Carpenter singing 'There's only one United' over and over again. As they neared his flat he remembered that he was the only one with a key to the front door.

Alison and Liz were sitting on the steps outside the house, both looking extremely cold. There were two empty bottles of red wine at their feet, and for a moment Carpenter thought Liz was going to lift one of them and crack Duffy over the head with it. He hastily opened the door and ushered them inside.

He was standing there, helpless, listening to the mounting argument between Liz and Duffy when Alison took his wrist and led him into his bedroom. She had not spoken since his arrival but had not shown any obvious signs of irritation. Why don't you ever get angry? Carpenter murmured drunkenly to her as they collapsed on the bed and he tried to undress her. I'm cold, was her only response; let's get into bed.

Carpenter undressed as quickly as he was able, watching Alison strip off the rest of her clothes. She did so without modesty or provocation, but the sight of her naked body was enough to inflame his befuddled mind. He wanted to bury his head between her breasts, to cup her bum in his hands, to smother her delightful face with large, wet, blubbery kisses . . .

He joined her under the sheets and found that her body was indeed cold to the touch. He held her close to him and began to rub her all over while thanking the stars that he had not been obliged to undertake an interminable Karen-type bout of striptease wrestling before getting down to the essentials. He paid special attention to her breasts, bottom and thighs while she stroked and clutched him and began to make the kind of noises he had heard through the bedroom wall on his unforgettable first night with Veronica. Soon she was warm all over, and when he slipped his hand between her legs he found a wetness beyond his previous experience or imagining.

Carpenter began to curse his own stupidity, for he knew he was too drunk to do anything about it. He started telling Alison how much he wanted to ravish her, to possess her, to fill her up until she couldn't take any more; this was accompanied by an increasingly emphatic simulation of the sexual act, the headboard of the bed starting to bang against the wall under his thrusting. But it was no use. Finally Alison grabbed him and pressed him against her, telling him to slow down, it was all right, they had the whole night and she didn't mind at all if they just kissed and cuddled. Carpenter was profoundly relieved to hear it, for his gyrations had started to make him feel sick.

So they simply held one another and did a lot of kissing and stroking. This was far pleasanter than Carpenter could have imagined. Alison was making no great demands on him while at the same time being so responsive that he felt like the world's greatest lover. Now she was stroking his back in a way which made him feel languid, drowsy, just drifting away . . .

The sound of the doorbell brought him abruptly from sleep. It was morning, and the bedside clock showed five past eleven. Immediately his head started to pound and he remembered the night before. He became aware of the rest of his body: his mouth felt like a rancid drain, his lungs were caked with cigarette smoke and there was a peculiar sensation in his stomach. A sensation, he realized, of the enormous Chinese takeaway which he had eaten on the way home with Duffy: it seemed to have turned into a lump of warm cement overnight.

The doorbell rang again. Carpenter levered himself to a sitting position. The pain in his head now resolved itself into a pervasive dull pulsation coupled with sharper spasms which radiated up from the base of his skull to collide with the backs of his eyes. He was at once parched and desperate to pee. Alison remained asleep beside him, her face pressed into the pillow. Again the doorbell rang.

Doing his best not to move his head an inch more than was necessary, Carpenter got out of bed and donned his dressing gown. He moved out into the corridor, where he ducked in an attempt to avoid the band of sunlight radiating through the fanlight above the door. This was a mistake, the rapid movement causing blood to rush before his eyes. When his vision cleared the spasms of pain grew stronger: it was as if Naas Van Dyk's spectral hands were inside his cranium, kneading both hemispheres of his brain.

Even as he was opening the door, it dawned on him that he was making a mistake. He should have stayed in bed, pretended that no one was home. Now it was too late.

Hello, said Karen, I didn't think you'd be back yet. Had Carpenter had his wits about him he might have asked her why in that case she had come to the flat. But his head was pounding, his stomach had begun to churn and his lower intestine had joined his bladder in signalling that he should visit the bathroom immediately. It was the kind of hangover that cried out for a complete transfusion of blood or even a brain transplant to another body.

I've been ill, Carpenter heard himself say, I couldn't make it to my grandmother's. You do look awful, Karen agreed, is it flu? Before he could think of a reply, a hot flush enveloped him and for a moment he thought he might pass out. But when the mists cleared he was still standing there and Karen was asking him if he had anyone with him.

With a mounting sense of panic he opened his mouth, not knowing what he was going to say. Suddenly he realized that there was nothing for it but the truth. Yes, he told her; three friends. They're staying with me. Who are they? she wanted to know. University friends, he replied, gripping the doorknob as his bowels contracted. Can I come in? she wanted to know. He hesitated, embarrassed despite his desperate need to visit the bathroom. It's a little difficult just now, he said, everyone else is asleep. I see, she replied, then gave him a bright smile. I'll come back later then. She kissed him quickly on the cheek and hurried away.

Her plucky response to his snub made him feel like an utter shit. He wanted to call her back, to apologize and explain. Then his stomach turned over and he bolted for the bathroom.

Twenty minutes later he crawled back into bed, bloated with water and Alka Seltzer. Alison felt warm and soft as he snuggled up beside her. Where've you been? she murmured. Someone called to read the gas meter, he told her.

When he next awoke Alison was gone from the bed. It was a quarter to three. Next door the Bonzo Dog Band were singing 'Canyons of Your Mind'; Duffy was a great fan of the Bonzos. All three were dressed and ready to leave. Duffy and Liz had mended their quarrel, but it was Alison who dominated his attention. She was as cheerful and relaxed as ever, and Carpenter wanted to drag her back into bed and ravish her. But he knew it was too late. He persuaded them to have a belated lunch with him, and then it was time to depart. He wanted to kick himself when Alison gave him a big wet kiss on the cheek as she left.

Karen did not appear that evening, or the evening afterwards. But somehow Carpenter felt confident that she would show up again, and he wondered what he would say to her when she did. Should he confess all and apologize for not having been honest with her in the first place? Or should he be firm and use the incident as a springboard for telling her that it was better if they didn't see one another any more? But was this what he really wanted? As ever, he vacillated.

Karen appeared late on Wednesday evening, flushed and bright-eyed. She seemed quite cheerful, and her tongue was probing his mouth within seconds of her arrival. The peculiar minty/medicinal flavour of her mouth was stronger than ever – so strong that he belatedly began to suspect its origin.

She did not refer to the events of the weekend, and he did not broach the subject either. Wanting to seem his normal self, Carpenter felt compelled to go through the usual motions of undressing her on the settee; but he took his time, actually hoping that she would soon fall asleep. At length she did.

Delicately he disengaged himself before reaching for her duffle coat and exploring its pockets. On several previous occasions he had been aware of a solid object in one pocket which he had always taken to be some cosmetic item; but he was not surprised when he withdrew a small bottle of Smirnoff vodka which was only a third full. Accompanying it was a tube of Sharp's Extra-Strong Mints.

He went to bed, wondering what he should do. Suddenly the whole situation seemed absurd. Did Karen need to get a bit sloshed whenever she visited him? Was she only capable of granting him sexual favours when she was lubricated with liquor? And if so, why was she bothering in the first place? What was she getting out of it apart from the odd meal and a settee for the night? Was life with her grandparents so unbearable that she would do anything to get away for the occasional evening, even if it meant spending it with someone she could only bear when benumbed by drink?

Carpenter did not know whether to be angry or offended. It couldn't be that simple, he was sure, for there had been times when she had been perfectly sober in his company. And hadn't she wanted to spend the weekend of Duffy and Alison's visit with him?

He lay awake for some time, restlessly seeking a plausible rationale for her behaviour. But by the time sleep had claimed him he had come to only one firm conclusion: he was going to have to end their dalliance for the sake of his peace of mind.

He was awoken early the following morning by the sound of the front door closing. It was only six-thirty. By the time he had risen and gone to the living room window, there was no sign of Karen. And apart from the rumpled blankets on the settee, there was no trace of her presence.

Some instinct made him glance towards his record collection, which he kept in a long cabinet in an alcove. He was finicky about keeping his records in alphabetical order, and he could immediately tell that Karen had been riffling through them. And yet they had played no music the previous evening.

Ten minutes later he had established that at least a dozen of his LPs were missing, among them several of his favourites. His immediate instinct was to pursue Karen to the factory, grab her by the throat and demand that she return every one. But instead he sat down and lit a cigarette, smoking it furiously and wanting to break things. If he followed her to the factory he would be late for work, and his uncle had been in a bad mood of late. Better if he slipped away later and caught her during her lunch break.

At eleven-thirty his uncle deposited the scribbled draft of a memo on his desk which exhorted the men in the workshop not to whistle at or make lewd suggestions to women who passed by on the street. His uncle's command of grammar and tone was virtually negligible, and if the memo had been transcribed as written it might have precipitated a mass walk-out. But Carpenter's modified text was rejected as too wishy-washy, and several drafts were required before his uncle declared himself satisfied. It was then too late to catch Karen at lunch. And her shift ended at four o'clock, an hour and a half before he left work.

Carpenter resolved to go to her grandparents' house immediately after work. It was a rainy evening, and Carpenter huddled in the doorway, hammering on the knocker for several minutes against the blaring sounds of a TV panel game. Finally Karen's grandfather opened the door. He stared at Carpenter for long moments before demanding to know who he was and what he wanted. Carpenter tried to explain, doing his best to insert rapid phrases in the brief pauses between bursts of television laughter or applause. Even then the old man frequently failed to apprehend what he was saying and would stare at him with a kind of wilful ignorance. Meanwhile the rain continued to pour down and, in the absence of an invitation into the house, Carpenter got wetter.

It appeared that the old man had no recollection of him, and Carpenter guessed that Karen had said nothing of their relationship. Either that, or she had primed the old man for his visit: he was now telling Carpenter that he didn't know where she was, he hadn't seen her in weeks. In weeks? said Carpenter sceptically. He had studiously refrained from mentioning why he wanted to see her, and the old man either wasn't interested or already knew and had been instructed to play dumb. He wondered if she was upstairs in her bedroom at that very moment.

But the old man would not be drawn further when Carpenter tried to establish exactly when he had last seen her and where she might now be living. He began to complain to Carpenter that it was wet and cold and that he couldn't stand there all night; they never knew what Karen was doing from one minute to the next, she used the house like a hotel, none of the family had ever been able to do a thing with her and that was the trouble with kids in this day and age, they didn't know the meaning of the word discipline. Then the door closed in his face.

There were no lights burning upstairs at the front of the house, so he went around to the back. It was also dark. The rain was falling more heavily now, and he rejected the idea of knocking again, deciding it was futile. On the way home, both his shoes developed leaks.

Carpenter had just removed his shoes and socks when the doorbell rang. Barefooted, he hurried to answer it, convinced it would be Karen. The instant he opened the door a fist thudded against his cheek. He reeled back from the blow, glimpsing a dark, thickset young man who immediately fled.

By the time he had composed himself, his attacker had vanished. He was pretty sure it had been Derek. Pursuit was impossible in bare feet, even if he had felt so inclined, which he didn't. Instead he closed the door and returned to the living room, sitting down beside the fire and nursing his jawbone while wondering what he should do next.

By the following morning he had done a lot of thinking on the general subject of Karen but had arrived at no firm conclusions. It was possible that she had never actually been living with her grandparents – he had only her word on that – but had been staying with Derek all the time. But if this was so, why did she periodically visit him and stay overnight? Did they perhaps have regular arguments which made her walk out on Derek and get drunk before seeking sanctuary with him? This did not quite fit in with the fact that Derek appeared not to have seen her for some time when he, Carpenter, had called on him with her letter. So had they perhaps made up in the last few weeks or months? And was the theft of the records and the punch from Derek retribution for him having snubbed her at the weekend? Or had Karen only just revealed that he had been her secret lover, thus spurring Derek to redeem his honour by belting him in the face? Had Karen only thrown herself back on Derek's mercies because of the snub? Carpenter was pretty sure the grandparents weren't directly involved: Derek's attack had come within minutes of his return, as if he had been waiting for him nearby. Was it significant that the first record Karen had played at his flat had been by *Derek* and the Dominos? Or that Karen's initials spelt KON?

Anything and everything might be significant if he chose to make it so. It was quite possible that he might obtain unambiguous answers to most of his questions if he went to Derek's flat or waited for Karen after work. Assuming that she did work at the Wills factory.

That morning he asked his uncle about her without giving him any hint of their recent liaison. Typically his uncle was unable to provide Carpenter with anything more than a thumbnail sketch of her; he knew nothing about her family background or her personality outside the office. Carpenter had suspected as much; he would have been more surprised if his uncle had told him anything revealing.

By lunch-time Carpenter had reached a decision: he was going to do nothing. It simply didn't seem worth it. There had never been anything remotely satisfactory about his relationship with Karen, and if she had used him, it was all he deserved since he had only ever craved her company in the hope of satisfying his lust. Better to close the book completely on the whole unfortunate episode by making no further effort to contact her. The stolen records could be replaced simply by buying new ones.

That afternoon he rang the Students' Union in Cardiff, knowing that Duffy and Bullivant often took a liquid lunch there. His abortive night with Alison had at least shown him what he was missing, and he intended to arrange a visit to Cardiff as soon as possible.

It was Bullivant who eventually came to the phone. The first thing he told Carpenter was that Alison and Naas Van Dyk had just got engaged. Carpenter didn't hear what he said immediately after that because he went momentarily deaf. *I don't understand it*, he was thinking. *I don't understand any of it.*

When Bullivant finally stopped talking and asked him why he had rung, Carpenter pretended that his uncle had just returned to the office and that he couldn't talk further. He said that he would call back later, though several years were to pass before he spoke to Bullivant again. That evening he bought a local paper and started scanning the accommodation advertisements. A few weeks later he moved into a new flat in a different part of the city. He gave only his uncle and his parents his new address. That same weekend United were relegated to the Second Division. Denis Law, Carpenter's football hero throughout his teens, scored the goal for their arch-rivals Manchester City which sent them down.

*

'Has everybody got that?' said Blvthe.

Carpenter saw that everyone else looked as incredulous as he. Blythe had just been explaining the new routine which he expected them to go through. It entailed giving each of the walls of the gym a number from one to four. If Blythe shouted 'One' they were all to rush off and touch that particular wall with the flat of their hands before doing likewise to the other walls when their numbers were called. 'Five' meant sit on the floor.

'Two!' shouted Blythe.

No one moved.

'Two!' he shouted again.

Still no one moved. Everyone looked as if they didn't quite believe that Blythe meant it.

'One!' he yelled.

Sinnott was twitching like a conditioned rat, but even he remained rooted to the spot.

'One!' shouted Blythe, going redder in the face. 'Two! Three!'

'Four! Five!' finished Riley. He flopped into a heap at Blythe's feet.

Blythe regarded him, his lower lip beginning to tremble, his face going even redder. Was this to be the longed-for moment when he would succumb to a heart attack or apoplexy? Carpenter bombarded him with nasty thoughts. He was more keen than ever to escape the gym that morning since both his nostrils and his digestive tract were still in a tender state.

'Are you going to get up?' Blythe demanded.

'Five,' said Riley. 'Five means sit on the floor.'

'I didn't say five!'

'I was waiting for you to. I wanted to be first.'

Blythe stalked across to Snider, who was chaperoning Wright at the entrance to the gym.

'They won't do the routines I've developed for them.'

'Routines?' said Wright. 'What do you think they are? Schoolchildren? You can't order grown men – '

'Shut up,' said Snider.

'It's part of the programme,' Blythe told him, a whining note in his voice.

Snider studied him with his usual impassivity.

'I think that will do for this morning,' he said.

*

Treadwell and Sinnott were making approving noises about Snider over the breakfast table. They took the view that Snider was stern but fair.

'You're so easily pandered to,' said Wright. 'Don't think that just because he didn't let Blythe have his way he's on your side. His sole concern is with maintaining discipline.'

Carpenter put a piece of black pudding into his mouth. The food was back to its usual standard, which only tended to confirm his suspicion that Harris was adulterating their evening meals. In a sense this was preferable to the possibility that the food might be genuinely bad, for a dose of laxative-induced runs was better than the prospect of genuine food poisoning.

He veered away from this line of thought and tried to shut out the sound of Wright's voice. Wright was now telling them that Snider had been worried by their refusal to do the exercises and that a planned campaign of disobedience would really put the wind up him. At this point Hemmings entered and handed Carpenter a fresh packet of Silk Cut. It was accompanied by a new disposable lighter to replace the empty one Carpenter had left in the lounge the previous night. The new lighter was red instead of blue.

*

MALE STRIPPERS IN CHURCH HALL, read one headline in Carpenter's tabloid. DO HICCUP CURES WORK? read another. Carpenter scanned the latter article, which was described as an in-depth investigation of such common hiccup cures as drinking from the wrong side of the glass and getting your lover to give you a shock. Over two hundred readers had been interviewed in the survey. No firm conclusions were drawn.

Carpenter turned the page. ROCK STAR IN DEATH PACT WITH INCURABLE MODEL. What was an incurable model? he wondered, and learned that it was a secretary who had once been photographed for a Halifax tool manufacturer's company calendar and was now dying from leukaemia. Her boyfriend, the rock star of the headline, played bass guitar in a local cabaret group. Since the girl had only months to live, the couple had decided to do away with themselves by driving their car over the edge of a cliff. But the plan had misfired. The girl had escaped unscathed from the wreckage of the car, while her boyfriend had suffered spinal injuries which were likely to keep him confined to a wheelchair for the rest of his life.

Carpenter studied the unopened cigarette packet on the coffee table in front of him. He desperately wanted a cigarette, but the moment Hemmings had put the new red lighter on the table he had told himself that he wasn't going to smoke again in Limbo. The renewal of the lighter meant a renewal of his sentence; it carried the message 'Another three months'. He did not think he could bear this.

He put the newspaper aside, telling himself that the story about the couple had almost certainly been made up by a bored reporter who was short of copy. But it made no difference: the story was true in some larger symbolic sense because the things that happened to people were often bizarre and pathetic. It was not a question of unfairness, for that was to presume some underlying principle or force which operated with a moral purpose, and he could no longer believe in such a possibility. It was simply a question of being dismayed by the blithe cruelty of nature.

'Look at it this way,' Wright was saying to Sinnott, 'when Treadwell and I succeed in breaking through the wall, you'll want to come with us, won't you?'

Sinnott made a noncommittal movement of his head. He looked uncomfortable to be the object of Wright's persistence, Wright having resumed his efforts to enlist his help with the tunnel. Treadwell had just taken Hemmings aside on a pretext so that he would be out of earshot. They stood in the games room doorway, with Treadwell talking loudly to cover the sound of Wright's voice in case the room was bugged.

'All we're asking for is a few minutes of your time each day,' said Wright. 'That's not too much to ask for something that's intended to benefit us all, is it?'

Carpenter was surprised by the relative moderation of Wright's tone and the fact that he was not bringing weighty moral principles to bear on Sinnott.

'All that's required is for you to spend five minutes extra in the toilet every time you go. What's unreasonable about that?'

But Sinnott was looking everywhere except directly at him.

'Do you know why toilets have WC on their doors?' Riley asked him.

Sinnott was keen to disengage himself from Wright. 'Why?'

'The Normans invented them. It stands for William the Conqueror.'

Wright's mouth opened and closed in one swift movement. He gave a tolerant smile.

In the games room doorway Treadwell was talking to Hemmings about plumbing. Carpenter listened for a while, wondering why Hemmings was so interested in the subject. Treadwell was discussing U-bends and septic tanks. It was obvious that he didn't know what he was talking about, but he clearly knew he was waffling and was determinedly playing a role which could not have come easily to him either temperamentally or imaginatively: it was for the good of the cause.

Meanwhile Riley was explaining to Sinnott how the Normans had invented the water closet. The story involved the prevalence of naturally occurring self-flushing water holes in the Norman homeland – Norway – whi·h they used as lavatories and which had provided the inspiration for the toilet as we know it today. When William the Conqueror had invaded England and discovered that there were no such water holes there, he had sent some of his engineers back to Norway to find out how they worked. Eventually they had returned with the necessary plans, and William had immediately set about having one installed in the new castle which was being built for him at the time.

'The Tower of London,' concluded Riley, 'was the first building in the world to have a custom-built flushing lavatory.'

★

Carpenter read a newspaper article which told him that it was possible to be allergic to a whole range of foods from potatoes to bread; often a person's favourite food was the one to which he was most allergic. This was just one more aspect of his health about which he could now worry. There was a wide range of diseases and illnesses which he had been convinced he was succumbing to over the years. Cancer and heart failure remained the front-runners, depending on whether he was smoking too much or suffering twinges in the chest which he could never quite convince himself were indigestion. Given the complexity of the human body and the host of things that could go wrong with it, it sometimes amazed him that anyone survived to a ripe old age.

He knew that he was a hypochondriac and had often been criticized for it, not least by Veronica. But he'd always felt that hypochondria was much maligned since it seldom made you feel so ill that you couldn't be comfortably sorry for yourself while at the same time being non-infectious.

Riley was asleep opposite him, Treadwell and Sinnott were playing pool, and Wright had departed for a protracted visit to the toilet. Carpenter flung the newspaper aside and switched on the television.

By a stroke of misfortune he caught the end of the afternoon news broadcast and had to sit through a summary which told him that fierce fighting had once again broken out in the Middle East, that two British soldiers had been killed in an ambush near the Ulster border, that hundreds had died in a famine which was affecting large areas of India, and that the international banks were gloomy about the prospects of world economic growth in the coming year.

Happily the news was followed by a children's programme featuring the activities of animated puppets in a model village of gingerbread rusticity. This was much more to his taste, and it soon made him wistful about his vanished childhood. One of his most secret and prized possessions was an old picture book which he had had from an early age and which contained colourful drawings of the same kind of cheery, apple-faced folk as those on television. In their worlds problems were never more acute than cats stranded up trees or children temporarily lost, and when they were rescued the whole village celebrated. He could not forgive the real world for containing such things as war, disease, mental illness and, above all, death.

He watched the hearty postman help the friendly fireman extract a talking cow from a marshy field. The essential difference between characters in children's stories and people in real life was that real people had interior lives: they spent a lot of time thinking, which inevitably meant that a proportion of it was spent in worrying, scheming and other unwholesome mental activities. Characters in children's stories were exactly as they acted, and you could always count on them. Real people were devious and elusive. They also had pasts, which made them unpredictable. This was particularly true of women, and particularly true of women with whom he became involved. They tended to have things like old boyfriends, as in the case of Karen, or even husbands, as with Eleanor.

'Not disturbing you, am I?' said a voice.

It was Hemmings. He sat down next to Carpenter.

Carpenter tried to give his full attention to a soap opera episode which was now showing. A man with a broad Australian accent was talking to a whey-faced woman about another person called Sidney R. Borbridge. It seemed strange that he should continue referring to the man by his full name; then it dawned on Carpenter that he was talking about *Sydney harbour bridge*. Carpenter began wondering how the presence of an Australian guard in Limbo might have affected Wright's calculations as to its location. Would they have ended up in the middle of the Mediterranean?

Meanwhile Hemmings was conducting a monologue about his conversation with Treadwell on the subject of plumbing. He was apparently dubious about the advice which Treadwell had given him. Eventually Hemmings got around to explaining that the conversation had started as a result of him mentioning plugholes.

'Water always swirls down the plughole in one direction, right?' he said to Carpenter. 'I tried it in my house, and it always goes the same way. Except in my kitchen sink. I tried it there, and guess what? It goes down the *wrong* way.'

*

Carpenter played Sinnott at snooker. With his new haircut, Sinnott looked a true prisoner. His fingernails were bitten right down.

'My mother always threatened to put salt and lard on my fingers if I bit them,' Carpenter said.

Sinnott studied his fingers as if hitherto unaware that he had been biting them.

'She told me I'd get gangrene and they'd drop off.'

Carpenter smiled benignly at him. Sinnott fluffed his shot, as Carpenter had intended.

'It's a habit,' he said. 'I can't help it. It's like smoking, I suppose.'

Only then did Carpenter realize that he had lit up and half-smoked a cigarette without being fully conscious of it.

'Do you like it here?' he asked.

Sinnott glanced nervously at him.

'No one's listening,' Carpenter said. He hadn't really talked to Sinnott about anything important apart from football since they'd been in Limbo.

'It's not fair,' Sinnott said in a low voice. 'We shouldn't be here. We haven't done anything wrong.'

'How do you know?'

A worried look appeared on Sinnott's face. Carpenter missed an easy red.

'Perhaps we've done something wrong that we don't know about.'

This time Sinnott did not miss. He lined up the blue, and potted that as well.

'Do you want to get out of here?' Carpenter asked.

'I wish they would.'

'Would what?'

'Let us go. I'm fed up being here.' He sank another red.

'Then why don't you help Wright and Treadwell?'

'I don't want to escape. I want to be set free.'

*

On his way to his cell, Carpenter encountered Wright in the corridor.

'You're going to regret not helping us, Carpenter.'

'Everything going well?'

'I'm confident we'll be through the wall in another few days.' Wright spoke in a low voice.

'And then what?'

'Then we're getting out of here.'

'When will you make your move?'

Wright suddenly looked suspicious. 'I don't think it would be wise to tell you that.'

'By night would be best. If the cells weren't locked. By day you'd only manage to get about ten minutes' start on the guards before they realized you were gone. Perhaps less than that with two of you.'

'You're a defeatist, Carpenter. You'll be here until you rot.'

Wright walked off. Carpenter entered his cell, closing the door behind him. He wanted to be alone.

*

Carpenter had been lying on his bed for about half an hour when Snider swung his door open.

'How long have you been in here?' he asked.

Carpenter sat up. 'I thought my activities were being constantly monitored.'

Snider said nothing to this. Carpenter put his pillow behind his head and settled back. Snider seemed to be studying him.

'Is something wrong?' Carpenter asked.

'I hope you're not contemplating anything foolish.'

'What sort of thing?' Did he know about the escape tunnel?

Snider was peering around the cell as if searching for clues.

'Leave the door open when you're in here,' he said.

'Why? What are you afraid I'm going to do?'

Snider stared hard at him, then said, 'Just be careful.'

He turned and walked out, leaving the door ajar and Carpenter unsure of whether his parting comment had been a warning or an oblique expression of concern.

Carpenter had been thinking about his father, whom he was seldom able to imagine in any other context than sitting beside the fire in the leatherette armchair with a newspaper on his lap. Some people were always strongly associated with a given situation in your mind: it was hard, for example, to think of Snider living an ordinary life in the real world outside Limbo.

Carpenter plumped up his pillow and made himself comfortable again. It was his father's death that had finally brought about his departure from Bristol. Just when you thought you were comfortably settled into a routine, something came along which changed your life completely.

After the Karen fiasco he had managed to retreat into a sheltered world of his own making; ensconced in his new flat and relieved of the possibility that she, or indeed anyone else, might turn up unexpectedly on his doorstep, he was able to settle down to a quiet life. Reading in particular gradually took up more and more of his time; he began to tour the city's bookshops on Saturday afternoons, returning home with carrier bags full of books. Soon his days became focused around the moment when he could finally close his door behind him after the mindless hours of the office and settle down to his solitary communion with other minds.

His reading tastes remained eclectic, though he went through a phase in which he devoured dense Russian novels. It was impossible to emerge from a book by Dostoevsky or Solzhenitsyn and not feel that his own life was hopelessly cosseted and trivial. Later he became fascinated by psychology textbooks and quickly realized how little he had understood of the unconscious forces which motivated people. The more he read, the more it seemed that he was gaining a broader perspective of the world and how to deal with it; it was all tremendously exciting and liberating.

Looking back on it now, Carpenter saw that his confidence in his maturing of outlook had grown in inverse proportion to the amount of contact he was actually having with real people in the everyday world. And as the weeks turned into months, he had become further entrenched in his insular habits. He visited Manchester briefly at Christmas but saw none of his friends. Graham's group was touring Scotland over the holiday period, and Gail had gone with them. In their absence Carpenter felt disinclined to go out, and he spent the four days of his visit at home with his parents. Nothing had changed in the sedate routine of their household and he had little to say to them. It was a relief to return to Bristol and the comforts of his own routine. If only he had known it was the last time he would see his father. If only he had known.

Winter gave way to spring, and it seemed that he might continue for ever amassing books and seeing no one. He hardly even noticed that United were prospering again, though he did treat himself to a few celebratory beers when they finally secured promotion as Second Division champions. Then, one morning in June, his uncle entered the office and told him that his Aunt Muriel had phoned with an urgent message: his father had died suddenly during the night, apparently of simple heart failure.

It seemed to him that he was never able to anticipate important events in his life or deal with them effectively when they occurred. The news of his father's death provided him with his first intimations of his own mortality, accompanied by an uncomfortable sense of obligation. As he sat on the train to Manchester, watching the placid green countryside slip by his window, he wondered what would be required of him and whether he would be able to face up to it.

As it turned out, all that was required of him was his presence. His mother had immersed her grief in a flurry of organization, and there was nothing for him to do. He sat around the house, feeling inadequate, disconnected; there was an absence of real grief in him, a sense that he was only going through the motions of bereavement. His father had always been a remote and colourless figure to him, and his passing affected him most in his fears of what it might do to his mother.

She insisted that she was all right, and during the month in which he stayed with her she tended to his every need, cooking his food, doing his laundry and even making his bed. Muriel, her younger sister, lived only a few streets away; her own husband, Alf, had died when Carpenter was eight. Carpenter had spent many evenings at their house as a child, and Alf now seemed more vivid in his mind than his own father: he had been a whimsical man who used to captivate the young Carpenter with imaginative tales of how spiders' webs were made (they spun them out of dust and dew) or where the tooth-fairies got their sixpences from (there was a silver mine on the Moon). Muriel, by contrast, tended to scare him with stories of vain children seeing demons in mirrors or young boys whose bones crumbled to dust because they didn't eat their greens. Was this the same Muriel? She treated him as an adult now, and was even slightly deferential in her manner towards him. This unsettled rather than flattered him, the onus of responsibility and maturity which it implied not resting lightly on his shoulders. But her sympathy and supportiveness gratified Carpenter. His mother looked shrunken and vulnerable, and he wanted to take hold of her and hug her to him. But they had never been a demonstrative family, and he could not shrug off the weight of his reserve.

His uncle, a young brother to his father, had attended the funeral but had returned to Bristol immediately afterwards. Carpenter took his speedy departure as something of a snub and realized that he had no desire to continue working for him. Then he received a letter from Gail which told him that she and Graham and the rest of the group were living in a large house in Ludlow with a recording studio in the basement where Graham and his group – who now bore the exotic name Xenon Sunrise – were laying down tracks for a concept album financed by the owner of the house, a young businessman who was intending to set up his own record company. She'd heard about his father's death, sent her commiserations and suggested that he come and stay with them for a while.

He was to spend sixteen contented months there, living off his savings and supplementing them with stints working in pubs and doing odd jobs around the town. Most days he simply sat in on the group's recording sessions, occasionally helping them to shift equipment around. Graham had added a keyboards player and a saxophonist to the group's original line-up, and he was writing most of the songs for the LP, provisionally entitled 'Art Attack' and telling the story of a talented young painter who survives drug addiction, public hostility and an assassination attempt to become a famous artist before his suicide by setting fire to himself at an exhibition of his work in London.

It was, Carpenter thought privately, rather a derivative theme, though he said nothing to Graham and was carried along by his boundless enthusiasm for the project. Once again Carpenter felt drab and conventional compared to him; once again Graham was full of plans for the future, intending to tour Europe when the album was complete, to record with a full orchestra and to organize a dramatic presentation of 'Art Attack'.

Meanwhile Gail was working as a supply teacher in the local area. She appeared as devoted to Graham as ever, though Carpenter thought he detected an undercurrent of discontent in her which was never quite articulated. He still felt all his old familiar longings for her, but he did his best to give her no hint of this. Mostly everything was placid and idle; they would drink beer, smoke grass and sit out in the spacious garden on warm afternoons, staring out over the rolling Shropshire hills. When winter closed in, they lit fires inside the house, drank mulled wine and played marathon games of Monopoly, poker and Call My Bluff.

The weeks and months slipped by, and soon it was spring again. United reached the final of the FA Cup, but lost to Southampton. Graham and the rest of the group had recorded only four of the ten tracks for the prospective album, but there was no sense of hurry; Graham would not be satisfied until everything was absolutely right, and the rest of the group followed his lead. The songs themselves struck Carpenter as solid, intricate and well-played but somehow lacking that spark of originality or inspiration which would have made them special. But he kept his counsel, telling himself that he was being overly critical because he knew Graham so well.

The summer which followed was a long and remarkable one, with day after day of unrelenting sunshine and blue skies. Everyone lazed about and developed nut-brown tans, and there were many philosophical conversations which basically entailed expressing a profound satisfaction with their circumstances and asking one another why everyone else allowed themselves to be caught up in the rat-race. It was one of the happiest times of his life, and consequently he now had few specific memories of it.

Then, in late September, their backer, who had been in America, returned home with the news that he had cash-flow difficulties and had abandoned his plans to set up a record company. The whole deal was off, and they were obliged to be out of the house within the week.

Graham responded typically to the disappointment by dispatching demo tapes to several record companies in London soon after their return to Manchester. By Christmas, only two companies had replied, both expressing a polite lack of interest. It had been a miserable autumn, both in terms of the weather and the mood of discontent which seemed to infect everyone. In the interim two of the group had left to join other bands, and by the turn of the year Xenon Sunrise were no longer in existence and Graham had departed to London to seek work as a session musician.

Meanwhile Carpenter was unemployed and living in Crumpsall. Lacking Graham's moral support for the bohemian life, he felt a renewed pressure to get a regular job and earn a decent wage. The problem was that there were no decent jobs to be had, or at least none he could aspire to. The dismal prospect of having to return to the biscuit factory began to loom. Then he met an old schoolfriend who was teaching in Stockport and who asked him if he had ever considered that line of work. There was a shortage of science teachers, and he happened to know that a boys' comprehensive school in Blackpool where he had previously worked was advertising for one. No, he wouldn't need a formal teaching qualification.

Carpenter had never remotely contemplated teaching before, but he was desperate to escape Crumpsall and decided to apply for the job without really expecting to be given an interview. But his friend had promised him a reference, and evidently this did the trick, for he was duly summoned. United had reached the Cup Final again that year, and on the Saturday before he was due to visit Blackpool they defeated Liverpool and carried off the Cup. Carpenter took this as a good omen.

At the interview he old the assembled local dignitaries how he had always been interested in children, wanted a job which allowed him to use his initiative, believed education to be the only hope for the future of civilization, and much else in an improvisatory vein. Perhaps his crowning piece of waffle was his claim that his variegated and intermittent working career to date had been a planned campaign designed to give him the widest possible experience of life outside the academic world before he finally took up his chosen profession.

Faced with such inspired lying, his interviewers could only nod and make approving noises. It came as no surprise to him when he was offered the job, and he immediately wrote back a letter of acceptance before he could have second thoughts. Even a scale one teacher's salary was quite respectable, and think of all the holidays.

Within days of dispatching the letter, however, he began to wonder what he had let himself in for. Would he be able to stand in front of a classroom full of boys and hold forth for half an hour at a time? What about the kids themselves? Would he be able to manage them? And think of all the preparatory work he'd have to do before he even started – brushing up on his secondary school science, working to a syllabus, then the actual lessons themselves, with homework to mark and exam papers to set . . .

But there was no going back now; he realized that he'd already committed himself when he'd had his hair cut for the interview. He had worn it shoulder-length for the last several years, and the haircut had made him suddenly appear much older, not least because it revealed that he had begun to recede at the temples. In recent years he had been clean-shaven, but now he decided to grow a full beard in compensation. The beard proved so schoolmasterly that he immediately shaved it off again.

A month before term was due to start he moved to Blackpool and managed to find himself a two-roomed flat above a café less than a hundred yards from the seafront. The rooms were grubby and in dire need of redecoration, but the place was serviceable enough for the time being. The school itself was only fifteen minutes' walk away, a solid Edwardian building of grey stone and red brick, with cream-tiled corridors and classrooms containing large, fixed blackboards and stout wooden desks which were dark and scarred with age.

The head of the science department, Mrs Teasdale, proved very helpful and considerate. Carpenter did not have to worry about constructing his lessons from scratch: he simply had to follow the school syllabus. His duties as a general science master included giving chemistry and biology lessons. These were subjects he hadn't studied in years, but Mrs Teasdale gave him lots of useful advice on how best to organize his lessons. She was a small, gentle woman in her late fifties who was due to retire the following summer.

Carpenter felt extremely self-conscious when he was introduced to the school at assembly on the first day of term, but surprisingly less so when Mrs Teasdale introduced him again to class One Beta half an hour later. (There were four streams at the school, their A to D grading ineffectually disguised with Greek letters.) His first lesson was to be on the expansion and contraction of solids with heat; it was a double period with plenty of practical work for the children. Mrs Teasdale departed, abandoning him to his fate.

Carpenter comforted himself with the knowledge that most of his classes were with the first and second forms. These, Mrs Teasdale had counselled him, were generally more amenable to the principle of being taught than third- and fourth-formers who were feeling the effects of puberty and had grown resentful of the whole idea of school. The fifth and sixth forms, being examination orientated, were also favoured by teachers, though Mr Rawcliffe, the headmaster, demanded two years' apprenticeship with the lower forms before a teacher was allowed to take any of these classes.

Carpenter started slowly and hesitantly, aware of twenty-eight eyes on him. But gradually he warmed to his theme when he realized that the class was merely curious rather than potentially hostile. He handed out the worksheets which gave details of the practical experiments the class were to conduct, and from then on the lesson practically ran itself.

By the end of the day he was feeling good. All his lessons had gone well, and he seemed to have established a reasonable rapport with each class. And so it continued in the days that followed. By the end of the week he was quietly delighted with his performance. He'd had no disciplinary problems whatsoever.

The second week was just as easy, and in the third week he began to remember names and faces. By the fourth week he could glance at his timetable for the day and know exactly what classroom he would be teaching in and what the class would look like. Each working day passed remarkably quickly; he would recall how long a lesson had seemed to him when he had been a pupil and how short it seemed now that he was the teacher. Even so, he found the job very tiring and was usually in bed long before midnight. His evenings and weekends were taken up with background reading and marking homework; he was determined to sustain his auspicious start.

Before he knew it, his first term was over and he returned to Manchester for Christmas feeling as if he had finally found his true vocation. Graham was still in London with Gail, and he saw neither of them. His mother was suitably pleased with his new-found enthusiasm for teaching and wondered aloud why he hadn't gone into it in the first place since he'd always had a way with children. This was news to Carpenter, for he had always found children a pain in the neck; but he appreciated the sentiments.

In his second term small matters of discipline began to intrude on his lessons, with children talking at the back of the class or making faces at one another or firing rice grains through Bic biro tubes. Mr Rawcliffe was a proponent of the cane, but Carpenter had no intention of delivering up miscreants to him. Instead he attempted to be reasonable and would take the offenders aside and give them a gentle lecture on the merits of good behaviour and mutual respect between teacher and class. These lectures always sounded trite and unconvincing even to himself, and they had no effect on the children.

Mrs Teasdale had earlier cautioned him that he could expect a few problems once his novelty value had run out with the boys, and so it proved. By the summer term he was having to deal with water pistols, paper pellets, whoopee cushions, cap guns, live frogs, and much else. During practical lessons he would encounter hands deliberately coated with potassium permanganate solution, worksheets conveniently burnt in bunsen burner flames, chewing gum dropped into beakers of boiling water, and so on. It was worst with the few third- and fourth-form classes which he took: their faces developed a glazed expression of boredom and resentment, fashioned like a protective sheen between themselves and himself. His own schooldays were close enough for him to recall the general temper of the adolescent mind, with its short attention spans, its views of adults as intrusive, and its limited ability to project beyond the immediate future. Education as well as youth was wasted on the young.

It was necessary, and inevitable, that he develop some technique for stopping or at least stifling dissent. The child psychology textbooks he was reading emphasized that he should try to deal with each problem child as an individual, seeking to understand the particular anxieties underlying his disruptive behaviour and adopting a sympathetic and tolerant approach. This was fine in theory, but what did you do in practice when a group of boys went into a frantic simulation of masturbation every time your back was turned?

Loath to resort to physical intimidation or the futility of assigning extra homework, Carpenter moved the worst offenders to the front of the class and adopted the tactic of the cold, silent stare. Sometimes this worked, but in every class there were at least two or three boys who were simply beyond the disciplinary pale. They were inveterate delinquents who would probably grow up to become nightclub bouncers, soldiers or policemen.

Despite these problems, the pressure of work actually declined as he grew more familiar with it. He now found that he had more leisure time, and he started taking walks along the blustery seafront, buying himself a stick of rock in memory of more uninhibited days. Mr Rawcliffe was always cordial to him on their rare meetings, and the inspector who visited to watch him at work seemed satisfied with his approach.

Mrs Teasdale collected antiques, and at the end of term Carpenter bought her a Victorian marble-cased clock as a retirement present. At £50 it was an expensive present, but it was a measure of his gratitude for all the help she had given him. After the presentation she took him aside and told him that in her opinion he would go on to become a fine teacher.

Both Graham and Gail were back in Manchester when he returned there for the summer holidays. Graham looked totally transformed: he had had his hair cut short, shaved off his beard and was wearing ragged drainpipe jeans, baseball boots, a grimy white T-shirt and a black leather biker's jacket. He was in the process of forming a new three-piece group with a young drummer and bassist which would be devoted to playing New Wave music. Carpenter had been out of touch with the music scene since his move to Blackpool, but he soon discovered that the New Wave was basically a fresh generation of young groups who were playing raw but often exciting music with a keynote of disdain in the lyrics for everything that had gone before; they tended to have names like The Demonics and The Still-Born. The New Wave, Graham told him, was the coming thing, and London and Manchester were the two main places where it was happening. Carpenter sat in on one of the group's sessions, in which they played songs with titles like 'Axe Murder' and 'City Shits'; Graham, hitherto a pacifist whom Carpenter had never even known to swear, could not decide whether to call the group Eyes Scream or The Dynamic Yawn.

With his neat haircut, bell-bottomed jeans and aged parka, Carpenter felt hopelessly out-of-date and bourgeois in the face of Graham's radical new lease of musical life. Within a month Graham and the group – finally christened Fiasco – had departed to London to play gigs with Gail in tow. She had been conspicuously silent about the new group, but Carpenter knew that she would have followed Graham to the ends of the earth if necessary. He had been tempted to accompany them to the capital, but his mother looked pale and unwell and he decided to stay with her.

In August a letter forwarded by his uncle in Bristol arrived. It was from Veronica. Since she'd last written to him she had spent a year working on a kibbutz near the Sea of Galilee which had been strafed by Migs several times during her stay. Much of the letter was taken up with a favourable description of life on the kibbutz, though to Carpenter it sounded grindingly tough and monotonous. She extolled the gaunt beauty of the landscape, the stolid fortitude of her fellow workers, and generally gave the impression that she had enjoyed doing her bit for beleaguered Israel. Thus he was confounded by her final paragraph, in which she informed him that she had joined an anti-Zionist group on her return to Britain and was now living in the East End of London and working at a Drug Rehabilitation Centre.

Carpenter kept the letter, but he did not write back. Things were running so smoothly for him just now that he felt sure Veronica would disapprove of him should he write and tell her what he was doing. If only people would leave me alone, he found himself thinking; if only I could do without them.

The new academic year in Blackpool began with him being interviewed by Mr Rawcliffe, who liked to discuss the previous year's achievements and the coming year's prospects with each of his staff. The interview proceeded blandly enough, with the headmaster praising his work in his first year at the school and saying that he had made an auspicious start. Carpenter responded equally blandly by saying that his work had been made easier by the support he'd received from other members of the staff, and in particular Mrs Teasdale, whom he was going to miss. Yes indeed, Mr Rawcliffe replied in a rather abstracted manner, then asked him if he was having any particular problems with discipline. Carpenter told him that he wasn't, especially. I see, said Mr Rawcliffe, sounding distinctly unconvinced. I merely ask because I note that you did not have occasion to send any boys to me at all last year. Before Carpenter could reply he added that most teachers found it necessary to dispatch at least one or two boys to his office when full disciplinary measures were called for and that this seemed to him an accurate reflection of the kind of problems that one could expect at a school of this nature. Wouldn't he agree?

It was immediately clear to Carpenter that he was being given a veiled ultimatum: deliver up your share of sacrificial victims, or else. Carpenter stared at the selection of canes which were stacked in an umbrella rack behind Mr Rawcliffe's desk, then at his headmaster's small, adamant face. A weasel face, he thought, wondering what he was going to say in reply.

He was not required to say anything. Mr Rawcliffe smiled, said he was sure he appreciated how maintaining standards of discipline depended on co-operation from members of staff before adding that he felt confident a successful year lay ahead for everyone. Then he rose from his desk. The interview was over.

In the first few weeks of term Carpenter had more pressing problems than that of fulfilling his canee quota. He had paid a retainer on his bedsitter during the summer, but had returned to find that the café over which it stood had been converted into an amusement arcade. The arcade was open until midnight, and Carpenter was kept awake by the *ping ping ping* of pinball machines, the pecuniary crash of one-arm bandits and the shouts, squeals and choruses of delight or frustration from their demonstrative players. It was worse late at night, when an influx of boisterous drunks from local pubs swelled the arcade's population and the noises rising through his floorboards sounded like rehearsals for a riot.

Soon Carpenter was feeling tired and frayed by day. But Mr Weatherby, his new head of department, was the antithesis of Mrs Teasdale and showed little sympathy for his plight; he was one of those teachers who saw his job as a constant battle to ram home facts into the skulls of schoolchildren despite themselves: teaching for him was less a vocation requiring patience and devotion than an endurance test in which the chief object was to get through the day with a minimum of fuss.

Bereft of Mrs Teadale's wise and gentle patronage, Carpenter began to find some of his lessons an increasing trial. In purely presentational terms he could cope well enough, having now familiarized himself with his various syllabuses and having developed a suitably pedagogic classroom presence. But the persistent problem of discipline began to nag at him as the weeks wore on and he became increasingly convinced that his familiarity to the boys was breeding their contempt for him. He already knew that he had at least one nickname – 'Woody' – and that jokes were circulating about his penchant for jiggling the small change in his pocket during classroom orations. But the chief source of his vexation was the persistent offenders who misbehaved during his classes. And the chief amongst these was Terrence Torrance.

This was the unlikely name of a pupil in Four Delta whom Carpenter had begun to teach that term. Carpenter supposed that the boy hated the awful assonance of his name and wanted to revenge himself on the world as a result; little else could explain his obnoxious behaviour. Terrence was a large, fat individual with a rather piggish face and small, crafty eyes. He liked to pull his classmates' hair, twist their fingers, stick compasses into them, push, pinch and punch them whenever he thought Carpenter wasn't looking. If challenged he would respond with a sullen, obdurate stare. When pressed to explain himself, he would always claim that he had done nothing; and none of his classmates could ever be persuaded to inform on him.

Carpenter could not understand their reticence, for Terrence was paradoxically the biggest sneak whenever anyone else misbehaved, being only too eager to name the guilty party. But far from despising him, his classmates seemed to find his unparalleled awfulness a quality worthy of esteem, as if by flouting all the rules of decency and camaraderie he put himself beyond normal criticism. Until his acquaintance with Terrence, Carpenter had always considered himself essentially understanding of the adolescent mind, but he was now forced to admit that in some respects children of any age were, as far as adults were concerned, really an alien species.

Terrence proved a persistent vexation to Carpenter, the more so because his activities were not primarily directed at him but at his classmates. One afternoon during a practical lesson Carpenter caught him jabbing the end of a spatula into the hand of a smaller boy whom he was holding by the wrist. Before he had pause to think, Carpenter grabbed him by the arm and marched him off to Mr Rawcliffe's office. The headmaster listened silently to Carpenter's indictment, a faint but unmistakable expression of satisfaction growing on his face. When Carpenter was finished Mr Rawcliffe said that he could leave the matter with him and return to his class. But something made Carpenter linger outside his office, and he heard the cane swish three times before he hastily departed. When Terrence reappeared he looked suitably chastened and was silent for the rest of the lesson. But Carpenter felt no sense of victory.

Terrence was subdued in the days that followed, but the next week, in the same practical lesson, Carpenter returned from a brief visit to the staffroom and found him tormenting the same boy in exactly the same fashion as before. There was a brazen, challenging look on his face when he saw Carpenter, and he made no attempt to disguise what he was doing. Carpenter strode forward, snatched the spatula from his hand and jabbed it into his palm so hard that it grazed the skin.

Terrence jerked his hand away and inspected the damage before looking up at Carpenter with a mixture of astonishment and hatred. Carpenter had intended to give him a mild dose of his own medicine, but in the heat of the moment he had overdone it. I'll get my father on you, said Terrence. Carpenter was profoundly aware that the eyes of the whole class were on him. He experienced a sinking feeling, like a spy in a foreign country whose cover has just been blown.

For days afterwards he was nervous of a summons to Mr Rawcliffe's office and a confrontation with Terrence's indignant parents who would immediately demand his resignation. He was moody and distracted in the staffroom, his brittle frame of mind compounded by the fact that all of Blackpool's aspiring Hell's Angels now seemed to have chosen the amusement arcade below his bedsitter as a meeting place where they conducted nightly symphonies of motorbike revving into the small hours. None of his colleagues seemed aware of his difficulties, and he found that he could not talk to any of them about his private problems. He began to find the atmosphere of the staffroom smug and philistine, and took to having lunch alone in a pub nearby.

It was a staffroom tradition to cut out *The Times* crossword every morning and pin it to a board so that the staff could pass it around during their breaks. Carpenter had proved himself a star performer at deciphering clues, his reputation being bolstered by the fact that he never actively sought the crossword; he was viewed by his colleagues as an expert to be brought in when all else failed. During one mid-morning break he was sitting in the staffroom when Eleanor Netherton, the buxom geography mistress, presented him with a recondite clue. He merely shrugged and said that he had no idea as to the answer.

At lunch time he was sitting alone in the pub when Eleanor entered and sat down beside him. She told him she thought he had looked preoccupied earlier, and was there anything she could do to help? She was a friendly, busy woman in her early thirties; the hearty organizer type, Carpenter thought, and quite attractive in a smart, respectable way.

The threat of Terrence's father had by now receded in his mind, but he was left with a nagging dissatisfaction about his work which he couldn't pin down. It's nothing really, he heard himself say, I'm just a bit fed up generally. Eleanor studied him with understanding eyes and told him that disillusionment often set in during the second year of teaching; it had happened to her and he wasn't to worry, he simply had to stick with it and it would soon pass. She told him several horror stories about her own first two years in teaching which made his present difficulties seem trivial by comparison.

She insisted on buying him a half of bitter and returned with a slimline tonic for herself. They continued talking, and when Carpenter cited Terrence Torrance as the archetypal source of pupil irritation, she nodded and informed him that Terrence had been a thorn in the flesh of even the most experienced teachers since his arrival at the school. But he wasn't to worry, she insisted, he would be surprised at how quickly Terrence and his ilk passed through the school and departed. The important thing was to remember that particular pupils were only temporary vexations.

Carpenter returned to his lessons that afternoon feeling more cheerful. He had needed to talk to someone, and Eleanor had proved the perfect person, being of a similar age but having the experience necessary to put his problems in perspective. She was married to the school's PT teacher, a towering, ginger-haired man called Frank; they lived on the outskirts of nearby St Anne's. On hearing that Carpenter did nothing in his leisure time except read and take walks, she shook her head and told him that he must come to dinner sometime.

Christmas was now approaching, and the end-of-term party was in prospect. This was traditionally held in conjunction with the equivalent girls' school close by, and there was to be a dance in the assembly hall there. Carpenter had been detailed to supervise the affair with several other members of staff, including Eleanor.

It was not something he had been looking forward to, and he spent most of the evening standing in the shadows at a corner of the hall, watching clusters of girls warily eye aloof clusters of boys while the sixth former who was in charge of the disco played records by Status Quo and The Supremes and vainly exhorted everyone to dance. Carpenter felt as if he had entered a time-warp and was fifteen again.

Meanwhile Eleanor was supervising the buffet tables which had been set up in the opposite corner of the hall. It had been essential to organize everyone into a queue in order to prevent the immediate formation of a mêlée, and Eleanor was doing her best to ensure that not too many sausage rolls were trodden into the varnished floor. Another member of staff was handing out paper plates to the queue. Several boys had fashioned these into hats and were doing impersonations of demented Chinese peasants.

Carpenter had been warned to keep an eye on the cloakroom and ensure that no alcoholic drinks were being brought into the dance. He needn't have worried; around nine o'clock several older boys started arriving already tanked up. Carpenter studied their eyes, made them utter a sentence or two, then admitted them, deciding that none was so inebriated as to be a risk to the stifling decorum of the occasion. In fact, they quickly proved an asset, being sufficiently emboldened by drink to ask girls to dance. Soon there were upwards of a dozen couples gyrating on the floor. Presently Eleanor approached him and said she thought things were going well. At that moment Terrence Torrance arrived.

He, too, had clearly been imbibing alcohol; he came swaying down the corridor with the single-minded expression of the hopelessly plastered. Carpenter moved quickly to head him off, taking him by the shoulders and steering him outside. I can't let you in there, Carpenter told him, you're drunk.

Terrence looked up at him with gleaming eyes, cidery fumes issuing from his mouth. For several moments he did not appear to recognize Carpenter. Then he heaved, stepped back, and vomited over Carpenter's desert boots.

Five minutes later Carpenter was sitting in the staff toilets in his bare feet while Eleanor sponged the vomit from his shoes and rinsed out his socks. She had followed him outside with Terrence, and had promptly arranged for the boy to be taken home by another teacher before marching the hapless Carpenter off for much-needed ablutions. Now she was insisting on driving him home in her car. The buffet was finished and the rest of the staff would be able to cope without them.

Carpenter reluctantly invited her in for coffee, conscious of how shabby and disorganized the place looked; he had never found time to do any decorating, and dirty clothes and old newspapers were strewn everywhere. Eleanor perched herself on the end of his unmade bed, her smart blue gabardine overcoat still buttoned to the neck. Carpenter selected his two best mugs and made the coffee. As they settled down to drink it, the bikers arrived and any immediate possibility of conversation was forestalled by their ritual of assembly, which entailed riding around and around for several minutes while emitting shouts of greeting heavily larded with swearwords and rodeo-like whoops.

Eleanor demurely sipped her coffee while this was going on, maintaining a studiously unconcerned expression. Carpenter took advantage of a brief hiatus in the noise to tell her that this sort of thing happened most nights and often went on until well after midnight. How can you stand living here? she asked him. Carpenter admitted that it was becoming an increasing strain.

Eleanor put her mug down on the dusty bedside table and insisted that they leave immediately and drive to her house; he could spend the night there. No, it wasn't too late, and Frank wouldn't mind at all once she had explained what had happened. There was a spare bedroom where he could sleep and get some proper rest. He looked exhausted.

Carpenter was not exhausted but he was feeling rather sorry for himself and was not relishing another night trying to sleep to a chorus of motorbike engines and prehistoric repartee. Besides which, Eleanor made it sound as if he would be doing her a favour by accompanying her home, and he could never resist people when they were being nice to him.

Her house proved to be a modern semi-detached on a quiet estate; it had pebble-dash walls and a red-tiled roof. The frosted glass panel in the front door showed a deer or some similar animal standing on a mountaintop while the sun set behind it. A wooden panel mounted among curlicues of wrought iron on the wall beside the door announced that the house was called 'Avalon'.

Eleanor opened the door and led him inside. They passed through a hallway filled with potted plants, and entered the living room. A turquoise carpet covered the floor, the wallpaper was in floral patterns of sea green, while the drapes and upholstery were peacock-blue paisley. A small white fur rug stood in front of the cream-tiled fireplace, and there were glass flamingos and brass cannons on the mantelpiece. A huge dark pebble stood on the gilt-framed coffee table, and Carpenter belatedly realized that it was an ashtray. The room was very warm.

A Siamese cat entered, and Eleanor immediately swept it up into her arms and began stroking it. His name's Oscar, she told him. Footsteps sounded on the stairs and then a large man wearing a two-tone brown silk kimono entered. It was a moment before Carpenter recognized Frank Netherton, for he had never before seen him wearing anything but a blue tracksuit and training shoes. The kimono was of standard size, but on Frank's massive frame it looked like an exotic sort of pinafore.

Although he was red in colouring and did not resemble him facially, Frank Netherton was very much in the Naas Van Dyk mould, being extremely tall and built like a shot-putter. Like Van Dyk he was taciturn in temperament, and he and Carpenter had scarcely exchanged more than a handful of words during his whole time at the school.

Eleanor explained that she had invited Carpenter to stay the night in the spare bedroom because he was having disturbances at his own place. Frank merely grunted, saying that he had been about to go to bed himself when they had arrived. Was it all right then? Eleanor enquired, something in her manner making it sound less like a request than a question to which he was expected to give the correct answer. It's all right by me, Frank said without enthusiasm, I'm off to bed.

It was only ten o'clock. He always goes to bed early, Eleanor explained, stroking the cat and heedless of its attempts to escape her embrace. Would he like a drink before she showed him where the spare bedroom was? A drink would be nice, Carpenter told her. Sherry? Martini? Or perhaps he fancied something stronger such as scotch or vodka? Or even a beer?

She fetched him a can of Carlsberg Special from the fridge, still holding the cat, who was by now writhing frantically in her arms. It escaped as they sat down in matching armchairs, fleeing out into the hallway. Well, said Eleanor, here we are. Yes, said Carpenter, gulping down his lager. Did he want some music on? An immaculate stereo stood in a glass cabinet at one corner of the room. No, no, I'm fine, Carpenter assured her, having already noted the Perry Como and Tom Jones LPs in her collection. Besides, Frank would be trying to sleep.

For some reason it was an awkward moment, but then Eleanor began to talk about the school party and soon they were conducting a postmortem of the evening and agreeing that it had been quite successful overall. They reaffirmed their belief in the general awfulness of Terrence Torrance, and Eleanor bemoaned the appalling fate of Carpenter's desert boots, which would have to be thrown out. Still, you had to laugh, didn't you? Yes, said Carpenter, simulating a hearty chuckle and thinking of how he'd like to give the little shit a boot up the backside.

His can of lager was empty, but he declined the offer of a second one, having fallen prey to the potency of Carlsberg Special on several occasions in the past. He pretended to yawn, and Eleanor got the hint. Was he tired? Well, he had to admit that he did feel a bit weary. In that case she would give him a brief tour of the house then let him get to his bed.

The tour was conducted on the pretext of letting him know where everything was, but Carpenter knew that Eleanor wanted to show off the place. They passed through the sliding glass doors into the kitchen, which proved to be a monument to culinary technology in white tile, brushed chrome and smoked glass. An array of domestic appliances had been fitted into every bit of free space, and they ranged from a humble toaster to a huge liquidizer which looked capable of turning a human head into pulp within seconds.

The hallway was decorated with bamboo-effect wallpaper and pea-green paintwork. Potted palms flanked the front door, and ferns hung from the ceiling. This rustic flavour gave way to deep red walls and Persian carpeting on the landing upstairs which made Carpenter imagine that he had suddenly wandered into some exotic oriental opium den. The bathroom was all yellow tiles and gold-plated taps, with furry brown carpeting on the floor and toilet seat cover. Everywhere it was hot.

Eleanor led him into the spare bedroom. It was decorated in pink, blue and white, with a small single bed at its centre. The headboard of the bed had a heart cut out of its centre and it looked like something out of *Alice in Wonderland*. Do you like it? she asked him. Carpenter gave a broken-backed nod. She handed him a pair of Frank's pyjamas, which were copper-coloured and with a mosaic motif. There was also a fragrant bathtowel for his personal use. Sleep well, she told him, and then she was gone.

He slept badly, awakening from dreams in which he was gulping down water without slaking his thirst. Finally he rose and crept out to the bathroom, where he drank his fill. It was stiflingly hot in the bedroom, even though he slept naked. In addition the bed was so small he had to bend his legs so that his feet didn't stick out over the edge of the mattress. It was a long night.

I slept very well, thank you, he told Eleanor as she put a bowl of porridge down in front of him the next morning. Carpenter had always hated porridge but he knew he would have to eat it. He contracted his nostrils and started spooning the stuff into his mouth as fast as was politely possible. Frank was not at the table, having risen at seven o'clock to depart for the three-mile run with which he always greeted the day. Eleanor poured tea for them both, then attended to her boiled egg and slice of Ryvita.

Carpenter still felt groggy as a result of the heat. Evidently the central heating system was on around the clock, and kept at a tropical temperature. Sometime during the night he had thrown off all his bedclothes, and when he had finally been roused by Eleanor tapping on his door to call him to breakfast, the bed looked as if he had spent the night wrestling on it.

Carpenter emptied his bowl of porridge, then relaxed his nasal cavities. Immediately its taste registered on him, the glutinous aftermath clinging to his teeth and gums. At this point Oscar suddenly leapt up on his lap, causing him to slop some of his tea down his chest. He likes you, said Eleanor, as the cat proceeded to nuzzle his groin.

Frank returned from his run shortly before eight-thirty and went straight to the bathroom to shower without greeting either of them. He rode a bicycle to work each morning. After breakfast Eleanor got the car out of the garage and she and Carpenter departed. Frank had not yet emerged from the bathroom, but Carpenter half-expected him to pass them on his ten-speed derailleur along the way. Meanwhile Eleanor was telling him that he really had to find himself a new place but was welcome to use their spare bedroom if ever he found himself in difficulties again.

Term ended a few days later and Carpenter returned to Manchester to find that Gail had left Graham and was now going out with a market researcher from Prestwich whom Carpenter had never met. He was apparently five years older than her, and Gail had known him for some years. The news was unprecedented and seemed quite contrary to the laws of nature: Carpenter had never really imagined that Gail would ever give Graham up. He was also disappointed that she had not turned to him in the event; it was confirmation that his infatuation for her was hopeless. He saw neither Gail nor Graham over the holidays and was thus unable to discover what had caused the split; Gail had gone to the Peak District to stay with her new boyfriend's relatives, while Graham was still playing with Fiasco in London and by all accounts had accommodated himself to life without her.

He bought his mother an electric blanket for Christmas since she had begun to complain of the cold. She looked haggard and her hair was turning white, though she continued to insist that there was nothing wrong with her. It was a chilly, rainswept holiday, with Carpenter feeling like a stranger in all his old haunts. He wrote to Veronica just before his return to Blackpool, telling her that he was now teaching and describing the job in enthusiastic terms which were more applicable to his most optimistic phase a year previously than his present uncertainty. This was less deceit than a desire to see what criticisms she might have to level against the job when presented in its best light. Only much later did it occur to him that he had been seeking from her cogent reasons for removing himself from the school altogether.

On his return to Blackpool he discovered that the few letters which had been delivered over the holiday lay damp and yellowish on the doormat at the foot of the stairs. Someone had pissed through his letter box while he had been away. He put the letters in the oven on a low heat and sat morosely on his bed, thinking that he would have to find a new place to live.

Still morose on the first day of term, he came upon Eleanor in the corridor outside the staffroom. They exchanged pleasantries, and then Eleanor announced that she had been talking to Frank over Christmas and he had agreed that they would rent him the spare bedroom in their house at ten pounds a week until he could find a new place of his own to stay. She really hoped he would accept the offer and at least stay there until the end of term; apart from anything else, the extra income would be useful to them.

Carpenter immediately said yes. He felt too weary to face the prospect of traipsing around Blackpool in search of a new place, the motorbike crowd having resumed their midnight meetings at the amusement arcade the day after his return and having added klaxon horns to increase their nuisance value. Any misgivings which he felt about the idea of lodging at Eleanor's – and they were several – were outweighed by the prospect of being able to sleep in peace.

They did the moving in stages, Eleanor filling up her car with his belongings each evening and ferrying them to her house. By the end of the week everything had been transferred, and Carpenter formally moved in that Sunday. Eleanor had provided him with a small desk at which he could work in the evenings, and she assured him that he would have all the privacy he needed while at the same time insisting that he feel free to use the facilities of the house as his own. Carpenter, abashed by her hospitality, managed to persuade her that he preferred not to eat breakfast and would settle for a simple cup of coffee. But Eleanor was adamant that he join her and Frank for dinner in the evenings.

Frank had been conspicuous by his absence during the week of his moving, and it transpired that he spent most evenings either training with a local basketball team or attending judo classes at a sports centre in Lytham. Carpenter never discovered whether the latter activity was conducted in the capacity of trainee or instructor; he felt it better not to ask. When Frank was at home he seemed to accept Carpenter's presence in the house without resentment or enthusiasm, seldom initiating any conversations between them. At first Carpenter took his stolidness as a sign of disapproval until he realized that he behaved in a similar way towards Eleanor. He was a man of few words and emotions whose only passion seemed to be the maintenance of his muscle-bound body.

Frank seldom arrived home in the evenings before nine o'clock, and consequently dinner was postponed until then. Carpenter used the time to attend to his homework, growing ever more ravenous until Eleanor tapped on his door with a cup of tea and a plate of biscuits around seven-thirty. Afterwards he would hear her preparing dinner downstairs. Frank preferred food of the plain and wholesome variety so that each evening they sat down to large portions of steak and kidney pie, liver and bacon dumpling or Lancashire hot-pot, followed by custard tart, rice pudding or strawberry flan. It was like a more elaborate version of school dinners. Frank always retired by ten-thirty at the latest, and Carpenter would sit making polite conversation with Eleanor in front of the television for a further half hour before he, too, climbed the stairs and went to bed with a book.

He got used to the smallness of the bed, but his bedroom, like the rest of the house, remained hot, and no amount of fiddling with the dial on the radiator under the window succeeded in reducing the temperature by any noticeable margin. He would eventually lapse into a drugged sleep, filled with anxiety dreams in which he was being ridiculed by his classes or had spilled his dinner over Eleanor's best upholstery. In the morning he would be roused by Frank's noisy ablutions in the bathroom preparatory to his run. Afterwards he would lie there in his cocoon of twisted sheets, feeling parched and just as soporific as when he had gone to bed.

On Saturdays he rose early, made his excuses and departed, ostensibly to go sightseeing. In fact he took a bus into Blackpool and spent most of the day in public libraries, recapturing the fervour for reading which had possessed him during his second year in Bristol. Afterwards he would go to see a film or have a few drinks in pubs along the Golden Mile before his return to Eleanor's.

Sundays were rather more difficult. Frank's one concession to indolence was to lie in bed on Sunday mornings until Eleanor summoned him to lunch, but although Carpenter tried to emulate him, he rarely managed to stay in bed beyond eleven o'clock. After a cup of coffee he would accompany Eleanor on a constitutional which usually involved making a circuit of the nearby golf course while discussing the weather. Sunday lunch tended to be a traditional affair of roast beef or lamb with huge helpings of vegetables and gravy. Afterwards they would sit around watching television, with Eleanor instantly rising and switching channels the moment *The Big Match* was announced.

He noticed that Frank and Eleanor seldom sat together on the sofa, Frank preferring to lounge in an armchair, Eleanor favouring an upright studio chair in tubular steel and white canvas. Frank would stare at the screen with a disinterested fixity, while Eleanor usually had Oscar draped across her. She would absently stroke the cat in a manner designed to ensure that it remained firmly on her lap. She and Frank seemed less a married couple at these times than two strangers who had been thrown together in some over-furnished airport lounge, whiling away the time before they received calls to their separate flights.

Eventually it would be time to eat again, and Eleanor would emerge from the kitchen with scones or crumpets, followed by a variety of home-made cakes. Like most dedicated cooks, she ate little of her own produce, and the lion's share usually fell to Frank, who was capable of putting a whole slice of gateau into his mouth without looking away from the television screen. At some stage Oscar would migrate to Carpenter's lap, and happily settle down under his lack of molestation. Unfortunately it had a habit of exuding noxious farts into his face just as he was about to bite into a coconut kiss or a slice of lemon meringue pie. Carpenter showed great self-control on these occasions by resisting the urge to hurl it across the room. Comatose from too much food and heat, he was then a captive audience to the television and to Eleanor's conversational forays until he finally summoned the energy to climb the stairs to bed. What I need, he would tell himself, is some obsessive hobby such as writing poetry or building model aeroplanes so that I'd have the excuse to spend hours alone in my room. Sundays weighed heavily on him, as they had always done.

Meanwhile at school the boys in his classes were growing increasingly insolent, and when he arrived one morning for a class with Four Delta and found Terrence Torrance hammering down his lectern top with three-inch nails and half a sandbrick, he had no compunction in marching him off to Mr Rawcliffe and demanding six of the best. But he sensed that it was too late, that the boys in the school had finally got his measure and saw him as a soft option whom they could take liberties with. Carpenter resented this because he knew it was essentially true; he was a weakling who could only deal with gross acts of misbehaviour by passing the responsibility on to someone else.

In February his spirits were briefly raised when his mother forwarded a letter which turned out to be an invitation from Nick Bullivant to attend a reunion party at his parents' house in Wiltshire over Easter. Nick was inviting most of the people he had known in Cardiff and indicated that they would have the run of the house since his parents would be holidaying in Jamaica. Carpenter determined to attend.

The weeks drifted by, and Carpenter grew plumper on Eleanor's cooking. Frank's fanaticism for exercise now seemed more understandable as a means of preventing complete inertia from setting in. Meanwhile Eleanor showed a growing inclination to have candid conversations with him about matters of concern to her. These covered a wide range of subjects from the pros and cons of marriage to gossip about various members of staff at the school, but two main preoccupations emerged. The first was that people shouldn't become slaves to their possessions, and the second involved the subject of having children. On this latter topic Eleanor was eloquent, telling Carpenter that while she wasn't against the idea of having children *per se* – for heaven's sake she had chosen a job which involved working with them – she and Frank had thought hard about starting a family before deciding against it, at least for the time being. Frank in particular was adamant that children tied you down; he took the view that they should wait a few years until they were both settled and financially secure in their careers.

It was hard to imagine Frank being adamant about anything, except in a purely physical sense, but Eleanor's stroking of the cat would redouble as if to emphasize the point. Carpenter always indicated tacit agreement with whatever she was saying, though he could think of equally good reasons for amassing huge amounts of property and filling the world up with as many children as possible. Children and possessions were not subjects which had ever preoccupied him greatly because he tended to avoid thinking about marriage and the idea of settling down.

One evening, an hour before Frank was due home from a training session, Carpenter was marking books when Eleanor tapped on the door and entered with his tea and biscuits. She set them down beside him then sat on the corner of the bed, giving a small sigh which seemed to indicate a general sense of dissatisfaction with the world. When she said nothing, Carpenter asked her if something was wrong. She shook her head and urged him to continue with his marking as if she wasn't there. Somewhat sheepishly, Carpenter obliged, but the silence made him increasingly nervous. Then Eleanor asked him in a quiet voice if he didn't think that most people led lives of quiet desperation.

Some faint tremor of alarm passed through Carpenter. He considered a number of responses before saying he supposed they did. Eleanor gave a further contemplative sigh, then said that if one accepted this, did he not think that people should try to grasp moments of happiness or even ecstasy whenever they could and no matter how difficult the circumstances might be?

This was an even thornier question, the presence of the word 'ecstasy' making it fraught with danger. Carpenter hesitated, then agreed that this seemed quite a reasonable policy to him in situations where moments of happiness and pleasure tended to be rare or absent in the normal course of events.

Eleanor smiled and told him she was pleased he felt the same way. And didn't he think that if two people were strongly attracted to one another then they owed it to themselves to express this attraction if it was possible to do so without harming anyone else? Carpenter didn't like the sound of this at all, but he had no choice but to affirm that he could see nothing wrong with this notion in a theoretical sense.

Eleanor rose, smoothed down her pleated skirt, and said she was glad they understood one another. Then she announced that she had to go and get dinner ready, whereupon she departed.

Carpenter spent the rest of the evening in a mild state of apprehension, but nothing untoward happened. He went to bed at the same time as Frank, pleading the onset of a cold.

The following morning he was awoken when someone sat on his arm. It was Eleanor, dressed in a purple quilted housecoat. Carpenter sat up groggily, asking her the time and wondering if she was wearing anything under the coat.

Eleanor told him that it was seven-thirty; she was sorry to disturb him but she needed his help. Later today she was taking a class on a nature ramble along the beach, and she kept the worksheets for such occasions in a large suitcase on top of the wardrobe in her bedroom. The suitcase could only be reached by standing on the stepladder which she had already brought upstairs for the purpose, but it was rickety and could he hold it for her while she climbed up? She'd meant to ask Frank before he went out on his run but she'd forgotten.

Carpenter told her that he would be quite happy to oblige, and could she pass him his dressing gown, which was hanging on the back of the door. He managed to get it on without revealing any intimate parts of his body to her. By now he had decided that she did not have anything on under the housecoat, which was secured around her waist by a loosely tied rope belt.

Her bedroom was decorated in shades of lilac and mauve, the bed having an elaborate padded headboard and a purple quilted coverlet which exactly matched Eleanor's housecoat. The stepladder was indeed rickety, but Eleanor declined his offer to mount the steps, saying that the suitcase was unlocked and that she only had to reach inside and grab a handful of the worksheets. But on the way up she stumbled and overbalanced into his arms. There was a still moment in which her face was mere inches from his, and he knew he had no option but to kiss her.

At first he ensured that it was the kind of kiss which could immediately be broken if necessary, but her mouth opened wide at the touch of his lips, eager, welcoming. As the kiss went on her hands came up and rested lightly on his waist, while her housecoat fell open, revealing her tremendous bosom. She began to tremble, then took his wrists and put his hands on her breasts. Oh Mike, he heard her gasp as she pressed herself to him.

They made love on the purple coverlet, with Eleanor still wearing her housecoat, though Carpenter managed to throw off his dressing gown. Eleanor was extremely responsive, trembling and making affirmative noises throughout while peering into his face with an adoring expression. At first this was sufficient to inflame Carpenter, but as their lovemaking went on he noticed that she had not once closed her eyes or looked away from his face so that he began to feel as if she was assessing his performance.

Then she gave a loud gasp and went limp. He realized that she had come. This quickly precipitated his own climax, which he signalled with a similar gasp. In the aftermath he slumped across her and she hugged him tightly. Immediately he started to think of Frank with a mixture of guilt and fear. What have I done? he thought. What if he finds out?

Eleanor stroked his hair while continuing to hug him. He became preoccupied with the possibility that Frank might return at any moment, and he tried to think of a tactful way in which he could extricate himself from her embrace.

I know you're worried about Frank, Eleanor said out of the silence, confirming his notion that any woman whom he so much as kissed immediately developed the ability to read his mind. She went on to assure him that there was no need to feel guilty; the thing was, in the last year or so she and Frank had been living together more as brother and sister than man and wife, and while she was still fond of him and didn't want to do anything to hurt him, the passion had gone out of their marriage. For some reason Frank no longer had any appetite for the physical side of things. But most women needed to be loved as well as having companionship, and she had increasingly found herself prey to unsatisfied urges. She had recognized that he, Carpenter, was an emotional and compassionate man, and was it a crime that she had turned to him for the physical gratification which Frank no longer provided her?

Before Carpenter could answer this the doorbell rang. He hurled himself off the bed, dashed across the landing and locked himself in the bathroom, his heart pounding. Then he realized that he had left his dressing gown in a heap at the foot of the bed. He had begun to envisage an enraged Frank tearing the bathroom door off its hinges when it occurred to him that Frank would not have rung his own doorbell.

Emotional and compassionate, thought Carpenter as he eased open the door; neither adjective seemed remotely applicable to him. He crept to the head of the landing and peered down the stairs. Eleanor was taking delivery of a parcel which proved to be a new tracksuit for Frank. It was at this point that Carpenter remembered he had once again forgotten to ask about contraception.

Later, when she was driving him to school, she assured him that he need have no worries on that score. She looked flushed and delighted by what had happened, telling him that they would have to be discreet but that they had discovered something too rare between themselves to turn back now. Carpenter was unclear as to what exactly was rare or had been discovered, but he thought it better not to ask. What was clear was that he had committed himself willy-nilly to an affair with her.

As soon as they entered the school gates Eleanor reverted to her traditional role as the busy and efficient schoolmistress. The day passed uneventfully. Then he learned that by coincidence Frank had no sporting commitments that evening and had decided to leave his bicycle at the school and travel home with them in the car.

Carpenter sat in the back seat, convinced that he knew something. Eleanor was self-possession itself, but somehow this only made Carpenter more nervous that at any moment Frank would turn and accuse him of cuckoldry. And then what? Then Frank would probably fling himself over the passenger seat and beat the shit out of him.

Nothing of this sort happened. Carpenter stayed in his room that evening, marking homework until his dinner was on the table. Afterwards he immediately returned to the task, claiming pressure of work. He was aware that he might succeed in arousing Frank's suspicions by his very avoidance of spending time with Eleanor, but The Secret Lover was not a role into which he could settle easily, especially when he had to share the same living room with his lover's husband. That night sleep was a long time coming.

The next morning he was woken by Eleanor's call to coffee. Frank had already departed, but she made no reference to what had happened the previous morning and he wondered if she had had second thoughts about the whole incident and preferred to forget it as an unfortunate lapse which would not be repeated. This notion made him feel at once relieved and disappointed. Then she leaned forward and squeezed his shoulder before planting a kiss on the top of his head.

That evening they made love on the sofa in the living room while Frank was at his judo class. It happened quite unexpectedly, with Eleanor sitting down beside him while he was drinking the cup of tea which she always provided for him on their return from school. She put her arms around his neck and drew his mouth on hers. The tea grew cold in the cup as they hastily removed their clothing and fell upon one another. While they were in the throes of the act, Oscar entered and sat down on the fur rug, watching them with a disinterest which Carpenter found quite off-putting. Eleanor came twice before he attainec his own climax.

With this second bout of lovemaking Carpenter knew that their affair had been formally launched and that he could not turn back now. He always left Eleanor to take the initiative, and from then on she would either come to his bedroom in the morning when Frank was out running, or they would make love in the living room before he came home for dinner. In purely physical terms, their lovemaking was exciting in its illicitness and in Eleanor's responsiveness to him: she invariably came within minutes of penetration. Although they never deviated from the missionary position, they maintained a certain variety by doing it on armchairs or on the floor or even, on one occasion, at the top of the stairs.

Over a period of weeks Carpenter's fear that Frank would discover their affair diminished through simple habituation; but a corresponding problem arose in that it began to take him longer and longer to reach his own climax. Eleanor's habit of staring at him throughout their lovemaking was disconcerting and tended to inhibit his spontaneity and capacity for erotic fantasy. Then one evening while they were doing it on the sofa in the front room he suddenly imagined Frank entering through the front door and about to catch them in the act. His climax came in a rush. He was to evoke similar fantasies whenever they made love from then on.

The Easter holidays arrived, and Carpenter departed to Manchester with a renewed confidence born of his affair with Eleanor. He felt insouciant, worldly-wise, tempered in the furnace of experience. There was a letter from Veronica awaiting him at his mother's in which she informed him that she was now going out with an eclectic pyschotherapist at a clinic in London. She was working as an aide in his psychodrama group, and he was helping her towards a discovery of her orgasm through gestalt techniques which involved invoking her parents and having imaginary conversations with them in which she told them how they had mindfucked her as a child. In the final paragraph she announced that she had profound reservations about traditional teaching within the typical repressive school context; she hoped he wasn't employing stereotyped role-models or relying on institutional pressures to achieve his aims; it was essential to see the difference between good examination results and a child's real growth.

There was no mention of Nick Bullivant's reunion party in the letter, so Carpenter dispatched a short note saying that he hoped to see her there. He saw neither Graham nor Gail that holiday: Graham was still playing in London with Fiasco, while Gail had gone off for a rambling holiday in the Peak District with her market researcher boyfriend, whom Carpenter discovered was called Desmond Ormerod. Somehow it was hard to imagine Gail going out with anyone called Desmond Ormerod, but there it was.

Nick Bullivant's parents' house turned out to be a small mansion near Savernake Forest, set in spacious grounds. Carpenter arrived late on the Saturday afternoon, having decided to hitchhike from Manchester and having somehow contrived to get himself stranded at Spaghetti Junction for over two hours. The party was already in full swing, with Bullivant drunk on champagne and scarcely capable of recognizing Carpenter, let alone having a conversation with him. Duffy was also there, newly married to someone Carpenter had never met before and looking tanned and wealthy in a three-piece suit. He had been working in Bahrain for the last eighteen months, and told Carpenter that he had bought a house in Croydon which had sitting tenants while he was living abroad whose rent paid for his mortgage and left him with a small profit into the bargain. He talked of investments, of tax dodges and insurance schemes, and the more he talked the more Carpenter realized that Duffy had become a stranger to him.

He kept expecting Veronica to appear, but there was no sign of her. Then Alison arrived with a short, bespectacled man whom she introduced as her husband, Ray. Ray wore a check sports jacket and a diffident smile. He told Carpenter that he was a computer engineer; he and Alison had married six months previously and were living in Wisbech. He seemed a pleasant enough man, though he was clearly in awe of the increasingly drunken revelries around him, into which Alison was soon throwing herself. Later Carpenter managed to get a few minutes alone with her and she told him that she had gone to live in South Africa for a few years with Naas Van Dyk after their engagement. No, she hadn't married him, and she had eventually come home because she didn't like the country and things hadn't worked out between them. She had met Ray shortly after her return.

Alison was friendly and seemed pleased to see him, but Carpenter sensed an absence of the humour and spontaneity which had once marked their friendship. As the evening wore on a vague melancholy descended on him; he felt isolated, abandoned, unable to connect with people who had once been among his closest friends. Then a young female cousin of Bullivant's started taking an interest in him for no obvious reason he could discern. She was short, pretty and energetic, dragging him on to the floor in the drawing room. Carpenter sustained himself with swigs of Newcastle Brown in between dances and found it easier to surrender to the present as it became clear that the girl, whose name was Cicely, was genuinely attracted to him. He felt the confidence he had brought with him from Blackpool returning as he gyrated to old favourites like 'Hi-Ho Silver Lining' and 'Reelin' in the Years'.

Later, during a riotous conga around the house, Cicely detached him from the throng and led him into an empty bedroom in a quiet part of the house. Within minutes they were both naked, but Carpenter's usual problem of first night nerves was compounded by brewer's droop so that penetration proved impossible. He was saved prolonged embarrassment by the fact that Cicely was even drunker than himself and finally passed out while he was breathing passionately in her ear. Later in the night he awoke to find her fondling him and was erect within seconds. She proved just as energetic and demanding in lovemaking as in dancing, and a grey dawn had broken before they subsided into sleep.

When Carpenter woke again the afternoon was well advanced and Cicely was gone from the bed. He wandered around the house, where only the stragglers of the party remained. Both Duffy and Alison had departed, while Bullivant was still abed and not expected to emerge until it was dark again. He found Cicely drinking white wine in the spacious kitchen with a small group of people who were obviously her close friends. While she was not unfriendly to him, he understood within seconds that there was to be no resumption of the intimacies which they had shared the night before. He surprised himself by accepting this quite matter-of-factly.

There was a spare seat in a car which was headed for Sheffield, and Carpenter immediately accepted the offer of a lift. He sat in the back seat during the long drive north, staring through the window with the glum frame of mind of someone who knows that the past is a foreign country. The probability that he would never see Duffy or Bullivant again depressed him less than the realization that he did not particularly want to, while people like Alison and Veronica were now leading lives which could only diverge more and more from his.

His mother was looking healthier than she had done in the past year, and he was consequently more relaxed in her presence. Through a mutual friend he received an invitation from Graham to go to London for a few days and watch Fiasco perform. He was tempted, but decided against it, not wanting to risk any further disillusionment after the bittersweet experience of Bullivant's party. He realized that he had grown so accustomed to thinking of Graham and Gail as a unit that he did not relish the prospect of meeting either of them alone. Instead his thoughts were focused on Blackpool, where at least Eleanor awaited him.

He spent the rest of the holiday at home with his mother, and returned to Blackpool three days before the start of term to find that Frank was visiting relatives in Leicester and was not due back for two more days. He and Eleanor made love all over the house while he was away. Carpenter was filled with sexual energy, his enjoyment of Eleanor being considerably enhanced by visions of the nubile and eager Cicely, in comparison with whom Eleanor now seemed just a shade matronly and domestic.

The school term proceeded with Carpenter determined to assert his authority over his classes. He structured his lessons more rigorously, doing less talking and more dictation, reducing the amount of practical work in favour of demonstrations, and generally contriving to ensure that there was minimum opportunity for mischief. Whenever someone did misbehave he made the offender stand in the corner with his face to the wall for the rest of the lesson; hardened offenders were summarily dispatched to Mr

Rawcliffe. Carpenter justified these measures to himself on the principle that firmness now would enable him to relax his regimen later, when his pupils had learned that he was not to be trifled with.

Meanwhile Frank had joined a weight-lifting club and was now spending even less time at home. Far from seeing this as a bonus which gave him more opportunity for adultery with Eleanor, Carpenter was immediately suspicious that Frank had purposely arranged to be absent from the house in the evenings as much as possible. It was as if he didn't care what Eleanor did while he was away. At the same time Carpenter felt sure that Frank was not the sort of man who would countenance her having an affair without making a very physical protest. He finally decided that Frank hadn't stepped aside to let him, Carpenter, in; he had done so to give himself some air.

Carpenter came to this conclusion by virtue of his growing intimacy with Eleanor in all her aspects. At school she had always been a great organizer and orchestrator, and it was clear that she was also master of her household. Carpenter knew that the house had been furnished to her specifications, not excluding Frank as an essential part of it; he could not imagine Frank wearing a kimono except under the influence of a persuasive and insistent wife. One Saturday afternoon while Frank was playing basketball Eleanor persuaded him to accompany her on a shopping expedition, and Carpenter found himself standing outside a branch of Burton's while Eleanor told him how nice she thought a particular Norfolk jacket looked and how much it would suit him. Similar selections of a shirt, trousers and tie followed, all notable for being the kind of clothes he wouldn't be seen dead in. Suddenly, like a small mammal scenting danger, he wanted to bolt for cover.

In various small ways from then on he found Eleanor attempting to remake him in an image more suitable to her. She never did more than hint or suggest changes in his wardrobe, but he was sure that if they had been husband and wife she would have made her case more forcibly. He realized that their affair had now passed beyond the exciting getting-to-know stage where sheer novelty and a sense of discovery is sufficient; now she had his measure, and hence a measure of what she saw as his shortcomings, to be appropriately remedied. He remembered only too well how Veronica had tried to remake his mind; now here was Eleanor, who wanted to find him a new tailor.

Carpenter said nothing, though a sense of impending doom continued to grow in him. From that time on his trysts with Eleanor began to seem more like a chore than a pleasure; her watchfulness in their lovemaking more off-putting than ever.

He did his best to give himself as much free time alone as possible. That spring United reached their third Cup Final in four years, and Carpenter felt that the gods had smiled on him when Eleanor and Frank chose to spend the weekend of the game visiting Eleanor's parents in Doncaster. He got in supplies of beer and prepared to settle down for a comfortable afternoon. But earlier he had piled far too much cat food into Oscar's dish, and ten minutes before the game started the cat regurgitated it over the white rug in front of the fireplace. By the time Carpenter had cleared up the mess, United were 2–0 down to Arsenal, and they went on to lose 3–2.

Alone in bed at nights, Carpenter found himself reading intricate novels about difficult love affairs and psychology titles on interpersonal relationships. One Saturday afternoon he even took a train to Leeds to hear one of his favourite authors give a talk. The man produced witty and insightful novels, but in person he proved to be pompous and utterly devoid of charm. Carpenter felt cheated, betrayed: the man was nothing like his books and had learned none of the lessons contained in them.

The experience so disillusioned him that he decided to give up serious reading for instruction. He came to the conclusion that real life was far more intractable than any novel or psychological theory and that books could provide no answers to the practicalities of living. But he only grew more dissatisfied. At school he became irritable and short-tempered, finding his lessons a growing strain. One afternoon towards the end of term he was doing a routine demonstration of the properties of the alkali metals which involved dropping a piece of sodium metal into a trough of water. Normally the sodium promptly reacted with the water, melting into a small blob which fizzed along the surface, generating hydrogen and steam. But on this occasion he used too large a piece, so that when he dropped the lump of metal on to the water, it exploded, splattering his face with water.

When the steam had cleared he saw that all the class were stifling giggles, but he focused on a boy at the front of the class who was red-faced and vibrating with suppressed laughter. Before he knew it, Carpenter had grabbed him and was marching him off to Mr Rawcliffe's office.

On their admission Carpenter announced that the boy had been impertinent and disruptive. The headmaster studied the damp lapels of Carpenter's jacket and drew his own conclusions. He asked the boy if he had anything to say. The boy, dumb with bewilderment and fright, shook his head.

At this point Carpenter recalled that the boy was one of his more diligent pupils who never gave him any trouble. He left the office feeling like Judas Iscariot. And when the boy returned to his class minutes later, his eyes bright with tears, he was ashamed.

The next morning he and Eleanor were lying on his bed, having just made love, when Eleanor announced that she was thinking of asking Frank for a divorce. Carpenter sat up slowly, suddenly wanting to be as far away from her as possible. In recent weeks he had been taking an inordinate time to reach orgasm, and detumescence often left him feeling nothing but a vague disgust with himself. Now his whole situation came into stark focus, and he saw Eleanor as a lonely and insecure woman who had been used by him for sexual release. No matter that it was she who had initiated the affair, for he had allowed it to happen; he would never have moved into her house in the first place had he not secretly recognized that she was attracted to him and that an affair was more or less inevitable once he was on the premises. But his chief source of pleasure in the affair had not been Eleanor herself but the thrill of bedding someone else's wife. She, however, had obviously assumed a greater commitment than he was prepared to make.

Dismayed with himself, he also saw the kind of teacher he had become. He realized he had grown so obsessed with establishing his authority in the classroom that his methods were becoming callous. He lacked a real sense of commitment to the work, and it was only a matter of time before he turned into the kind of teacher he had always hated when he had been a schoolboy.

He looked at Eleanor, then told her he was intending to leave teaching at the end of the term and return to Manchester. Eleanor stared back at him for a long while without speaking, and he felt like a worm. I see, she said finally, then rose from the bed and wrapped her housecoat tightly around her before departing to her own bedroom. He heard the door close pointedly. Though he knew the only decent thing to do would be to follow her and try to explain his decision, he did not move.

The two remaining weeks which he spent at Eleanor's were difficult, but he bore them as a penance. She treated him with conspicuous politeness, even continuing to drive him to school each morning; but their conversations remained scrupulously prosaic and she never referred to their affair. There were numerous occasions when Carpenter felt that he should broach the subject, but he could never summon the courage to do so. At the same time he remained apprehensive that she might seek to revenge herself on him by telling Frank about their relationship; but somehow this never seemed very likely. Frank remained his phlegmatic self, unmoved by or conscious of the tense atmosphere around him. The dismal conviction grew in Carpenter that in twenty years' time they would probably still be married.

Mr Rawcliffe was suitably surprised when he tendered his resignation, telling him that he had been making steady progress and wanting to know what had precipitated his decision to leave teaching. Carpenter replied that it was a personal matter which he did not feel he could discuss. Mr Rawcliffe enquired if there was any way in which this matter could be resolved without him having to resign. No, Carpenter informed him, there was not; he had thought long and hard about it and his decision was final. Mr Rawcliffe nodded and immediately became more businesslike, briskly dashing off a reference which extolled Carpenter's qualities as a teacher and all-round human being.

Insincere though the reference was, it would be useful to him in practical terms. Showing rare foresight, Carpenter had already replied to an advertisement in the *Guardian* for an Assistant Product Manager with a canned food manufacturer based in North London. He had promptly received an application form which he had even more promptly completed and returned, giving his permanent address as his mother's. He had practically no idea what the duties of an assistant product manager entailed, but he wanted to get as far away from Blackpool as possible, and the salary was certainly attractive.

Carpenter had arranged for a friend from Manchester who owned a van to drive him and his belongings home at the end of term. His friend duly arrived shortly after lunch on the appointed day, and everything was quickly installed in the back of the van. It was a Saturday afternoon, and Frank had forgone a basketball game to bid him farewell. Eleanor was at her most subdued and hence appealing, making him feel despicable all over again. She found a private moment to take him aside and ask him if he would write to her. He promised that he would. It was his final lie.

*

'Coffee, Carpenter,' said Peacock as he rattled past his cell with the trolley.

Carpenter hadn't even realized that the guards had changed. He got off his bed and went to the bathroom. The right-hand cubicle door was closed.

'It's only me,' he said.

'What do you want?' came the irate voice of Wright.

'I don't want anything. I just came to use the facilities.'

He entered the cubicle next door.

'Where's Treadwell?' Wright asked.

'Probably in the lounge, waiting for his coffee.'

'He's supposed to be keeping alert.'

'Is he supposed to warn you about my movements?'

'We have to keep an eye on everyone if we're to ensure that we won't be disturbed.'

'I thought you told him not to panic.'

'I don't see what business this is of yours, Carpenter. You're doing nothing to help.'

'Sorry I spoke.'

'It's a matter of principle. If you don't participate in something you can't expect to have a say in how it's run.'

Carpenter marvelled at how effortlessly Wright could elevate a passing comment into a lecture on participatory democracy. He sat down on the toilet seat cover, waiting for Wright to clear up and leave. He'd always had difficulty relieving himself when there was anyone else around, whether they were able to see him or not. It was silly, really, but there was nothing he could do about it. He'd once missed most of the second half of a match at Old Trafford while lingering outside the toilet with a bursting bladder, waiting for the place to empty. Veronica claimed that the problem was rooted in his fear of other men's sexuality. Perhaps this was true; but it was of no practical help at all.

*

While washing his hands, Carpenter experienced the urge to scrawl graffiti over the white-tiled walls, to make some profound or scathing or simply obscene statement. But he could think of nothing appropriate. And besides, he had no pen.

He'd once read a book about graffiti which had taken over three hundred pages to reach the startling conclusion that it was rooted in the fundamental human urge to express oneself. Carpenter had seldom felt the urge to deface public surfaces himself, but he had always thought that everyone would benefit from being able to make a concise statement of his or her basic beliefs. This had once led him to invent the idea of Personal Philosophy slogans which were to be printed on T-shirts to improve communication between people. The idea was that every person had a particular sentence or phrase which summed up his general attitude towards life. Each Personal Philosophy slogan was to be selected very carefully by the individual in question for the express purpose of self-description. The slogan would then be emblazoned on a T-shirt, to be worn at social gatherings or anywhere else so that people knew how you felt about things in general.

Carpenter first mooted the idea one evening at the house in Ludlow when he was sitting around with Graham and the rest of them, smoking grass and feeling in a frivolously philosophical frame of mind. Soon everyone was engrossed in the game of selecting slogans for themselves. One drawback quickly emerged when it became clear that a person's own choice seldom corresponded with what close friends might select for him; but this in itself was revealing, allowing pertinent comparisons to be made between self-image and public persona. It was also agreed that people's slogans might change during the course of their lives, reflecting changing circumstances and attitudes. But as parlour games went, the idea had a certain loony appeal and it kept them entertained for the rest of the evening. From time to time since then Carpenter would amuse himself by inventing such slogans for people he knew.

He considered his fellow inmates. Treadwell had already proffered his own slogan with *Time and Patience*, and this seemed as apt as anything. Wright was a clear case of *That's not the point*, while Sinnott lived the plea *Don't hurt me*. But Riley stumped him; even after considerable thought Carpenter could think of nothing that satisfactorily described his quirky and elusive character.

Everyone was assembled in the lounge when he entered, and happily there was no sign of Harris. The coffee breaks were now back to normal, and today there was a large plate of Jaffa Cakes accompanying the trolley. Carpenter took three, checking them for signs of adulteration before popping one into his mouth.

While he munched, he contemplated Limbo's staff vis-à-vis his Personal Philosophy slogans, and finally drew up a mental list:

Naughton: *I won't stand for it*
Dr Dempster: *How are you feeling?*
Snider: *Watch your step*
Hemmings: *Not bothering you, am I?*
Peacock: *This is beneath me*
Harris: *I hate your guts*

Carpenter did not delude himself that these slogans reflected anything more than his own perceptions of the staff, but the game was interesting for its very subjectivity. Ideally, though, each person's slogan was the most reliable, providing that it was chosen as honestly and as accurately as possible. Carpenter had derived his own from his conviction that the accumulation of knowledge and experience did not bring wisdom or peace of mind. His slogan was: *It doesn't help*.

*

Carpenter watched an Open University programme in which a man in a beige safari jacket and horn-rimmed glasses was gesticulating at a complicated mathematical construction on a blackboard while talking with considerable rapidity about sets and transformations. The man was communicating great enthusiasm for his subject, but Carpenter had no idea what he was talking about.

Everyone else was in the games room, but presently Wright emerged and took a seat opposite him. Carpenter kept his eyes on the screen, but he immediately knew that Wright wanted to talk to him.

'I've come to ask you a favour,' he said at length.

'A favour?'

Wright mumbled something.

'What?' said Carpenter.

'We need your help.'

'My help? What for?'

'The tunnel,' Wright murmured.

'The tunnel – '

'Keep your voice down.' Wright looked around him like a character from an espionage film.

'I thought you were making good progress,' Carpenter said. 'I thought you were going to be through the wall in another few days.'

'We are,' said Wright. 'We fully intend to. But we've reached the stage where we consider it prudent to have a third party involved.'

Carpenter was tempted to make a joke about third-party insurance, but he thought better of it. He fished out a cigarette and lit up, hoping it would make Wright go away. But he was still waiting.

'Why don't you try Sinnott again?' Carpenter said.

'You know he's too frightened to do anything to help himself.'

'What about Riley?'

'Riley? You must be mad. He'd be more of a hindrance than a help. We need you, Carpenter. The guards are getting suspicious.

With only two of us it's easier for them to notice our absence. With three of us it wouldn't be so obvious.'

'What wouldn't be so obvious?'

'That we were making frequent visits to the bathroom.'

'If you'd eaten the baked apple last night you'd have every excuse to spend half the day in there.'

'You simply refuse to take this seriously, don't you? Your attitude mystifies me, Carpenter. You're not a coward like Sinnott or an idiot like Riley, and yet you're content to sit here and do nothing.'

'How do you know I'm not a coward?'

Wright gave a small sigh. 'Is it just that you dislike me personally? I am aware, you know, that not everyone sees things as I do. I don't see that that's any reason for us not to work together when we have common interests and goals. I can't believe that you're content to do nothing to gain your freedom.'

'What's the point of boring a hole through a wall unless you know where it leads? What if you're right about us being underwater? What if you break through the outer wall and have the whole Channel pouring in here?'

'I don't think that's very likely. I've revised my original calculations and I now think it's more probable we're in the London area.'

Very convenient, Carpenter thought; no one else had ever seriously imagined they were anywhere else. But Wright was not the type to accept a consensus view unless he could pretend to have arrived at it independently.

'What if we're twenty floors up in a skyscaper?' said Carpenter. 'Boring a hole in a wall isn't going to help much if we are.'

'Why do you persist in being so negative? We have to explore every option available to us. At least Treadwell and I are doing something constructive.'

'I can't see anything very constructive about digging a hole in a wall without knowing where it's going.'

'It's going out, Carpenter. And we're going through it to freedom.'

'No you aren't,' Carpenter said dully.

Harris had just walked into the room behind Wright. He was

holding a bathroom tile in each hand, and there was a broad smile on his unpleasant face.

*

Naughton was wearing a floral tie in crimson, violet and pink. His suit was of some shiny blue material which tended to shimmer in the strip lighting, generating the impression that he was a starship captain about to dematerialize in a matter transmitter.

I wish he would bloody dematerialize, Carpenter thought as Naughton went through his usual parade of clichés about their irresponsibility, wanton destruction of public property, and all the rest of it. Even Wright looked moribund and bored. In fact he looked positively morose.

Meanwhile Sinnott was doing his best to avoid the attentions of Mordred, who had begun its forays on his feet within seconds of him entering the office. Its lead looked badly frayed, and it seemed that it might break free at any moment and promptly lunge for Sinnott's throat.

The cat's unerring instinct for Sinnott was proof that animals could smell fear. In a similar manner, Carpenter was convinced that most people could sniff out the sort of person you really were, even when you were doing your damnedest to present yourself differently. Women in particular had arcane powers which enabled them to expose the weaknesses in his own character within a short acquaintance. He was always doing his best to appear more forceful or confident or nonchalant or whatever, but under the slightest pressure he would collapse into his old habits and attitudes of mind. Having a personality was like owning a particular model of car; you could sometimes add accessories or remove bits to streamline it, but you couldn't really do anything about the basic design. And the only facility for changing models was madness.

'Carpenter,' said Naughton, 'you're not listening to a word I'm saying, are you?'

'No,' said Carpenter.

Harris stood at Naughton's shoulder, looking very pleased with himself. Why, of all people, had he been the one to discover the hole in the wall? There was no justice.

'I am not going to ask for any explanations,' Naughton told them, 'since it is perfectly clear what was going on. As far as I'm concerned you are all in this together. Therefore I'm closing the games room forthwith and there will be no more television.'

'All in it together?' said an incredulous Wright. 'There were only two of us involved, as you know only too well. Don't try to pretend that you haven't been aware of what we've been doing from the start. It's quite obvious that you have an informer. And I know who it is. Him.'

Wright's finger pointed unambiguously at Carpenter.

*

'What time is it?' Carpenter asked Peacock.

Peacock glanced at the Rolex on his wrist. 'Twenty-five past six.'

Dr Dempster had not shown up that evening, and Carpenter craved her company. A funereal atmosphere prevailed in the lounge, with Sinnott in particular looking as if he didn't know what to do with himself. Treadwell was engrossed in some elaborate piece of origami on a newspaper, and everyone else was doing his best not to watch him. Riley, slumped in an armchair, had draped the *Radio Times* across his face as though to blot out the world.

Only Wright was absent. He had stalked off to his cell earlier after refusing to accept Carpenter's assurances that he had said nothing to Naughton or any of the guards about the escape tunnel. Treadwell had also tried to intercede on Carpenter's behalf, but this had only made Wright declare that he wouldn't trust any of them any more. Then he departed in a huff of indignation and self-righteousness.

The trouble was that Wright's accusation had made Carpenter feel like a traitor in spite of himself. The others had assured him that they gave no credence to it, but it was noticeable that none of them had spoken much to him since. Had Wright planted a seed of doubt in them?

'Fancy a game of snooker?' Carpenter asked Riley.

'No games,' said Peacock, who was sitting at the back of the room with his feet up on a chair.

Carpenter had forgotten that the games room had been locked on Naughton's orders. He sighed.

Treadwell had completed his origami, which resembled a human figure. He managed to stand it upright on the coffee table.

'What is it?' asked Sinnott.

'Harris,' Treadwell told him. Then he tore its limbs off.

*

Over dinner Wright's silence was eerie. He sat at the head of the table and refused to speak to anyone. The rest of them did their best to ignore him, but Carpenter continued to feel uncomfortable under his angry eyes. In a way he wished he had been guilty of informing so that he could confess and at least clear the air. But there was nothing he could say.

Peacock was doling out the tomato soup when Harris entered. He stood beside the table, surveying them with an air of amusement.

'Too bad,' he said. 'No TV. No fun and games. You've all been naughty boys.'

He patted Riley hard on the back just as he was about to put a spoonful of soup into his mouth.

Riley managed to avoid spilling the soup on himself. Without looking at Harris, he dipped the spoon in his bowl and flicked it at his face.

Harris stepped back as if he had been slapped. Carpenter saw rage welling up in him, but Peacock intervened to stop him from attacking Riley. Then Wright swept his own soup bowl off the table and walked out.

Harris went off in pursuit of him. No one else moved, and there was a lengthy silence. Then Riley began to tuck into his main course, which was roast chicken and chips with peas. There was a banana for afters.

*

Sitting before the grey television screen, Carpenter took the banana from his trouser pocket and pointed it at the light fitting, making shooting noises. Harris had locked Wright in his cell for the night after he had refused to clear up his mess, and the rest of them had been made to perform the duty, washing the whole floor of the dining room until Harris was satisfied. They had not protested and had even taken their time over the task, knowing that the evening would weigh heavily on them without the TV. Sinnott had retired to his cell immediately afterwards. Riley and Treadwell were playing dominoes on the coffee table – a concession granted by Peacock on their return to the lounge. Peacock had looked distinctly nervous since dinner.

Carpenter considered the banana, which he had saved in case he became peckish later on. According to a recent magazine article it was Mother Nature's pre-packaged convenience food, designed to be consumed with a minimum of fuss and providing a wide range of essential nutrients. Hence the continued survival of desert-island castaways in the absence of fish-and-chip shops or Chinese restaurants. From a modern packaging point of view its only drawback was apparently its shape: a rectangular banana would have been more acceptable in terms of storage efficiency.

Carpenter wondered if any genetic engineers were working towards this end. Perhaps they would also introduce a range of different flavours, so that you could get smoky bacon bananas, cheese and onion bananas, prawn cocktail bananas, and so on, with appropriately coloured skins to identify them. Brownish-red for smoky bacon, yellow with white stripes for cheese and onion, pink for prawn cocktail –

'Carpenter.' It was Harris. 'You're wanted.'

Carpenter slipped the banana into his pocket and followed Harris down the corridor, keeping his distance. What next? he wondered. What more did Harris want? Then he saw that Dr Dempster's office door was open. She was waiting for him inside.

*

Carpenter took his usual seat while she went through the familiar ritual of pouring tea. Today she was wearing a cream silk blouse under her white coat, with slightly more make-up on her face than normal – redder lips and darker eyes. The effect was very elegant, and he wondered if she was late because she had just come from some social engagement in the outside world. Or perhaps she was due to attend one immediately after seeing him. He had to keep reminding himself that the staff of Limbo led lives outside its walls.

He tried to imagine her domestic circumstances and decided that she was probably married to a solicitor or barrister who would be called Charles or Edward. They would have, say, two children, both daughters in their teens. Annabelle and Victoria, he decided. They would be pretty and intelligent and would attend good schools.

She passed him his tea, and he thought of suggesting that they share his banana with it until common sense got the better of him. But this didn't prevent a brief fantasy of her slowly peeling it, then beginning to suck it in a very suggestive way . . .

'Is something wrong?' she asked. 'You look preoccupied.'

Carpenter shrugged, then told her what had happened since the discovery of the escape tunnel. It all came pouring out of him, like a confession. He spared her no details, even telling her of Wright's accusation that he had been an informer to Naughton.

She studied him over her cup. 'And were you?'

'No,' he said, hurt. 'Do you think I would?'

She smiled. 'I think you would be quite loyal to the others.'

One of their silences ensued. She offered him more tea, which he accepted.

'Are you angry?' she asked.

'Angry?'

'About what's happened.'

He considered. 'Worried's more like it. Everyone's getting a bit on edge.'

She said nothing, but continued staring at him. Carpenter could smell her perfume again, and it made him want to bury his head in her neck.

'Tell me about your job,' she said abruptly.

'My job?'

'Your last job. Before you came here. It was in the food industry, wasn't it?'

'Sort of.'

'How did that come about?'

'It's a complicated story.'

'Just give me the essential details. What exactly did it entail?'
'A kind of institutional madness.'

*

In fact he had been surprised when the company had invited him to London for an interview, given his lack of qualifications for the job. He was even more surprised when he was actually offered the post.

At the interview he had sat in front of four smart, very company-looking men who had asked him all sorts of questions about marketing, sales forecasts, wholesalers, and much else about which he knew nothing. He had blathered and bluffed, feeling that the job was slipping away from him the more he talked. Then the questions had got around to his interests outside working hours, and when he had mentioned that he had always been a keen football fan the bearded, thickset man at the end of the table who had not previously spoken asked him what team he supported. Carpenter immediately recognized a hint of Mancunian in his accent. Mentally crossing his fingers, he announced that he had been a Manchester United supporter from an early age.

The man said nothing, but Carpenter saw the brief flicker of approval in his face, and he knew he had found a kindred spirit. Though he was never to see him again, he later learned that he was a cousin of the company chairman, and he felt certain that the job had been his from that moment.

A week later he received a letter asking him if he could start work within the month. He had only been back in Manchester for two weeks, and had been hoping to spend the best part of the summer lazing around. But his mother, who had been worried about his future, urged him to accept the job, and he did not want to risk spending another dismal winter in Manchester without work.

Ten days later he was stepping off an Inter-City train in London, and he promptly booked himself into a cheap hotel near King's Cross. Hoping to contact Veronica, he rang the number of the institution which she had given him in her last letter. But a brusque male voice informed him that she was no longer associated with the establishment, had left some months ago. No, there was no forwarding address.

He had just over a week to find a place to live before he started work. The company was based in Kilburn, and he spent several days prowling the streets of North London before finally finding himself a two-roomed flat on the first floor of a house near Kilburn underground station, only five minutes' walk from his place of work. At forty pounds a week the rent was exorbitant, but he had been warned about London prices and was eager to escape his sleazy hotel, where he was kept awake half the night by the scabrous bickerings of prostitutes and their clients on the street below. The landlady, who lived on the top floor, was due to depart to Australia for six months, and the only other tenant was a young photographer named Kenneth who occupied a bedsitter on the ground floor. The flat was unpretentious and cosy in a pleasantly suburban way. It suited Carpenter, who felt that London had to be taken a little at a time. He paid the landlady half a year's rent in advance and moved in two days before he started work.

We call it The Jungle, said Piggott, his immediate superior, as he showed Carpenter around the large open-plan office building on his first morning. Carpenter had been given a conducted tour of the whole place after his interview, but Piggott, a nervous, thyroidal man in his mid-thirties, seemed keen to act as guide and mentor, so he was suitably attentive. Piggott led him from desk to desk, introducing him to people whose names and functions he immediately forgot while giving him a commentary on working practices, office personalities and current gossip. The Jungle was situated on the ground floor of the administrative building, looking out on the older and more ramshackle factory where the goods themselves were produced. It contained upwards of thirty desks, carefully screened from one another by movable partitions and large potted plants. The ceiling was low and strip lighting burned fiercely overhead, the varnished wood-panelled walls gleaming under its light. Well-tailored men and women sat at desks or negotiated the spaces between them with an air of purposeful efficiency.

The company manufactured a range of canned and bottled foods which were marketed primarily in the southern half of England and Wales. Carpenter's role as Assistant Product Manager made him directly responsible to Piggott, the Product Manager, while Piggott was in turn responsible to the Sales Manager, who reported directly to the Managing Director. The Sales Manager was a grey-suited and grey-haired man of middle age named Prendergast; he wore gold-framed glasses and had a smile that was not at all friendly or encouraging but more a baring of teeth. Piggott and the four other Product Managers privately called him Prenderghastly, and it was immediately clear to Carpenter that Piggott was terrified of him.

The company's range of products was divided and ranked according to sales into five sections, each having a Product Manager at its head. First, and by far the largest and most important section, was Baked Beans. Next came Jams & Preserves. Third was Meat & Fruit Pie Fillings. The fourth and fifth sections were subject to fluctuating sales and hence rankings, but Pickles, Onions & Chutneys under Piggott was currently outselling Tinned Fruits & Vegetables by a narrow margin.

The product manager's job was to ensure that those lines for which he was responsible maintained or preferably improved their share of the market, and to this purpose he needed to work closely with the salesmen who were actually travelling around the country arranging orders with wholesalers and retail outlets. It was necessary to monitor sales figures constantly, ensure that deliveries were made promptly, look for new or under-exploited markets, consult with the marketing department on matters of promotion and advertising, liaise with R&D, and so on. The assistant product manager's role was simply to shoulder a portion of this work, thereby gaining the experience by which he might eventually rise to full product managership.

Such was the theory, but in practice Carpenter soon came to realize that Piggott was not a delegator. He was so concerned about the prospect of sales falling or of Tinned Fruits & Vegetables under Nigel Denton overtaking him and relegating him to last place in the hierarchy that he was incapable of trusting Carpenter to work on his own or of giving him anything but routine tasks. There was considerable rivalry between the five sections, and Denton often irritated Piggott by claiming that he was only outselling him because his brand-range included pickled onions, which were guaranteed a healthy turnover regardless. Piggott would counter that in such products as stewed prunes and tinned strawberries Denton had a ready-made market in pensioners, who were forming an increasing proportion of the country's population. Meanwhile everyone was envious of Mark Quick's unassailable position at the top of the heap with Baked Beans.

Piggott worked long hours, being always at his desk when Carpenter arrived at nine in the morning, and being still hard at it when he departed shortly after five-thirty. Office rumour had it that a night watchman had once found him at his desk at ten o'clock, though Carpenter suspected the anecdote was apocryphal. Nevertheless, Piggott showed a remarkable capacity for hectic overwork, and the general feeling prevailed that he would soon succumb to a heart attack or a nervous breakdown, two not uncommon ways of ending one's career in The Jungle. His previous assistant, a woman, had lasted only six months before she left to join the Forestry Commission.

Carpenter felt under little pressure himself; since he was rarely given anything interesting or challenging to do, his chief problem was staving off boredom. He spent much of his days chatting with other product managers, all nattily dressed men with cars, houses and ambitions wholly financial in nature who showed varying degrees of commitment to their jobs. Carpenter was pleased to note that Mark Quick proved the most relaxed and personable; he liked to think that simply being pleasant gained its own rewards. Piggott had formerly been Quick's assistant on Pickles, Onions & Chutneys before Quick had been promoted to Baked Beans. Carpenter's section was known as POC in office parlance, the others being BB, JAPE, MFPF and TV. Carpenter was never able to use any of these acronyms without wincing.

When it was necessary to be on duty at his desk, Carpenter would do his best to look busy; but there were too many hours in the day. His desk was back-to-back with Piggott's but noticably smaller, so that it seemed as if he was doing the office equivalent of kneeling at Piggott's feet. When Piggott was not at his desk making frantic phonecalls or furiously checking sales figures, he would be meeting incoming salesmen in the lobby of the building in case their sales reports were bad and overheard by Prendergast. Every day Carpenter felt as if he was sitting in the still eye at the centre of a storm.

Meanwhile he was settling into his new flat. His landlady had departed for Australia leaving him two large tins of suspiciously unlabelled emulsion with which to redecorate the place. Happily both proved to contain brilliant white paint rather than the puce or dayglo orange which he had expected. Carpenter spent the next several weeks transforming the flat from the dowdy digs of a staid bachelor into the quietly fashionable abode of an eligible young man: the antique furniture sat well against the white walls.

The redecorating so absorbed his spare time that with its completion he was suddenly at a loss and realized that his social life was non-existent. The football season had started, but somehow he no longer had any enthusiasm for attending matches, even though United would be visiting London to play Spurs, Arsenal and West Ham. There was no attraction in the prospect of standing on a cold, windy terrace for an hour and a half, being jostled and crushed; the spark was gone. It was a similar story with music: he still enjoyed all his old records but he hadn't bought a new LP in months and wondered if his tastes had ossified. He felt no inclination to attend any of Fiasco's gigs, or even to contact Graham. Was he already drifting into crabbed middle age?

He determined to be more outgoing, and took to visiting local pubs in the evenings. But most of them were inhabited by expatriate Irish, and he always felt that he was an outsider whose presence was tolerated but not really welcomed. At nights he would lie awake listening to the late trains rattling by on the underground, and he would remind himself that his twenty-ninth birthday was approaching. The years were slipping by, and it seemed to him that his life had no more focus or direction than when he had been nineteen. What he needed was some excitement and romance to offset the boredom of his job and the solitude of his evenings and weekends.

One Saturday afternoon he bumped into an old colleague from Cardiff while out shopping on Kilburn High Road. It was one of those awkward moments of instant recognition immediately followed by the realization that they had hardly known one another but could not turn away now. After exchanging self-conscious greetings, they lapsed into hesitant small-talk. Carpenter could not even remember his name, though he learned that he was now married with two children, worked for an insurance company and had been living in Cricklewood for the past five years.

Carpenter gave a potted account of his own career and present circumstances, unable to resist adding that he'd found London somewhat a lonely place since his arrival. To this, Jeff (the name came to Carpenter suddenly) agreed that London could indeed be difficult when you first moved there, but he was quite settled now and had made quite a few friends. In fact he was off to a dance this evening, and why didn't Carpenter come along? The dance was being held at a social club in Maida Vale to celebrate the local cricket club's successful season, and he would be more than welcome. Carpenter duly made a note of the address.

They parted with Carpenter having no intention of attending the dance; but by seven o'clock that evening he had changed his mind, unable to bear the thought of another Saturday night alone. The place was already crowded when he arrived, with several men wearing cricketing blazers, the rest looking like any party crowd. He found Jeff at the bar – several pumps attached to trestle-tables – with his wife, a small blonde woman named Sonia who looked a little alarmed when Carpenter insisted on buying Jeff a pint of Fuller's Extra Special Bitter. People were already dancing at the centre of the floor to 'Satisfaction'.

Five pints and two hours later, he and Jeff were sprawled around a table in the company of several other people, male and female. Jeff was the wicket-keeper with the cricket team, and they hadn't lost a match all season. He had loosened up considerably since imbibing the beer, though Sonia looked correspondingly more anxious the drunker he became.

Carpenter, too, was in high spirits by now and had been regaling his audience with a series of sporting anecdotes which he was implying were original to him but which he had in fact heard many years previously from Graham's father, who had always had a good line in droll stories. He recounted his favourite one about a match United had played at Old Trafford in poor visibility and to atrocious refereeing. Finally someone in the crowd had called for a white ball to be used, whereupon a voice in the Stretford End had yelled that it should be accompanied by a white stick for the referee.

Carpenter was never more adept at telling these stories than when he was drunk, and the tale was suitably well received. As the laughter subsided he noticed that the very attractive, dark-haired girl who was sitting at the end of the table was looking at him with what seemed to be admiration. He had been aware of her when she had first sat down at the table because she was strikingly good-looking and had a perfectly formed body. Her curly hair fell about her shoulders, and she wore a black silk dress with a halter-neck which made him long to caress her bare arms and back. He had been doing his best to ignore her, knowing that such an attraction was fatal; but now, in his moment of glory, he decided that there was nothing for it but to take the plunge.

Rising slowly from his seat in case the drink had affected his balance, he asked her if she fancied a dance. When she said yes, he was genuinely surprised; it seemed impossible that anyone so pretty could be interested in him. But she scarcely took her eyes off his face as they leapt about to 'Purple Haze' and 'Virginia Plain', and she laughed at all his jokes. She told him he had a lovely accent, and said that she'd always found Northern people warm and friendly. Now her arms were around his neck and his hands had slipped to her waist as they swayed to 'A Whiter Shade of Pale'.

Her name was Penny, she was twenty-four and worked as a secretary-cum-assistant to a senior accountant at an estate agent's office in South Kensington. She shared a flat just off Hampstead Heath with another girl, and originally hailed from Canterbury, where her parents still lived. There was no mention of any regular boyfriend, and Carpenter could scarcely believe his luck. You're beautiful, he told her in his drunkenness. She smiled without coyness or complacency.

Penny was a fluid and energetic dancer after the fashion of Cicely, though she did at least stop for a rest every fourth record or so. She seemed as buoyed up with drink as he, and he bought her a rum and coke when they sat down to gather their breath for a few minutes. During a later break she insisted on buying him a beer in return. He kept expecting her to be waylaid at any moment by some suave and handsome type who would immediately carry her off in his E-type Jaguar, but she returned from the bar as promised and seemed to have eyes and ears only for him.

They remained on the dance floor until the very last record, a smooch to 'The Long and Winding Road'. On their return to the table, Penny went into a huddled consultation with a girl friend before telling him that she was getting a lift home. Carpenter immediately started cursing himself for not having asked her earlier if he could take her home, but she was already enquiring if he wanted her telephone number.

Carpenter wrote the number down in his pocket diary with only a slightly trembling hand. Meanwhile Penny was suggesting that he give her a ring tomorrow, perhaps they could go out somewhere together. He wanted to hug her there and then, though typically he did nothing. She gave him a brief kiss on the cheek as she departed, leaving him feeling wonderful. His last memory of the dance was of Sonia leading a teetering Jeff from the bar. See you again, Jeff, Carpenter called heartily, whereupon Sonia glowered at him and said, His name is John.

Carpenter woke the next morning with the best sort of hangover. He always did things when he was drunk which made him want to cringe the following day, but on this occasion these were forgotten in the triumph of Penny's phone number. He decided to play it cool and not phone her until after lunch; but by ten-thirty he could stand the suspense no longer.

A female voice answered the phone. Is that Penny? he asked. No, just a moment. He heard the receiver being put down, and then he waited for what seemed like a long time. Finally the same voice returned, telling him that Penny was still in bed. Could he leave a number so that she could ring him back later?

Carpenter duly recited it, but a blush of embarrassment was rising up in him as he did so. He felt sure that Penny had had second thoughts and simply didn't want to talk to him: there would be no return call. Idiot, he told himself, idiot. It had just been a one-off party fling. So much for the Great Romance.

Two hours later he was slumped morosely in an armchair, reading about atrocities in South-East Asia in the *Sunday Times*, when the telephone started ringing. The phone was a coin-box affair on the landing between his own flat and Kenneth's. Kenneth, a quiet young man who did free-lance work for a mail order catalogue, was seldom at home on weekends, though hitherto all the incoming calls had been for him. Carpenter dutifully descended the short flight of stairs and picked up the receiver.

It was Penny. She was sorry she hadn't been able to talk to him earlier but she had been feeling a bit iffy from too many rums the night before and had needed a lie-in for a few hours. Hadn't the party been fun? Would he like to come to a wine bar that evening with her and a few of her friends?

Ten minutes later Carpenter was lying happily in a foamy bath, his earlier resolve never to have anything to do with women again entirely forgotten. Penny had sounded much brighter, and the very fact that she had phoned him back proved that she was interested in him.

The wine bar was in a narrow side street off East Heath Road. It proved studiously dark and cramped, a rabbit's warren of corridors and alcoves. Carpenter kept banging his head against the lanterns which hung from the eaves. The lanterns gave off a murky yellow light which scarcely illuminated the rough wooden tables and benches. There was sawdust on the floor, and a feeling that cobwebs lurked in shadowy corners. Yet it was all somehow studied, cosmetic, and the patrons all looked modishly elegant and comfortably off.

He arrived shortly after the appointed time of eight o'clock, but a brief tour of the place revealed no sign of Penny or her friends. He stood at the bar, quickly swallowing three glasses of white wine. He had never been much of a wine drinker, except when he was already too drunk on beer to care. But when in Rome . . .

He was just about to put the fourth glass to his lips when Penny appeared at his side. We're all out in the back room, she told him. Carpenter hadn't even realized there *was* a back room. She led him down a narrow stairway which he had previously assumed had led to the toilets.

There were four other people at Penny's table, and Carpenter made a concentrated effort to remember their names as he was introduced to them. This was Colin, who worked in banking, this was Jilly, who was with London Weekend Television, this was Henry, who was in antiques, and this was Geraldine, who didn't do much of anything, really, apart from the odd spot of modelling.

Geraldine, a statuesque and elegantly thin young woman, certainly looked as if she might command a model's fees. Jilly was shorter and plumper, with a stubby nose, freckles and a broad smile. Colin was pale, rather horsey, and somewhat nervous in manner, his eyes darting away from anyone else's. Henry was much older than the others, in his late thirties; he wore a tweed jacket over a white shirt with a paisley cravat at his neck, and his hair was cropped short around his ears. Jilly had been with Penny at the cricketing party, though Carpenter had no recollection of her.

Carpenter sat down and let the conversation flow around him. At first he assumed that Penny's two girl friends were paired off with Colin and Henry, but it quickly transpired that there were no couples at all. Colin was clearly attracted to Geraldine but was too shy to do anything about it even if Geraldine had shown some interest in him, which she didn't. Jilly was obviously enamoured of Henry, but Henry had eyes only for Penny. Penny seemed quite friendly towards him, but she did not reciprocate with the kind of lingering looks and smiles with which Henry was constantly trying to engage her attention. In fact she presently moved her leg so that her thigh was resting against Carpenter's own.

Most of the talk seemed to be about their respective jobs, and Carpenter was content chiefly to listen and interject the occasional affirmative grunt when called upon to do so. Penny kept trying to bring him into the conversation, but then Henry would steer it away again to another subject about which Carpenter knew nothing. Henry obviously resented his presence.

Carpenter felt that he had little to contribute to the conversation but he was relaxed – relaxed no doubt by the wine he had already drunk and was still drinking at quite a respectable pace. He had bought a round for everyone, then was abashed that he was empty again before the others had taken more than a few sips of their drinks. Henry had started talking about the dangers of alcoholism, studiously not looking at Carpenter as he did so. Carpenter equally studiously ignored him, and when Penny insisted on fetching him another glass of white wine he felt that he had been vindicated.

This, however, only seemed to make Henry more disgruntled. A few polite questions had earlier been asked about his job, which he had answered as briefly as possible. But now Henry wanted to know *exactly* what he did from day to day. I sit at a desk, Carpenter told him. Really? said Henry. And did the job satisfy him, did he feel fulfilled by it, and was the welfare of the company important to him? Carpenter replied that he wasn't especially concerned about the company's welfare but rather about the welfare of his bank balance. Wasn't that a rather selfish attitude? Wasn't it rather mercenary? Yes, said Carpenter, that's exactly what it is.

This admission seemed to take the wind out of Henry's argumentative sails, and he fell silent. I've got this one taped, thought Carpenter; he's a pushover. But a few minutes later the conversation had got around to hair styles, make-up and other methods of enhancing one's facial appearance when Henry started talking about hair transplants. In his view they were quite disgusting and he would never have one if his hair started to fall out, though of course he was lucky, he had quite a mop of hair, it ran in the family and his grandfather had had a white mane at the age of ninety. But what did he, Carpenter, think?

Carpenter wanted to come up with a tart and devastating response, but in truth he felt profoundly self-conscious and outraged. Hitherto he had not been overly sensitive about his receding hairline, chiefly because no one else had ever commented on it. But he was aware that his father had had a very high forehead, and he could not honestly pretend that a similar prospect appealed to him. He had not receded *that* much, he was sure, but Henry was calling attention to the fact that he *was* receding, and Penny was hardly likely to think it a favourable attribute.

Henry had a pleasant, toothy smile on his face, and Carpenter wanted to hit him. It was as simple as that. He heard himself saying that he'd never thought much about hair transplants himself, though he'd always been interested in the change in facial appearance brought about when a person had his front teeth knocked out.

Henry's smile vanished, and Carpenter knew he had struck home; Henry was far too civilized to contemplate settling an argument by brute force, and the prospect clearly intimidated him. Carpenter continued staring at him until he looked away; at the same time he could feel his face growing hot. An awkward silence had descended on the table, and Carpenter knew he had committed a dreadful breach of etiquette. But he didn't care; all that had mattered had been shutting up the pompous oaf.

The glow of victory soon faded, however. A stiffness entered the conversation from that point onwards, with Colin, Jilly and Geraldine all talking carefully around him, while Penny looked tense and embarrassed. He knew he had blown it with her and he began to wish he could have defeated Henry with some piece of verbal adroitness rather than his sledge-hammer approach. He felt hopelessly crass and provincial.

When it was time to go, Carpenter tried to make his goodbyes as quickly as possible, only to have Penny ask him if he would like a lift home. He hadn't been aware that she had a car, but a red Ford Fiesta was parked outside, and she explained that she hadn't brought it to the cricket club party because she had known she would be drinking. Carpenter thought that she did not seem entirely sober tonight, but nothing would have made him refuse her offer. Henry made a big show of kissing her goodnight, but Carpenter was immune, victorious.

As soon as they were inside the car, Penny told him he had been wonderful, Henry could be such a pain at times and not many people could get the better of him. But he was a dear at heart, really, once you got used to his crustiness. Carpenter wanted to know how she had become friends with him, and she explained that he was an old friend of the family and had looked after her like a sister when she first moved to London. He's mad about you, Carpenter told her, to which she replied that while she thought a lot of him as a friend she wasn't attracted to him in that sort of way. *He* was more her type.

She smelt of expensive perfume, and Carpenter would have liked to smother her face with kisses. He might have done so had she not been driving. He was a bit drunk, he realized, but not *that* drunk, and it felt wonderful.

She declined his invitation to come in for coffee, telling him that she had to get up early the following morning. But they arranged to meet that coming Wednesday to see a foreign film which all her friends had been telling her was marvellous. Her eyes were dark and bright, and she looked utterly beautiful sitting there beside him. He leaned forward and put his lips on hers. She responded immediately, her mouth enveloping his. Is this real? Carpenter asked himself as he luxuriated in the kissing of her. Am I really here?

Her breathing came faster and faster until she finally broke away and told him that she really had to get home. She made it sound as if to continue kissing him might make it impossible for her to resist anything he would want to do to her. Carpenter, ever cautious and leery of spoiling a good thing, duly bade her goodnight and got out of the car. He climbed the stairs to his flat feeling triumphant.

The film turned out to be a subtitled Czechoslovakian satire of decadent Western capitalism. Carpenter didn't understand any of the jokes and soon lost the thread of the story. His lack of concentration was only partly due to the subtitles; he was also profoundly conscious of Penny's head, which rested against his shoulder throughout. Then she slipped her hand on to his knee, whereupon any form of concentration became impossible.

Afterwards she drove him back to her flat for coffee. It proved to be a spacious four-roomed affair on the ground floor of a house which looked out on Hampstead Heath. All the rooms had unobtrusive wall-to-wall carpeting, the furniture was in oak and mahogany with heavy cotton upholstery in buff and khaki and olive green. There were patchwork scatter cushions everywhere, and on the walls hung framed prints and delicate watercolours. Her flatmate, Sally, was not at home.

Penny was in the kitchen a long time before she emerged with the coffee; it turned out to be freshly roasted. Carpenter diluted it with plenty of milk while she sat down beside him on the sofa, looking ravishing in a frilly white cotton blouse and a navy-blue satin skirt. She had taken off her shoes, and he wanted to stroke her legs from ankle to thigh before slowly peeling off the dark tights she was wearing. She told him a little about her parents: her father was a solicitor in Canterbury, while her mother managed a clothes shop. Then she put her coffee mug aside and looked at him in such a way that he knew she wanted him to kiss her.

Ten minutes later they were still locked together, and Penny was breathing hard and fast each time they paused between kisses. As a result of their entanglement her skirt had become raised by several inches, and when Carpenter finally put a hand on her knee she did not protest.

Five minutes later his hand had progressed half-way up her thigh and her breathing had grown even more rapid. Then he heard the front door to the flat being opened. Penny immediately sat up and adjusted her clothing, though Carpenter noted with satisfaction that she was still breathing heavily.

It was Sally, who proved to be a fair-headed girl who was taller and bonier than Penny. She had had an argument with her boyfriend, and she scarcely acknowledged Carpenter before launching into a threnody of woe and frustration. Penny listened attentively and at length began to proffer suggestions on what to do. Carpenter knew it was time to go.

Penny insisted on running him home. As they drove to Kilburn she explained that Sally's boyfriend was a salesman who did a lot of travelling and was thus often not around when Sally wanted to see him; this was the fundamental cause of the strains in their relationship, though she had no doubt that Sally was in love with him and that everything would work out for the best.

The following Sunday afternoon he accompanied her to Camden market, where she bought an antique mirror which he dutifully carried around until they got back to the car. That evening her parents were visiting her, so Carpenter made himself scarce. They went out again in midweek to the cinema, and this time the film was a Turkish production which Carpenter found utterly incomprehensible. He suspected that Penny hadn't got much out of it either, since they did not discuss it afterwards. She drove him back to his flat, and when he invited her in for coffee, she said yes.

Half an hour later they were entwined on the divan in Carpenter's front room, and this time he was sure they would go the whole hog; Penny was gasping and murmuring and panting as he stroked her body and kissed her face and neck. He ran his hand up and down her spine. She shivered and went *Mmmmm*. He continued downwards, stroking her bottom and hips. She gave a further murmur of pleasure. His other hand moved slowly to her breast. She gasped and hugged him to her.

He undid the buttons of her cheesecloth blouse. The bra underneath was of the variety with the clasp between the breasts, so that undoing it was easy. She began to tremble as he cupped a breast in his hand, the nipple quickly hardening beneath his palm. This was bliss. Sheer bliss. She continued to murmur under his attentions, and he thought he heard the words 'Oh yes' and 'Want you'. This was enough to spur him into moving his other hand beneath her skirt.

Even as he was doing so, some instinct was telling him that it was all too good to be true and that something was bound to happen to prevent him from making love to her. She would stop him on some pretext, or he would get the nervous droop, or the Fire Brigade would arrive on a hoax call and axe down the door. Then he realized that she was unzipping him, while at the same time telling him that she was on the pill.

It was wonderful. Penny writhed and gasped and scratched at him throughout, and Carpenter did everything in his power to delay his ejaculation. But it was not easy: Penny looked perfectly gorgeous in a state of dishevelled abandonment, and he could feel the irresistible pressure to explode building in him.

Then she screamed: a long, loud scream, just as if she was being murdered. It was quite bloodcurdling, and Carpenter immediately wilted at the sound of it. She was gripping him hard and hugging him to her. He froze, wondering what to do. The most advisable policy seemed simply to lie there for a moment and see what transpired.

That was wonderful, she told him presently out of the silence, and made him turn his face to hers. She was smiling. Do you always scream when you come? Carpenter asked her, and she nodded and said, I just lose control. This was an exciting thought, but Carpenter profoundly hoped that Kenneth was not already phoning the police.

From then on they began to meet regularly, once in midweek and on Sundays. Penny made it clear from the outset that she valued a certain independence and needed time to herself. Friday night was women's night, reserved for socializing with Sally and Jilly and other female friends; Saturdays she liked to keep free for her parents or unexpected visitors – people were always dropping in. They both agreed that many couples saw too much of one another to start with and soon got bored.

At first Carpenter was quite happy with their schedule, pleased that Penny was not seeking to tie him down as he felt other women in his life had done. Under her prompting he applied for a provisional driver's licence so that she could give him lessons in her car. When they met in midweek they always ended up at his place and made love before she departed. On Sundays Sally was usually absent until late evening (the disagreement with her boyfriend had soon blown over) and they made love there, too, on sofas and beds and armchairs and even standing up in the kitchen. Penny quickly revealed herself as having a great appetite for sex and a liberated approach to it. Hitherto Carpenter had considered himself quite sexually experienced, but she soon introduced him to a variety of different positions and the exquisite delights of oral sex in all its glory. Carpenter was amazed; it was not that he had been unaware of such variations, merely that he would never have imagined anyone like Penny permitting him such liberties. He never quite got used to her screaming at climax, no matter how much he tried to prepare himself for it in advance, but in all other respects she was a dream lover, capable of a wantonness which never failed to inflame him.

Carpenter was bowled over. To have a girlfriend who was very attractive and easy-going was miracle enough, but to have one who was also lewd and abandoned when they were alone together was unbelievable. As the weeks went by he found himself reflecting upon her in odd moments and wishing that they saw one another more often. By her very lack of demands on his time and mind, she gave herself greater appeal to him. This was not to suggest that everything was perfect between them – she was sometimes moody, absent-minded and was often late arriving for their dates – but overall he could not believe his luck.

About a month after they had started going out together his provisional driving licence arrived. They arranged an extra meeting during midweek for his lesson. At first he had been worried that Penny might prove a finicky and critical instructor, but the reverse was true: she seemed to take the barest interest in what he was doing as soon as she handed over the car keys to him. This was unnerving since he showed no natural aptitude for driving whatsoever and could barely manage to steer the car in a straight line, let alone keep an eye out for the numerous hazards and complexities of the typical London road. Soon the idea of spending the rest of his life without learning to drive began to seem more attractive than the increasing likelihood that they would both be mangled in an accident.

But Penny insisted that he was doing well and only needed more practice to gain the necessary confidence. They began to meet regularly on Saturday afternoons and would spend the rest of the weekend together, staying either at his flat or at hers and going their separate ways on Monday morning. Gradually she was giving him more and more of her time, and Carpenter was quietly delighted.

Eventually he took her up to Manchester for the weekend. He made the visit on the advice of Muriel, who had rung him to say that his mother was a bit poorly and that a visit from him would probably buck her up. When he mentioned the idea to Penny, she immediately asked if she could accompany him; she'd never visited Manchester and would love to meet his mother. Carpenter knew that taking a girlfriend home would be tantamount to the intention of marrying her in his mother's eyes, but this didn't make him hesitate: he wanted to show her off. And it would do his mother no harm if she jumped to the conclusion that they had marriage in mind; recently he had found himself contemplating the prospect at odd moments, and it was not without its attractions.

His mother did indeed look a little pale when they arrived, but otherwise seemed her normal self. They arrived at noon on Saturday, and soon his mother had them seated at the dinner table, eating large home-made pasties with huge helpings of crinkle-cut chips. She was busy and talkative and took a great interest in Penny from the outset, asking her questions about her home and family and job. The questions were asked casually, as if in the normal course of conversation, but Carpenter knew she was being vetted in a very motherly way. However Penny did not demur in the slightest and showed a positive interest when the family photograph albums were produced.

Carpenter sat there squirming as she studied photographs of himself as a plump seven-year-old in short trousers and braces, in a US cavalry outfit at nine, in a maroon and lime-green knitted jacket at eleven, in baggy jeans and brothel-creepers at thirteen. On and on it went, this embarrassing visual catalogue of his formative years, and in every photograph he looked idiotic. Somehow it was more cringeworthy the older he was: here was the shiny black Beatle jacket he'd been so proud of at fifteen, here was the purple paisley shirt and the back-combed hairstyle he'd had two years later, and here was the scraggly shoulder-length hair and the wispy Fu Manchu moustache he had grown in his first year at Cardiff.

Penny lingered over every photograph, her eyes drinking in all the details as if they were later to be used in evidence against him. But she said nothing disapproving, and the general tenor of her remarks was that he looked 'nice' or 'cute' or 'lovable'. None of these descriptions was addressed to him but rather to his mother, with whom she already appeared to have established a strong rapport. Carpenter had the odd feeling that they would somehow be able to talk more frankly together if he left the room.

United were playing at home that afternoon, and he had planned on taking Penny to the game. But shortly before they were due to leave Muriel turned up and remained until tea-time. Carpenter quickly sensed that Muriel did not take to Penny, but there was no tension. His aunt had always been a fount of gossip, and he was soon brought up to date on the most recent doings of people known to him. Chief amongst Muriel's tidings was that Graham and Gail were back together; Graham had returned to Manchester for a few weeks in September and Gail had gone back to London with him.

Although unexpected, this news had an air of inevitability about it, a sense of the natural order of things reasserting itself. And he realized that he no longer felt jealous of Graham's claim on Gail's affections; with Penny beside him Gail had ceased to be the epitome of all that was desirable in a woman.

Before Muriel departed she took him aside and asked him how he thought his mother was looking. He told her that she seemed a little pale but in all other respects healthy. Muriel looked dubious, but when pressed admitted that she had no evidence to support any major illness.

That evening Carpenter took Penny to one of his old locals. Since they had been going out together most of their drinking had been done in Hampstead wine bars, but Penny was keen to sample an evening at a typical Manchester pub.

A beefy man wearing a collarless shirt, serge trousers and a waistcoat was sitting at a piano in the bar playing 'As Time Goes By' when they entered. Carpenter steered Penny through the smoke-thick air to a corner table and departed to the bar. When he returned with the drinks he found that Penny had been joined by a tall, emaciated-looking woman in a floral dress and a pale green cardigan. She wore copious make-up and her hair was bleached. She was telling Penny about the three sons she'd raised. Penny was capable of looking interested whenever anyone was talking to her, but a frown began to form on her face the more the woman talked. She had already explained that one of her sons was a policeman who had helped catch the Great Train Robbers before going on to say that her second son had become a surgeon at Crumpsall Hospital and had performed open-heart surgery on various celebrities. Now she was telling Penny how her third son was in America, at Cape Canaveral; he had trained as an astronaut and was soon to set off for the moon.

At this point a small woman wearing a dark blue gabardine coat took the blonde woman by the arm and made her get to her feet. The blonde woman clearly wanted to continue her conversation with Penny, but the short woman was equally insistent that they leave. Unable to resist her, the blonde woman nevertheless had a parting message for Penny before she was whisked away. She leant her face close to Penny's and whispered confidentially: They look through windows.

And then both women were gone. Carpenter rapidly explained that the blonde woman was probably an inmate of Springfield mental hospital and that the short woman was probably her nurse. None of the inmates was dangerous, and it wasn't unusual to find them in the pub. Really? said Penny, in such a way that he knew he would be advised immediately to change the subject.

Carpenter could hear a pounding noise coming through the ceiling, and presently he discovered that a dance was taking place upstairs. Penny had been glancing nervously around the bar ever since her encounter with the blonde woman and she seemed keen to join the dance.

He led her upstairs. There was a small stage at the far end of the room, on which he could just see a middle-aged drummer and organist over the heads of the middle-aged and elderly dancers who were crowded on to the tiny dance floor. The drummer and organist were playing a rumba, and this was followed by a cha-cha, a tango, a quickstep and a foxtrot. It was difficult to discern much variety in the movement of the dancers to the changing rhythms and tempos. By now he and Penny had squeezed into another corner table next to an old man wearing a flat cap and the puckered leer of someone wholly lacking teeth.

Carpenter had been looking around for someone he knew, but there was no one under thirty-five whom he recognized. Penny was gazing at the dancing with the expression of a Victorian missionary witnessing some Polynesian fertility rite, and she sat very close to him. The old man had made several attempts to talk to her, and she had tried to talk back; but there seemed to be some fundamental problem of communication which transcended speech. Penny was already embarked on her third gin and soda, and Carpenter was doing his best to keep pace with her on beer.

At length the organ and drums fell silent and a short man with glasses and a squint came to the microphone to introduce the evening's singer, Tony Verdi, who had apparently just finished a very successful season at Morecambe. To a smattering of applause, Tony came on to the stage. He wore a scarlet shirt with a low-cut black waistcoat and bell-bottomed trousers with a high waist and silver ribbing up the seams. He looked like a matador gone to seed, a pot-belly straining against his waistcoat, his long sideboards and greased-back hair giving him the facial appearance of a forty-year-old teddy boy.

When Tony spoke his voice betrayed his Italianate surname: his accent was pure Rotherham. How do you make a cat sound like a dog? Tony wanted to know. The question was rhetorical: you pour petrol over it, put a match to it and it goes woof. At this Penny swallowed the rest of her drink and offered the glass to him with a pleading expression.

Tony was singing 'Release Me' when he returned from the bar. His basic singing technique seemed to involve shouting as loudly as possible from the back of his throat and modulating the resulting sounds with puffed-out cheeks and quivering lips. He also possessed the essential attribute of any pub singer by being able to hold a note far longer than seemed humanly possible until his audience was rapt, suspended, silently willing him to complete it.

'Release Me' was followed by 'Spanish Harlem', 'I Did What I Did for Maria', 'Amarillo', 'Edelweiss', 'Viva L'Espana', 'I Remember You' and others. 'I Remember You' was particularly striking for the remarkable quality of Tony's yodelling, its basso vibrancy quite unlike anything Carpenter had ever heard before, or ever wanted to. The old man sitting beside them was attempting to talk to Penny again, and presently she grabbed Carpenter's wrist and insisted that they dance.

There was little room for manoeuvre on the dance floor, and the air was hot and filled with cigarette smoke. Nevertheless Penny danced vigorously to 'Yellow River', 'I Left My Heart in San Francisco', 'White Christmas' and 'The Green Green Grass of Home'. Carpenter kept bumping into older people whom he knew vaguely and to whom he gave a vague nod of apology and recognition. None of his friends had shown up.

Penny had danced him into exhaustion by the time Tony was bidding them adieu with 'We'll Meet Again'. Not if I can help it, thought Carpenter, holding Penny in his arms and feeling abominably sweaty and disgusting. Penny's face nestled in the crook of his neck and he could feel her hot breath on his skin. She had drunk eight gin and sodas.

His mother had gone to bed by the time they got home. Both he and Penny were drunk and randy, and Carpenter had been making lewd suggestions to her all the way home, knowing that this always stimulated her. He had been unable to pluck up the courage to tell his mother that he and Penny wanted to sleep in the same bedroom, so she had naturally provided them with separate bedrooms at opposite ends of the landing with her own bedroom in between. The floorboards creaked.

They crept up the stairs and went directly to his room. Everything was silent, but Carpenter knew the walls of the house were relatively thin and that his mother was a light sleeper, instantly brought to consciousness by the slightest nocturnal sound. He and Penny fell gently on to the bed and started kissing. Carpenter was erect within seconds. There was no way either of them could stop now, though Carpenter wanted to suggest to Penny that he gag her for the duration of the act to prevent her orgasmic shrieking. But bondage had never been a part of their sexual repertoire.

Penny had started to undress him, and he did likewise to her. Soon they were both completely naked, and Carpenter had an erection harder than any he could remember. But he also desperately needed to pee. For a while he tried to ignore it, but the pressure on his bladder was insistent, not to be denied.

Reluctantly breaking their clinch, he told her that he wouldn't be a moment. He crept gingerly along the landing in an elaborate path which was designed to minimize the possibility of encountering the floorboards which creaked. He managed to make it into the bathroom without incident, gently and gratefully closing the door behind him.

Now a further problem presented itself: though painfully in need of emptying his bladder, he was still remorselessly erect and was faced with the problem of arranging himself so that he could aim directly into a toilet bowl that stood abnormally high in the first place, being mounted on a small cement block. Bending his organ proved impossible, and eventually there was no alternative but to climb up on the bathroom stool and drape the upper half of his body over the cistern. This was not a particularly comfortable position, and for long seconds he could generate no hydraulic pressure whatsoever. Then finally the blessed flow began. At that moment he heard his mother calling his name and wanting to know if he was in the bathroom. Yes, he called back in a half-choked voice, yes he was, but he wouldn't be long. Was everything all right? his mother asked; was Penny settled comfortably in her bed? Yes, yes, Carpenter assured her, everything's fine.

The flow diminished to a trickle and finally stopped. A silence had descended but Carpenter hadn't heard his mother closing her door and he wondered if she was waiting for him to come out. Perhaps she wanted to use the bathroom herself. He climbed down off the stool and flushed the toilet, wondering what he was going to do.

Ten minutes later he was still perched on the toilet seat flap, shivering in the chill air, his erection utterly vanished. There had been no sound outside during that time and it seemed inconceivable that his mother would still be waiting silently in her doorway for him to emerge. Yet even if he made it safely back to the bedroom, Penny would be waiting for him to continue where they had left off, and his mother might have a heart attack when she came.

After another five minutes he could stand the cold no longer and cautiously eased open the door. There was no sign of his mother, and her bedroom door was closed. He did a balletic dash across the landing, reaching the sanctuary of his bedroom to find that Penny was fast asleep on the bed.

They rose late the following morning, Penny coming down the stairs a studied half an hour after Carpenter himself. Carpenter knew that his mother knew they had slept together, but she surprised him by making no reference to the fact and was as pleasant to Penny as she had been the day before. It was Carpenter who felt rebuffed and disapproved of, sitting silent and ignored at the dinner table while his mother chatted to Penny about families and houses and the problems young couples had today in setting up home, what with inflation and the cost of everything and the difficulties in leading a settled life in such a competitive age. There was no direct reference to himself and Penny as a couple in this context, but he knew his mother was hoping for some hint of an engagement or plans for marriage. While saying nothing specific herself, Penny seemed to agree with most of his mother's comments, and he wondered if she had also begun to contemplate a more permanent arrangement between them.

They left for London shortly afterwards. On the way back, Carpenter considered the idea of getting engaged, but he did not have the nerve to ask Penny what she thought of it. She dropped him off at his flat, and before she drove home she told him that she'd had a marvellous weekend, his mother had been lovely and she was so glad she'd been able to visit his home. The travelling had tired them both, and on Penny's suggestion they decided to forgo their usual midweek meeting so that they could catch up on such things as sleep, the laundering of clothes and other routine necessities.

Carpenter arrived at work on Monday morning to discover that Piggott had resigned. He had phoned Prendergast at his home over the weekend and had announced that he'd consulted his doctor about the migraines he'd been suffering. His doctor had advised him to take things more easily, and after discussions with his wife he had decided to take a complete break from work and was tendering his resignation forthwith.

Carpenter knew nothing about any migraines, but apparently Piggott had insisted that they were unbearable and had been resolute in his decision not to return to work. It was not the kind of end that anyone in The Jungle, Carpenter included, had envisaged for Piggott, but it certainly was a better way out than a heart attack or a nervous breakdown. Carpenter spent the rest of the morning making bewildered efforts to look busy. Shortly after lunch Prendergast summoned him to his alcove and announced that he was promoting him to Piggott's job.

You've got to be kidding, Carpenter thought, but it was clear that Prendergast was not. He was telling Carpenter that he had been pleased with his progress thus far, he seemed to have brought an improved efficiency to his section and Prendergast took the view that he was ready for the extra responsibility. Unfortunately he would have to manage without an assistant for a few weeks at least while they advertised and interviewed for his old position; but his colleagues would be on hand to give him advice and help if he needed it. Of course there was always a measure of risk in promoting someone who had only joined the company two months previously, but Prendergast was confident that he would rise to the challenge.

It did not occur to Carpenter simply to refuse the job, even though he knew he wasn't up to it; Prendergast was the kind of man who made you an offer you couldn't refuse. And there wasn't really any other contender for the post: Denton was intent on improving the status of Tinned Fruits & Vegetables, and his assistant was very loyal to him. And the assistants to the other product managers would have regarded a move to Carpenter's section as a demotion; they were hoping for better things by staying where they were.

Half an hour later Carpenter was sitting at his desk when it dawned on him why Prendergast had promoted him. Piggott had obviously considered his own job to be under threat following Carpenter's appointment as his assistant, so he had begun to work even harder and had boosted his section's sales as a result. But from Prendergast's perspective the improved sales had coincided with Carpenter's arrival and were therefore due at least in part to his efforts. And he clearly expected Carpenter to maintain the improvement.

The first week in his new dispensation proved hectic and exhausting. Carpenter had to attend meetings and seminars, interrogate salesmen, check with accountants, liaise with the marketing department, ring wholesalers and raw materials manufacturers, reply to reports from R&D, and much else. Most of the faces he encountered or the voices he listened to over the phone belonged to people he had never met before. He had no idea whether he was succeeding in fooling any of them that he was informed and understanding of their various problems. Each evening he went home feeling more exhausted, and Friday loomed like a release date from a prison sentence.

He had phoned Penny on Monday evening to tell her of his promotion, and they had agreed to go out for a celebratory meal that coming Saturday. She usually rang him shortly before she went out on Friday evenings to arrange their meeting the following day; failing this, she would call early on Saturday morning, so Carpenter was not worried when the phone remained silent that evening. He went to bed early, and immediately lapsed into a deep sleep. When he woke the bedside clock told him that it was approaching noon.

He ate a late breakfast and waited for Penny to ring, thinking that he had perhaps slept through an earlier call. But the telephone remained silent, and at two o'clock Carpenter went downstairs and rang her flat. The phone rang and rang, but there was no answer.

He usually did his week's shopping on a Saturday afternoon but he was reluctant to leave the flat in case Penny called while he was out. He phoned her again at three o'clock, and again at four, but there was still no answer. Kenneth was invariably absent on Saturdays – he did wedding photography to boost his income – so Carpenter could not leave a message with him.

He continued his hourly phone calls with a growing sense of unease until finally, at seven o'clock, his call was answered. It was Sally. She told him that she didn't know where Penny was, she hadn't seen her all weekend. After checking the flat for any messages, she returned to the phone and informed him that there was none; but Penny had taken a small suitcase and some of her clothes, which usually meant that she would be away for a few days. She had probably gone to her parents. Perhaps there was some emergency; perhaps she would ring him from there.

Sally didn't have their number, and Carpenter knew only that their surname was Brown. He rang off, already feeling crushed. He was sure that Sally had not been lying, but if Penny had had to leave unexpectedly she would surely have rung to tell him before she left, or phoned from her parents' house by now, or at least left a message with Sally. It all smacked of the abrupt change of heart, the sudden rebuff, the cold, cold shoulder. There was a sick feeling inside him comprised of betrayal, a sense of his own foolishness and a strong conviction of the futility of all things. He immediately went out to a local off-licence and returned with two four-packs of Carlsberg Special. Then he proceeded to drink himself into a stupor.

He woke the following morning with a pounding head and saw to his dismay that it was only eight o'clock. He rolled over and tried to go back to sleep, but his misery immediately began to nag at him, compounded by his hangover. It was a long, dismal and utterly empty day, the quintessence of all the unhappy Sundays he had ever spent. At noon he rang Penny's flat again, but there was no answer. It was the same story at three o'clock, and again at six. By now he was convinced that Penny was betraying him with another man. He was tempted to take a bus to Hampstead and hide in the vicinity of her house until he caught her in the act. But this sort of dramatic gesture was alien to his temperament, and he did nothing.

That night sleep deserted him while his restless mind rooted for reasons why Penny had rejected him. Had it been the Manchester visit? Had she, despite what she had said, actually hated every minute of it and had decided that his background was so different from hers that they could not possibly continue together? In a rare moment of detachment Carpenter saw that if this was true then the fault lay with her and not with him. But somehow it seemed too pat an explanation. The visit might have precipitated her withdrawal from him, but he was sure it was not the basic cause.

His fretful mind explored every possibility, exhuming minor

details which he had considered of no importance when things had been going well but which now became fraught with significance. Chief amongst these was the fact that Penny had never given him her work number. She had claimed that her boss disliked his staff taking personal calls and that she didn't want to risk antagonizing him since she was only a humble secretary. At the time this had seemed quite reasonable to Carpenter, but now he began to wonder if she had not wanted him to ring her there for some more Machiavellian reason. He didn't even know the name of the place.

Work was a vexation the following day, the more trying because it demanded every moment of his time; he felt brittle, distracted. That evening he resisted the temptation to ring Penny's flat and went to bed early with *One Day in the Life of Ivan Denisovich*. He read until his eyelids began to droop.

The following day he was in slightly better spirits, and when he got home that evening it occurred to him that he was behaving very foolishly and melodramatically. He had no evidence whatsoever that Penny hadn't really had to go to Canterbury on some family emergency and simply had been unable to contact him.

Before he had time to dissuade himself he went downstairs and telephoned her flat. After several rings, someone answered. It was Sally. No, Penny wasn't back yet. No, she hadn't rung to leave any messages or to say what was going on. No, Sally didn't know her work number. Did he want to leave a message? Carpenter took a deep breath, then said, Just tell her I phoned.

He went back to his room, feeling crushed all over again. That was it. That really was it. Finito. Kaput. Balls.

Somehow he endured the week, keeping himself constantly occupied at work – an easy undertaking – and visiting the local pub immediately afterwards with the group of regular drinkers from The Jungle. He told no one about Penny, but was content to sit there and listen to office gossip or private grievances, relishing the sheer fact of company, of voices addressing him. Later he would go home and slump in an armchair, watching television until the screen went blank.

He had given up hope that Penny would ring him, but each evening the silence of the telephone weighed upon him, and the urge to call her or visit her flat came and went like the craving for a cigarette. But he denied it; he had done all he could and now it was up to her. He knew he was displaying his usual self-destructive passivity in the face of emotional crisis and that he should go to her flat and confront her or continue ringing her until she was forced to speak to him; but his pride would not permit him to do either.

The next weekend was even more miserable than its predecessor, all the hours he had lately spent with Penny on Saturdays and Sundays now like voids filled only with his morbid awareness of her absence. He told himself that he had been far happier before he had met Penny and had been content to spend his weekends pottering about on his own. Relationships made you dependent; they took over a large part of your life, and when they ended you were left feeling like an emotional amputee.

The next day he began to find some respite from his private turmoil in the remorseless responsibilities of his new job; the more he had to grapple with its demands, the less time he had for gloomy cogitations about Penny. On Tuesday almost the whole morning went by without him even thinking of her, and that evening he went straight home from work for the first time in over a week. He found himself wondering if his abrupt departure from Blackpool had had a similar effect on Eleanor to Penny's abandonment of him, and this small departure from his obsession with his own misfortune seemed to mark some kind of progress. On Wednesday morning he awoke more cheerful, with the feeling that the worst was over. That evening he came home to find Penny waiting outside his flat in her car.

She immediately opened the door and came running over to him before flinging herself into his arms and starting to sob. Carpenter stood there, dumbfounded, wrestling with the contradictory feelings that he wanted to hug her and fling her away from him with a maximum of force.

Then she started saying sorry over and over, while telling him that he had to let her explain. She seemed genuinely distraught, and eventually there was nothing for it but to take her upstairs and make her a cup of tea. She sat on the edge of the divan, looking timid and bleary-eyed. When he was seated opposite, with two mugs of tea on the coffee table between them, she announced that her disappearance was all to do with Gordon.

Gordon? said Carpenter. She nodded and explained that Gordon was a married man with whom she had been having an affair for several months. He was her boss, in fact, the senior accountant she worked for. It all happened by accident, really; Gordon was very unhappy in his marriage and she felt sorry for him and they just fell into an affair. But then she had met him, Carpenter, and things had started to change. She had never had the nerve to tell him about Gordon because there had never been the right moment; and the more important he, Carpenter, had become to her, the more difficult it had become to tell him the truth.

Carpenter felt as if he had been hit in the gut with a lead-filled sock. Shit, shit, shit, he was thinking. Then Penny told him that Gordon had somehow discovered that she had gone to Manchester for the weekend with another man; he had been furious and had made her life hell in the office, demanding to know where he, Carpenter, lived so that he could confront him. By the end of the week she had been so terrified that he would follow her to Carpenter's place and cause a scene that she had phoned her father, who had driven to London and taken her back to Canterbury. All she wanted to do was to get away for a while. It turned out that her parents were setting off for a holiday in Normandy the following morning, and on the spur of the moment she had decided to go with them. She had needed time to herself to think things over.

Penny paused, looking at him expectantly. Carpenter remained silent. She assured him that there had been no opportunity to ring him before she departed; she had set off at six-thirty in the morning with her parents, and they had stayed at a remote farm with no postal facilities. But the solitude had helped her come to a decision: when she had got back she had immediately resigned her job and broken off the affair with Gordon. If he didn't believe her he could phone him and check for himself. She had realized that he, Carpenter, was far more important to her, and she couldn't bear to lose him.

Again she paused, and again he remained silent. It was all true, she insisted; he had to believe her. She'd never been able to cope with any unpleasantness and she always ran away from it, ran away and hid until everything had blown over.

Carpenter knew that this, at least, was true. He recalled how tense and silent she had been during his verbal sparring with Henry in the wine bar, and his subsequent familiarity with her had made him realize that she was always uncomfortable with any extreme displays of public emotion; on those occasions when there had been a hint of discord in the air, she had always looked as if she was wishing she were somewhere else entirely.

There were real tears trickling down her cheeks now, and her lips were quivering. For a moment Carpenter did not move. His illusion of their perfect affair had been abruptly dispelled, and he felt humiliated that Penny had been continuing an affair with this Gordon all the time she had been going out with him. After what had happened with Karen and Derek he could not bear the thought of again being the unwitting third party in any love triangle. But at the same time he recognized that Penny had been no more deceitful with him than Eleanor had been with Frank when he had been the other man. At least Penny had had the courage finally to explain everything to his face. And she had decided in his favour in the end.

Confused though his emotions were, his prevailing feeling was of great relief. Penny was still waiting. He rose, went over to her and hugged her to him.

She stayed with him that night, and they made love as passionately as they had ever done. There was a renewed urgency in her affections, an eagerness to placate him and resume their relationship on its former footing. Carpenter responded in kind, and yet a small part of him remained detached, inured to her. He still found her as physically desirable as ever, but the wholehearted, uncritical desire he had once felt was gone.

She remained at his flat until the following Monday morning, doing his shopping while he was at work and greeting him with a cup of coffee when he arrived home in the evenings. She disliked cooking, and Carpenter was always too weary to prepare a meal for the two of them himself, so they dined out in local restaurants and afterwards went to bed early. On Saturday they drove out to Hampton Court for the day, and on Sunday spent a crisp and bright afternoon at Kew Gardens, Penny giving her camera to a stranger so that he could photograph them outside the Palm House. It was like being on holiday, and Carpenter was almost disappointed when they parted on Monday morning, she returning to her own flat before she began her search for a new job.

A few days later she phoned him with the news that she would be starting work as secretary to the head of a design studio in Covent Garden the following Monday. It did not surprise him that she had found a job so quickly, for she was not only personable but also had an air of capability and efficiency. They went out for a celebratory meal on the Saturday evening. Sitting opposite him at the candle-lit table and dabbing at her lips with a white napkin, she looked simply adorable.

The weeks went by, and everything was fine. Carpenter had persuaded her to suspend his driving lessons, but they continued to meet during the week and always spent Saturdays and Sundays together. Still somewhat cautious at first, he managed to take Sally aside one evening and ask her about Gordon. Sally knew no more than him, and if Penny had been lying to him about what had actualiy happened between them, she had apparently told Sally the same story; though they were flatmates, they led separate lives and Penny had never confided in her about personal matters. One afternoon while at her flat, he came across some company notepaper which gave the address and telephone number of her old employers. An unworthy instinct made him fold up one of the sheets and slip it into his pocket, just in case. Otherwise he felt content and amply rewarded by Penny's renewed devotion to him.

This was just as well, for work was proving ever more troublesome. Several people had been interviewed for the post of his assistant, but all had been declared unsuitable and no appointment had yet been made. Carpenter struggled on, but by December it was abundantly clear to him that Piggott had left him unequipped to master the job, and this was now apparent to Prendergast as well. Prendergast had allowed him a certain leeway during his running-in period, but his patience was wearing thin. Carpenter's bluffs and obfuscations had become less and less convincing, and it was only a matter of time before his basic ineptitude was exposed. In mid-November the October sales figures had been issued, and while the figures for his section showed some residual buoyancy from Piggott's efforts, there were indications of a definite downturn. Soon the November sales figures would follow, and the prospect filled Carpenter with trepidation. He kept his worries to himself, but was ever more grateful for Penny's companionship. Then she disappeared again.

He had arranged to meet her outside Tottenham Court Road tube station at noon on a Saturday afternoon; they would have an early lunch, and then go Christmas shopping in Oxford Street. When she had not arrived by one o'clock, he rang her flat, but there was no answer. At one-thirty he abandoned his vigil at the station and went directly to her place. No one answered the bell. He waited outside her flat all afternoon before finally going home.

She was not waiting for him there, and the phone remained silent all evening. He tried ringing her again at intervals throughout the evening, but no one replied. At ten o'clock he gave up. There was a four-pack of lager in his fridge, but he left it untouched and went to bed early with a copy of *Penthouse*. The magazine failed dismally to arouse him.

The next day Sally answered his call. No, she had absolutely no idea where Penny was, wasn't she with him? No, Carpenter told her, and when she asked him if he wanted to leave a message he said, Yes, tell her that I don't want to hear from her again.

He was surprised how fatalistic he felt. This time there really would be no going back; he'd had enough. Kenneth was away on an assignment in Brighton, so Carpenter took the phone off the hook, not intending to replace it until he returned. But that night he began to wonder if Penny had been injured in an accident. Was she lying broken and unconscious in some hospital bed even as he was vilifying her memory?

He rang her new work number the following morning, but was told that she had not yet arrived. He tried again towards noon, but got the same answer. When a third call later that afternoon produced the same response, the possibility of an accident began to seem more real: surely nothing else would have prevented her from going to work on her first day in a new job? But at the same time he rejected the idea, telling himself that it was only his over-developed sense of guilt that was making him think the worst. That evening he made a point of going to the pub immediately after work. He stayed until closing time, went for a late meal at a local curry house, and did not turn on any lights at the front of the house when he got home.

The next morning the November sales figures were issued, and they proved worse than Carpenter had anticipated. Every one of his product range, pickled onions included, had shown a slump. Soon afterwards Nigel Denton came by to offer smiling commiserations: Tinned Fruit & Vegetables had outstripped Pickles, Onions & Chutneys in sales for the first time in six months, and Carpenter knew he was doomed.

His summons to Prendergast's alcove came that afternoon. Prendergast had the sales figures spread out on his desk, and he did not ask Carpenter to sit down. Carpenter waited while he shuffled the papers around with a studied air of distraction. At length he gave a heavy sigh and looked up at Carpenter before asking him if he knew why he had been summoned.

Yes, said Carpenter, deciding that there was nothing for it but bluntness; you want to know why my figures for this month are down. He was about to say that this was because the original improvement had been nothing to do with him in the first place and that he just wasn't equipped to do the job. But before he could continue he heard Prendergast telling him that this was not the reason at all; he knew perfectly well why the figures were down. They were down because Carpenter wasn't doing his job properly. Did he not agree? Carpenter replied that he did, but before he could elaborate Prendergast was asking him if he did not think he should get himself in order for the sake of the company who had placed him in a position of responsibility in the first place?

Carpenter wanted to say that he was doing his best. He wanted to add that even if he had been experienced and efficient at his job he would still have found it hard to get worked up about the sales of piccalilli in Peterborough or the market potential of mayonnaise in Morden. But already his original intention to be honest had faded away in the face of Prendergast's stern, unyielding expression. Prendergast wanted results; excuses were of no interest to him.

There followed a short lecture in which Prendergast reminded him that he had put his faith in Carpenter in the first place and would be severely disappointed if Carpenter continued to demonstrate that he had erred in his judgement. So disappointed that he would not possibly be able to recommend that Carpenter continue in his present position. Carpenter nodded and duly promised to do better. Then he made the tactical blunder of asking about the Christmas holidays. Christmas Day fell on a Tuesday that year, and Carpenter was hoping to take two extra days off so that he could spend a whole week in Manchester and return to London in the New Year. But Prendergast was adamant that he be at work on Thursday the 27th and Friday the 28th.

When Carpenter arrived home that evening, Penny was waiting for him.

He spotted her Fiesta as he came down the road, and his first instinct was to turn on his heels and flee. But he stopped himself and instead strode manfully up to the car. Penny was sitting in the driver's seat and did not notice him until he was opening the door.

She stared timidly at him with her small cornered animal expression. Oh Mike, she said at last, it was terrible; and then she flung her arms around his neck.

Carpenter banged his head against the roof of the car as he jerked back, but he was immune to the pain. He loosened her arms from his neck and crouched in the doorway, saying nothing.

Tears began to roll down her cheeks as she told him that Gordon had bundled her into his car outside his flat on Friday evening and driven her to a bedsitter in Paddington. He wouldn't accept that their affair was over and had told her that he was never going to let her go. She'd been fed and given a bed to sleep in at the flat, and he hadn't laid a finger on her; but he'd kept her locked up all the time and had only released her that afternoon when she finally persuaded him that she would go to the police if he didn't.

Penny fell silent, still crying and not looking at him. Now it was Carpenter who felt like a cornered animal. This is insane, he thought; she can't be expecting me to believe this. Then Penny turned towards him again and he saw an intensity in her eyes which told him that she did. It was as if she had already convinced herself and expected no less from him.

Carpenter heard himself asking her if she didn't think she ought to go to the police, to which she replied that she simply couldn't. She had promised him she wouldn't and he had been so good to her in the past that she couldn't bear to let him down. And after all, it was her breaking off their affair that had made him so distraught and irrational in his behaviour so that what had happened was partly her fault. Carpenter pointed out that he had locked her up for four days and that this was kidnapping, a criminal offence. Didn't she think she would be doing him a favour by informing the police? It was obvious that Gordon was emotionally disturbed and he would be able to get proper treatment when he was in the hands of the authorities.

Penny was adamant that she could do no such thing; it would be like betraying him. She was sure she had at last succeeded in convincing Gordon that there was no prospect of them resuming their affair; when he had finally set her free he had been profoundly apologetic, like a little boy who knew he had done wrong, and she was confident that he would not bother her again. All she wanted now was to forget it and concentrate on him, Carpenter; she was looking forward to them spending Christmas together.

A sense of futility and impatience overtook Carpenter. He was merely consolidating her fantasy by pretending to go along with it, and this would do neither of them any good.

She was waiting for him to say something, but he allowed the silence to extend before telling her that the whole story was preposterous and he couldn't understand why she imagined he would believe a word of it. For all he knew this Gordon might not even exist, but if he did then it certainly wasn't at all plausible that he would kidnap her. He didn't know why she was lying to him and quite frankly he no longer cared, his patience was exhausted. The whole pantomime was an insult to his intelligence.

He walked off. Crossing the street to his front door, he had the prickly feeling that she was staring after him. He opened the door, entered, and closed it behind him without looking back. Then he darted up the stairs and let himself into his flat before going to the window of his front room, which overlooked the street. Her car could be seen across the road but its roof blocked any view of her. What he dreaded most at that moment was that she would get out, come to his door and start ringing his bell. But even as he was thinking this, she drove away.

With her departure Carpenter immediately began to feel guilty, as if he had judged her far too harshly. What if her story were true in spirit if not in fact? What if this Gordon had been pestering her in some way which made her want to run away and not see or talk to anyone? He shook his head. Even if this were true, he had reached the point where he simply could not deal with it any longer. Enough was enough.

Something made him put the receiver back on its cradle that evening, and he kept expecting the phone to ring and to hear Penny's imploring, apologetic voice at the other end of the line. Long after he had got into bed he was still primed for its sound; but there was only silence.

As soon as he had a spare moment the next morning he took his wallet from his jacket pocket and removed the sheet of headed notepaper with the telephone number of Penny's old workplace. A brisk female voice answered his call. He asked to speak to Gordon, his tone designed to suggest that Gordon was an old friend of his. Carpenter did not in fact know his surname, but as luck would have it the woman immediately transferred the call.

Hello? said a male voice which sounded responsible and mature. Would that be Gordon? Carpenter wanted to know, and was informed that yes it was and who was this? Well, said Carpenter, you don't actually know me but I wanted to talk to you about Penny, your former secretary.

There was a silence at the other end of the line. The thing is, Carpenter went on quickly, we've been going out together recently and she's been talking a lot about you and I was wondering . . . He faltered, stopped. Still the other man remained silent.

The thing is, Carpenter began again, I don't want to pry but she told me that the two of you used to go out together and she gave me the impression that you've seen one another lately. He stopped again. This was much too subtle, and if he was going to get anywhere he would have to muster his courage and be blunt. He took a deep breath and said that Penny had told him that he, Gordon, had kidnapped her and held her captive at a bedsitter in Paddington over the weekend. Until Tuesday afternoon, in fact.

There was another silence, much longer than any before. Then Carpenter heard Gordon ask him what his name was. Mike, he said, Mike Carpenter.

Well, Mr Carpenter, said Gordon, sounding very professional

and utterly in command of the situation, Penny's story bears no relation whatsoever to the true facts. He had no idea what she had said about him, but the fact was that he had been forced to sack Penny several weeks ago because she had developed an infatuation with him which had become deeply embarrassing for himself and for everyone else in the office. He had done his best to discourage it, but Penny would not see reason and was continually pestering him to take her out. At no point had he ever done so; there was no question of any sort of involvement with her, let alone a full-blown affair. He was a married man with two children, and Penny's repeated telephone calls to his home soliciting his company had caused his wife considerable distress. It was not he who had kidnapped her – the idea was absurd – but she who had camped outside his house all evening, pleading with him to see her until he had threatened to telephone the police. In his considered opinion she had serious emotional problems and was in urgent need of psychiatric help.

There were other questions which Carpenter had intended to ask, but they now seemed irrelevant. Gordon had spoken in a rather guarded fashion throughout, presumably because there were other people in earshot, and Carpenter did not want to strain his goodwill. He thanked him for his frankness, apologized for disturbing him and rang off.

That afternoon Carpenter was in the middle of a consultation with Prendergast when his phone rang. He picked it up automatically – half his working day seemed to be spent on the phone – and heard Penny's voice say, Mike, is that you?

She had never telephoned him at work before. Carpenter immediately adopted a nasal drawl and asked her who she required. Prendergast was standing in front of his desk, having paused to allow him to take the call. They had been discussing the new line in cucumber and sweet corn relishes which were due for test launch in South Wales at the turn of the year (Carpenter had been making much of his familiarity with that part of the country). In the same peculiar voice he told Penny that unfortunately Mr Carpenter had gone to a sales conference and was not expected back for the rest of the week.

He did not dare look at Prendergast. Mike, Penny was saying, I know it's you, we have to talk. Still speaking through his nose, Carpenter insisted that Mr Carpenter would not be available until the end of the week. Then he remembered that next week was Christmas week. Mike, Penny said again, a sob fracturing the word, why are you doing this? I have to see you. We have to talk.

Prendergast's face was a study in deadpan outrage. Carpenter smiled helplessly at him. Penny was sobbing loudly now, and Carpenter was sure that Prendergast could hear every sniffle. Please Mike, she implored him. Please. Prendergast walked off.

Carpenter waited until there was a pause in her sobbing before informing her that he had spoken to Gordon, who had told him everything. She was silent. Goodbye Penny, he said, feeling like a character in a soap opera. Then he put the phone down.

That evening there was a pre-Christmas drink at a local pub, and Carpenter was more than happy to be part of it. He managed to regulate his drinking so that he was not totally blotto by the time he got home; he might need to have his wits about him if Penny was on the prowl. Entering his street he scrutinized the parked cars on both sides of the road for a red Ford Fiesta before cautiously approaching his front door. All seemed well, though at any moment he expected Penny to leap out from behind a lowering privet hedge. But he made it inside without incident, and soon he was safely in bed, the telephone off the hook again. Sleep came swiftly.

He fully expected her to ring him at work the next day, but she did not. It proved a day blissfully free of harassment, Prendergast being ensconced in a high-level meeting for most of it. That evening the department had its Christmas party in the cafeteria on the second floor, and Carpenter managed several dances with secretaries and tea ladies before he became too drunk to continue. Mark Quick, who had been far more restrained in his drinking, ran him home in his Lotus Elan. The car windows were misted up, and Carpenter could not see straight in any case so that it was impossible to establish whether or not Penny was lurking nearby when they pulled up outside his house.

He flung the car door open and stumbled out into the street. The only sign of life was a woman putting out milkbottles opposite, yet the neat houses with their tidy front gardens looked menacing in the stark orange glare of the streetlights. He thought he heard

Mark Quick tell him to drive carefully before he departed in a cloud of carbon monoxide. Carpenter teetered towards his front door.

The telephone was ringing even as he opened it. He climbed the stairs saying, I'm not going to answer it, I'm not going to answer it, then snatched up the receiver as soon as he was within arm's reach. Mike? Is that Mike? It was Penny. He said nothing. Mike, we have to talk, I need to see you; Sally's gone home for Christmas and I'm on my own here, and I'm feeling depressed, I just have to see you. Still he remained silent. She started to cry, then told him he had to come, she'd taken something. What? said Carpenter. I've taken something; tablets. He told her he wasn't falling for that, she wasn't playing him for a sucker again. There was a silence at the other end of the line. He really was finished with her, he insisted, and it was better if they both left one another alone from now on.

There was a further silence. Goodbye, Mike, she said in the most forlorn voice he had ever heard, then cut the connection.

Ten minutes later Carpenter was on his way to her flat. He simply couldn't take the risk that she was faking; given her obvious mental instability, anything was possible. The idea petrified him.

There was no possibility of any public transport at that hour, and he didn't think of calling a cab. Instead he ran the whole way there. Soon his head was pounding, he had a stitch in his side and felt as if he was about to throw up. But he did not stint in his efforts to get there as quickly as possible, hurrying through street after street, all anonymous and leached of colour under a ubiquitous sodium glow.

When he finally reached Penny's flat he was breathless and fiery-lunged, but he felt utterly sober. He rang the bell, not expecting her to answer and wondering what he would do if she didn't. But presently the door opened to reveal Penny standing there in her dressing gown. She looked woozy, and hardly seemed to recognize him. As he stepped inside, she slumped against him.

Carpenter laid her out on the sofa in the front room. She smelt sickly and he checked the bathroom. Sure enough, she had vomited in the toilet bowl. On the shelf above the washbasin he found a packet of soluble aspirin, and from the torn foil strips was able to estimate that she had swallowed no more than twelve tablets. He felt at once relieved and annoyed, judging that it hadn't been a serious suicide attempt at all. She'd probably even stuck her fingers down her throat to make sure she was sick.

But she looked pale and out of sorts. He fetched a blanket from the bedroom and wrapped it around her. Then he went into the kitchen and made her a mug of Horlicks. She had said nothing to him since his arrival, merely gazing at him with a doleful expression. He put the mug down beside her and took an armchair opposite, lighting a cigarette and waiting.

She shivered and drew the blanket more tightly around her shoulders. Without looking up at him she whispered that she was sorry, it was all her fault, she hadn't meant to drag him all the way over here at this time of the night; she felt much better now and he could go if he liked. She understood that it was all over between them, even if she didn't understand why; she wasn't going to bother him any more.

Just drink your Horlicks and get some sleep, Carpenter told her. We can talk about it in the morning. She made no reply to this. But soon she was asleep.

It took him far longer to drift off. His trek to the flat had sobered him up, but it had also brought on a hangover; his head was throbbing and he felt nauseous every time he closed his eyes. He fetched another blanket from the bedroom and draped it around himself, huddling in the armchair with his feet up on a floor cushion. It would have been easier if he had put Penny to bed and slept beside her, but he didn't want to disturb her now.

He slept fitfully, waking at regular intervals throughout the night from vague, threatening dreams which left him anxious and disorientated. Once he got up and checked Penny's pulse, which was normal as far as he could tell. At length a deeper sleep overtook him.

He woke to noises in the kitchen. Presently Penny emerged with a plate of bacon and eggs and a cup of coffee. She told him what a lovely day it was, then threw back the curtains to reveal a cloudless winter sky. She was bright and cheerful and made no reference to what had happened the night before.

Carpenter felt awful. His head was still throbbing, he felt weary from insufficient sleep, and he had a stiff neck from lying awkwardly in the armchair. The bacon and eggs were both undercooked and wallowing in grease. Penny brought him toast and marmalade before departing to the bathroom.

He heard the shower being turned on. He took his plate into the kitchen and scraped the bacon and eggs into the flip-top bin. In the bathroom Penny was humming to herself as she showered. Was she going to pretend that nothing had happened? If so, would he be advised to do likewise and depart with a minimum of fuss? He was inclined to do just that. He checked his watch and saw that it was already eight-fifteen. It was going to be difficult enough to face his working day without engaging Penny in a heart-to-heart conversation as a prelude. But he knew he had to go through with it.

Ten minutes later she emerged, fully made-up and dressed in a white cotton blouse with a tweed jacket and a fawn skirt. She looked a picture of administrative prettiness, but he was determined not to let that sway him. She was saying that they ought to be leaving if they were both not to be late for work. He shook his head and told her to sit down. She was the one who had been insisting that they had to talk, and now they were going to do just that.

He made her sit down in an armchair, then began by asking her if she realized what she had tried to do last night. Her head was bowed and she said nothing. He asked her again, and this time she gave a brief nod. He wondered to himself if she had tried this sort of thing before – with Gordon perhaps? He asked her as much, and she shook her head; Gordon had never meant as much to her as he did.

Carpenter did not believe this for a moment, but he said nothing. Unable to think of a better tack, he told her exactly what Gordon had said to him, not omitting his judgement that she was emotionally disturbed and needed expert help. At this point she looked up, a mixture of hurt and outrage on her face.

And you believed him? she said. You believed everything he said? Then she proceeded to insist that none of it was true, that it was Gordon who had been pestering her and she who had been doing her best to make him leave her alone. Didn't he see that Gordon was just trying to protect himself at her expense? Of course he wasn't going to admit that he had abducted her and kept her locked up for four days. Of course it was in his interest to pretend that she was the guilty party. Gordon always sounded rational and convincing, the more so when he was in the wrong. She was not surprised that he, Carpenter, had believed his every word. But it simply wasn't true.

Throughout this recital her tone had varied between the aggrieved and the indignant. But Carpenter was unmoved. She started to cry again, and he found himself incapable of offering her any sympathy or reassurance. He rose, taking his coat off the back of the chair and putting it on before telling her that it would be best if they didn't see one another for a while. In fact he had no intention of ever seeing her again; the fierceness with which she seemed to want to cling to him was frightening not least because it was unconnected with any genuine fondness for him. Or so it seemed; he was not sure he understood anything of her real feelings. He knew that he was leaving without having properly tackled the question of her suicide attempt, but he felt inadequate to the task and wanted only to get away. She was staring at him, looking wounded and forlorn. He turned away and departed without a further word, without looking back.

It was approaching ten o'clock before he arrived at work, but happily Prendergast was nowhere to be seen. When he did appear Carpenter was primed with an excuse for his lateness: having earlier been asked by Mark Quick why he was carrying his head so stiffly, he had told him that he'd strained a muscle in his shoulder while helping his landlady carry her wheelchair-bound grandfather up the stairs that morning. Carpenter took the view that an excuse was more likely to be convincing the more preposterous it sounded, and it seemed to work: Prendergast merely blinked at him and walked off, as if nothing Carpenter said could surprise him.

By lunch time Carpenter had had pause to reflect on Penny's version of the Gordon affair, and he was no longer quite so convinced that she had been lying. True, Gordon's story made more sense than hers, but what if his hesitancy in the telling of it had not been due to the proximity of a colleague but a result of evasiveness? What if Gordon really was the guilty party and had simply been covering up for himself?

He could not bring himself to phone Gordon again, but decided to seek the advice of an interested third party: Henry. He had not seen Henry since the night at the wine bar, but Penny had often spoken of him and Carpenter had managed to remember both his full name and the name of the antiques shop which he ran. It was a simple matter of consulting the telephone directory.

He rang later that afternoon. The woman who answered asked for his name, and there was a long pause before he heard Henry's officious voice say, Yes, Mr Carpenter, what can I do for you?

Carpenter was sure that Henry remembered him, but he was determinedly pretending otherwise. Carpenter reminded him of their first and only meeting, but this proved a mistake for a brisk note of resentment entered Henry's tone as he informed Carpenter that he did not have much time for social calls during his working day.

Carpenter explained that he was ringing about a matter of mutual interest and was seeking his advice. Lately he had been having a few problems with Penny and he knew that he, Henry, was close to her and probably knew her as well as anyone; she certainly always spoke highly of him. He, Carpenter, was rather worried about her and felt that he needed to talk to someone who would also have her welfare at heart.

Henry responded grudgingly to this flattery; when Carpenter asked if it would be possible for them to meet for a quiet drink that evening, he grumbled that it was very inconvenient, Christmas being a busy time of the year and he having numerous pressing commitments. But he did not actually say no, and Carpenter duly gave him leeway to sigh and then reluctantly condescend to spare him an hour. Carpenter suggested that they meet at the wine bar, but this was immediately rejected, with Henry favouring a pub on Hampstead High Street.

The meeting proved inconclusive. Carpenter arrived ten minutes early, but Henry was already waiting for him, a half-pint of beer on the table in front of him. He declined Carpenter's offer of a further drink, reminding him that he was pressed for time. Carpenter hastily departed to the bar. When he returned to the table he immediately gave Henry a precis of what had happened between Penny, himself and Gordon in recent weeks. He couched it all as tactfully as possible but spared Henry no facts, even mentioning the suicide attempt. Then he admitted that he was confused and did not know whether to believe Penny or Gordon's story about what had really been happening between them. What did he, Henry, think?

He had been hoping that Henry would give him some hard facts about Penny, but this was not to be. Henry shook his head before telling Carpenter that Penny was a complex and emotionally vulnerable person who needed stability and security in her life; she needed someone who could offer her understanding, warmth, patience. Too many men were drawn to the superficially attractive features of her but they were always the ones who weren't prepared to stand by her when the going got tough. The real problem was not with her but with the men she became involved with; she had a self-destructive urge for choosing boyfriends who always let her down.

Henry went on in this vein for some time, and it soon dawned on Carpenter that he was defining Penny's ideal man as himself. Far from offering Carpenter advice or information about her character, Henry was secretly pleased by his difficulties and saw them as confirmation that he, not Carpenter, was the only man for her. He would not tell Carpenter anything that he might be able to use to his own advantage.

The telephone was ringing when Carpenter arrived back at his flat. He let it ring, difficult though this was, then took the phone off the hook when it fell silent. Go away, he thought; leave me alone. His heart was pounding in his chest, his gut felt taut, and the morning's headache had returned. One more day, he told himself; just one more day. He spent the rest of the evening packing; tomorrow, after work, he would take the train home to Manchester for Christmas.

He slept fitfully again that night, but went to work cheerful in the thought that everyone would be relaxed and in the festive spirit. This proved grossly optimistic; Prendergast was waiting for him when he arrived with a sheaf of sales forecasts which did not bode well for his section. Carpenter was forced to spend the morning huddled in his alcove while Prendergast told him What Had To Be Done, or else. What had to be done was beyond Carpenter's capabilities, and he thought only of his imminent escape to Manchester, a few days' respite.

He had hoped to get away early that afternoon, but around three-thirty Prendergast arrived at his desk with a party of Japanese visitors. He announced that Carpenter was to escort them around the department. Carpenter knew that he was probably the least qualified person in the place for the job, but there was nothing he could do. Five expectant faces regarded him. I hate you, he thought as Prendergast departed.

He attempted a whirlwind tour, but the Japanese proved so curious and interested in every detail of The Jungle that it was well over an hour before he finally returned the party to Prendergast. By the time he was ready to depart it was six o'clock. Prendergast was on hand to remind him that he was expected to be at work on the 27th.

When Carpenter opened his front door Kenneth emerged from his flat, suitcase in hand, and presented him with a Christmas card. He was off to Lincoln to spend the holiday with his parents. Carpenter felt guilty, for he had forgotten to buy a card for Kenneth. In fact he had bought no cards for anyone at all, or any presents. He would have to do all his shopping in Manchester tomorrow.

Carpenter checked that everything was switched off in his flat before locking up his suitcase. Then the doorbell rang.

He crept to the window, but there was no sign of Penny's car. The bell rang again, but he did not move. At length someone stepped out of the doorway – a woman with short fair hair and large glasses. As she turned to walk away, he saw that it was Veronica.

She had obtained his address from his mother, she told him when she was inside and seated. She had tried to ring him the previous evening but kept getting an engaged tone, so she had decided to look him up personally. A canvas rucksack sat at her feet. She explained that she had a few days off before Christmas but would be manning the emergency desk at her workplace during Christmas week itself. She wore white baseball boots and a baggy olive-green jump suit over a black long-sleeved vest. Her hair had been cropped unflatteringly short, and her gold-rimmed grannie glasses had been replaced by large, pink-framed spectacles with lenses shaped like miniature television screens. Yet somehow she seemed remarkably unchanged, her grey, questioning eyes still disconcertingly intense, her face as pale and unblemished as ever.

She informed him that she was now living in a mixed house in Stepney working for a community aid group who dealt with the problems of ethnic minorities in the London area. She had left the psychotherapy institute and split up with her counsellor boyfriend when it became clear to her that the underlying tenets of Eclectic Therapy were sexist and designed to bolster male supremacy. On weekends she helped out at a feminist co-operative called AWOL, for Active Women's League, a pressure group dedicated to exposing instances of sexual discrimination and to achieving fair and equal treatment for women in all spheres of life.

Carpenter felt distinctly reluctant to talk about his own job, but when prompted he gave her a vague and dismissive account of what he did, saying that he had just drifted into it really and found the whole thing hard to take seriously. She studied him, then informed him that his company had subsidiaries in Black Africa and were currently under suspicion of paying native workers subsistence wages. I didn't know, Carpenter said feebly.

When she asked him what else he had been doing he shrugged, not having the heart to tell her that he had been about to depart for Manchester. He had already revised his timetable, deciding that he would set off early the next morning.

She had not seen any of their old friends from Cardiff in recent years, so he made small talk about Nick Bullivant's party for a while. But it soon became clear that Veronica was not really interested in any of it; she had never been one to dwell on the past. But she did surprise him by asking if he was having a relationship with anyone at the moment. No, Carpenter told her, thinking of Penny at her most ravishing. No one.

Had she eaten? She wasn't hungry. Carpenter had earlier stuffed himself with sandwiches from the company cafeteria preparatory to his train journey, so that problem was solved. He lit a cigarette and asked her if she fancied a drink down the road. Not particularly, she told him, and he remembered that she had never especially liked pubs. But he could have done with a stiffener himself; though he was genuinely pleased to see her again, he inevitably felt that he was being weighed in her critical balance and found wanting. Already he was self-conscious about smoking in front of her.

She noticed his suitcase, and he explained that he was intending to depart for Manchester on the morrow. That's a shame, she said; she was hoping they would be able to spend the weekend together. She was free till Sunday. Well, said Carpenter, why not? He was flexible and could take a train to Manchester on Sunday night. (He'd still have Christmas Eve on which to buy presents.)

He saw that Veronica was smiling at him. This was a phenomenon almost as rare as a wet weekend in the Atacama Desert, and it always seemed less an expression of pleasure or friendliness than one of concession, as if she was acknowledging an adroit point in a debate. You haven't changed, Mike, she told him. It's rather comforting.

The telephone started ringing. He did not move. Aren't you going to answer it? Veronica wanted to know. Carpenter told her that it was probably for Ken, the photographer who lived downstairs, and then proceeded to portray him as a hell-raiser and womanizer who was always getting calls from cast-off lovers. He, Carpenter, was tired of making excuses for him and preferred to let the phone ring.

Veronica gave no indication of whether she believed this little fiction, but the phone presently stopped ringing. She delved into her rucksack and produced a dark brown bottle with an ornate label covered with incomprehensible script. She had brought it to toast the holiday with him, she said; it had been a present from a friend of hers who had recently returned from Eastern Europe.

The drink was some kind of Bulgarian liquor, and Carpenter made the mistake of taking a large swig. It went down the gullet like napalm and brought tears to his eyes. Did the average Bulgarian drink this stuff as a matter of course? he wondered. Or did they do the sensible thing and use it for sterilizing the U-bends of their toilets?

Five minutes later he essayed a second sip, and this time it did not taste so bad, possibly because his mouth had been anaesthetized by the first dose. Veronica had started to query him about his love life, and he knew she was leading up to something.

He gave her a potted and very selective account of his liaisons with Karen, Eleanor and Penny. He also mentioned Cicely and made a few passing references to fictitious one-night stands with numerous other women. Veronica listened without comment for the most part, and Carpenter was convinced that she knew exactly when he was lying or elaborating. She studied him for a while as if sifting through everything he had told her. Then she began to ask him about Penny.

Carpenter did his best to present their relationship as a passionate and happy-go-lucky affair which had ended several weeks previously by mutual consent. But the Bulgarian cleaning fluid was beginning to take its effect, and Veronica kept asking pertinent questions until finally Carpenter was unable to conceal the problems he had had with her. In the end he revealed all about Penny's disappearances, his telephone conversation with Gordon, Penny's suicide attempt and her subsequent insistence that Gordon had kidnapped her. The more he talked, the more he became convinced that he was giving Veronica ammunition for some damning indictment of himself. But he couldn't stop: he was confessing, and while he did not expect Veronica to be gracious or forgiving, he hoped that she would tell him what to do.

She offered neither advice nor criticism. When he was finished she merely extended a hand and rested it lightly on his own before saying that he felt better now that he had talked about it, didn't he? Carpenter frowned, wondering. He felt only that he had been given some strange form of benediction by her. Then it came to him that he had been playing patient to her psychotherapist.

At this point she suggested that they go to bed.

From the moment she had indicated that she wanted to spend the weekend with him he had assumed that she intended to sleep in the front room. But she obviously meant them to share the same bed. This was a complete surprise; true, they had once slept together regularly, but he had never imagined that she would want to do so again.

While she was in the bathroom he undressed quickly and got into bed. He had switched off the light, remembering that she had always preferred their intimacies to be conducted in darkness. But when she entered she turned the light on and undressed in front of him, tossing her clothes in the lap of an armchair. Last of all she removed her glasses.

She got in beside him, and he felt her perennially cold feet touch his. With her short haircut, she looked like a complete stranger beside him, and yet he knew it was the same old Veronica underneath. He felt like a virgin all over again.

During their time together in Cardiff Veronica had never had a great appetite for sex or been greatly demonstrative during it. She would lie practically motionless beneath him as if partaking in a ritual which was necessary but not especially enjoyable. Only on rare occasions had she ever shown stronger reactions, occasionally clutching his arms so fiercely that he had thought she was finally about to come. But it had always proved a false alarm, and in general she had seemed far happier when discussing sexual politics in the abstract than actually having sex in the flesh.

But now she surprised him with the energy of her attentions. She was not only mobile and vigorous as they kissed and stroked one another but also took the upper hand, straddling him and placing her hands on his shoulders as she guided herself on to him.

Carpenter decided to relax and let her dictate matters. He had drunk sufficient alcohol to remove his nervousness but not so much as to impair his performance. After a time Veronica began to urge him towards his climax with words as well as movements, something she had never remotely done before. The vulgar expressions startled him at first, but he closed his eyes and began to fantasize that she was some voluptuous creature consumed with passion for his body. When he finally delivered, Veronica gave a gasp and pressed herself down hard on him.

Afterwards she slumped face down on the pillow, still lying across him. Long minutes passed. Carpenter could feel her heart fluttering against his chest, but otherwise everything was still and silent. He studied the ceiling and wondered if he should try to move his left arm, which was trapped beneath her in an awkward position. The arm had gone numb before he realized that she was sleeping.

He awoke in the depths of the night to find Veronica performing fellatio on him. For a moment he thought he was dreaming, but there was no doubt about it. It was another first for her, and he wondered if she intended to demonstrate her entire sexual repertoire. They made love again, and at length. He was seldom able to come twice within the space of a few hours, but presently Veronica crouched on her hands and knees with her fanny raised to him. Carpenter could scarcely believe it. Through Penny he had discovered this to be one of his favourite positions and the one most guaranteed to bring about a rapid ejaculation; but it was a submissive posture and he would never have imagined Veronica permitting him such liberties. Scant seconds after entering her, he came.

They lay in bed the following morning until noon, making love yet again before they got up. It was all so unlike the Veronica he remembered, but he wasn't complaining. She did not appear to have overcome her inability to attain orgasm but was certainly putting more effort into the task. The phone rang again during mid-morning, but they were in the throes of lovemaking, so he had a good excuse not to answer it.

That afternoon they took a walk around the local area, and it did not surprise him when Veronica proved much more knowledgeable about it than himself. When they got back she rummaged in his larder and eventually mustered the ingredients for a vegetable curry.

The telephone started ringing as they sat down to eat. Veronica stared at him, then asked if he was sure he wasn't expecting a call from someone. Carpenter insisted that he was not, though he was convinced it was Penny who was ringing. Didn't he think he ought to answer it, in case it was an emergency? Through a mouthful of rice and red peppers Carpenter said that he didn't want his food to go cold.

Veronica told him all about AWOL that evening, and it seemed that her general opinion of men was lower than it had ever been. But in bed that night she was as ardent as ever, urging him to thrust deep and whispering so coarsely in his ear that he felt himself blushing. She woke him again in the small hours, taking the dominant position once more and peering down at him with tightly drawn lips as if she was engaged in an act which required maximum concentration. This time Carpenter was unable to achieve orgasm; he felt exhausted, a failure in some rigorous test of sexual stamina.

When he awoke again a pale dawn was filtering through the

curtains and Veronica was already up and dressed. She told him that it had been good to see him again, she had enjoyed their weekend. Still sleepy, he watched her buckle up her rucksack and sling it over her shoulders. Only then did he realize that she was leaving. She moved to the door, then turned to face him again. It was only fair, she said, that she explain to him her full reasons for seeking him out.

Then she announced that she intended to have a baby.

It was not a decision which she had arrived at lightly, she went on, especially since she had no intention of getting married or even living with another man. But it had been important that the father be someone for whom she felt affection and whom she knew well. So she had chosen him. He was not to concern himself about the outcome because she had decided to accept full responsibility for the upbringing of the child and there was no question of him being under any moral or financial obligations towards it. In fact she positively didn't want him to be involved in any way since the whole idea was to raise the child herself, alone. She looked upon it as a form of artificial insemination with the added bonus that the sperm provider was a close friend and a person she respected. She would not even have mentioned it if that hadn't been the case.

Carpenter was too stunned to say anything, or even move. Veronica adjusted her rucksack, said that she would look him up again some time. And then she was gone.

He lay there for several minutes, thinking that he didn't believe it but knowing only too well that with Veronica anything was possible. And there was nothing he could do; it was too late. He was always forgetting to check on matters of contraception beforehand, and he had finally gained his comeuppance.

He had a bizarre and tasteless image of one of his sperm fusing with one of Veronica's ova even as she was walking down the street. Little wonder that she had been so urgent and passionate in bed with him; little wonder that she had wanted to make love at every possible moment. The whole weekend had been designed by her to maximize the possibility of fertilization.

There was a small part of him which had always relished the idea of fatherhood, but not with her, not like this. He tried to imagine what would happen in the future, if she bore his child. Would she send him photographs of it, regular letters informing him of its progress? Or would there be nothing – no contact, no mention of it? Either possibility seemed intolerable.

The telephone started ringing. Carpenter tried to ignore it, but this time the ringing went on and on, on and on. He wanted to pursue Veronica and shout his outrage at her, but he knew that this would have been utterly futile. His only hope was that he had somehow failed to impregnate her.

The phone rang again that afternoon while he was lying like a drowned man in the bath. It rang and rang. That afternoon, as daylight began to fade, he took a long walk, going nowhere and so wrapped up in his thoughts that he registered nothing of his surroundings. On his return he could hear the phone ringing on the landing even before he had opened the door. He bounded up the stairs and snatched the receiver off its cradle, intending to yell at Penny that he wanted to be left alone. But it was his Aunt Muriel. She had been trying to reach him all weekend. His mother had died.

*

Carpenter looked up and saw that Dr Dempster was waiting, her silver ballpoint pen resting between her lips. He had no idea of how much he had told her, but he felt as if he had been talking for hours.

'Would you like some more tea?' she asked.

He nodded, and she refilled his cup. The tea was practically cold, but he drank it down in one. He saw her glance at her wrist-watch.

'Am I keeping you from something?'

'Nothing that won't wait.' She smiled. 'What happened then?'

Carpenter sighed, then shook his head; he couldn't talk any more.

Dr Dempster waited. Carpenter grew uncomfortable with her silence; he felt that he had overstayed his welcome. Then there was a brisk knocking on the door. Peacock entered.

'We've been instructed to check all the rooms,' he said. 'The cat has escaped.'

Carpenter turned in his chair. 'Mordred?'

‘There’s no other animal on the premises. Would you by any chance have seen it?’

‘No,’ said Dr Dempster, ‘we haven’t.’

Her tone was brusque. Peacock stiffened.

‘Carpenter will be required to help with the search.’

‘When we’re finished here.’

She outstared him and he withdrew, closing the door behind him. His footsteps receded down the corridor.

A silence descended. Carpenter was gazing at the white telephone on her desk.

‘Is there someone you wanted to call?’ she asked.

When he said nothing, she picked up the receiver. Carpenter could hear an ordinary dial tone.

‘Would I need to dial 01 for a London number?’

She smiled, shook her head.

There were footsteps outside, and he heard Harris’s voice.

‘I’d better go help,’ he said.

*

Everyone except Wright was assembled in the lounge; Wright had refused to participate in the search and had been locked in his cell again once the guards had established that he was not harbouring the cat there. Mordred had finally succeeded in gnawing through his lead and had escaped from Naughton’s office some time between him going off duty at five o’clock and returning at seven. A brief reconnaissance of Limbo had already been made without any trace of the animal being found; but it had to be on the premises somewhere, and now a search would be conducted in earnest.

They were organized into two groups, with Carpenter and Sinnott being led by Harris, and Treadwell and Riley under Peacock’s command. Naughton himself did not emerge from his office, but Harris told them he had given orders that they would not be allowed to go to bed until the cat was found.

They began to check every room, each team moving in an opposite direction from the lounge. Particular attention was to be paid to their cells, they were informed, and no one was allowed to search his own. If anyone was found to have been hiding the cat, severe disciplinary measures would be taken.

It was hard to imagine where the cat could be, Carpenter thought as they went along; aside from Dr Dempster's office, each room in Limbo had a minimum of furnishings and all were box-like affairs without alcoves, niches or any architectural falderal. Perhaps someone had finally strangled it and flushed it down the toilet.

They were in the library when Harris asked him if Wright was still accusing him of having told Naughton about the excavation in the toilet.

Carpenter said nothing. Harris chuckled.

'Too bad. He's got the wrong man.'

Carpenter feigned a lack of interest. He glanced at Sinnott, who shook his head vigorously, as if denying that he had anything to do with it.

'Don't you want to know who really shopped you?' Harris was plainly enjoying himself. 'It was Riley. Riley's the informer. What do you think of that?'

Carpenter remained silent. He decided that Harris was simply trying to make mischief. And yet the idea was not beyond the bounds of possibility.

Presently the two teams met up outside Naughton's office. Neither had so much as caught a glimpse of the cat.

On hearing this news Naughton, resplendent in a burgundy suit and a chocolate-and-cream polka-dot tie, immediately ordered them to retrace each other's paths.

Half an hour later they reconvened in the lounge, still empty-handed. Harris and Peacock went off to report to Naughton while the rest of them slumped in chairs, fed up with the whole endeavour.

Without the television on, the room lacked a focus, and it was as if they were strangers gathered in some desolate dentist's waiting room. Carpenter studied Riley, searching for evidence of guilt in his manner. He did not really believe that Riley had said anything to Naughton about the escape tunnel, but Riley's elusive character made it impossible to be sure. What if he had been working for the other side from the outset?

The games room door was open. Carpenter went inside. The dartboard was shuttered up and the grey covering sheet had been draped over the pool table. He tried the cupboard where the rest of the games were stored: it was locked. For the first time since he'd been in Limbo Carpenter felt trapped, stifled by the place.

Sinnott came in behind him, looking equally frustrated. He stared at the snooker table, then threw back the cover.

Mordred was hiding underneath. It immediately leapt at him and landed on top of his head. For an instant Sinnott looked like a Mohican Indian; then he keeled over, shrieking, the cat still clinging grimly to his scalp.

They fell out of Carpenter's view for a moment. There was a scuffling sound, a further shriek, a hissing and spitting, then more scuffles. Sinnott scrambled to his feet, his head catless. He lunged for the table and began grabbing snooker balls. Mordred darted out of the room as he hurled a red ball after it. Carpenter saw it go scurrying out into the corridor.

Sinnott scooped up more balls, dropping several on the floor in the process, and went running in pursuit of the cat. 'I'll kill it!' he screamed. 'I'll kill it!'

Treadwell tried to stop him, but as he moved forward he put his foot down on a ball and fell, cracking his head against the door jamb.

Carpenter rushed to his aid, helping him sit up.

'Are you all right?' he asked.

Treadwell's eyes flickered open, but his gaze was unfocused and there was a stupid smile on his face.

'Warmble,' he said. 'Fimble farble.'

*

Mordred was cornered outside Dr Dempster's office by Harris and Peacock, who had been alerted by Sinnott's screams. Peacock fetched a towel from the storeroom which Harris threw over the cat before bundling it up and carrying it away.

Sinnott was devastated that the revenge he craved on the animal had been denied him. Carpenter helped Peacock take him to his cell, where they made him lie down. Peacock went off for an aspirin while Carpenter tried to console the trembling Sinnott. He was torn between grief and rage, and he looked broken. 'Please,' he said in a whimper. 'Just leave me alone.'

Carpenter went out, closing the cell door behind him. He intercepted Peacock and turned him away, saying that Sinnott was sleeping. Meanwhile Harris and Riley had carried the concussed Treadwell back to his cell. Treadwell was still mumbling nonsense words, and proved too oblivious to drink the mug of hot milk which was rustled up for him. Harris finally ordered everyone out of his cell before locking him in for the night.

Throughout all this Wright had been pounding on his door, demanding to know what was going on. No one paid him any attention.

★

Carpenter sat down opposite Riley in the lounge. They were all alone. Riley was perusing a copy of *New Scientist.*

'According to this, everything in the world is held together by gluons.'

'Riley, we've got to get out of here.'

'They hold quarks together. And quarks are what make up atoms and all the rest of it.'

'Are you listening to me?'

'What I want to know is how do they know that gluons and quarks aren't made up of something else. Once you start this sort of thing there's no end to it.'

Carpenter snatched the magazine from him.

'I want you to listen to me. We can't stay here any longer.'

Riley settled back in his chair.

'I'm serious,' Carpenter told him. 'It's slowly driving us all barmy. Wright's getting paranoid, Sinnott's a nervous wreck and Treadwell's concussed. Sooner or later we're all going to be strait-jacket cases if we stay here.'

Riley said nothing to this. He was studying his feet. Treadwell had tied double knots in both his shoelaces.

'We've got to get out,' Carpenter said. 'All of us.'

'Not me. I'm all right here.'

Carpenter paused, studying him.

'You're serious, aren't you?'

He shrugged. 'What do you want to escape for? It's easy here. We're fed and looked after – it's not so bad. I can put up with all the rest of it for the sake of a quiet life.'

He was not looking at Carpenter, but Carpenter knew he was speaking sincerely. He finally understood that the secret wisdom which he had always imagined was hidden behind Riley's veneer of flippancy was not really there. Riley was just a tired old man who had given up the ghost; his wit and whimsy were merely designed to deflect attention from the real issues.

Carpenter could find no dismay in himself at this realization; he had spent too much of his life seeking exemplars and being disappointed when they turned out to be ordinary people with ordinary frailties.

'Did you tell Naughton about the escape tunnel?' he asked.

'Eh?'

'Harris said you did. He told me you went to Naughton and told him what was going on in the bathroom.'

'Harris. I wouldn't trust him with a blunt instrument.'

'Did you?'

'You've got to be kidding. What do you take me for?'

Carpenter tossed the magazine on the table but said nothing. Riley sat up, looking earnest for the first time in the months that Carpenter had known him.

'Listen,' he said, 'Wright's got about as much sense as a strawberry, but I'm not going to stop him from doing anything he wants to do as long as he doesn't drag me into it. Why should I grass to Naughton? It makes no difference to me. Wright can make an idiot of himself without my help.'

'An escape tunnel would make a difference to you, whether you were helping or not. Naughton would assume that we'd all had a hand in it. Unless you've been in his pocket from the start.'

Riley stared at him. 'You think that?'

'I don't know what to think.'

A silence fell, and lengthened. Then Riley rose and stretched before shuffling out, leaving Carpenter alone in the lounge. As soon as he was gone, Carpenter realized that at last he had a slogan for him. It was, *Why bother?*

*

Carpenter lingered in the lounge, eating his banana and ostentatiously carving his initials on the plyboard armrest of his chair with a fifty pence coin he had found in the library during the search for Mordred. It felt strange to be handling money again, and at any moment he expected Harris or Peacock to appear and take the coin from him. But no one came.

He finished the banana and tossed the skin aside. It fell in the doorway to the corridor. With difficulty he managed to scratch out the full stops after each initial with a pointed end of the coin. The quietude of the place weighed heavily on him, but still no one came.

The newspapers scattered about the place told him of conflict and crisis at home and abroad, while magazines exhorted him to buy or be enlightened or better himself. In essence they represented one week's catalogue of the familiar disparity between human aspirations and achievements, part of the continuing pattern of muddling through despite greed, corruption, brutality, neglect and all the rest of it. A paper aeroplane presumably fashioned by Treadwell lay on a chair. Carpenter picked it up and threw it at the light-fitting. It veered away at the last moment and went sailing towards the door just as Peacock appeared.

'Bedtime, Carpenter,' he said, and promptly slipped on the banana skin, sitting down hard in the doorway.

*

Sleep would not come: he was far too alert for it, as if this was not the time for rest at all. He lay in the half-light for a long while, his thoughts gradually and inexorably drawn towards his mother.

She had died of heart failure, just like his father, except that her doctor had apparently warned her that her time was limited several months previously. Muriel had only discovered this from the doctor himself after her death; his mother had said nothing to anyone.

The coffin was lying in Muriel's front room, but Carpenter could do no more than stare at it from the doorway. The thought of touching it was unwelcome, that of actually lifting the lid was inconceivable. Why didn't she say anything? he kept asking himself. *Why didn't she tell me?*

He was grateful for Muriel's organizational abilities. She had already taken care of all the funeral arrangements and there was nothing for him to do. He had returned to Manchester on the Sunday evening, and the funeral was to be held the following day – Christmas Eve. His mother had expired in her bed some time between Thursday night and Friday afternoon; she had been found there by Muriel when she called in at tea-time. There had been no opportunity to phone him at work that afternoon.

He slept in the spare bedroom directly above the coffin that night, and was so exhausted that sleep immediately claimed him. But he woke early, before it was light, and was possessed with the terrifying feeling that he was now utterly alone in the world.

As dawn began to break, he dressed and left the house without disturbing Muriel. He had a spare set of doorkeys to his mother's house – his house now, he supposed. He let himself in through the front door, nodding to a neighbour who was passing by on the street. Home for the holiday? the man said, smiling; she'll fill you up with turkey and mince pies.

Everything was exactly as he remembered it except for the yawning absence of life. His father's armchair still sat in the living room, unoccupied since his death. The kitchen proved the easiest room in which to linger, and he stared out at the garden, his domain in childhood, a place of camps, bonfires and holes in the ground. It was overgrown and derelict now, the flagstone path succumbing to encroaching grass, the small vegetable patch choked with weeds and urban litter.

The wildlife calendar which he had bought his mother a year ago was pinned on the wall above the sink – a white stoat for December – and a dishcloth hung on the hot-water tap. To him both these objects represented continuity, for every year he bought his mother a new calendar and every day there were cups and saucers and plates for her to wash and dry and put away in the cupboard. Things went on. They didn't just stop.

His eyes filled up with tears. He had intended to inspect every drawer and cupboard in the house but found it impossible to stay there any longer. Next door's cat, his old enemy, was preening itself on the pavement outside. It was an old and scrawny tabby now, a frail reflection of its predatory prime; but it still clung to its animal life and had outlasted both his parents.

Somehow he endured the funeral, endured all the delicate expressions of condolence from family and friends – endured them because he had no choice. Relatively few people were in attendance, for it was an unseasonable time of the year and the funeral had been arranged at short notice. There was a wreath from his uncle in Bristol, and a card from Gail and Graham with a message saying that he should let them know if they could do anything to help.

It was a grey day and it drizzled throughout the service. His mother's coffin lay on milky plastic sheets before it was lowered into the grave. Mr Fearnley, the minister, spoke at gentle length, but Carpenter absorbed little of it. He felt hollowed out, inert.

That evening he told Muriel that he had to return to London on Boxing Day because he was needed at work but would come back again the following weekend to do whatever was necessary in the aftermath of his mother's death. He supposed that he would have to execute her will, dispose of her property, and all the rest of it. And what about the house? Would he have to sell it if he was intending to remain in London? He tried not to think about any of it, and was grateful when Muriel told him that nothing needed to be done immediately.

He knew that the simplest thing would be to phone Prendergast on the 27th and tell him exactly what had happened; even Prendergast wouldn't refuse him compassionate leave under the circumstances. But for some reason he was determined to return to London and fulfil his duties at work.

It was a dismal Christmas Eve, with Muriel and himself sitting disconsolately in front of the television, unmoved by the festive posturings of celebrities in panel games and variety shows, mocked by the silver Christmas tree festooned with chocolate ornaments and shiny coloured balls. He slept badly that night, hardly at all. In the morning Muriel presented him with a desk diary and a pair of socks. He had nothing for her.

At one o'clock they sat down to Christmas dinner: a small turkey with roast potatoes and vegetables, followed by two individual

Christmas puddings. Somehow he got all the food down, though he had no appetite. Later, when they were sitting around watching a routine war film, the telephone in the hall rang. Muriel had only had the phone installed a matter of weeks ago, partly prompted by his mother's increasing frailty; she immediately hurried to answer it.

The caller turned out to be Gail. Her voice sounded distant, infinitely sympathetic, and Carpenter smiled at the sound of it. When she asked him how he was feeling he told her that he was all right, coping, though in fact he felt peculiarly unable to assess his frame of mind. It emerged that she and Graham had been back in Manchester since late September; Graham had disbanded Fiasco and was now playing with a local group. In fact they had a gig tonight, at a pub Carpenter knew well. Why didn't he come? He must be feeling miserable and it might take him out of himself for a few hours. Besides, she and Graham would very much like to see him.

Carpenter told her he would think about it. At first he was disinclined, but after several hours of mind-numbing television he changed his mind.

He was late arriving, but got in without difficulty. Bing Crosby was singing 'White Christmas' as he went down the narrow corridor to the large back room where everyone was gathered for the evening. The room was dimly lit, for which he was grateful; he felt stigmatized by his mother's death and was desirous of remaining unseen by anyone who might know him. He bought himself a pint of lager and found a free chair at a corner table beside the door.

A series of festive records issued from the speakers on either side of the stage. Most people were wearing paper party hats, and there was cigar smoke in the air. Carpenter spotted several people he knew, but luckily he was hidden from them; the bulk of the audience comprised middle-aged people, and everyone sitting around him was a stranger. Now Slade were singing 'So here it is, Merry Christmas, everybody's having fun'. Carpenter sipped his lager and huddled in the shadows.

At length the records ceased and the group was announced: they were called The Abominable Showmen. Gail had told him nothing about the group, but they came on stage wearing dark suits and frilly white shirts with black lace ties. All, that is, except the singer, who appeared after the group had launched into an instrumental version of 'Ghost Riders in the Sky' wearing a long overcoat, a cowboy hat and a leering rubber mask. He immediately went into a routine designed to illustrate that he was The Fastest Flasher in the West. This basically entailed leaping off the stage, rushing up to young women sitting at nearby tables and flapping open his overcoat to reveal the message taped across his crotch. It read: STICK 'EM UP!

The group then played a few songs – 'You've Got Your Troubles', 'Massachusetts' and 'Knock Three Times' – before the singer went off stage and returned dressed as a harridan in a floral dress, hairnet and handbag. A routine to the song 'Poison Ivy' followed in which the bass guitarist and drummer were repeatedly beaten about the head with the handbag, much to the audience's amusement. Then the drummer slipped away and came back on stage wearing short trousers and a school cap. The singer immediately started chasing him around the stage while Graham and the bass guitarist played 'My Boy Lollipop'.

There was a further stint of straightforward songs such as 'Tie A Yellow Ribbon', 'Bachelor Boy' and 'Sweet Caroline' before strobe lights were activated on the stage for a Laurel and Hardy routine involving the singer and the bass guitarist. Graham stood in the shadows, playing intricate backing music on his guitar. Carpenter could not see him clearly, but his hair had grown longer since their last meeting and he looked completely transformed from his punk image. All the group appeared to be in their late twenties or early thirties, and the drummer was an old schoolfriend who had played with Gray Stone and the Rockrollers and had been a stalwart on what was loosely termed the cabaret circuit for several years. Carpenter recognized none of the others.

The Laurel and Hardy routine was later followed by a Santa Claus sketch in which the audience was showered with fake snow. The Christmas spirit had by now overtaken everyone, and there was much good-natured raillery between the group and people sitting at the tables closest to the stage. There was also a queue to the gents which extended in front of Carpenter, blocking his view. He didn't mind, but simply concentrated on the backing music which Graham was providing for the skit. His guitar playing was fluid, precise, impeccably timed, but no one else in the audience cared; to them it was just a bit of fancy background music to add spice to the action.

By the end of the evening a vague depression had settled over Carpenter which was quite distinct from the desolation of bereavement. He had bought only one drink all evening, and an inch of lager still remained in his glass. He swilled it down, finding it disgustingly warm and flat. The lights were on, and most of the audience had already filed out. Then he saw Gail approaching his table.

She had presumably been backstage, for he had not seen her all evening. She wore a mauve knee-length dress under a brown suede coat. Her hair was longer than when he had last seen her, and it had a tousled yet utilitarian look to it, as if it was a style which she had chosen because it required a minimum of maintenance. Without knowing why, he felt that there was something staid in her appearance.

She planted a kiss on his cheek then sat down beside him. Where had he been? She'd been looking for him all evening. Carpenter explained that he had arrived late and had taken the only seat he could find. On the stage Graham and the rest of the group were hauling away drums and amplifiers. Gail said that it had been a terrible shock about his mother and that probably nothing anyone could say or do would be much comfort to him at the moment. No, Carpenter agreed, but never mind. He smiled and wished her a Merry Christmas.

When he told her that he was intending to return to London the following day she insisted that he come back to the flat she and Graham were renting and have a few drinks. It was only a stone's throw from Muriel's. She had a car now, a battered old Avenger, and they could be there in no time once Graham had finished helping the others load all the equipment into the van.

She departed backstage and returned ten minutes later with Graham, who had changed into jeans and a grey V-neck sweater over a check shirt. He had thickened somewhat both in frame and face since they had last met and had developed lines about the eyes and mouth. To Carpenter he had always seemed eternally youthful, but now he looked his age.

How you doing? he asked Carpenter somewhat awkwardly. Carpenter told him that he was bearing up, remembering that Graham had always been ill at ease when faced with tragedy or loss. There was something in his face which unsettled Carpenter – a bloatedness, a lack of the remembered intensity in his blue eyes. Or was this merely a reflection of his morose frame of mind?

It was a short drive to the flat, and Gail sustained the conversation with gossip about how they had obtained the place through a cousin of hers and how she was now working for a travel agency. Graham interjected the occasional comment, but he was mostly silent. Carpenter suspected that he was unsure how to behave with him because of his mother's death.

The flat occupied the ground floor of a terraced Victorian house which looked seedy and dilapidated. The furniture and fittings had come with it: frayed floral armchairs, post-war austerity wardrobes, worn mottled carpets. Gail had put up Christmas decorations in the front room, and there were a few ornaments and prints which he remembered from their old flat; but the place had an air of being squatted rather than properly lived in. There was no sign of Graham's stereo or his huge collection of records.

I sold them, Graham told him, before we left London. Gail handed them their drinks – a gin and tonic for Graham, a can of Guinness for himself – and Graham explained that they had been broke at the time and had needed the money to get back to Manchester and pay the deposit on the flat. He shrugged and told Carpenter he wasn't too bothered; he'd get another stereo and replace the records when he had some money again.

He fell silent, and the burden of the conversation once again fell to Gail. It was she who told Carpenter how Graham had finally tired of playing with Fiasco and had decided to get a job in Manchester. He was presently working in the library at Cheetham Hill and playing with The Abominable Showmen. It was useful extra cash.

Graham sat with his legs draped over an arm of the sofa; he wore a smart and functional pair of brogues on his feet. Carpenter felt that there must be more to the story than this, but Graham was defensive about the group, telling Carpenter that he'd had enough of playing in cramped and sweaty London clubs and was now happier to play guitar more as a hobby. There was a different sort of challenge and discipline in playing with a showband which he found just as rewarding. He didn't care much for current musical directions, and you couldn't keep beating your head against a brick wall.

There was no sense that he was offering excuses or justifications, for he spoke matter-of-factly, and Carpenter had no reason to doubt his sincerity. What dismayed him was the indifference in his voice, the sense that he had become utterly accepting of whatever befell him. There was no talk of future plans or ambitions, none of the restless enthusiasm which had always marked his conversation. The spirit had gone out of him.

But the spirit of what? Of youth? Innocence? Passion? Inspiration, even? Was this what getting older meant, that you lost your idealism, your urge to strive, and became fatalistic, drab, inured? Or had Graham simply come to terms with his own limitations and reached an adult decision to lower his horizons so that they were commensurate with his abilities?

The conversation remained halting and awkward. Finally Carpenter said that he ought to be getting back to Muriel's. Although it was only a short walk, Gail insisted on driving him home.

Graham did not rise from the sofa as they made to depart, but merely asked Carpenter when he would be back in Manchester. On hearing that Carpenter intended to return the following weekend, he said he hoped he would look in on them again. I will, Carpenter promised. It was rough about your mother, said Graham; I hope things work out.

He had drunk three gin and tonics while talking to Carpenter, and Carpenter remarked on this as Gail drove him home. Graham had never been fond of alcohol in the past, and Carpenter was already imagining that some shattering experience had caused him to abandon all his musical ambitions and turn to drink. The truth proved more prosaic. It's Christmas, Gail reminded him, then went on to say that while Graham had developed a fondness for the occasional gin she had never known him to get really drunk drunk. He had disbanded Fiasco because their audience had comprised aggressive young punks who had hurled insults, cigarette butts and beer cans at the group while they were performing. One night Graham had come off stage covered in spit and had decided that enough was enough.

Carpenter could tell that Gail had mixed feelings about the change in Graham. She was clearly uneasy about his loss of energy and enthusiasm, but she was also happier with the more settled life which he now seemed satisfied to lead. Carpenter managed to ask her about the hiatus in their relationship. She told him that she had simply felt Graham had been taking her for granted and that she had needed some distance from him and the contrast of another partner so that she could get things in perspective. It was Graham who had finally brought about their reunion by going to her house and insisting that she return with him to London. Just before Christmas he had suggested that they get married in the summer; they were hoping that he, Carpenter, would be the best man.

For the first time Carpenter noticed the engagement ring on her finger; it was typical of him to miss such small and significant details. He felt a sense of loss – not because he finally knew that he could never replace Graham in her life, but because he no longer wanted to. For years he had secretly desired her above all other women, but something had changed since he had last seen her. When she had appeared earlier that evening there had been no stirring of his old infatuation, and he knew that somehow he had finally laid her ghost. She had become what she had always really been: a close friend who happened to be a woman. He was able to look at her without any of his old longing and say quite sincerely that he would be delighted to be Graham's best man.

They had arrived at Muriel's. She gave him a big hug before he got out of the car. Graham's always admired you, she told him through the window before driving off, leaving him stunned at the idea. He stood in the road, staring after her car and feeling all the liberation and loneliness which follows the passing of a cherished illusion.

He woke late the following morning with a headache and a general feeling of weariness. When Muriel asked him what time he was intending to leave he told her that he had changed his mind and would take the early train to London the following morning instead. He had decided that he was going to spend a few hours browsing through all that remained in his parents' home.

That afternoon he systematically searched the house for memorabilia. Among the first things he found were his mother's photograph albums in the bottom drawer of the dressing table in her bedroom. Even as he was turning the stiff and odorous pages it occurred to him that he had never exhibited much curiosity about his family background while his parents had been alive. Because he had always found his father stolid and drab, his mother over-inquisitive and preoccupied with trivia, he had never thought to enquire what their lives had been like in their youth and heyday. The photographs of himself as a child he had seen far too often, and he was familiar with his parents' wedding portrait, which had hung in the front room ever since he could remember. He knew that they had married early in 1947, in the depths of a terrible winter, and that his father had been grey-haired even then; he knew, too, that his mother had worked as a midwife before she married and that his father had owned an old black Austin in the 1950s before he had given up driving altogether. Beyond these facts, he knew little.

Here was his mother, dark-haired and vivacious-looking in a white cotton dress, standing on a sea-front. The inscription said EASTBOURNE, 1946. Here was his father, in a short-trousered Army uniform with braces and socks, a grey haze of foliage in the background: SINGAPORE, 1941. There were photographs of relatives and friends, group portraits, blurred images of children at school, on holiday, posing stiffly for some professional photographer. But he found himself primarily drawn to photographs of his parents which showed them in late youth or early adulthood, in their physical prime.

His mother was well represented – in a spotted summer frock at eighteen, in a pinafore and headscarf while working at a munitions factory during the war – but there were relatively few photographs of his father. One showed him as a young man standing rather self-consciously in front of a stone wall. It was dated 1938 and his hair was dark in it. Another revealed him in his shirtsleeves, his hair severely shorn, putting a spade into the earth of some allotment.

The date was 1939. Aside from this and the single photograph of him in uniform, there were no others covering the war years.

Carpenter lingered over the photographs for some hours before finally returning the albums to the drawer; he would inspect them again when he came back from London. He continued his search, finding all his school exercise books preserved in a bedroom cupboard (he did not dare open them), finding documents, knitwear patterns, handwritten recipes and newspaper cuttings whose significance was often obscure to him. He found nothing surprising.

All the while he did his best to harden his mind against any wellings of grief, but it was not easy and he knew that he was snatching at fragments of two lives which had ended before he had fully recognized their importance to him: the paradox was that it had taken their deaths to reveal it. He would have given anything to have his mother and father resurrected for just five minutes so that he could tell them how much they had meant to him and to plead for their forgiveness that he had not been as loving or considerate or worthy a son as they deserved.

It had grown dark outside and he did not want to linger much longer in the empty house. Neither his father nor his mother had ever talked about the war, and Carpenter had never asked them about it. But from the moment he had seen the photograph of his father in Singapore he had become convinced that his father had been captured by the Japanese and endured terrible years of imprisonment. But there was nothing to support this conviction.

Muriel told him later that his father had been an adjutant to a colonel and that he had been flown out before the garrison fell to the Japanese in 1942 and had spent the rest of the war in England. He had seldom talked about the period, but she understood that he had had several friends who had been interned by the Japanese in a prisoner-of-war camp and had not survived the war. Carpenter wondered if his father had been haunted by guilt that he had escaped; but at the same time he knew he was trying to invest his father's life with a romantic drama which it had probably never possessed. There was little likelihood that he would ever know either way.

He overslept the next morning and missed the train he had intended to catch from Crumpsall station. As a consequence he was an hour late departing to London and did not arrive in work until ten-fifteen, his suitcase still in his hand. The long journey south had done nothing to settle him: he felt weary, frayed, not up to the day that was ahead of him. His mother's death was now affecting him far less profoundly than the feeling that she and his father had always shielded much of their lives from him. True, he had always been self-absorbed and often dismissive of them, but there had never been a sense that they would readily discuss anything about themselves that did not directly concern him. And he would never be able to understand why his mother had not wanted him to be with her when she died. This was what pained him above all else.

Prendergast was nowhere to be seen, but the telephone on his desk was ringing and there were messages and memos waiting for him. Most of the staff were still on holiday and he could not believe that anyone would have business to discuss with him the day after Boxing Day. But it proved to be a call from one of his more zealous salesmen.

*

When Prendergast appeared Carpenter immediately apologized for being late and said that he would work on that evening. Prendergast did not look mollified, but Carpenter felt unable to tell him that his mother had died. He did not know why. Possibly it was because he felt he had not quite come to a full understanding of what it meant to him; possibly it was because he could not bear the idea of sympathy from a person he disliked.

Carpenter operated on automatic throughout the day, but although it proved to be a relatively quiet one, a sense of strain continued to build in him. That afternoon he took a call from the creative director of the advertising agency who handled the accounts of most of his products. Normally the marketing manager dealt with such calls, but he was away and Carpenter was expected to cover for him. But as the man started talking about budgets and campaign strategies and peak-time slots Carpenter found his words turning into an unintelligible drone. The more he tried to understand them, the less sense they made. He felt a sweat break out all over his body and had to keep swallowing down a rising panic.

Eventually a silence fell, and he knew the man was waiting for some response. He could do nothing but slam the phone down.

At five-thirty Prendergast called him to his alcove and without preamble told him he was completely dissatisfied with his performance. He was seriously thinking of transferring pickled onions to another product manager; the only alternative was immediately to advertise for Carpenter's post and have Carpenter return to his former position as assistant. Neither option gave him great pleasure, but he really didn't think he had any other alternatives under the circumstances.

Carpenter stared at him without speaking, then walked out. Where do you think you're going? Prendergast called after him. Carpenter went home.

The flat felt dank when he arrived, and he huddled beside the gas fire with his bag of fish and chips, eating without relish. Later he drank a four-pack of Guinness and swallowed two valium tablets from a bottle he had found in his mother's bedside cabinet. Soon the drug had enveloped him in a soporific calm. He went off to bed and immediately slept.

Morning was well advanced when he woke, but he still felt unutterably weary. He ate a late breakfast, then took the underground into the city and spent the rest of the morning wandering around Regent's Park. After lunching in a pub opposite the British Museum, he wandered up Oxford Street. It was filled with eager shoppers abroad for the winter sales. He continued on to Hyde Park and sat on a bench until it grew too cold for him to linger any longer. On the train home he felt lightheaded, adrift from the world at large.

An hour or so after his return the telephone downstairs started ringing. When he put the receiver to his ear he heard Penny's voice say, Mike? Is that you? I have to see you, can you come over right away? It's very important. He cut the connection before dropping the receiver back on its cradle.

Later, when he was in bed trying to read a paperback about the war in the Japanese theatre, the phone rang again. It rang for several minutes. He had replaced the receiver because the telephone was his only link with the outside world. But he wasn't going to answer it.

At length he subsided into an uneasy sleep. He dreamt that a telephone was ringing, then awoke to hear it on the landing below. Gradually the sound faded and he drifted into sleep once more, only to wake again from the same dream and to the same sound. This went on throughout the night until his befuddled mind could not tell whether the dreams were induced by real sounds or the sounds a projection of his haunted imagination. Then he began to hear Penny's voice pleading with him to help her. She had slashed her wrists, was lying dead in a bath with an electric fire blazing beneath the water, had taken a massive overdose and was spread-eagled across her bed when he burst into her room. At the same time he was imploring her to leave him alone. He wanted to flee somewhere safe and shut himself away from everyone. Suddenly he was doing just that, crawling into the cubby beneath the stairs in his parents' house as he had often done as a child, when he had been naughty. He closed the door behind him and was enveloped in utter blackness, sealed and secure from the whole world. The next morning he had woken to his cell in Limbo.

*

Carpenter flung back the sheets and got out of bed. He studied the dim half-globe of the light for several moments before finally dragging his bed to the centre of the room and climbing up on it.

The light covering unscrewed quite easily, to reveal an ordinary bulb beneath. There was, as he had suspected for some time, no spy camera. There never had been. Not in his cell or anywhere else in Limbo. No one was watching him.

'Sinnott!' he whispered loudly through the wall.

There was no reply.

'Sinnott!'

He heard a muffled groan.

'Sinnott! Wake up!'

'What . . . who is it?'

'It's Carpenter.'

'What do you want?'

'We've got to get out of here. Tonight. Now. I've checked the lights and there's no spy cameras. We're not being watched. No one's even listening.'

'I'm tired. Let me sleep.'

'You've got to help me. You're the only one who can.'

Earlier, when Peacock was escorting him to his cell, Carpenter had noticed that the guards had neglected to bolt Sinnott's door.

'Your cell's open,' he said. 'I want you to come and unlock my door.'

'Leave me alone.'

'Sinnott, you've got to help.'

'I want to sleep.'

'If we don't try now, we might be here for ever.'

He waited, but Sinnott was silent.

'Is that what you want? Do you want to stay here?'

'Please. Leave me alone.'

'Sinnott!' Carpenter shouted, his voice rising above a whisper for the first time. 'If you don't come and open my door I'm going to beat you up tomorrow.'

'I'll tell the guards.'

'I don't care what you do – I'll still get you sooner or later.'

He paused. Sinnott remained silent.

'Just come and unlock my door. That's all I'm asking.'

The silence continued, and then Sinnott began to make ostentatious snoring noises.

'Sinnott!' Carpenter yelled, 'I'll keep you awake all bloody night if necessary!'

'You'll bring the guards if you keep shouting.'

'Too bloody right I'll bring them. I'll tell them you were trying to escape and picked the bolt on your door.'

'They wouldn't believe it. They'd remember that they forgot to lock me in.'

'It'll be the night shift, you dolt. Your word against mine.'

'I won't do it.'

Sinnott sounded apprehensive but resolute. Carpenter sighed, wondering what to do. Neither sweet reason nor bullying had worked.

'Please,' he said quietly. 'I need your help. I'm asking you to help me.'

A long silence followed. Carpenter waited. Then he heard the bolt being slowly drawn on his door.

Sinnott was standing there in his blue-striped pyjamas, his eyes wide and nervous. He looked like a waif who had just been caught stealing food. Carpenter immediately grabbed him by the arm and hauled him off to Treadwell's cell.

Treadwell was sleeping soundly, and Carpenter had to shake him hard before he sat up.

'Wamma?' he murmured. 'Hoot?'

'Come on,' said Carpenter, helping him to his feet. 'We're getting out of here.'

Treadwell still looked dazed. Sinnott was huddling in the corner beside the door.

'I'm going back,' he said.

Carpenter grabbed his wrist before he could bolt and pushed him against the wall. 'You're coming with us whether you like it or not. We're *all* getting out of here tonight.'

'Goan,' Treadwell seemed to be saying. 'Flout.'

'Treadwell's still gaga. You're going to have to help him.'

'I don't want anything to do with this.'

'It's too late to turn back now.'

He made Sinnott take Treadwell by the arm and help him out into the corridor. There was no sign of any guards, and it was as if the place had never truly been inhabited.

'Carpenter?' came a voice through the wall. 'Is that you? What's going on?'

It was Wright. 'Be with you in a minute,' Carpenter told him. He was going to leave Wright until last. He helped Sinnott support Treadwell along to Riley's cell.

Riley proved even more difficult to rouse than Treadwell, and Carpenter had to drag him half out of bed before he stirred.

'We're leaving,' Carpenter told him.

'Leaving? Where are we going?'

'Out. We're getting out of here.'

'Carpenter!' Wright shouted from next door. 'Carpenter! Unlock my door!'

Riley tugged his pyjama jacket down over his potbelly and tried to climb back into bed.

Carpenter yanked him to his feet and pushed him towards the door.

'You're coming,' he insisted. 'We're all going.'

'Whoat,' said Treadwell. 'Gloo.'

Carpenter unbolted Wright's door. He immediately surged out and began demanding to know what was going on.

'Keep your voice down,' said Carpenter. 'You'll have every guard on the premises here.'

But Wright was galvanized for action. 'What's your plan?' he asked. 'I think we should – '

'I'm in charge,' Carpenter said firmly. 'You'll do exactly as I say or I'm locking you back in your cell right now. Is that clear?'

Wright was too surprised to say anything.

'Give Sinnott a hand with Treadwell.'

Wright studied Treadwell's oblivious face. 'And what will you be doing?'

'I'll be making sure that Riley stays by my side. If you don't like it, say so now or keep your mouth shut.'

The domineering role was not one which came easily to Carpenter, but he knew he was the only person who could lead them all out of Limbo since Riley and probably Sinnott would never follow Wright.

Wright seemed to realize this too, for he took Treadwell by the arm. Carpenter led the way down the corridor to Naughton's office, keeping a hand on Riley's back to urge him along. Sinnott looked scared, but he seemed to have accepted that there could be no turning back now.

Carpenter was relieved that Wright hadn't pressed him for details of his plan, because he didn't have one; he was merely following an intuition and hoping for the best.

They reached Naughton's door. Carpenter turned the handle, thinking, please don't let it be locked.

The door opened.

Naughton's office was empty and in darkness, but a light was burning in the adjacent room. Carpenter crept to the door.

'Leet,' said Treadwell.

Sinnott clamped a hand over his mouth. Carpenter waited a moment, then eased the door open.

An elderly guard whom none of them had seen before was asleep in front of the blank television screen. He looked to be in his late fifties, with a lined face and hair shot through with grey. He wore the usual slate-blue coveralls, his name-tag hidden in its folds.

Carpenter moved slowly to the door which led into the corridor. This, too, opened without fuss. The others tiptoed through, Sinnott still with his hand over Treadwell's mouth. Carpenter had to give Riley an extra nudge to get him through the door.

He closed it behind him and immediately led the way down the corridor. It was long and of bare concrete throughout its length, with bulkhead lamps set at intervals along the ceiling and providing just enough illumination for them to make their way without difficulty. The tunnel smelt musty, unused somehow; it tended to confirm Carpenter's suspicion that Limbo was underground. He said nothing of this to the others.

Presently they came to a T-junction. The right- and left-hand corridors looked identical. Riley and Wright wanted to go off in opposite directions, so Carpenter took the fifty pence piece from his pyjama pocket and tossed it, calling heads for right and tails for left.

It came down tails. They moved off again, Carpenter still urging Riley along, Wright and Sinnott still supporting the dazed Treadwell.

'Someone's following us,' Sinnott said presently.

They stopped and listened. All was quiet. Too quiet, Carpenter couldn't help thinking. They moved on.

'The Russians are coming,' said Treadwell.

For an instant he appeared fully conscious, but then the vague, glazed expression descended once more. But he was moving more easily now, requiring only the occasional nudge from Wright or Sinnott to keep him on course.

After about a hundred yards Riley slumped against a wall, panting.

'I can't go on,' he told Carpenter. 'Just leave me here.'

Carpenter yanked him upright and dragged him off again. Ahead was a short flight of steps, leading upwards. The impression of pursuit was far stronger now.

The stairway led to a small landing, and then they turned at right-angles up another short flight of stairs which led to a door. It was padlocked.

Riley slid to the floor. All of them were panting apart from Treadwell, who appeared to be enjoying the exercise. Sinnott looked close to panic.

Carpenter noticed a metal aperture about two feet square set low in the wall beside the padlocked door. It proved to be some kind of service lift with two buttons at its side labelled UP and DOWN. He pressed the latter.

Immediately there was the faint rumbling sound of the lift descending. Everyone looked expectant, but no one spoke.

The rumbling grew louder and finally expired in a grinding sound. The metal door slid open to reveal a low rectangular chamber just big enough for one person to squeeze into if he lay flat. There was nothing for it.

'OK,' said Carpenter, 'who's going first?'

Wright immediately stepped forward and climbed inside. Carpenter did not hesitate in pressing the UP button. The door slid shut and the lift started to ascend.

After what seemed like a long time, it fell silent. Carpenter waited several seconds, then pressed DOWN again.

When the lift arrived the door opened on an empty chamber. No one said anything.

'Treadwell's next,' Carpenter announced. 'Help me get him inside.'

This proved easier than Carpenter had anticipated, for Treadwell appeared to grasp what was required of him and allowed himself to be manoeuvred into the chamber without protest.

'Aloha,' he seemed to say as the door closed on him.

Sinnott kept glancing anxiously down the stairs while they waited, but neither he nor Riley moved. It was cold on the landing, and Carpenter began to feel shivery. There was a faint draught of air from somewhere – stale, indoor air.

The lift returned, again empty.

'Right,' said Carpenter. 'Who's next?'

Sinnott looked away from him, and Riley was studying his feet.

'Sinnott. Your turn.'

Sinnott shook his head.

'Get in there. If the guards catch you now they'll have your guts for garters.'

For a moment Sinnott did not move; then he bundled himself into the lift. Carpenter punched the button, glimpsing his frightened face before the door closed.

'I'll go last,' Riley said as they waited.

'You're next.'

'Let's toss for it.'

Carpenter simply stared at him.

'I hate lifts.' Riley began to tap his toes together. 'Why do they call them lifts when they go down as well?'

'Shut up, Riley.'

A silence descended and persisted until the lift returned. To Carpenter's surprise Riley climbed inside without prompting.

'Nothing to say?' Carpenter asked. 'No parting shot?'

Riley shook his head. Carpenter punched the button.

And then he was alone on the bare concrete landing, listening to the lift wind its way upwards. Only now did he allow his own profound apprehensions to surface. He was not at all relishing the prospect of having to squeeze himself into the chamber. It was too much like being buried alive.

The gears finally stopped turning. He waited a while, then pressed DOWN. This was it. Escape time. Apparently they had not been followed, or else their pursuers had gone off in the wrong direction. He felt sure that nothing would now prevent him from making the ascent as the others had done. If only he could go through with it. If only he had a cigarette.

The lift came to a halt and the door trundled open. Without giving himself pause to hesitate he punched the UP button and scrambled inside. The chamber was even smaller than he had imagined, perhaps only eighteen inches high and wide, and no more than six feet long. He lay flat on his back with his arms straight at his sides as the door slid shut.

He was enveloped in total blackness – something which he had not taken into account. After the chill of the landing, he found the air stuffy, redolent of body heat; it felt starved of oxygen.

The lift ground slowly upwards. Carpenter closed his eyes and tried to quell the claustrophobic feeling which was rising in him; he concentrated on the rumbling of the gears and the sensation of upward movement. It seemed to be taking a long time to reach its destination. Then abruptly it stopped.

He waited for the door to open, for the flood of light, for his release. But nothing happened. Seconds went by in absolute silence, and still nothing happened.

A panic began to swell in him. He was trapped, stuck between floors, or even at his destination but unable to escape until someone outside pressed a button to open the door. But the others would have gone, fled as soon as they emerged from the lift, he was sure. There was no one to release him.

The air in the chamber now seemed to be pressing down on him, making it impossible to breathe. His entire body started to prickle, and it was no longer possible to suppress his terror. He would be immured in the chamber until he ran out of air, buried alive by default, helpless, alone. He started yelling and pressing his hands and feet against the walls of the chamber, wanting to burst out into space and light and air. But the walls were unyielding before his onslaught, and panic overwhelmed him. He passed out.

3
Out

The ceiling was either a yellowed white or a faded cream; the question of which absorbed him for several minutes before he finally sat up in bed. He wore blue-and-white striped pyjamas, and there was a fawn quilted bedspread and too many blankets on top of him; he felt weighed down by them.

The room was modern-functional, with cream-plastered walls, white woodwork and white blinds above the window. Outside the sky was grey. The only ornamentation was an abstract painting on the wall opposite which showed geometrical shapes in shades of purple, mauve and pink. It was an amateur effort in oils, framed but without glass. He imagined that its surface would feel rough to the touch.

A table stood under the window – metal-framed with a white formica top – and his combat jacket had been draped over the back of the chair accompanying it. His jeans lay folded on the seat with a pair of blue briefs, and his desert boots were underneath, a black sock stuffed into each. On the back of the door hung his check lumberjack shirt and a black crew-neck sweater. They were the clothes he had been wearing the day before Limbo.

There was water in a glass-topped carafe on the white bedside table. He swallowed a few mouthfuls – it was stale and dusty-tasting – before getting out of bed. For some reason he had expected his legs to be wobbly, but they were not. He felt somewhat weary though, like waking from a long night's sleep after an exhausting day.

He went to the door and tried the handle. It opened. A buff-coloured corridor floored with shiny brown tiles ran to the junction with another corridor. Doors were set at intervals along both sides of it, and there was a skylight in the ceiling. The air smelt sterile, centrally-heated. He heard the muted sound of someone coughing. Then one of the doors started to open, and he abruptly shut his own.

He crossed to the window and saw that he was several floors up in a modern, monolithic building of concrete and glass. A squat rectangular wing stretched out at right-angles to his window from the right, its bitumen roof dotted with aluminium ventilator ducts. Directly below him was an area of grass demarcated by curving paved walkways; muddy trails crisscrossed it at various points. A central driveway to the left divided this from a crowded car park. Beyond, a dual carriageway ran parallel to the window, and beyond this a line of bare poplars formed a backdrop to a row of shops in concrete and redbrick: a Tesco supermarket, a Barclays Bank, a laundrette, a newsagents, a hairdresser's salon, an off-licence and a William Hill betting shop. It could have been almost anywhere.

A light rain was falling from a uniform layer of cloud, staining the concrete abutments of the building and speckling his window. Cars passed by on the road, and three children were clustered around an ice-cream van parked at the end of the row of shops. An old woman wearing a blue plastic mac emerged from the supermarket, and a man in a donkey jacket entered the betting shop.

He yawned and wished that he could open the window; but it was double-glazed, the inner pane screwed into place. Since awakening he had needed to pee but was reluctant to leave his room. Cautiously he opened the door again and found the corridor empty. The second door along to his right was labelled with the silhouette of a man.

He crept out and entered the toilet. It was white-tiled and white-walled, though not without its quota of graffiti, scrawled at eye-level for the convenience of the patrons. THE HUMAN BODY IS A MACHINE FOR TURNING LIVING THINGS INTO WASTE, read one. Someone else had scribbled out the last word and replaced it with WAIST. Other examples ranged from the familiar – LIFE IS A SEXUALLY TRANSMITTED DISEASE – to the elliptical – THE HEAVENLY HOST SEND APOLOGIES FOR THEIR ABSENCE. Directly in front of him was a message in red marker pen which exhorted him to LOOK STRAIGHT AHEAD AND HOLD YOUR OWN.

He crept back to his room and returned to the window. A red GPO van was now parked outside the post office, and two of the three children had gravitated to it from the ice-cream van and were watching a postman load mailbags into its back. A young woman came out of the newsagents holding a magazine which promptly slipped from her hands into a puddle. He sat down on the edge of the table without taking his eyes from the window.

Sometime later he heard footsteps in the corridor outside. His door opened. It was Dr Dempster.

'Michael,' she said. 'You're up.'

'What time is it?'

'After ten. How are you feeling?'

He almost smiled. 'Alive if not exactly kicking.'

She joined him at the window, stared out.

'Nasty weather,' he remarked.

'Yes, isn't it?'

'April.'

'Yes. I suppose we can't expect too much at this time of the year.'

He wondered what to say next.

'Is it all right if I get dressed?'

'Of course. Would you like some breakfast?'

He was hungry, he realized, and nodded.

She departed. While she was away, he donned his clothes. She returned with a tiny tray bearing orange juice, two Weetabix in a bowl with milk and sugar, and two slices of toast with a pot of tea.

'I'll leave you in peace to eat,' she told him. 'We can talk later.'

He attended to his breakfast. It was drab, institution food, but his appetite was hearty enough. Presently it stopped raining and patches of blue appeared between the clouds. He returned to the window, wishing he had some cigarettes.

About an hour later, Dr Dempster reappeared.

'There's someone here to see you.' she told him. 'A young woman. Do you feel up to it? She asked me not to give you her name; she wanted it to be a surprise. But that's up to you.'

He shrugged. 'It's all right by me.' It would probably be Veronica or Penny, he guessed; Penny, most likely. He did not relish the prospect of confronting her again, but it was necessary, inevitable.

'She's waiting in the reception area. Shall we go down?'

He stood up, then paused as she opened the door.

'Can I ask you a personal question?'

She turned back to him. 'Of course.'

'What's your name? Your first name?'

It was a moment before she said, 'Elizabeth.'

'Is that what people call you? Your friends and family?'

'Usually. Sometimes Beth. Why do you ask?'

'Just curiosity. Do you have any children?'

'You are inquisitive this morning.'

There was something in her tone which indicated that it was a sensitive subject.

'I'm sorry,' he said. 'I didn't mean to pry.'

The awkward moment passed, and she smiled. 'Shall we go? I'd take your jacket, just in case.'

He followed her down the corridor. Most of the doors were closed, but they passed one which was half ajar, and he glimpsed a fair-haired man in a blue denim jacket talking to another man in a hound's-tooth suit seated at a desk. They might have been Snider and Naughton, but he didn't pause to confirm this.

She led him along several corridors until they came to a lift. It turned out that he was on the sixth and topmost floor of the building. The lift was spacious, lined with wood veneer, brushed metal and mirrors. Its soft yellow lighting made him look suntanned. A familiar, formal silence had descended between them.

They emerged into a small reception area with wiry brown carpeting, sliding glass doors and trays of potted plants along the walls. A young woman wearing a brown suede overcoat and brown leather boots was standing with her back to him in a wide alcove, gazing at a noticeboard. She turned. It was Alison.

'Mike,' she said immediately, a smile spreading across her face as she came forward.

'Alison,' he murmured, smelling musky perfume and leather as she hugged him. 'How the devil are you?'

She smiled in acknowledgement – this last expression had once been a catch-phrase amongst their group at university. (It was part of a whole routine, conducted in very plummy voices, which went: 'Cynthia, wonderful to see you.' 'Niles, darling, how the devil are you?' 'Mustn't grumble, old girl.' 'What are you doing in this neck of the woods?' 'I was just passing by and I thought I'd drop in for a snifter.' And so on – and on. Very undergraduate.)

Alison looked little changed from their last meeting – thinner, perhaps, and with a shorter hairstyle, but otherwise she was much as he remembered her. A black-and-white CND badge was pinned to the lapel of her coat.

'Well, you must excuse me,' said Dr Dempster. 'I've got things to do. Your room is 66 in the west wing, Michael.' She departed.

'Get your kicks in room 66,' said Alison.

'I wish she wouldn't call me Michael. It makes me feel about ten years old.'

'What's she like? Bit of a sergeant-major?'

'She's OK really. Her heart's in the right place.'

He stood by the doorway, staring out. It had clouded over again, but the rain was holding off.

'Fancy a walk?' he said. 'I could use the fresh air.'

'OK.'

He put his jacket on and zipped it up. Dr Dempster must have anticipated that he would want to take a constitutional.

'It was good of you to come,' he said.

'It's good to see you again, Mike.'

Outside it was a typical April day, a bit blustery and raw, yet promising milder weather. Purple crocuses were dotted about on the grass.

'I never expected to find you here,' Alison said presently. 'What happened?'

He considered. The full story would have taken hours to tell, so he explained as briefly as possible how the pressures of his job, the confusions of his affair with Penny and finally his mother's death had conspired against him. He did not mention Riley or any of the others, but tried his best to give her some idea of what it had been like in Limbo.

Alison listened attentively but said nothing. In a way Limbo had been the special destiny which he had always felt lay in store for him. Perhaps that was why it had taken him so long to get out of it: nothing was more difficult to disavow than a fate which you felt you deserved. But in the end a constant diet of guilt had simply become dreary, and this had been his salvation.

They had reached the main road, and he glanced back at the building. It was a monument to brute modern functionalism, with horizontal slabs of concrete enclosing adjacent lines of windows. Like a glassed-in multi-storey car park.

They walked on down the road, Carpenter beginning to wrestle with his still confused feelings about his mother's death.

'My mother didn't say a word to me, that's what I can't get over. She knew she was on the way out, but she kept it to herself. I didn't even have a chance to do things for her, prepare myself, or even say goodbye.'

'Perhaps she wanted to spare you,' Alison said. 'Perhaps she couldn't bear the thought of telling you.'

'All she spared me was the chance to be a proper son to her at the end, damn it.' He could feel himself becoming emotional, and did his best to compose himself. 'She could have had me back there on some pretext, made sure I was around at the end. I could have helped.'

Alison slipped her arm through his. It had started to rain again.

'They never made much fuss of me, even when I was small. Do you know something? I always felt that I was really an orphan they'd adopted, not their proper son at all.' He peered at her. 'I've never told anyone that before.'

Alison smiled. 'That's not so unusual, you know. When I was little I was convinced my mother was a witch.'

Suddenly he felt that he had absurdly inflated all his problems. There was nothing remarkable or unique about his destiny to date; he was merely the victim of an unlucky conjunction of misfortunes.

Cars rushed past them on the road. Carpenter craved a cigarette, but he knew Alison didn't smoke and he couldn't bring himself to borrow money from her to buy some.

'How's Ray?' he asked.

'We split up. Last November.'

He looked at her. 'I didn't know.'

She shrugged. 'It was just one of those things. He's a nice man, gentle to a fault. But I just found I couldn't go on living with him. I don't know why. I woke up one morning and thought, "That's it, I've got to get out." So I told him I was leaving.'

'Was he upset?'

'He wasn't exactly dancing with joy. But I think he saw it coming, things hadn't been right for some time. He was such a gentleman about it, though I could tell he was really hurt. He told me he didn't want to do anything to interfere with my happiness.' For a moment she looked thoughtful. 'If he'd fought a bit to keep me, I might have stayed.'

'No chance of you patching it up?'

'No.'

'Do you feel guilty?'

'Of course I do. The more so because he didn't deserve it. But he'll be all right. People are usually more resilient than you think.'

Carpenter had the feeling that this last remark had been made for his benefit. They continued on in silence for a while, the rain falling more steadily. A coach went by, trailing red and white scarves.

'I came to London after Christmas,' she said, 'and moved in with guess who?'

He had no idea. 'Who?'

'Veronica. There was a spare room in her house, and you know what Veronica's like for waifs and strays.'

'How is she?'

'The same as ever. Well, not exactly.'

He felt a pang of apprehension. 'She's not pregnant, is she?'

'Pregnant? Not that I know of.'

Carpenter was loath to tell her about Veronica's pre-Christmas visit, but it was necessary since Alison might be able to put his mind at rest. He explained exactly what had happened.

'That's very odd, Mike,' she said when he was finished.

'I thought so, too.'

'No, it's odd because she told me she'd spent the week before Christmas in Yorkshire with Katrina. Katrina's her flatmate. Only she's not just her flatmate, as far as I can gather.'

'What do you mean?'

'I think they're having an affair as well.'

'She's a woman? This Katrina?'

'I think so. If you'd met her you'd know why I'm not sure. She certainly dresses like a woman.'

Somehow Carpenter was not surprised. Was it possible that Veronica had finally discovered contentment and perhaps her orgasm in the attentions of another woman? Was this why she had wanted him to be the surrogate father of her child, so that it could be raised in an all-female household? And had she spun Alison the yarn about going to Yorkshire to keep it a secret? He was profoundly relieved that she did not appear to be pregnant.

'It's an amazing place to live,' Alison was saying. 'About a dozen people in as many rooms, and not much privacy anywhere. People are always dropping in for meetings or midnight discussions about women's rights or left-wing politics. It's like a Worker's Revolutionary Party squat.'

He touched her CND badge. 'Have they recruited you?'

'I was wearing this before I came to London. It's probably the main reason they let me stay at the house.'

'It sounds just the sort of place Veronica would thrive in.'

'Not for much longer. The landlord gave everyone a month's notice to quit last week. He's selling the place off to a property developer.' She looked wry. 'In a way I'm almost relieved. Veronica sends her best, by the way. She would have come with me but she and Katrina were already committed to a conference in Brighton on radical womanhood. Veronica's a delegate.'

'I bet she'll love every minute of it. Veronica, the eternal champion.'

'She has a theory about you, you know.'

'I bet she does.'

Alison was grinning at him.

'What is it?'

'Are you sure you want to know?'

'She's been analysing me for years. I think I can bear it.'

'She says you've got a castration complex. You're secretly afraid of women.'

'There's nothing secret about it.'

They both laughed.

'And what do you think?' he asked.

She considered. 'I think there's hope for you.'

The rain had started to come down in earnest, and they would be soaked even if they immediately turned back. A few yards ahead was a public telephone box. He suggested they make a dash for it.

The air inside was rank with stale cigarette smoke, but at least it was dry. Raindrops splattered the tiny windowpanes, and the heat from their bodies soon caused the windows to mist up, shutting out the world. He and Alison huddled close, partly because there was not enough room to do anything else, partly because it was nice to feel one another's warmth. He put his hands into the pockets of her coat.

'How did you find me?' he asked.

'Veronica gave me your address. I went there yesterday. The young lad downstairs told me where to find you.'

'That would be Kenneth.'

'He didn't tell me his name. He said he fancied your girlfriend.'

'He's welcome to her.'

But the thought of Penny unsettled him. He checked his pockets, but the only coin he had was the fifty pence piece he had taken out of his pyjamas.

'Have you got any change?' he asked Alison. 'I want to make a quick phone call.'

She found him a ten pence piece. He dialled the number from memory and then the pips started. After a furious effort he finally managed to get the coin in.

A female voice he didn't recognize answered, giving the name of the design studio. He asked to speak to Penny.

'Hello?' another voice said presently.

'Is that Penny?'

'Speaking. Who is this?'

She sounded relaxed, even cheerful in an efficient secretarial way. He hesitated, then replaced the receiver.

Alison was looking at him with something of the old twinkle in her eyes.

'A bit of unfinished business,' he told her. 'Now satisfactorily concluded.' The very fact that Penny had not recognized his voice was enough to convince him that he had already been relegated to her past.

Cars swished by on the road, and the rain beat against the kiosk windows with a renewed intensity.

'What are you going to do about the notice to quit?' he asked. 'Have you found somewhere else to live?'

'Veronica and Katrina are planning to move into another communal house in Wandsworth. They've offered to fix me up with a room there, but I'm not sure.'

'You can stay at my place if you like. Dr Dempster will probably want to keep me in for a while longer. I can give you the keys.'

She studied him, her face serious. 'I'll think about it.'

'Remember Bristol?' he said in an access of boldness. 'The night we went to bed together and I was so drunk I passed out on you?'

'That was Cardiff, Mike. At my birthday party. You came over from Bristol one weekend when Naas was away.'

He frowned. 'Naas was at your party. You were flirting with me and I locked myself in the toilet in case he decided to get physical.'

'That was another time.'

'But you visited me in Bristol. With Duffy and Liz.'

'And Liz was keeping an eye on me to make sure I didn't misbehave. So I didn't.'

'It was Bristol. I remember it.'

'Cardiff, Mike.' Her tone was gentle but firm.

His face became hot. Was Alison's memory at fault, or did he have a few things muddled? Was it all jumbled up in his mind – the business with Veronica, and all the rest of it?

'The details don't matter,' she said.

'Sometimes they do. Sometimes they do.'

He had spoken vehemently, and immediately felt embarrassed. She took him by the arms and made him look at her.

'Perhaps it was Bristol. It really doesn't matter, you know. The important thing is that we both remember it.'

He was silent, still confused and mortified.

'Poor Mike,' she said. 'You've always been so scared of disappointing people.'

At that moment the door jerked open and a man made to enter the kiosk. On seeing them he mumbled an apology and withdrew.

'Two's company,' Alison said.

They exchanged smiles, and everything went away except the present moment. He listened to the cadences of the rain without taking his eyes off her face. It was mere inches from his own, and there was a hint of mischief in her expression, just like the old Alison. Somehow he had managed to put his arms around her, and he knew she was waiting for him to do something.

'Give us a kiss,' she said.